Counter-Coup

Counter-Coup

MICHAEL BRADFORD

FREDERICK MULLER LIMITED
LONDON

First published in Great Britain 1980 by
Frederick Muller Limited, London, NW2 6LE

British Library Cataloguing in Publication Data

Bradford, Michael
    Counter-Coup.
    I. Title
    823'.9'1F   PR6051.L5395/C

    ISBN 0–584–31052–8

Printed in Great Britain by Biddles Ltd., Guildford, Surrey

PART ONE

Balembi

One

On Sunday 6 June, 1965, Philip Morgan flew from London to Cairo in a de Havilland Comet 4; he was on his way to Balembi.

Philip was seen off at Heathrow by an old friend from his army days, Jonathan Courtney. As green young second lieutenants, Jonathan and Philip had fought together against the communist guerillas in the Malayan jungle, ten years earlier; the experience had formed a lasting friendship between them.

When the time for Philip's departure drew near, Jonathan extended his hand. 'Well,' he said with a smile, 'take care of yourself.'

'Don't worry,' said Philip, smiling in return as he shook his friend's hand. 'I shan't come to any harm.'

'And think very seriously about going to work for Kasaboru.'

'I will,' Philip assured him. 'I could hardly do otherwise, since you've talked about nothing else for the last half-hour.'

'Well, why not? The job is right up your street. You've got the background for it, you know the country, and you'd enjoy it.'

'And I'd get a pension if I lived long enough to collect it,' said Philip with a grin. 'Well, I'll do as you suggest – I'll think about it very carefully. But I'm not making any promises.'

Forty-five minutes later the Comet 4 took off for Cairo. As it did so Philip Morgan leaned back in his seat, closed his eyes, and sighed. He felt as if he were starting life afresh – as if he were wiping away all the painful memories of the past and retaining only the happier recollections.

Philip Morgan was thirty years old. After national service in the army he had joined the Metropolitan Police; with seven years' police experience under his belt he had married and moved to Birmingham, where he became head of security at a large engineering works. But in January 1965 his wife, Caroline, had died tragically in a fire, and from that time on Philip had felt increasingly restless. If there had been any children to worry about he would naturally have stayed in England; as it was, he began to think about going abroad.

In the end it was a letter of condolence from his uncle, George Morgan, which finally helped him to make up his mind. George Morgan lived in Balembi, a small land-locked country in central

3

Africa; he had retired five years ago after a long period as Belmbi's Lord Chief Justice. Philip himself had lived in Balembi until he was ten, and his uncle's invitation to go out there for a holiday appealed to him strongly; in fact it confirmed in him the wish to get right away from England, at least for a while.

Almost immediately Philip decided that he would resign from his job in Birmingham and fly out to stay with his uncle. He wasn't sure what he would do in Balembi – whether he would stay and get a new job, or just have an extended holiday and then come back home. But one thing he was certain of: the only way to fill the void left by the death of his wife was to make a complete break with his present surroundings.

Philip wrote back to his uncle accordingly. He gave his firm the necessary one month's notice, put his house on the market, and generally began to tidy up his affairs.

A few days later he contacted his old friend Jonathan Courtney. Jonathan was a director of World-Wide Mining, and he had sole responsibility at the London end for WWM's extensive operations in Balembi. Philip had wondered if Jonathan might know of a vacant job out there, and as it turned out, he did. The President of Balembi, Paul Kasaboru, was looking for a chief security officer, and he had asked Jonathan if he could help to find someone with appropriate experience. Jonathan had therefore written back to the President, explaining Philip's circumstances and giving him a personal recommendation. Philip was by no means sure that he would take this job, even if it were offered to him; but he fully intended to make some enquiries about what it would entail, and the prospect of taking care of the famous African President was certainly an intriguing one.

When the Comet 4 reached Cairo, Philip flew on to Nairobi where he stayed overnight. Early the following morning he found himself sitting in Nairobi airport. His flight to Balembi was delayed, and to pass the time he glanced unobtrusively at his fellow passengers in the departure area.

They were a markedly cosmopolitan crowd: there were one or two children and a sprinkling of the elderly; Europeans, Americans, Arabs – black, white and every shade in between.

For Philip, however, one person stood out from all the rest, and he had to work hard to avoid staring at her. She was a young woman in her early twenties. By any standards this particular girl was exceptionally attractive: she wore a slim-fitting, dark green skirt with a cream-coloured blouse above it; both emphasised the rounded curves of her well-proportioned figure. She had brown hair and dark brown eyes; her skin was lightly tanned.

It occurred to Philip that he could do a lot worse than find himself

4

sitting next to this young lady on the flight to Balembi; he made a point of checking that she was wearing neither a wedding nor an engagement ring. However, for the moment the girl was absorbed in a lively conversation with an elderly clergyman sitting beside her. And with a wry smile at his thoughts Philip opened the paperback he had bought in London and tried, unsuccessfully, to concentrate on it.

Philip Morgan might have been slightly surprised if he had known that the young lady he had been looking at had also noticed him.

Jane Stuart was twenty-five and a doctor by profession. She was still single, and in fact since she qualified as a doctor she had been working far too hard to devote much thought to men at all. But now she found herself instantly attracted to the powerfully built, good-looking man sitting opposite her; and for some reason which she could not quite understand, she was very angry with herself for feeling that way.

She tried to shake free of her thoughts and listen to what the clergyman beside her was saying.

The Reverend Archibald Carter had introduced himself almost as soon as Jane sat down. He was in his early sixties, but he was so frail and white-haired that he looked much older. The prospect of the coming flight had made the Reverend Carter so nervous that any inhibitions he might have had about talking to an attractive young woman were totally banished.

'Of course,' he continued, 'I've lived in Africa nearly all my life, you know. Born and brought up in England, of course, most of my generation were, and then we came out here as young adults, saw it as our calling. What about you, my dear? Are you a newcomer to Africa, or are you an old hand like me?'

Jane smiled and turned to look at the stooped, elderly man beside her. He was such an obvious gentleman that it would have been churlish to cut him short. And besides, talking to Archibald Carter took her mind off that other man opposite, the one with the confident smirk on his face who stared at her frankly from time to time.

'Well, I'm *sort* of an old hand,' said Jane. 'But I've got a very mixed background, I suppose. My mother was English and my father was American. I was born in the States, and we lived in America until I was eleven. Then we came out to Balembi.'

'Ah yes,' said the clergyman. 'I thought I detected an American accent in the background there. If acquired in early life it's not easily lost. When did you come to Balembi did you say – when you were eleven?'

'Yes. My father was a doctor, and he had a brother who was involved in missionary work – he was with an Episcopalian group, I believe. Anyway, after my mother died my uncle pointed out that there was an urgent need for doctors over here – so, my father and I just upped and came.'

5

'I see, I see,' said the clergyman, with real interest. 'My dear, I've known so many people like your father over the years – salt of the earth they are. In fact I might even know him personally. Would you be very offended if I asked his name?'

'Not at all,' said Jane. 'It was Stuart – Bob Stuart. He died some seven years ago.'

'Hmm.' The Reverend Carter thought about it, and then declared that he had vague recollections of meeting a Dr Stuart but couldn't quite be sure. 'And what about you, my dear – have you had any thoughts of taking up medicine yourself?'

Jane laughed. 'Oh yes. In fact I'm already qualified. After my father died I went over to England to do my training.'

'Oh, I see. . . . And now you're going back to Balembi. Is that for a holiday, or are you going to work there?'

'Well, I expect I shall find a job of some sort – and stay for a year or two at least. I believe there's still a considerable shortage of doctors.'

'Oh, yes,' said the little clergyman with feeling. 'How right you are, my dear. You'll be very welcome in Balembi, I can assure you of that. Very welcome indeed.'

At last the Bristol Britannia left Nairobi en route for Digara, the capital of Balembi. Just before the end of the flight, however, the captain announced to the passengers that because of a heavy storm at Digara airport, the plane was being diverted; it would now land at Akaville, the capital of Gabuti, the adjoining state to the east.

'Oh dear, oh dear,' said the Reverend Carter, who was seated on Jane's right, in the aisle seat. 'Oh dear, oh dear, how very unfortunate. I had this happen to me once before – it's very upsetting. The Gabutis are communists, you know – they don't like clergymen at all, and they kept me waiting at the airport for hours last time. I do hope no-one's put out waiting for me at the other end.'

'I'm sure the airline will make an announcement at Digara airport,' said Jane, who was sure of no such thing. Neither was she particularly convinced by the captain's explanation of the cause of the diversion: June was a bit late in the year for a heavy storm at the airport. Before leaving England Jane had been doing some background reading, and it was her private opinion that the growing political instability in Balembi was a much more likely reason than the weather for the plane being unable to land; she would not have been at all surprised to hear that a bomb had gone off. However, she decided not to share her views with her travelling companion.

'Never mind,' she said. 'If I remember my geography correctly, it's only about eighty or ninety miles from Akaville to Digara. I expect they'll hire a bus for us.'

'Well, let's hope so,' said the Reverend Carter, obviously very

6

unhappy.

When they landed it became obvious that Akaville airport, in the middle of a massively humid African afternoon, was not exactly bustling with activity. It took an hour and a half to go through customs, but at last the bus which was to take the passengers to Digara began to ease its way through the Akaville traffic towards the border.

For over an hour the bus climbed slowly but steadily, leaving the low, humid plains of Gabuti and climbing into the slightly cooler hills of Balembi.

At the border there was further trouble with the Gabuti customs officers. Jane herself had no difficulty, but an American had his camera 'confiscated', and complained bitterly, which did him no good at all. Various other passengers also had possessions removed, but they chose to keep their thoughts to themselves.

Eventually, the bus driver managed to persuade the Gabuti authorities that they had had their fair share of booty for one day. The driver was a white Balembian in his mid-thirties, and he used a mixture of good-humoured banter in the local dialect and an occasional flash of official-sounding English. No doubt as a result of much practice, the tactic worked, and the bus resumed its journey.

There were no further problems for at least ten minutes. Then, suddenly, the late African afternoon became infinitely menacing.

The bus turned a corner and came on a car by the side of the road. The car was burnt out and smoking, the driver lying half out of it, face down. Jane had never seen anyone look deader, but the bus driver didn't give her a chance to exercise her professional skills. He put his foot down hard and accelerated.

Round the next bend, however, he had to brake even harder to avoid disaster. The road narrowed sharply at that point, running between two rock formations on either side. Blocking the gap completely was a lorry, parked sideways on.

The bus screeched to a halt and the driver grated the gears as he tried desperately to find reverse. But before he could attempt to turn the bus around, the door was thrown open and a black youth appeared on the step, his eyes wide and his teeth gleaming. He pointed an elderly Lee Enfield rifle at the driver and told him curtly to switch off the engine – or else.

'Oh dear,' said the Reverend Carter faintly. 'I don't like the look of this. I don't like the look of it at all.'

Two

Jane Stuart didn't like the look of the situation either, though from her position, four rows back from the front of the bus, there was nothing at all she could do about it.

The bus driver did his best to repel boarders. He started to get out of his seat to throw the black youth physically back through the door, but as he did so the youth fired the rifle straight at him.

Fortunately for the bus driver, the youth jerked the trigger, with the result that the barrel swung sharply to the right; instead of blowing a hole in the driver the bullet merely blew a hole in the window of his bus. But it shocked the driver into immobility, and by the time he had recovered his senses, the youth had rattled the bolt back and forth and was all ready to fire again. There were stifled screams from many of the women present, Jane included.

'Switch off engine! Everybody get out!' shouted the youth, articulating so fiercely that globules of spit scattered in all directions.

The Reverend Carter started to pray silently, and the babble of voices which had arisen when the bus first shuddered to a halt was now silenced.

'Everybody get out!' shouted the youth with the rifle again. 'Or you all get shot, double quick!' He stared fiercely up and down the bus, looking for opposition. There was none.

Jane glanced out of the window beside her: half a dozen other black youths, all aged between about sixteen and twenty, had appeared from behind the lorry; it was the same on the other side of the bus. The youths were all dressed in a ragged assortment of civilian clothing with scraps of military uniform attached. One of them, a pale-skinned mulatto, had a sergeant's stripes on a faded khaki bush jacket; on his head he wore a monkey-skin cap with a feather in it, and he too carried a rifle with bayonet attached. The others were armed with pangas (African chopping knives) or heavy sticks which they swung as clubs.

Jane wasn't at all sure who these people were or what they wanted, but she suspected that they were simply the Balembian equivalent of eighteenth-century highwaymen; unfortunately they appeared to be nothing like as chivalrous.

The youth with the rifle waved his weapon in the air, and shouted fiercely again. 'Out!' he yelled. 'Everyone out of bus, line up quick, or I shoot this lady dead.' He pointed his rifle at a woman sitting in the front seat.

For a moment there was a stunned silence. But it was broken by Philip Morgan, the man Jane had found so instantly and disturbingly attractive when she first saw him at Nairobi airport. He stood up from his seat three rows behind her and spoke clearly in a calm, authoritative voice.

'All right, everybody, I want you to listen carefully.' He paused until all eyes were turned in his direction. 'Now then – as you can see, we've been stopped by armed men. And if we don't do as we're told then it's obvious that someone is going to get hurt. So I'd like you all to co-operate. To begin with I want you to leave the bus in a quiet and orderly manner. I've no doubt that the young men who have stopped us are just as anxious to avoid trouble as we are.' (In his heart Philip didn't believe that for a second, but he felt it was the right thing to say.) 'Let's give them what they're after, which is no doubt our wallets and valuables, and then get back on our way to Digara. Now – I'd like the people at the front to lead the way out of the bus calmly and quietly.'

Nearly all the forty passengers shared Jane's reaction to this speech, which was one of immense relief. None of the passengers had the remotest idea who Philip Morgan was – in fact none of them even knew his name – but his voice and his presence were so obviously those of a leader and a man who could be trusted that they instantly followed his suggestion. In almost total silence the passengers filed nervously out of the bus and took up the positions indicated by the grinning black youths who had waylaid them.

Philip Morgan waited until the very end before leaving the bus himself. He wanted to take a careful look at all his fellow passengers to see how many of them could be expected to join in a fight if one developed. The depressing conclusion he came to was that there were only two men present, out of twenty-five, who could reasonably be called able-bodied: those were the bus driver and himself. Most of the others were elderly or obviously desk-bound executives.

None of the women looked particularly self-possessed either, but again there were two exceptions. The first was the outstandingly beautiful girl Philip had been cautiously ogling all along: she seemed to be in complete command of herself. The second was a very fierce-looking middle-aged white lady who was accompanied by a small black boy aged perhaps seven or eight. The woman was grey-haired, dimunitive, and wore spectacles; but she was clearly the no-nonsense type. The very fact that she was wearing a severe two-piece costume, despite the great heat, indicated that she did not buckle under easily.

As she moved down the aisle to get out, this middle-aged lady paused and spoke to Philip in a whisper; she had a strong Scottish accent.

9

'Now listen, young man,' she said. 'My name is Macintyre. Miss Macintyre,' she added. 'I'm secretary to Richard Chokwe, and this wee boy here is his son.'

Philip knew that he ought to be able to remember who Richard Chokwe was, but in the present circumstances it slipped his mind.

'If they split up the men and the women, as I think they will,' Miss Macintyre continued, 'I want you to look after the boy.'

Philip nodded. 'Leave him with me now,' he said, and took the boy's hand.

The boy's guardian hesitated for a moment and then continued towards the door.

The bus had drawn to a halt barely ten feet from the lorry blocking the road. At the point where the lorry was parked the road narrowed sharply, but to the left of the bus there was a small plateau, a level area probably cleared when the highway was being constructed, in order to allow drivers to pull off the road and park. Here the black youths assembled their victims, the men in one line at right angles to the bus, the women in another. Everyone was forced to stand with their hands in the air.

It became apparent that the young mulatto with the sergeant's stripes was in charge. He barked orders in an African dialect, and poked viciously with his bayonet at anyone who was slow in obeying instructions. Like all his companions, the Sergeant walked oddly, as if staggering under a heavy weight. Jane Stuart's diagnosis was that they were all heavily dosed up with marijuana or booze – or possibly both.

When everyone was out of the bus and standing exactly where the Sergeant wanted them, he gave a further order which the other youth with a rifle translated into English.

'Everybody strip,' he shouted excitedly. 'Everybody – all clothes off, double quick!' And to make the point clear he started pulling the jacket and tie off the man standing closest to him. All the other youths followed suit, yelling and cursing at anyone who was slow in obeying, particularly the women. One man began to object loudly, but soon changed his mind after a few heavy blows from a club sent him to his knees. The Sergeant watched everyone carefully, his finger never leaving the trigger of his rifle.

The screaming black youth in front of Jane left her in no doubt at all what would happen if she did not do what she was told: he gestured that he would cut her throat with his knife. With almost clinical detachment, Jane realised that her whole body was trembling violently; she also felt sick, her stomach churning with nausea. But she was determined not to panic. She forced herself to move slowly and carefully, to do things in an orderly and rational manner.

Her cheeks burning, she took off all her clothes, threw them forward in a heap in front of her, as indicated by the Sergeant, and resisted a strong urge to put her hands over her breasts and pubic

10

hair. She stared straight ahead, looking neither to the right nor to the left.

The black youths moved up and down the line, searching the bus passengers' clothes for money, jewellery, and whatever other trinkets they could find. One or two of them sniggered and pointed at Jane as they passed, but most seemed slightly in awe of her. That, Jane knew, would not last.

The only problem with staring straight ahead was that she found herself looking at the men opposite. And in particular she had difficulty in taking her eyes off the naked body of the man who had taken charge on the bus. Despite – or perhaps because of – the terrifying circumstances of the moment, Jane found her eyes following the contours of his muscles. He stood in a relaxed position, his feet slightly apart and his shoulders set back – like a soldier, Jane thought to herself. His eyes carefully observed the actions of the black hijackers. Occasionally he turned and addressed a word of comfort to the little black boy who stood beside him, anxiously clutching his hand. The man's body seemed whiter than ever in contrast with the boy's.

The human mind has a way of protecting itself from unacceptable reality, and for a full minute or more, until something happened to break the spell, Jane found herself taking stock of the man as a potential lover. He was clearly fit and hard; his stomach was flat, the arms and thighs well muscled. There was black hair on his legs and arms, but not on his chest. And best of all, his genitals were pleasing in appearance: the testicles heavy, the penis large even when flaccid, with a foreskin which was attractive to her.

A sudden scream from a teenage girl standing two places down the line brought Jane out of her reverie with a violent shock; the scream set her heart pounding at a greatly increased rate; her breathing shortened. She became instantly aware of what was happening to her – of the fact that her mind had temporarily switched itself off in order to escape the thought of rape and death which was undoubtedly present. But now she was back in control again, fully conscious of all her senses and able to think clearly.

The teenage girl began to scream, repeatedly, hysterically, her eyes tight shut, her hands clutching handfuls of her hair. A black youth approached her menacingly and shouted at her in dialect. It made not the slightest difference.

Jane glanced again at the man opposite, seeking an instruction from him with her eyes. Philip frowned at her and urgently pointed at the teenager, urging her to do something to stop the uncontrolled outburst before the Sergeant or one of his cronies grew tired of the noise and put a stop to it for good.

Jane swallowed once to try to get some saliva into her mouth. Then she stepped out of the line and went and stood in front of the screaming girl. Taking time to aim the blow properly, she slapped

11

the girl really hard across the side of her face.

The screaming stopped. The eyes opened, and then the sobbing began. The girl covered her face with her hands and wept bitterly.

Jane embraced her, clutching the girl's warm and slightly built body to her own. 'There, there, there,' she said comfortingly. 'It's all right now. You'll be all right now. . . .'

Philip Morgan breathed a deep sigh; there had been a real danger of the situation getting completely out of control. The teenage girl's hysterical outburst had threatened to trigger off a violent reaction. The black youths appeared to be after money, cameras and other valuables. But they were obviously very happy to humiliate their predominantly white captives as much as possible – and it only needed one of them to suggest rape or a killing and the whole gang would join in. Fortunately, the young girl's screaming had been silenced in time, and the youths returned to their looting.

Philip took the opportunity to review the situation. Despite what he had said on the bus, he found it impossible to believe that in a few minutes the passengers were all going to be allowed to resume their journey unharmed. The best they could hope for was being left here with a disabled bus while the hijackers escaped in the lorry. A much more likely outcome was rape for the women and torture for the men: Philip had been away from Africa for a long time, but he had read many accounts of events in the Congo to the north, and he had no illusions that these youths would behave any differently. No – if the lives and welfare of the passengers were to be protected someone was going to have to take positive action. And as far as Philip could see, that someone was going to have to be the bus driver and himself. The bus driver was standing right next to Philip, and the main problem at the moment was keeping the man on the leash until the right moment.

'Steady,' Philip kept saying out of the corner of his mouth, as he saw the man clenching his fists and tensing himself to jump one of the youths. 'Wait for the right moment. Wait till I tell you.'

Philip didn't know it, but the driver was an exceptionally fit man. He had represented Balembi as a swimmer in the 1948 Olympics, and two of his national records were still standing seventeen years later.

Philip glanced around and assessed the position yet again. There were twelve hijackers in all, mostly very inexperienced and probably cowardly young men who would run a long way rather than fight. There were twenty-five male passengers and fifteen female. The only problem was, the passengers were all naked and unarmed and the hijackers had two rifles, six pangas and four heavy clubs.

The rifles were the chief risk. They were very elderly Lee Enfields with vee backsights, which so far as Philip could remember meant that they were pre-World War I models. Nevertheless, bolt-action weapons would have stood up well to African climatic conditions, much better than many a modern semi-automatic – and one of the rifles had already been shown to be loaded.

The Sergeant, a tall, gangly youth of about eighteen, had so far proved to be highly alert; his shining, prominent eyes were forever moving, his finger constantly on the trigger; he was clearly the most dangerous of the entire group.

But now, as Philip watched, the Sergeant's attention lapsed for the very first time. He came across and bent down on one knee to go through the pockets of a man's jacket, standing the rifle on its butt and holding it with his left hand as he did so.

'Now,' said Philip to the bus driver beside him. He took four rapid steps across the hot rocks underfoot and rammed both feet into the chest of the Sergeant, sending him sprawling and the rifle clattering on to the ground. Out of the corner of his eye he saw the stocky bus driver slam a punch into the face of one of the other youths who was standing lead-footed with surprise at Philip's action. The bus driver grabbed the club which the youth had dropped and laid about him with it.

Before the Sergeant could so much as lift his head Philip had his hands on the Lee Enfield. The rifle was cocked and Philip thumbed off the safety-catch and pulled the trigger, not knowing whether there was a round up the spout or not. There was, and the Sergeant fell back on to the rocks with blood flooding on to his bush jacket from a hole in his chest.

Philip opened the bolt and the spent round span away, flashing gold in the sunshine. He checked the magazine and noted briefly that it looked full. Then he closed the bolt again and turned and looked for the only other youth who had a rifle, praying for a clear line of fire.

The other youth was over by the bus, where he had been trying unsuccessfully to break open a suitcase. At the sound of Philip's first shot he looked up, grabbed for his weapon and fumbled with its mechanism, shouting in panic.

Philip went down on one knee, took his time over aiming the shot, and hit the youth in the right shoulder, bowling him over backwards with a scream of pain.

Pandemonium ensued.

Almost all the women passengers started screaming. The black youths yelled at each other, and at the passengers, and then ran for cover; in two cases they bumped into each other in their haste. For a few moments passengers and hijackers were hopelessly intermingled, and if the black youths had had sufficient presence of mind to seize hostages Philip would have failed miserably in achieving his aims.

But the black youths did not have a cool head amongst them.

They just assumed that pangas and wooden clubs were no match for the rifle Philip had seized, and they ran in all directions. After a few moments the passengers' cries of distress and horror turned to relief and jubilation: their enemies had fled in disorder.

As quickly as possible Philip and the bus driver got everyone dressed and back on the bus.

'I do this trip every week,' said the bus driver as they hurriedly pulled their clothes on. 'We've had this trouble for months on this road – cars and lorries being stopped and robbed and so on. There are several gangs of black kids running wild in these hills – the *jeunesse*, that's what the Belgians in the Congo call them. Most of them have never seen the inside of a school in their lives – straight out of the bush they are. They pinch rifles and shotguns from farms and then hold up lorries and cars. I expect they pinched that lorry blocking the road, too. But this is the first time they've dared to hold up a whole bus.'

'Do they usually hurt anyone?' asked Philip, conscious of the fact that he had shot first and asked questions afterwards.

'Damn right they do,' said the driver. He tucked his white open-necked shirt into his black trousers and then put on his cap. 'Rape the women, as often as not – I was just waiting for them to start that – and humiliate the men, if they're lucky. If they're not lucky they tend to go home with some parts missing. All that business about stripping all our clothes off was just the beginning.' He patted Philip on the shoulder. 'You did the right thing there, my friend, don't you worry about that. I'm ready to testify in your favour any day.'

The second youth who had been shot by Philip had staggered off into the trees on the other side of the road, but the Sergeant was lying with his mouth and eyes wide open, the flies already buzzing around him. Philip and the bus driver went over to look at him, only to be pushed aside by Jane Stuart.

'Let me see,' said Jane, now back in her clothes like the men. 'I'm a doctor.'

Philip and the bus driver exchanged surprised glances as Jane examined the Sergeant.

'Well,' she said after a moment, 'he's dead all right. . . . Look how fast the blood is congealing – that's the effect of the marijuana. . . . What do you want to do with him, stick him in the luggage compartment?'

'Not on your life,' said the driver. 'We're going to leave him here. There's another corpse in a car just down the road. . . . No, we'll leave them here, and the first phone we come to I'll get the police out.'

14

The bus arrived at Digara airport some five and a half hours after the flight from Cairo had originally be due to land. Almost all those who had been waiting for passengers at the appointed time were still there, together with the police, who had been notified by the bus driver; also present were a score of pressmen. The result was chaos, with relatives struggling to greet each other through a mass of shouting reporters and photographers.

Philip collected his two suitcases as quickly as he could and was then escorted by a uniformed policeman to a quiet office on the first floor of the main airport building. There he made a full and detailed statement to a senior Balembian police officer.

He had just completed the statement and was in the act of signing it when the office door opened without warning and a man with an air of authority entered the room. He was black – a member of the Mibambo tribe, Philip guessed, if his childhood memories did not deceive him. He was slimly built and appeared to be in his mid-thirties; he wore a well-cut business suit, smart but not flamboyant. His face was handsome and intelligent, with a moustache and a beard which were neatly trimmed; judging by the set of his features there had been at least one European somewhere in his background. All in all the man appeared to be young, confident, able, and important.

The police officer present thought so too; he stood up.

'Ah,' said the newcomer. 'The right place at last, I believe.' He held out his hand. 'I'd like to introduce myself. My name is Richard Chokwe. I believe you're a newcomer here, so my name won't mean anything to you, but I'm the Foreign Secretary of Balembi.'

Philip stood up and shook hands. 'Philip Morgan,' he said.

'Philip Morgan,' Chokwe repeated, still holding Philip's hand. 'Well, Mr Morgan, I shall not forget your name.' He released Philip's hand after a moment and moved away towards the window. 'No, I shall not forget it. . . . I owe you a great debt, Mr Morgan. My secretary, Miss Macintyre, was returning from London today with my young son. I had sent him over there for medical treatment. And according to Miss Macintyre, and the bus driver, I have you to thank for saving my son's life.'

'Well, I think that's putting it a bit strong,' said Philip.

'Oh no.' Chokwe shook his head. 'No. Miss Macintyre, let me tell you, is a Scottish Presbyterian, and if Miss Macintyre says that you saved my son's life, then save it you did. And let us have no illusions. There are parts of this country at the moment where, regrettably, one cannot walk in safety. There are reasons for that which are well known both to me and to this police officer here. And believe me we would dearly like to take action – strong, firm action, such as you have taken, to correct the situation. But, again for reasons which I will not go into now, we are not always able to take the action we would wish. . . . As it is, I can only thank you most warmly for what you have done.'

Chokwe took a step towards Philip and seemed about to say something else. But then, suddenly, his eyes filled with tears. Instead of speaking he simply squeezed Philip's hand once more and then went out of the room, leaving the door open behind him.

Three

Jane Stuart deliberately took her time over getting out of the bus at the airport, and after a few minutes the worst of the crowd moved away. The reporters and photographers were concentrating on interviewing a small, grey-haired lady accompanying a black boy aged about eight – his father seemed to be someone important – and Jane was able to locate her luggage and slip away without trouble.

Before leaving England Jane had arranged to stay with her mother's brother and his wife, who lived in a district of Digara called Victoria Vale. She had never met her uncle and aunt, and would not have been able to recognise them had they been at the airport. But in any case their letter had suggested that on her arrival she should simply take a taxi to Victoria Vale. This she duly did.

Jane was feeling totally exhausted. It was twelve hours since she had left Nairobi, where she had spent a week with friends, and her experiences on the journey had left her with a blinding headache; consequently she was not particularly looking forward to meeting her hosts. Jane's grandmother, back in England, had insisted that her son would be only too delighted to have Jane as his guest, but Jane had been uncomfortably aware from the tone of her uncle's letter that he was less than thrilled at the prospect of having her to stay. However, Jane decided that the arrangement had been made and it would have to stand for the time being. All she wanted at the moment was a bath and a soft bed.

The taxi driver, a cigar-smoking Welshman, kindly carried Jane's suitcases to the front door when they arrived at the Greys' house. There was no answer to the doorbell and he suggested that Jane should take a look in the back garden.

'Probably playing tennis,' he said with a touch of envy. 'They've all got tennis courts here.'

Jane thanked him for his help and walked round the side of the house. It was a large, detached, two-storey building, set in a garden which was extensive at the front and proved to be even bigger at the back. There was not, in fact, a tennis court, but there was a private swimming pool, some ten yards wide and five yards long. The evening sun glinted and flashed off the clear blue ripples of the water, and for a moment Jane was dazzled by it. Then, with a start, she realised that there was a woman in the pool.

17

The woman swam towards her and came to a halt at Jane's feet.

'Hello! You must be Jane Stuart.' The greeting was friendly enough.

'Yes,' said Jane. 'And you must be Eileen Grey.'

The swimmer nodded. 'That's right. You'll call me Eileen, I hope, rather than Auntie.'

Jane smiled. 'Of course.'

'Good. . . .' Eileen Grey grasped the chrome rail of the swimming-pool steps and hauled herself out of the water; she was wearing a very small black bikini. Jane stood back to let her pass.

Jane knew comparatively little about the woman who was married to her uncle, and as Eileen towelled herself down Jane tried to decide what to make of her. She was in her early thirties – thirty-two, Jane's grandmother had decided, after careful calculation – of medium height, with a first-class figure. Her body was tanned all over, even when she peeled off the bikini, which she did without the slightest hesitation. She had long black hair, and her features were open and alert, though far from beautiful: the nose was too large and the chin too pointed for beauty, but she had dark, confident eyes and good teeth. All in all Jane got the impression of a very self-assured and determined character, a woman who had matured fully under the African sun and had few inhibitions.

In due course Eileen dressed herself in a pair of slacks and a blouse which both hugged and emphasised her figure. Then the two women went indoors and settled down over drinks. Eileen lit a cigarette; her manner remained friendly and cheerful, but very brisk. Sort of take me or leave me, Jane decided.

'Well now,' said Eileen, after a long pull at an enormous gin and tonic, 'let me see if I've got the story straight. I never was very good at keeping track of Duncan's relations, but as I understand it, your mother was Duncan's eldest sister.'

'Yes, that's right,' said Jane. 'I think she must have been about twelve years older than Duncan.'

'I see. And she was the one who went off to America and married a doctor.'

'Yes.'

'Ah yes, I've placed you now.' Another long pull at the gin. 'And you've just qualified as a doctor yourself, I believe?'

'Yes – I finished last year. I've done a few months in general practice, but I didn't enjoy it very much, so I thought I'd come back here.'

Jane was about to add that she thought she might very well go to work out in the bush, where the need for medical assistance was greatest. But somehow she sensed that a statement like that would not go down well in this house. She decided to change the subject.

'Tell me a bit about yourself, Eileen,' Jane went on. 'Are you English?'

Eileen hooted with laughter. 'No – not in the sense you mean, anyway. Thank God I'm not. No, I was born in Rhodesia – lived there all my life until we came up here. Duncan was born in England, of course. He was in the British army for a while, until they kicked him out – then he came out to Rhodesia. About the only place that would have him, I think. We got married after he'd been out here a year or so, when I was still young and stupid. After that we stayed in Rhodesia for nearly ten years, and then three years ago Duncan got offered this job in Digara – he's technical director of the national radio network.'

'Oh – that sounds a very responsible sort of job,' said Jane, groping for something to say.

Eileen gave a short laugh. 'Not nearly as responsible as Duncan would have you believe,' she said. 'He's the black sheep of the family – didn't they tell you that back in England?'

A few minutes later Duncan Grey arrived home. He too helped himself to a large gin and tonic, and then the three of them sat down to dinner.

During the meal Duncan led the conversation by asking Jane numerous questions about 'the old country' as he called it, and about his parents; Jane had lived with Duncan's mother and father while she completed her medical studies.

Duncan Grey was approaching forty years of age; he was of average build, with a tanned, rather red face and a military moustache. He was particularly neatly dressed: the crease in his trousers was quite unspoilt and his shirt looked as if it had just been pressed, even at this time of day; his well-polished shoes also reinforced the impression of a man who took care over small details. In terms of his appearance and general demeanour he appeared to be a perfect gentleman; but there was something about him which did not quite ring true. When he momentarily forgot his military training, his posture became positively round-shouldered and pot-bellied, and Jane began to see how Africa had sown the seeds of decay in him. Perhaps her reaction to Duncan was also coloured by the derogatory remarks which Eileen had already made about him. Whatever it was, Jane could not quite take Duncan at face value. He gave her an account of his youth and his life in the army which differed in significant respects from the outline which Eileen had already supplied. And whenever Duncan said anything which was at variance with Eileen's account, Eileen would look up across the dinner-table and wink at Jane with a smile. Duncan apparently did not notice.

'Well,' Duncan said towards the end of the meal, 'Eileen and I always meant to nip over from Rhodesia and introduce ourselves to you and your father, but somehow we never did. And eventually it was too late, of course – your father died, and you went off to

19

England to do your medical training. But, now you're back, and we're very pleased to see you at last, I can tell you.' He noticed a hard look from his wife and then continued in a much more hesitant tone. 'I – er – I suppose you'll be looking around for a bit, deciding where you're going to work and all that sort of thing. And then you'll get yourself a little place of your own – a little flat, something like that. Is that the idea?'

The question was extremely clumsily put, but despite her weariness Jane did not allow herself to become annoyed.

'Yes,' she said politely. 'Yes, that's more or less the plan. There are a few friends I want to look up, just to get the feel of where the need for doctors is greatest. And after that I shall have a better idea of where I'm going to be based. So one way and another I don't think I shall need to impose on you for more than a week or two at the most.'

'Oh, well, I didn't mean to imply that we wanted to get rid of you,' said Duncan hastily, his cheeks reddening. 'By all means stay as long as you like. You're very welcome, Jane. Very welcome indeed.'

Duncan Grey's confident manner totally evaporated from that moment onwards: he became extremely edgy and hesitant. Eileen, on the other hand, remained cool and impassive. The evening light suited her, emphasising her good features and reducing her faults: she became an undeniably handsome woman.

After dinner, coffee was taken in the living-room. Duncan drained his cup almost as soon as it was passed to him; he obviously wanted to say something to Eileen but didn't quite know how to put it.

'Are you – er – are you planning anything special tonight, dear?' he asked eventually.

His wife gave him a look of amused contempt. 'I'm going out,' she said. 'A little later on.'

'Ah yes,' said Duncan, his eyes wandering all over the room. 'Yes. . . . Well. . . . I – er – I've been invited to make up a four at bridge, down at the golf club. I think perhaps I ought to go. Business, you know,' he said with a weak smile towards Jane. 'You won't mind if I go out then, dear?'

'Not at all,' said Eileen, as if it were a matter of complete indifference to her.

And after a further half-hearted attempt to excuse himself for deserting his guest so soon, Duncan drove away in his car.

Eileen poured herself some more coffee, to which she added a liberal dose of Drambuie.

'You won't see much of Duncan and myself in the evenings,' she explained. 'There's very little to do here except drink and the other thing. And Duncan's no good at the other thing, so we tend to go our separate ways.' She raised her coffee cup in a gesture of good-will. 'Cheers. . . .' She drank deeply before continuing.

'I quite often spend the evening with a friend of mine,' she went on after a moment. 'He's black, of course, which raises a few eyebrows, even in Balembi. But then, what do I care? You're only young once, and he's a lot more fun than Duncan.'

Jane realised that since coming in from the swimming pool Eileen had drunk quite a lot. It was difficult to say whether the alcohol was the cause, but her conversation was certainly frank.

'I don't suppose you'd like to come out with us?' Eileen asked. 'A good-looking girl like you could go a long way in Balembi, believe me. Joro could find you a friend, no trouble at all. And there's a nightclub we go to where they have a really very interesting cabaret – show you a few things you never saw in medical school, I can tell you. . . . What about it?'

'Well, thank you very much for the offer,' said Jane, trying not to sound too prim. 'But I'd really much rather just have a bath and go to bed.'

Eileen seemed unruffled. 'Suit yourself,' she said, quite without malice. 'But you've only to say the word.'

Through the window Jane saw another car draw up in the drive, a red MG sports car. Out of it climbed a heavily built black Balembian wearing a yellow open-necked shirt and brown slacks. Even at a distance he was an impressive figure of a man.

'Oh – there's Joro now,' said Eileen, and went to the door to let the visitor in.

On her return Eileen seemed charged with energy: her eyes sparkled and she was smiling happily for the first time since Jane had met her. With her into the room came the man Jane was to come to loathe and fear intensely over the next three weeks.

'Joro Nyanga,' said Eileen as she introduced them. 'Joro, this is Duncan's niece, Jane Stuart.'

They shook hands and Eileen crossed the room to get Nyanga a drink. Nyanga smiled at Jane, and despite herself, she shivered in response: there was something menacing about the display of even, white teeth, something very disturbing in the black man's fearsome stillness. But the moment passed.

'Well now, Miss Stuart,' said Nyanga, 'I hear you had an eventful journey from Nairobi.'

'Oh?' said Eileen, turning round at the drinks table. 'You didn't say anything about that, Jane.'

'Well, naturally – no doubt she would prefer to forget it,' Nyanga continued shortly. 'But we had a bomb scare at the airport this afternoon, and the flight from Nairobi was diverted to Akaville. And as if that was not enough, the bus bringing the passengers from Gabuti was held up on road by the *jeunesse*.'

'Oh my God!' said Eileen. She seemed genuinely concerned. 'Was

21

anyone hurt?'

'Oh, the passengers escaped in one piece,' said Nyanga with a grin. 'Fortunately for Jane and her companions, one of the passengers was a Mr Philip Morgan. Mr Morgan is a most resourceful gentleman – is that not so, Jane?'

'If you mean the man who shot the ringleader, then yes, he is resourceful,' said Jane. 'But I'm afraid I don't know his name.'

'Morgan,' said Nyanga again, as he took his drink from Eileen. 'Philip Morgan. Yes, Mr Morgan is a man who will be watched with great interest in Balembi.'

'Everybody knows absolutely everything about everybody out here,' said Eileen, by way of explanation. 'And Joro is a politician, of course, so naturally he knows more than most. He can give you the details of any juicy scandal almost as soon as it happens.'

'Sometimes before it happens,' said Nyanga, and then roared with laughter.

Jane could not take her eyes off the man. She was not at all surprised to hear that he was a politician – he had the basic animal magnetism or charisma which marks out the natural leader. He was taller than the average Balembian, nearly six feet, with a heavily muscled upper torso, presumably the result of weightlifting or bodybuilding of some kind. His facial characteristics were those of the smaller of the two main Balembi tribes, the Fanda: he had a tall forehead, a broad, flattened nose, thick lips, slightly turned out, and tightly curled, close-cropped hair. The eyes were dark brown, with patches of yellow discolouration in the whites; his skin was extremely black. On his left hand he wore a diamond ring, on his right wrist a gold identity bracelet. Jane guessed that he was aged about thirty-five.

Nyanga took a drink, still staring at Jane with an amused expression. 'Well now, Miss Stuart, Eileen and I are going to go out to a nightclub a little later on – perhaps you would like to join us?'

Jane did her best to sound grateful. 'Well, that's very kind of you – in fact Eileen has already suggested it. But if you don't mind I'd just like to go to bed. I really feel quite exhausted.' Which was true.

As soon as she reasonably could, Jane made her way upstairs, unpacked a few belongings, and after a quick bath fell wearily into bed.

She was too tired to spend very long thinking about Eileen's obvious affair with Joro Nyanga. It seemed unusual, to say the least – even in Balembi, which was noted among African countries for its liberal approach to relationships between the races. But even among Europeans, Eileen's behaviour towards Nyanga would have appeared deliberately scandalous, and what Jane's grandmother would have thought of it didn't bear thinking about. At the moment, however, Jane was just too tired to care.

When she came out of the bathroom Jane was aware, from the

22

voices downstairs, that Nyanga and Eileen were still in the house. And just as she was drifting off to sleep she heard them come upstairs and enter the bedroom next to hers.

The windows of both rooms were open, and despite the screens to keep out the insects, Jane could hear Nyanga talking in a low voice and Eileen giggling in reply. After a few moments the talking stopped and was replaced by the inevitable rocking of the bed-springs. Jane covered her head with the pillow, but even that did not block out the mounting crescendo of squeaks from the bed, gasps and moans from Eileen, and savage, deep grunts from Nyanga.

Eventually, after what seemed like an age, there was silence, and Jane fell into a deep sleep.

Four

It was half past eight in the evening before Philip Morgan arrived at his uncle's house in King George VI Avenue.

George Morgan greeted his nephew warmly. He immediately took him into the dining-room for a cold buffet supper, served by his elderly Mibambo manservant, Imbasa. Afterwards the two men relaxed in the comfortably old-fashioned living-room; the chairs and the settee were all long past their best, but comfortable, and the walls were lined with original oil paintings, mostly landscapes of the green English countryside.

In view of the fact that his uncle was a former Lord Chief Justice of Balembi, and therefore concerned with law and order, Philip felt that he had to tell him about the events of the afternoon; it wasn't everyone who shot dead a Balembian citizen soon after his arrival in the country, even in self-defence. And having told his uncle the details of what had happened, Philip mentioned that at some stage he would have to attend an inquest on the dead youth.

'Well, I don't think you need worry unduly about that,' said Uncle George. 'What you've described sounds fairly typical of the sort of mindless terrorism we've had to put up with for some years now. Fortunately there are several precedents for people taking the kind of defensive action that you took – so I'm confident that you won't find yourself being prosecuted.'

Philip looked suitably relieved.

As his uncle explained the legal situation in depth, Philip noticed how much the old man reminded him of his father, who had died nearly ten years earlier. George Morgan was seventy-five now, and a widower. With the passing years he was shrinking gradually from his originally average height and build. He still had most of his hair, which was very white and neatly cut, and a snowy white moustache stood out on his lightly tanned face. The eyes were blue, and very piercing, and the old man held himself well, sitting up straight with cushions to support his back.

'Well now, young man,' said Uncle George eventually, 'assuming that today's episode doesn't land you in any difficulties, what are your plans? Or haven't you any?'

'Only very loose ones,' said Philip. 'As I think I told you in my letters, my main purpose in coming here was to get away from

24

England for a while. But, I've heard since then that there's a job going as security adviser to President Kasaboru – so I thought I might make some enquiries about that. It sounds to be my line of country.'

'Ah yes,' said Uncle George. 'I heard that Kasaboru was in the market for someone like that. At the moment he's got a Scotsman called Walter McCulloch assisting him, but only till he gets someone permanent.'

'Yes,' said Philip. 'I have a friend in England, Jonathan Courtney, who told me about McCulloch. He's an ex-World-Wide-Mining man, isn't he?'

'Yes, I believe so. Retired now, anyway. He's a bachelor, and as tough as old boots by all accounts. . . . Well, if you're thinking of becoming Kasaboru's security chief you certainly won't be bored. And if you're going to apply for the job perhaps I ought to give you a bit of a briefing – would that be a good idea?'

'Certainly – I'd be very grateful.'

'All right. Well, let's see now. . . . I'm not sure how much you'll have remembered from your boyhood days – you were only ten when you left, after all. But let me remind you of a few basic facts. . . . First of all, geography. To the north we have the Congo, where there is still almost total anarchy. To the east our communist friends in Gabuti, to the south Zambia, to the west Angola. Balembi is, of course, a former British colony, and perhaps inevitably we're still very British in many of our ways. For instance, we use the pound sterling for money, English is the official language, and we drive on the left. And a lot of British money and talent is invested here. But, having said all that, one has to remember that Balembi is still very much part of Africa. The Africans have been here for thousands and thousands of years, while the British only came here less than a century ago. So, you must never forget that the modern, westernised way of doing things is often just superimposed on centuries and centuries of African tradition.'

'In the old days the missionaries had a very big influence, didn't they?' asked Philip.

'They still do. But that, you see, is my point. The mission schools provide a basic education and a grounding in Christianity. But underneath all that, superstition and the belief in witchcraft remain very powerful indeed, even in the present day. You get these extraordinary contrasts. There is much in Balembi that is modern, efficient and beautiful. But out there in the bush, only four or five miles from this very spot, you can still find people who are living in the most primitive conditions. Poverty and ignorance are widespread. The *average* income is only about twenty pounds a year. Something like eighty per cent of the white European population of Balembi live in the towns – but about the same proportion of black Balembians live in the bush. And out there the women are still beasts of burden. Practically all black Balembians, even those with a mission-school education, are terrified of the dark. And so on.'

'How many of the African population go to school, then?' asked Philip.

'Well, virtually all the younger children go to primary school nowadays,' said his uncle. 'Mostly mission schools supported by government grants. But only one African child in six can get into a secondary school, even now. And I should say about half of those aged twenty have never been to a school of any kind.'

Philip raised his eyebrows. 'Hmm. Well, I see what you mean – I shouldn't judge the country as a whole by what I see in Digara.'

'No indeed. And the point I'm making really is that education – in the sense that we're talking about it – often doesn't alter an African's basic way of thinking. For instance, in the Congo a few years ago, a force of trained African soldiers was put up against a crowd of natives armed only with spears. And because the soldiers believed that their opponents had drunk a magic medicine called *dawa*, which was supposed to make them immune to bullets, they just threw down their rifles and fled. So the witch doctors are still very important here, don't have any doubts about that.'

Philip grinned. 'I'll bear it in mind. But tell me a bit more about the political set-up. I gather you played quite a large part in drafting Balembi's constitution.'

'Well, some part, anyway. Very briefly, Balembi became independent in 1962. The nation is a member of the British Commonwealth but the Queen is not the head of state – Balembi is a republic, following the precedent set by India. Balembi is also a parliamentary democracy, based on the Westminster model. We don't quite have universal suffrage, but almost everybody except the crudest savage can vote.'

'A two-house system?' queried Philip.

'Yes. We have an upper house called the Senate, and a lower House of Representatives which does the real work. Both are fully elective.'

'And the head of state is the President?'

'Yes. He's elected too, on American lines, and he's a working president – in other words he not only plays the same role as the Queen, but he's effectively the Prime Minister as well. He heads a Council of Ministers which is the equivalent of the British Cabinet. In Balembi we recognized for years that black majority rule was inevitable, and we did the sensible thing – we worked like hell to set up a stable political framework. There was a black majority in the House of Representatives long before independence.'

'Yes, I see. And what about Kasaboru – would he be a good man to work for?'

'Oh, very much so. In fact the whole stability of this country depends on Kasaboru remaining in power for a good few years yet.

Or I would say so, anyway.'

'Why's that?'

'Well, to begin with, he's honest, which is rare enough in an African politician at the best of times. He's doing everything he can to stamp out corruption. Secondly, his background makes him uniquely eligible to run the country.'

'Why's that?'

'Well, the main political division in Balembi is between the two big tribal units: the Mibambo and the Fanda. The Mibambo occupy most of the west of the country, and make up about seventy per cent of the African population; the Fanda live mostly in the east, and constitute the remaining thirty per cent. The Progressive party is based largely on the Mibambo tribe and the National party on the Fanda. And the Fanda, of course, have tribal affinities with the Gabutis to the east, where they're all solidly communist.'

'And hate our guts,' said Philip, recalling the surly customs officials on the border.

'Precisely.'

'Now Kasaboru is a Progressive, isn't he?'

'He is, yes, but he has an unusual background. His father was a Mibambo chief, and also a very intelligent man. He largely educated himself, and made a lot of money as a businessman – and not all of it from the Africans by any means. In those days, the Africans and the Europeans didn't mix on a social basis, but it was very much a case of careers being open to talents. Anyway, some fifty years ago old man Kasaboru got a bit sick of all the fighting between the Mibambo and the Fanda tribes, so he very sensibly married a Fanda princess, to put an end to it. The child of that marriage was Paul Kasaboru – the only leading politician with a foot in both camps, so to speak.'

'And I've been told that he was educated in England.'

'Yes, that's true. His father, with a bit of help from his friends, sent Paul to an English public school – about 1935 that was – and later to an American college. He was really grooming the boy for leadership, on the Joseph Kennedy pattern. And by that time the son needed no pushing – I believe he majored in political thought.'

'So he was in the U.S. during the war, was he?'

'No – college in America came after the war. Paul was in the King's Own Balembian Rifles from about 1940. He joined up in time for El Alamein and went all the way up through Italy. Came out as a Major.'

'And after college?'

'Well, about 1950 he came back here and went straight into politics – he won a seat in Sungbarta. After that it wasn't long before he became leader of the Progressive Party, then Prime Minister, and then President in 1962.'

'I see. So he's a man worth supporting.'

'He is indeed. He's the sort of man I admire very much – a pragmatist.'

'What's the opposition like?'

'Well, not very attractive I'm afraid. That's very unfortunate, to put it mildly, because any healthy democracy must have a viable alternative government waiting in the wings. And in Balembi we only have the National party, which is very much in a minority when it comes to votes. It also has the disadvantage, in my estimation, of being led by an unscrupulous thug.'

'Nyanga – isn't that the name?'

'Yes. Now Nyanga's background forms a very illuminating contrast to the President's. His father was just a Fanda village headman – a vicious piece of work by all accounts. He taught his son to look after number one at all costs. Joro Nyanga was a very bright boy, though – he worked his way up through mission school to teacher-training college, and I believe he taught in this country for a couple of years. Anyway, eventually he got a scholarship to take a diploma of some sort at London University. After that he taught in the East End for a while. That was when he took up left-wing politics in a big way. The next thing we knew he'd got whisked off to Moscow. He did two years over there. The M.V. Lomonsov State University, it was – he told me all about it once, at a party. He read history, at the Russians' expense, and came back with a master's degree, for what it's worth. Soon afterwards he got elected to the Lower House, and we've had to put up with him ever since. My own opinion is that he's an extremely dangerous revolutionary, but then I'm just a hopeless old reactionary, so I keep my views to myself. To give him his credit, though, he's quite an interesting chap to talk to. If it weren't for the fact that he intends to bleed the country dry for the benefit of his own bank account I could find myself quite liking him.'

Philip laughed. 'But he's done nothing illegal, I take it?'

'Well, not that we could get a conviction on, no. It's widely believed that Nyanga is stirring up the Fanda tribesmen by leading them to believe that Kasaboru is going to wipe them all out. But proving it is difficult. Not that that would matter in most African countries. The head of state would have locked Nyanga up years ago in most places. But here, for better or for worse, we believe in the free expression of opinion, innocent until proved guilty, and all that sort of thing. There are quite a lot of us in this country who can see the trend of African history quite clearly – Macmillan spelt it all out in his 'Wind of Change' speech in 1960. The trend is towards self-determination, quite rightly. And our aim is to see that it's self-determination on democratic lines, because that's the fairest way for everyone. And because it's the fairest, it's also the most peaceful.'

'And at the end of the day,' said Philip, 'I suppose the prize that the politicians are competing for is Balembi's great mineral wealth.'

'Yes, that's right,' said his uncle. 'That's what it's all about, as usual – who gets the money. Now, the situation here is quite simple. If Kasaboru survives, then every Balembian, black or white, will get a fair lick at the lollipop. But if Nyanga takes over, then he'll guzzle the lot – and the rest will have to make do with the stick.'

Five

Philip awoke soon after eight o'clock the following morning. He came downstairs to find that his uncle's servant, Imbasa, was waiting to serve his breakfast.

'Mr Judge not get up till later,' Imbasa announced, displaying an almost total lack of teeth when he spoke. 'He have breakfast in bed. But you say – me make.'

'Very well,' said Philip, rubbing his hands together cheerfully. 'Here's what I'd like.' And having ordered his meal he picked up the *Digara Morning Mail*.

He found that the story of the hijacking of the bus from Akaville was front-page news, together with a photograph of himself getting off the bus at Digara airport. Philip winced. Personal publicity of that kind was something he could well do without. Fortunately, the account of what had happened turned out to be reasonably accurate, and much emphasis was laid on the fact that Richard Chokwe's young son had been one of the passengers; there was a picture of Chokwe embracing the boy. The issue of what was to be done about the problem of the *jeunesse* terrorising travellers was taken up in an editorial, on an inside page.

Philip broke off at this point to tuck into the enormous breakfast provided by Imbasa; then he read the newspaper's account again. A number of details about himself were included, such as the fact that he was a widower, had just left a job in Birmingham, England, and was related to former Lord Chief Justice Morgan. Philip couldn't help wondering where the newspaper had got their information – not from his uncle, he was sure, or the old man would have mentioned it.

Another interesting item was a list of all the passengers on the diverted plane, together with their destination addresses in Balembi. A name which leapt to Philip's eye was that of Dr Jane Stuart; she was the only doctor listed so he was in no doubt that he had identified her correctly. Philip still had a very clear mental image of Dr Stuart – both clothed and unclothed, and particularly the latter. He hadn't had time to enjoy the view very much during the hijacking, but the memory of the shape of her full, heavy breasts gave him an erection now with no trouble at all – even at nine o'clock in the morning.

30

For a few minutes he toyed with the idea of ringing Jane up and asking her out to lunch. But then he remembered that her attitude had not been at all encouraging. And if he approached her now she would probably think that he was just trying to cash in on his temporary notoriety. So, for the moment, Philip abandoned the idea.

Instead he tried to telephone Walter McCulloch, the former World-Wide Mining security officer who had been mentioned to him in London by Jonathan Courtney. Unfortunately he could not get any reply, possibly because McCulloch was out at work.

Shortly afterwards, 'Mr Judge', as Imbasa called him, came downstairs. Philip noticed that in the full light of day his uncle looked all of his seventy-five years old. Indeed he looked distinctly unwell, though he cheerfully claimed to feel in the best of health.

Philip showed his uncle the newspaper account, and the old man was particularly interested to see Richard Chokwe's name mentioned.

'He's a most able young man,' he explained. 'If you've made a friend of him you've made a useful ally. He's a dreadful womaniser, of course, and that might yet be the undoing of him.'

'Is there a risk of divorce?' asked Philip.

'No, I don't think so. It's just that sooner or later he might offend someone important. You see, the trouble is, Chokwe's wife isn't his intellectual equal. That is so often the case with Africans. What happens is this: a young couple get married very young, and then the husband goes on getting himself educated and developing himself through his work, while the wife stays at home and brings up the children. The result is that the wife stagnates while the husband progresses by leaps and bounds. And then the wives get very unhappy, because they realise that they can't move with ease in the same circles as their husbands. I've seen such women absolutely shaking with nerves, wondering which knife and fork to use, that sort of thing – I feel very sorry for them. But don't get me wrong – Chokwe hasn't deserted his wife and family. Far from it – he's very devoted to them, and so he should be – his wife is beautiful and his children are a credit to him. But, show him a French lady diplomat or a girl from *Time* and he's as happy as the day is long.'

Philip smiled to himself. Who wouldn't be, he thought.

Later that morning Philip's uncle took him for a drive round Digara.

Philip was impressed. Many of the buildings were built in rich red brick, giving an air of solidity and permanence. In the residential streets the private houses were set back, deeply embedded in lush green vegetation; the streets were often lined with acacia trees and yellow-blooming cassias.

The business district was equally pleasing: even the new glass and concrete office buildings had style and grace. Outside restaurants there were tables on the pavements, topped by gaily coloured umbrellas, and the shops appeared to be full of good quality products. Separated from the shops and offices by a small park were the President's palace and the Parliament building, large modern structures in white stone which managed to be dignified without looking opulent. The overall impression was therefore of a spaciously planned, luxurious European city. The population, Philip gathered, was about 150,000.

On the outskirts of the city, the industrial area boasted flour mills, dairies, soft-drink plants, a car-assembly plant, and a cigarette factory. All in all the city looked a credit to civilisation, but George Morgan again repeated his warning that things were very different out in the bush.

The two men returned to the house for lunch. There they found that a letter inviting Philip to have dinner at the President's palace the following evening had been delivered by hand. Imbasa was very impressed by this, even when Philip explained that according to the letter all the other passengers on the hijacked bus had also been invited, presumably to try to help them to forget their unpleasant experience.

Philip himself was not too keen on accepting the invitation. It struck him as being more of a public relations exercise for the Balembi Tourist Board than anything else; and he certainly didn't fancy the idea of being lionised in any way. But his uncle convinced him that President Kasaboru would handle the whole affair in a very common sense manner, without embarrassment to anyone, and Philip wrote out an acceptance for Imbasa to take to the post. He found himself wondering if Jane Stuart would also be attending the dinner.

After lunch George Morgan retired to his bedroom, declaring that at his age he felt entitled to a siesta. And after the old man had disappeared upstairs Imbasa sadly explained the reason for his absence.

'Mr Judge not well at all,' Imbasa declared with a sigh. 'Last year Mr Judge in hospital two times. When he come out, he say he not go back any more. Die here instead. I look after him.' Imbasa nodded his greying head solemnly. 'Yes,' he said, 'I look after him good.'

Philip digested this information thoughtfully, and decided that he would have to keep a careful eye on the old gentleman from now on. In the meantime, however, he decided to take advantage of his uncle's offer of the loan of his car. He decided to drive round to Walter McCulloch's house to see if he was in: McCulloch had still not answered the telephone, but Uncle George had suggested that like many retired men McCulloch might be spending much of his time in the garden. In any case, it was only a five-minute drive to

32

McCulloch's house, and no great harm would be done if he proved to be out.

McCulloch's bungalow turned out to be at the end of a quiet and secluded cul-de-sac. Nothing was moving in the blazing afternoon sunshine when Philip approached, and as he mopped the sweat from his forehead he was reminded of the saying about mad dogs and Englishmen.

There was a blue Morris 1000 parked on the driveway, in front of an open garage. This seemed to indicate that McCulloch might be at home, but there was no response to repeated rings on the doorbell; nor was there any answer to Philip's shout when he pushed the front door gently and found that it swung open.

Eventually Philip decided that if McCulloch was anywhere on the premises at all, he was at the end of a very long back garden. He went round the side of the bungalow, threaded his way through thick tropical shrubbery, and came on a wide lawn. At the far end of the lawn was a white metal table with a large sunshade above it; beside the table was a white chair with a green cushion. On the chair was an open book and a pair of reading glasses. But no McCulloch.

Philip walked to the end of the lawn. Still no McCulloch.

Then he saw him.

McCulloch was lying sprawled on the ground behind a thick hedge, ten feet beyond the table and chair. Philip ran the last few steps to McCulloch's side, but already he could see that speed would not help. The Scotsman was dead.

Walter McCulloch had been heavily built, over six feet tall and about fifteen stone; his grey hair was cut short on the back of a thick red neck. Whoever had killed him – and Philip guessed that it would have taken at least two men – had done it with pangas, almost severing the right arm and the head in the process. The whole upper body was heavily slashed, the blood plentiful and thickly congealed.

By the side of McCulloch's body was a 9mm. Luger Parabellum with a checkered walnut grip. The extractor projected slightly above the bolt, indicating that there was a round in the chamber; the safety catch was in the 'on' position, exposing the engraved word 'Gesichert'. McCulloch had apparently been expecting trouble, but at his age the reflexes had not been quite fast enough to cope with it.

Philip left the Luger where it was. With a deep sigh he turned to go back to the house to ring the police. He had the feeling that the Digara CID were not going to be at all pleased to find themselves interviewing him again, for the second time in twenty-four hours.

Six

The invitation to dinner at the President's palace had stated that Philip's presence was requested at seven-thirty for eight p.m.; dress informal. At seven thirty-five, therefore, Philip brought his uncle's car to a halt at the heavy wrought-iron gates which marked the entrance to the palace. He was wearing a medium-grey light-weight suit which George Morgan had assured him would be appropriate.

A soldier checked his invitation card and indicated where he should park his car; Philip then walked across the courtyard to the inner gate.

So far, the security arrangements seemed to him to be quite adequate: the outer defences were a set of iron railings some eight feet high and not at all easy to climb. The palace itself was built in the shape of an enormous letter C; it was an imposing building in white stone, glowing now in the light of the evening sun. The open mouth of the C was blocked by a further gate, also manned by soldiers. There were no windows at all at the ground-floor level on the outer side of the C, and clearly some thought had been given at the design stage to excluding unwelcome visitors. The building would not, of course, resist a full-scale military attack for very long – but then neither would the White House or Buckingham Palace. The important thing was to exclude the lunatic fringe; and if the soldier who gave Philip a polite but very thorough body search was any indication, Kasaboru's men were doing that very effectively indeed.

From the second gate Philip was guided towards a broad staircase which led to the banqueting hall. The entrance to the hall was mildly intimidating, with huge oak doors topped by a Grecian pediment; but the doors opened on to a reception area, which proved to be a pleasingly small-scale room, cosy rather than grandiose. The banqueting hall proper lay beyond.

A very fit-looking middle-aged man, dressed in tails and white gloves, announced the names of all arrivals to those already present. President Kasaboru then greeted his guests personally before passing them on to an aide, who ensured that they were given a drink and were made to feel at home. In short, the reception of the guests was handled in a formal but friendly manner which succeeded in putting everyone at their ease.

Philip had relatively little opportunity to observe the President when he was first introduced, and almost immediately afterwards he found himself in conversation with Richard Chokwe, Balembi's Foreign Secretary.

'Delighted you could make it, Mr Morgan,' said Chokwe, shaking Philip's hand. Philip noticed that he spoke very clearly and precisely; the accent was Oxford rather than American or mid-Atlantic, but not at all affected.

'I was very pleased to be invited,' said Philip. He had already looked around the room and noticed more than a score of familiar faces from Monday's journey. 'I think most people seem to be here,' he added.

'Well, I think one or two were unable to accept, for one reason or another,' said Chokwe. 'But you're right, most of the passengers have come, and I'm very pleased they have. It just so happened that many of the passengers on your particular flight were tourists or businessmen rather than residents. Now a resident would be able to put the hijacking into some sort of perspective – unpleasant no doubt, but not an everyday event. Newcomers, on the other hand, might not be able to see it that way – so the President and I decided we'd show them a more relaxed side of life in this country.'

'Good idea,' said Philip. He took a sip of the President's excellent sherry.

Shortly afterwards President Kasaboru himself eased his way through the now crowded room to Philip's side. 'Mr Morgan,' he said, placing a hand on Philip's shoulder.

'Good evening, Mr President.'

'A word in your ear, if I may.'

Richard Chokwe turned tactfully away and Philip followed the President into a quiet corner of the room. Kasaboru was immaculately dressed in a blue lounge suit, white shirt and blue tie. By any standards he was a handsome and powerful-looking man: his deep black features had appeared many times in the western press and on television, and were easily recognisable.

'Mr Morgan,' said Kasaboru, 'I just want to do two things. First of all I want to thank you personally for averting what could have been a very serious incident on Monday afternoon. From the evidence which the police have collected we know that it was entirely due to your courage and initiative that many lives were saved. And quite apart from the personal tragedies which that would have involved, the reputation of this country as a whole would have suffered severely. As head of state I am naturally very grateful to you for helping us to avoid that disaster. So that's the first thing I wanted to say. The second point I want to make is to assure you that there will be no speeches made tonight which sing your praises – no medals awarded or anything like that. And I say that because I suspect, from what I have heard of you from Jonathan Courtney, that you would be deeply embarrassed by any such public gesture.'

'And you would be quite right,' said Philip.

The President nodded. He glanced around the room, checking on the welfare of his guests. 'Good. Then we will leave it at that. Incidentally, having discussed the matter in detail with the Attorney General, I know that at the inquest on the dead youth, which will be held on Friday, you will not find yourself in any legal difficulty. You will not, for instance, need to go to the expense of being represented by a lawyer.'

'Thank you,' said Philip. 'It's quite a relief to know that.'

The President gave a gentle smile. 'Yes, I'm sure it must be. It's always an awkward situation – going to a country one doesn't know very well, and getting involved in something which might prove very complicated legally and therefore very expensive. But in this case there will be no problems. There will, of course, be the newspapers to contend with – but that, you will appreciate, is something I can do nothing about.'

'Yes, I understand that,' said Philip.

The President paused to give his empty sherry glass to a passing waiter.

'And that, of course, leads us on to the distressing business of Walter McCulloch.' The morning's papers had naturally made the most of the fact that it was Philip who had found the dead Scotsman the previous afternoon.

The President's expression clouded over. 'McCulloch was a very good chap, no doubt about that, and I am very sad indeed that he should have come to such an end. He tended to deprecate his own talents, but in reality he was enormously experienced. And, once again, finding his body could be a potentially embarrassing situation for you. But I just want to say that I have been able to explain to the police personally how it was that you came to know of Mc-Culloch – through your connection with Jonathan Courtney. And I understand that the post mortem established quite definitely that McCulloch was killed at about eleven a.m. – a time when you were being driven around Digara by a former Lord Chief Justice.'

'Fortunately for me,' said Philip drily.

'Yes, I think you are right there,' said the President. 'Our police are a very determined crew, but at least their determination will not be addressed to you on this occasion. But that leads me on to my final point. McCulloch was, as you know, advising me on security matters. Neither he nor I viewed the appointment as a permanent one, and it's no secret that I am looking for a civilian to co-ordinate presidential security as a whole. Now – I gather from Jonathan Courtney that you might be interested in being considered for such a post. Is that so?'

'Yes, it is,' said Philip.

'Good. Well in that case perhaps you would like to come along tomorrow morning at about eleven o'clock, and we will discuss it?'

'I'd be delighted,' said Philip.

'Splendid. Tomorrow morning we'll talk for a while and then have lunch together. In the meantime, enjoy tonight's dinner.' For a moment the President's eyes lit up with amusement. 'I think you will find,' he said, 'that I have seated you in congenial company.'

The banqueting hall was impressive but not overwhelming, a wide room with a high ceiling, from which chandeliers provided the illumination. Philip's recollection of the old Governor-General's residence on the other side of Digara was that in that building everything had been very much more ornate.

The food proved to be excellent and the service faultless; the former military man who had announced names at the door was in charge of the racially integrated group of waiters, and everything ran very smoothly.

The congenial company mentioned by the President turned out to be Jane Stuart, who was seated on Philip's right. Jane had now had two days in which to recover from her journey; that, coupled with the sherry before dinner and the wine which accompanied it, made her a good deal more outgoing than she had been on Monday. She no longer felt annoyed with herself for finding Philip attractive. On the contrary, having discovered during the past forty-eight hours that she had virtually nothing in common with Duncan and Eileen Grey, she was only too pleased to find someone who shared at least some of her interests, such as squash and sailing.

By the time dessert came along Jane had decided that Philip Morgan wasn't at all the conceited and muscle-bound moron she had feared he might be. He gave every appearance of being intelligent and well read, and there was even a hint, from time to time, that he possessed a sense of humour. Jane decided that if Philip ever asked her to go out with him she would give the matter serious consideration. Philip, for his part, had decided that one day before long he would certainly ask her for a date. He sensed that Jane always erected a barrier of reserve between herself and relative strangers, but at least the atmosphere wasn't as frosty as in the past.

After dinner the lights were dimmed and curtains were pulled back to reveal a stage at the far end of the hall. Then the Balembi National Dance Company was announced, and the dancers came on stage to begin a one-hour display.

The culmination of the dancers' performance was a long and very energetic item featuring six young Balembian girls; they were accompanied by six very loud and equally energetic male drummers. The girls were all topless, and very nearly bottomless too, and their dance allegedly enacted a saga of village rivalries. Jane couldn't quite follow the details of the plot, and suspected that no-one else

37

could either. But the story was perhaps not the point of the exercise, and the sight of all that naked flesh being shaken about brought a number of memories back to Jane's mind which made her blush. She sneaked a glance at her companion to see if he had noticed; fortunately, but not surprisingly, his attention was otherwise engaged.

After the dance troupe had finished, the evening was rounded off with dancing in the orthodox European style to an equally orthodox European quartet; the leader was clearly an admirer of Victor Sylvester.

The President claimed the first dance with Jane, and to her chagrin he proved to be a very much more accomplished dancer than she was; she felt quite relieved when the music ended and Richard Chokwe took over. Eileen Grey had warned Jane to watch out for Mr Chokwe, but he proved to be entirely harmless, at least on this occasion.

Jane's third partner was Philip Morgan, who turned out to be a dancer of much the same level of competence as herself; it was a pleasure not to be the only clumsy one for a change, and to be able to relax.

The quartet would no doubt have continued playing for as long as anyone wished to dance, but towards one a.m. the President excused himself. From then on the guests gradually began to leave, and by half past one Jane was quite happy to accept Philip's offer to drive her to Victoria Vale. Jane had been brought to the palace by Duncan Grey, and no arrangements had been made for getting her home.

'What are you going to do tomorrow?' Philip asked, as he guided his uncle's car through the darkened streets.

'I'm going to look round Digara General Hospital,' said Jane.

'Think you might work there?'

'I might. Or I might go out into the bush. I'll tell you better when I've seen a bit more. . . . What about you?'

Philip explained about his appointment with the President. 'Oh, well, I should think the job is yours for the asking,' said Jane.

'Well, perhaps. . . . But, like you, I'm not sure whether I want it.'

For the first time since arriving in Balembi Jane felt entirely at ease. She felt as if she had known Philip Morgan for some time – and what was more important, she felt as if she could trust him. In the circumstances it seemed natural that before getting out of the car she should lean over and give him a friendly but entirely sexless kiss on the cheek.

'Goodnight, Philip,' she said.

'Goodnight, Jane,' he replied, and drove away into the darkness.

Seven

'Come on, come in,' said the President cheerfully, as Philip was shown into his office the next morning. 'Have a seat over there and I'll be with you in a moment.'

He pointed to a group of Scandinavian easy chairs spread out around a coffee table. Philip sat down and the President continued signing some letters; his secretary stood waiting to take them away.

Paul Kasaboru was in his early forties, at the peak of his physical and mental powers. His height and build were those of an ordinary man, but his presence was outstanding; there was an unmistakeable air of authority and dignity about him. He was dressed in a well-cut single-breasted suit which Philip guessed had probably been made in Savile Row. The accessories had all been carefully chosen, but, unlike many African politicians, Kasaboru carefully avoided anything at all flashy or ostentatious.

After a few moments the President finished dealing with his correspondence and came to sit beside Philip; he poured coffee for them both and then sat back.

'Well now, Mr Morgan,' he began, 'we're here to talk about the job of security adviser to the Balembian head of state, currently myself. And in order to be able to do that effectively I have to explain a few things first. . . . Now, to begin with, I'd like to try to put the problem of presidential security into perspective for you. In 1955, there were only five independent states in the whole of Africa. By 1962, when we became independent, there were twenty-four. A very rapid change in a very short period of time. What's more, independence brought with it some special problems. When the Congo achieved independence in 1960, it was a country eighty-eight times the size of Belgium – and it had only sixteen university graduates. So the first point I want to make to you is this – Balembi is not too proud to admit that we need European help. In short, we need people like yourself, particularly when they already know something of our ways, as you do.'

The President paused to drink some coffee before continuing. 'Ah – excellent. . . . Now then. Second point. . . . Balembi is quite a small country by any standards – roughly one hundred miles from north to south and three hundred from east to west. And it's also a divided country – divided in all sorts of ways. Divided first of all

39

tribally – as you may know I had a Mibambo father and a Fanda mother, so there's not much anyone can tell me about differences between the tribes. And one of the main reasons why I have never married is that making any choice at all would inevitably have offended one side or the other – so, I remain single. But even the tribal division is not just a simple matter of Mibambo versus Fanda – would that it were. The situation is complicated by all sorts of cross-breedings brought about by past migrations, wars, border raids, concubinage, and, very occasionally, intermarriage between two people of different tribes who just happened to fall in love. The result of all that history is a great mass of racial mixtures and genetic outcroppings, with sub-tribes here and family groups there, all sorts of layers of antagonisms and loyalties which no outsider could begin to imagine. Consequently, you can never be quite sure who your friends are.'

'Or your enemies,' suggested Philip.

'Yes indeed. . . . And as if that were not enough, there are also other divisions. English is the official language, but not everyone speaks it. There are over one hundred and twenty local dialects, even in our small area. But, perhaps we should consider ourselves fortunate – in Nigeria there are over three hundred languages. . . . Then, of course, there are economic differences – and please don't think I am speaking wholly racially. I should imagine that the difference between my life style and that of a tribesman living out in the bush is of the order of a thousand to one. No, the point I am making is that for most of my fellow countrymen, for most of the time, life is – to quote Hobbes – nasty, brutish, and short.'

'I suppose most of your people still live in villages do they?' asked Philip.

'Yes, that's right. The village headman or chief is still the only authority recognised by many Balembians. If I took off this suit and walked through most villages in my underwear, no-one would know who I was. Far from being hailed as the President, I should probably be stoned as a dangerous stranger. Most black Balembians, I am sorry to say, live in a state of chronic ignorance and superstition, coupled with massive ill-health. Malaria, sleeping sickness, leprosy and filariasis, in that order, are major health problems.'

'And so subsistence farming will still be the major preoccupation.'

'In many instances, yes. The women tend to be given the agriculture to deal with, plus any other hard work. They grow manioc, the odd banana tree, and keep cattle. The men may hunt, fish, or just fight amongst themselves. They also make palm wine, smelt a little iron, and prepare magical medicines. Even among the educated Balembians, the prevailing atmosphere is often one of inefficiency and incompetence. . . . In some respects, though, we are a practical and down-to-earth people. There is a story that the first European who came here was asked by a Mibambo tribesman if it were true

40

that he was immortal. Yes, said the European, that was true. So the tribesman shot him through the heart with an arrow.'

Philip sat back and roared with laughter.

'So you see,' continued the President, 'you should be careful that what you say to us will stand up to examination. . . .' He poured some more coffee for both Philip and himself.

'The reason why I am telling you all this, Mr Morgan, is not to denigrate my friends and relations, but to try to convey to you the circumstances in which I am working. Now let us look a little closer at the political situation, because it is there that threats to the President's safety are most overt. . . . My own party, as I'm sure you know, is supported largely by the Mibambo people and by most of the Europeans. We have our problems within the party, as inevitably all political alliances do. There are young men, even in the Progressive party, who if given their head would scare away all European capital and manpower first thing tomorrow morning. They are youngsters who have very often seen something of western Europe, particularly Britain, through educational scholarships. These young men, they go off to Europe and come back with all sorts of wild ideas. But, at the moment, I think I can handle them. So all my real opposition comes from the National party. Now the National party draws most of its support from the Fanda tribe and from the working-class Europeans – and its leader is Joro Nyanga. Nyanga is also supported by the Communist government of Gabuti: they make no secret of their moral support, and less openly they give him funds and other resources. In the last year or two the Russians have also begun to give Mr Nyanga a helping hand. In fact only a couple of days ago a new "adviser" appeared at the Russian Embassy – a man called Semenov.'

'What about the Chinese communists?' asked Philip.

The President was cautious. 'Well, at the moment they are keeping a very low profile – but I have reason to believe that they have begun to make overtures to one or two key figures on the fringe of Gabuti politics.'

Philip nodded. 'I've heard quite a lot about Nyanga,' he said, 'most of it bad. What's your view?'

The President smiled. 'Well, I don't froth at the mouth when his name is mentioned – it's not my style. All I can say to you is that you must stop thinking in European terms – more specifically, you must stop thinking in British terms. Nyanga, you see, is not just a debating opponent – he is a killer. He is undoubtedly prepared to kill at one remove, and probably prepared to kill in person. I am certain, for instance, that it was he who ordered Walter McCulloch's death – though I must ask you not to repeat that outside this room, because I shall never be able to prove it. Nyanga is greedy, cruel, and ruthless. There is enormous potential wealth in this country, as there is in much of Africa – we have copper, cobalt, manganese, radium, gold, silver – even diamonds – and ninety per cent of those mineral resources remain totally unexploited. Now Nyanga knows all this, and his basic tactic is to tell the poor that under a National government they would be rich – and they believe it. He also tells the Fanda tribesmen that I, Kasaboru, together with the Mimbambo tribe as a whole, intend to wipe them all out – and they believe that, too. It's not surprising that they believe it, because we have had several nasty murders of Fanda villagers this year. And I should tell you that many of my colleagues in the Progressive party believe that Nyanga is responsible. They also believe that he is undermining the credibility of my government by organising indiscriminate acts of terrorism – such as the hijacking of your bus.'

'But again, you can't prove that,' said Philip.

The President shook his head. 'Not at present, no. And I doubt if we ever shall be able to prove it in the strictly legal sense. If you quoted me I would deny having said it. But I want you to be quite clear that Nyanga is fully capable of such crimes.'

Philip nodded. 'Jonathan Courtney believes that Nyanga is planning a revolutionary coup. What's your view?'

The President smiled wryly. 'Well, Mr Morgan, if I were a member of the communist government of Gabuti, or an official of the Russian Embassy in Digara, both organisations which are devoting considerable amounts of time and money to propping up Nyanga, I would certainly hope and expect that he *would* be planning a coup d'état – otherwise I'd be wasting my time and money, wouldn't I?'

'What's he going to use for men – units of the army?'

'Probably. We tried to introduce tribal integration into the army, but it didn't work. So you have Mimbambo regiments and Fanda regiments, and the latter naturally view Nyanga as a hero. Most of the officers are still European, but they're human, after all – they can be bribed, or frightened, or replaced. Staging a coup is really very easy, you know – it's been done time and time again in Africa. In the Congo, Colonel Mobutu took over the capital with only two hundred men. In the Sudan in 1958, General Abboud mounted guns in a position to control two key bridges over the Nile, and he controlled Khartoum. It's very simple. You take control of the army – not too difficult because African soldiers are easily led. You seize the post office, the airport, the radio station, and you arrest the President, and that's it. Child's play. Of course it could be done in London as easily as here, but it won't be because British politicians and the British army have got more sense.'

'The real problem is, a coup in itself solves nothing,' suggested Philip.

'Exactly. In fact more than that, it makes things far worse. That's what really worries me about Nyanga and his friends. You see, there are some people supporting Nyanga who are naive enough to

42

believe that they can have a controlled coup. They imagine that there will be a short, sharp burst of military activity which will result in me being deposed and Nyanga being put in my place. Now that would be uncomfortable for me – I don't want to die, of course – but it would be no great tragedy if that were all that happened. But it can't possibly be held to that. If Nyanga launches a violent revolution, then this country will descend into total anarchy. We have enough trouble keeping the lid on the situation as it is – but if the constitutionally elected government is overthrown by force, then force will be seen as the way to settle all scores. It's not so long since one village used to raid another to supply the Arab slave traders – and the whole history of this country is one of tribal wars and blood feuds. So if once the fuse is lit, all that hatred will flare up all over again. Village will turn against village, the black soldiers against their white officers, Mibambo against Fanda, and so on. There will be a mixture of civil war, mutiny and riot – anarchy and bloodshed on a huge scale, just as there was in the Congo.'

The President was silent for some moments, lost in his own thoughts.

'What sort of time scale are you talking about?' asked Philip eventually. 'You seem to feel an attempted coup is inevitable – when do you expect it to take place?'

The President shrugged. 'Who knows? In another three weeks I have to attend the Congress of Independent African States in Accra – it could be then, while I am out of the country. Or perhaps it won't happen for years. . . . Of course, we are not entirely unprepared, Mr Morgan.' The President smiled and seemed to recover some of his good spirits. 'We have our ears pretty firmly to the ground, you can be sure of that.'

Philip grinned in return.

The President collected a folder from his desk. 'Well now, let us talk about you for a change. Your friend Jonathan Courtney gave me an outline of your career to date, and with your permission I'd like to go through it.'

'Of course.'

For the next hour Philip was subjected to a series of penetrating questions on all aspects of his life from his early childhood onwards. He discovered that the President had been exceptionally well briefed, and not only by Jonathan Courtney. He knew, for instance, that Philip's father had been obliged to leave the Governor-General's staff because he had favoured self-determination for Balembi at a time when such talk was practically treason. He also knew that in addition to his training in the army, Philip had been a police marksman and a member of a pistol club in civilian life. Another piece of information in the file was that Philip had taught judo and boxing for two nights a week at a Birmingham youth club. All in all, Kasaboru seemed to have far more data than he would have done if Philip had filled in an application form.

At last the grilling came to an end.

'Well,' said the President, 'I think the only thing I haven't told you already which you ought to know, is exactly what I want my security adviser to do. And that I think I can summarise very briefly. There is a tradition in the Mibambo tribe that the chief never dies a natural death. If the worst comes to the worst, he has to be suffocated during his last illness. It is a tradition which I do not think should be taken too seriously. So first of all I need a personal bodyguard, rather like the Queen has – someone who stands beside me and carries a gun. I'm not prepared to be a Papa Doc and surround myself with soldiers all the time, and in the final analysis there is no protection against assassination, as you know. If the American Secret Service could not keep Kennedy alive then there is no use pretending I am immortal. But while we cannot insure against the professional, we can and must insure against the amateurs. . . . Secondly, I need someone to co-ordinate all my security arrangements, in this sense. The army guards the palace, and the police are responsible for me when I travel about the country. What I expect my security chief to do is to take overall responsibility for checking and approving all security arrangements, and to make sure that certain basic standards are maintained. The security chief will be a member of my staff and will have no direct authority over either the army or the police. But, in practice, he will agree with me what has to be done, and will then ensure that it is done. It's a matter of using common sense and a degree of tact, and I don't anticipate any difficulty. . . . Is there anything you'd like to ask about that?'

'No,' said Philip, 'I think you've put that very clearly.'

'Salary – well, that of a Detective Chief Superintendent, I think. I don't know what that is at present rates, not to the last pound, but we can check up in a minute. What I can tell you now, Mr Morgan, is that as a result of our discussion today I will write to you formally and offer you a year's contract. But I expect you would like time to study the terms and to think it over before replying.'

'Yes,' said Philip, 'I think I would.'

'Good. Well in that case let us go and have lunch.'

The President led the way into his private dining-room, where he introduced Philip to Albert Thompson, the Director of his household staff. Philip remembered Thompson well from the reception the night before, when he had announced the guests' names in his best parade-ground voice.

'Mr Thompson is a man of many talents,' said the President as they sat down at the table. 'One of the earliest attempts on my life was made by a cook. He obtained some of the stiff white hairs from around a leopard's mouth, chopped them up, and sprinkled them into my soup. Fortunately, Mr Thompson noticed. If he hadn't I would not be here today. I gather that, if ingested, the small pieces of hair pierce the stomach wall and cause cysts. The cysts become inflamed and lead to peritonitis – not a nice way to die. . . . But don't let me spoil your appetite.'

Albert Thompson winked at Philip as he served the first course. Conversation turned to more cheerful matters.

'As you will understand,' said the President later on, 'I took the liberty of making a few enquiries about you before you came for interview.'

'Yes,' said Philip. 'So I gathered.'

'Well, you must excuse me for that. But I had several other applicants for this post, and all of them disappointed me in one way or another, so it was important that I should be sure of my ground with you. Jonathan Courtney described you as a man who believes in old-fashioned virtues – such as freedom, justice, and equality. Is that a fair description?'

'I suppose so,' said Philip hesitantly. 'But I don't often stop to think about it.'

'Nor me,' said the President cheerfully. 'And you did have other advantages too. You're related to our former Lord Chief Justice, for example, and he's a man I much admire. Years ago, before the war, he defended African politicians at a time when that was a most unfashionable thing to do – and as a judge he was totally uncorruptible. He has also supported many young Balembians financially while they were being educated.'

Philip looked up in surprise. 'Now that I didn't know.'

'Oh yes. . . . And finally, of course, you have one overwhelming virtue.'

'What's that?'

'Like me, you went to school at Tallmead.'

'Ah yes,' said Philip. 'I remember now – Jonathan mentioned that.'

'In the circumstances,' said the President, 'you will understand that I obviously have to give some consideration to the loyalty of my personal bodyguard – and I came to the conclusion that while one Balembian would cheerfully stab any other Balembian in the back, no old Tallmeadian could possibly betray another.'

Philip glanced up across the table with raised eyebrows. The President's face was entirely straight – but Philip had the impression that Kasaboru might have been joking.

Eight

After lunch with the President, Philip returned to King George VI Avenue. There he described to his uncle the post that the President had offered him.

George Morgan talked at length about what the job would entail. He was an enormously useful source of information and advice; but as Philip was well aware, in the end the decision whether or not to accept the offer would have to be his own. The discussion with his uncle only served to confirm his earlier view that the task would be challenging and immensely worthwhile. But it would also be highly dangerous: the murder of Walter McCulloch had made that absolutely clear.

Towards five o'clock Philip decided that he had spent enough time thinking about his future: what he needed in the immediate present was some light entertainment. He rang up Jane Stuart and asked her to go out with him that evening, and slightly to his surprise she accepted immediately.

Philip called at the Greys' house in Victoria Vale at seven o'clock, and Eileen Grey invited him in for a drink. She poured him a huge glass of Scotch, and for a few minutes Philip chatted to Eileen and her husband while Jane finished putting on her make-up. Both the Greys congratulated him on his action in rescuing the bus passengers, and Eileen Grey deliberately sat in a position where she could reveal an ample display of thigh.

Finally, when Jane was ready, Philip took her out to see a film at a cinema in central Digara; afterwards they had dinner at a small restaurant which George Morgan had recommended.

Jane talked about her visit that afternoon to Digara General Hospital. The hospital had turned out to be entirely up-to-date in its design and equipment, and there were certainly openings for recently qualified doctors on the staff. But as Jane explained, working there would be much the same as working in a hospital in London or New York – and she had not come out to Balembi with quite that intention. She had not yet made up her mind what to do.

Philip in turn described the choice open to him. 'I'm not going to decide immediately, either,' he said. 'I'll wait until tomorrow's over, at least.'

'Oh – what's happening tomorrow?'

'Well, there are the inquests on that black youth and on Walter McCulloch, for a start. I'm surprised in a sense that Kasaboru has offered me the job before the inquests are out of the way. There's bound to be more publicity, and possibly some awkward questions.'

'None that you haven't a good answer to,' said Jane. 'I imagine he just wanted to demonstrate his confidence in you.'

The following morning Philip received the letter which the President had promised him, setting out a formal offer of employment; he put it on one side.

At eleven a.m. the inquest on the youth with the sergeant's stripes was held, and at two p.m. the inquest on Walter McCulloch. Both enquiries took place in the Balembi Justice buildings, near the President's palace; George Morgan accompanied his nephew on both occasions, 'just to keep an eye on things', as he put it.

In the event there were no problems. A senior police officer gave it as his opinion that without Philip's intervention the passengers would have suffered serious harm; the much worse experiences of other travellers in similar circumstances were quoted in support of this view. The Coroner concluded by making it entirely clear that Philip had acted as he did only in the interest of protecting innocent lives; certainly no proceedings should be taken against him. There were murmurs of agreement from those present when this was announced.

At the afternoon session, a different Coroner took pains to establish Philip's legitimate reason for calling on Walter McCulloch at the time he did; he also obtained confirmation from the police that Philip was not a suspect. Verdict: murder by a person or persons unknown.

Numerous flash-bulbs were let off in Philip's face as he left the Justice buildings after both inquests, but the reporters' questions were noticeably friendly after what they had heard.

About an hour after he returned home Philip received a telephone call from Jane. She had been listening to the Digara radio and had heard a news bulletin describing the outcome of the inquests.

'I'm sure it must be a great relief to get it all settled,' she said.

'Yes, it certainly is.'

'Well now – you bought me dinner last night so what about me cooking dinner for you this evening?'

'That sounds interesting,' said Philip. 'Where are you proposing to execute this culinary triumph?'

'Right here in Victoria Vale. The Greys have gone away for the weekend – they left about half an hour ago, full of apologies for leaving me alone for two days, but not suggesting for one moment that I should go with them. So how about it?'

'Delighted,' said Philip. 'I'll be right over.'

47

Despite a lack of familiarity with Eileen Grey's kitchen, Jane managed to concoct a very pleasing salad, followed by peaches and ice-cream; to accompany the meal they shared a bottle of South African white wine. Jane carried their coffee into the Grey's living-room at the end of the meal.

'Actually,' she said, 'although I felt cross with Duncan and Eileen for deserting me, I was really rather pleased to see them go.'

'Oh – why so?'

'Well, to tell you the honest truth, I can't stand either of them. Duncan is my mother's brother, but I'd never met him before, or his wife either, and no-one in the family knows much about him. My grandmother – Duncan's mother, that is – always gets a very worried look in her eye when she talks about him, and Eileen told me herself that he's the black sheep of the family. So there's something not quite right somewhere. He drinks like a fish, and I have a suspicion he was drummed out of the British army – though he says he was retired on medical grounds.'

'I see. . . . Was he a career officer?'

'Yes, I believe so. He likes to be known as Major Grey. He just saw service at the tail end of the second world war, and he has a long string of stories about his experiences in Korea – mostly on the crude side.'

'Hmm,' said Philip. 'Well, I can't say I was very impressed with him in that brief conversation we had last night. He seems a bit lightweight compared with his wife.'

'Oh, she just regards him as a complete fool. She also makes a cuckold of him in the most flagrant manner I've ever seen. The only reason she's gone away with him this weekend is because they've been invited to a house party by a very wealthy man, and she doesn't want to miss an opportunity of bettering herself. She as good as told me that before she set off.'

'Yes, she looks a bit of a handful for any man,' said Philip thoughtfully. 'She's got a boy-friend, has she?'

'Oh, yes.'

'What's he like?'

'Oh, I gather he's quite a big man. He's a local politician called Joro Nyanga.'

Philip's eyebrows demonstrated his surprise. 'Well I'm damned. . . .'

'Why – do you know him?'

'Not personally, no. But I've heard of him. And you're right, Jane, he is an important man.' Philip explained Nyanga's background.

'Oh, well, no wonder Eileen is so hot for him. Everyone knows about their affair – the neighbours were all dropping hints and asking me questions about it five minutes after I got here. And God knows I'm not a prude, but they indulge in the noisiest love-making

I've ever heard.'

'Oh? Tell me more,' said Philip with interest. And Jane described how she had been kept awake on the night of her arrival, and on the Tuesday night too, by the sounds from the bedroom next door.

Philip was highly amused. He put his arm round Jane's shoulders and pulled her closer to him. 'Speaking of love-making. . .' he said, and there was silence for some time.

A few minutes later Jane led the way upstairs to her bedroom; there was, after all, no point in being uncomfortable downstairs. As she took off her clothes in the soft light of late evening Philip could see the shape of her breasts which had given him such pleasure earlier on; his erection became so hard that it was almost painful.

As soon as they were both undressed they sat down on the edge of Jane's bed. Philip stroked her nipples and kissed her deeply, tasting the sweetness of her mouth; she was deliciously soft and yet firm all over.

Before long Jane lay back and opened her legs, her arms laid flat above her head in submission; Philip entered her at once. It was too hot to lie directly on top of her and he supported most of his weight on his hands. He forced his way far into Jane's body, rocking her whole frame with the force of his strokes; she gasped with pleasure at the limit of every thrust. In the half-light he could see intense physical delight flickering across her face; and when it had passed its peak he relaxed his own control and let the climax come spurting and throbbing out of him.

Almost immediately the energy drained out of Philip in a flood; his arms suddenly threatened to give way. He disentangled himself from Jane and sprawled across the bed, his heart pounding fiercely as the blood roared in his ears.

For a long time neither of them moved. Then Jane sat up on one elbow and kissed his cheek. The sight of her breasts moving, and the feel of them on his chest as she leaned over him brought Philip's body back to life again: his penis began to stiffen and rise.

Jane laughed softly and reached down to take hold of him. 'You know,' she remarked, 'back in the States, where I grew up, calling a man a two-timer is considered an insult. But personally I think there's a lot to be said for it.'

To avoid scandalizing the Greys' neighbours any further, Philip eventually went home that Friday night, but not before he and Jane had made arrangements to spend the rest of the weekend together.

After breakfast the next morning Philip explained his plans and asked his uncle if he knew anything about Duncan and Eileen Grey. He related briefly what Jane had told him.

'Well, I don't know them personally,' George Morgan replied. 'But I've heard of them. Your lassie is right – Duncan Grey is widely regarded as a weak fool, and his wife is Nyanga's moll, or whatever they call it nowadays. A white wife or mistress is a sort of status symbol for many Africans, particularly the ambitious ones – and the attraction works both ways, of course.'

'Well, I don't suppose Jane will have to put up with them much longer,' said Philip. 'She'll move out as soon as she decides where she's working.'

At his uncle's suggestion Philip brought Jane round to meet him before they left Digara to spend the weekend together. Imbasa served coffee in the living-room while Jane and the old man talked, and he was able to make a number of suggestions about where a doctor could make the biggest contribution. Then, towards noon, Philip and Jane drove off in a hired car.

They headed north, towards the Balembi National Park. The Park was too small to be a self-contained eco-system, but it contained a wide cross-section of African wildlife which could be seen in safety and relative comfort.

During the Saturday afternoon Philip and Jane joined the large numbers of tourists and Balembian citizens who were also admiring the giraffes, the elephants, and the various species of antelope; they even saw a quagga, a species of zebra which was on the verge of extinction.

Saturday night was spent in a beautifully air-conditioned hotel in the heart of the National Park. For the sake of appearances they took separate rooms, but slept together none the less.

On Sunday morning they visited the Bailey Falls, another major tourist attraction. The falls were named after the explorer who was the first white person to discover them, and the African name for them, in translation, was 'the smoke that thunders'.

The river that gave rise to the falls was a quarter of a mile wide at the point where the river bed fell sharply away, and the water dropped 130 feet into a deep pool called the Boiling Pot. The spray rose 500 feet into the air and was sometimes visible for twenty miles.

The falls were an awe-inspiring sight, and Philip and Jane were almost reluctant to leave. But the time came when they felt that they ought to return to Digara.

'Well,' said Jane, as they began their journey, 'have you decided what you'll do yet?'

'Yes,' said Philip. 'I'm going to take the job that Kasaboru's offered me. . . . What about you?'

'Well, tomorrow I'm going to go out into the bush and stay with an old friend of my father's – a lady doctor. She and my father were very fond of each other – though whether they ever became lovers I don't know. Anyway, I'm going to go and stay with her for a few days and get the feel of things.'

'What's this place called?'

'Opana – it's about twenty miles away.'

'Is there a cottage hospital out there?'

'Well, you could call it that. I gather her house is the only brick building in a good many square miles. It's not a hospital really, it's just a place where the very poor go for medical assistance.'

'Who pays for it?'

'Oh, I believe it's financed by a mission of some kind, but Enid's run it on her own for about twenty years. She's very dedicated, as you can imagine, and it's medicine right at the grass roots. So it'll be interesting to compare it with Digara General.'

'Yes, I bet it will. How will you get there?'

'Oh, I'll hire a car and follow my nose.'

Philip took his eyes off the road and glanced at her. 'Well just mind how you go, Dr Stuart. I'd like to see you again before long.'

Nine

'Mr Morgan?'

'Speaking.'

'Kasaboru here.'

For one awful moment Philip didn't recognise the voice or catch the name – it wasn't every day that he received a telephone call from a head of state, and it was only half past eight in the morning. But mercifully the penny dropped at last.

'Oh – good morning, sir,' Philip managed to stutter.

'Good morning. I've just opened your letter, which I was very pleased to receive, and I was wondering if you'd like to start work immediately?'

'Well – yes – by all means.'

'Good. In that case please come round to the palace when you're ready, and we can spend the day together. I have a long-standing engagement to go out to the World-Wide Mining Works at Tikiro later today – but at least the journey will give us an opportunity to talk.'

'I'll be with you in about an hour,' said Philip.

The President, Philip decided, was certainly a fast mover. On his return to Digara on the Sunday evening Philip had written a letter accepting the President's offer of a one-year contract; he had delivered it by hand to the palace gate late that night. And now, at half past eight the following morning, Kasaboru wanted him to report for duty. Well, fair enough.

By ten o'clock Philip had been introduced to the President's personal secretary – white, female, and very forbidding – and was sitting in Kasaboru's office. The President had been hard at work for two hours, and had succeeded in clearing his desk in good time for a ten-thirty departure.

'You've already met Kelly Thompson, haven't you?' asked Kasaboru. 'The head of my household staff,' he continued, when Philip looked a bit blank.

'Oh, yes.'

'His real name's Albert Thompson, but he had an Irish mother and we all tend to use his middle name. You'll find that Kelly is a

52

very useful man in many ways. He also has a close friend called Bob Fuller, who acts as my transport officer and personal chauffeur. Now Fuller and Thompson you ought to know a bit about. They're both British, and they both came out here with the army, back in colonial days, to train our soldiers. They were both non-commissioned officers but absolutely at the top of their particular tree. Thompson left the army about six years ago, and having got to like Balembi he decided to stay on here. He got a job as assistant director of the Governor-General's household – and then, after independence, when there was a bit of a reshuffle, he took over his present post.'

'What's Fuller's background?' Philip asked.

'Much the same. He comes from South London originally – a fairly modest background I should say. He did seventeen years in the army, where he learnt everything there is to know about motor vehicles. And, like Thompson, he decided to stay on here when his time in the army came to an end. He's now responsible for all my transport arrangements. We've got four cars altogether, and we usually travel by road. Fuller and Thompson share a flat together incidentally – neither of them is married.'

'Do they live in the palace?'

'No, they live outside, so they're not on the premises all the time. But from a security point of view they're still quite a useful pair. Absolutely loyal, I have no doubt about that, and for men of forty-plus they're both very fit. They both saw active service in the war, so they obviously know which way to point a gun, and Walter McCulloch made sure that they were provided with the right weapons. I don't think Walter did anything more than suggest that they should help to defend the palace if it were ever attacked. But perhaps you'll have a chat with them and find out exactly what arrangements Walter did make.'

'Right, I will. Speaking of where people live, that reminds me – is there any chance that I could be found a room in the palace?'

'Certainly, if you wish.'

'I think it would be just as well,' said Philip. 'At least until I get the feel of the security situation as a whole. At the moment there seems to be a good deal of tension.'

'Well, perhaps that's just because you're new here,' said the President. 'Personally I think the situation is much the same as it always was – in Africa we live in a perpetual state of crisis. But, in any case, finding you a comfortable room here is no problem. I'll get Kelly to see to it. Incidentally, I've sent a memo round to all my staff, briefing them on who you are and what you're up to – so once you introduce yourself you'll get all the co-operation you need. If not, you'll let me know, of course.'

Philip nodded. 'What about the army unit stationed here?'

'There's a Colonel in charge, Colonel Webb. I've arranged for you to meet him when we get back this afternoon.'

Bob Fuller, the President's chauffeur, was a small dark man with clear blue eyes and a permanently cheerful expression. He wore a smart grey uniform which was cut close to his trim and compact frame. He looked almost alarmingly fit and wiry, and despite an advantage in size, Philip would not have cared to come up against him in a fight.

Fuller paused only to show Philip that under the rear seat of the President's Rolls-Royce there was a drawer containing two Mark 5 Sten guns and a large quantity of ammunition.

'If there's any trouble on the road you and the President help yourself,' said Fuller. 'The President's seen plenty of action in his time, by the way, so he won't need any coaching. He's a dab hand with one of those.'

Then they were off, heading south-west from Digara on the road to Tikiro.

A police car travelled ahead of the President's Rolls, in constant radio communication with police units stationed along the route; another police car followed up behind. Not a hundred per cent foolproof, thought Philip. But then – what was?

The President waited until they had left Digara before speaking. Then he crossed his legs and relaxed in his seat.

'If I remember rightly,' he said, 'we were talking the other day about Balembi's mineral wealth. Well, the object of this visit today is to enable us to look at some developments in the mining world. It will also, incidentally, enable you to meet a singularly dangerous man – but we will speak of him in a minute. . . . In the meantime, what do you know about the relationship between African governments and mining companies, Mr Morgan?'

'Not as much as I should,' said Philip. 'But by and large you co-operate, don't you? In other words, you share both expenses and profits.'

'Well, in broad terms, yes, though some countries favour nation-alisation. In the Congo, for instance, I have the feeling that Mobutu is about to lose patience with Mr Tshombe – before long he will throw Tshombe out and nationalise the Union Minière. But that is not something I would favour myself. No, in Balembi we adopt a compromise, in the true British tradition. In our case, the state finances exploration, and once feasibility has been established, pri-vate enterprise is invited in to actually dig the minerals out of the ground. It's quite a common arrangement, as a matter of fact. Togo's phosphate and Swaziland's iron ore are exploited in exactly the same way.'

'And in your case the chief firm concerned is World-Wide Mining.'

'Yes, that's right. There are others, but World-Wide is the biggest. Jonathan Courtney, as you know, is the director responsible for the Balembi operation at the London end – and very helpful he is too. Drives a hard bargain, but fundamentally he is interested in our development. Here in Balembi, however, the WWM subsidiary is headed by a very different man. . . . His name is Conrad Hall. Have you heard of him?'

'Not by name,' said Philip. 'But I gathered from Jonathan that he had his doubts about the man's honesty.'

'So he should have. Hall is one of those people I was telling you about last week – one of those idiots who think that they can stage a brief coup d'état without unleashing chaos. He's a Nyanga supporter – gives him both money and advice. Fortunately I found out about Mr Hall quite a while ago, and I have had my intelligence people do a careful study of him. They're still working on his early life, which is interestingly difficult to find out about, but we already know quite a lot. He's forty-five now, and he claims to have been brought up in South Africa. But there's no real record of his having existed until 1946, when he began a B.Sc. course in engineering at the University of the Witwatersrand in Johannesburg. The story goes that he was unable to serve in the South African forces during the war because of a back injury sustained when he was thrown from a horse. Personally I doubt it. Anyway, he got his B.Sc. in 1949, and qualified as a chartered accountant at the same time, which gives some indication of his ability. For the next twelve years he worked in three different mining companies in South Africa, where he rose to very high positions. After that he joined WWM in Balembi.'

'So he's good at his job,' said Philip. 'But what's he like as a man?'

'A snob, and a racialist.' The President spoke sharply, but then turned to Philip and smiled. 'I try not to let my prejudices show, but really he is one of the most unpleasant men I have ever come across. He has a large number of African servants, whom he abuses both mentally and physically – in the sexual context he is a sadist, by the way. Men dislike him, women fear him, and he sneers at everything. I suppose he must have some redeeming characteristic, but offhand I can't imagine what it is.'

'Perhaps he contributes to charities,' suggested Philip.

'If so, he does a remarkably good job of keeping it secret. No – the truth, I suspect, is quite the opposite. I believe he steals rather than gives away. Neither Jonathan Courtney nor I can prove it – yet – but we believe he is using WWM funds and facilities to further the political ambitions of Mr Nyanga. And his whole motive in supporting Nyanga is to make himself richer than he is already – though God knows he lives like a mediaeval baron as it is.'

'I don't quite follow that,' said Philip. 'From the way you describe him he sounds like a right-wing capitalist – but he's supporting a communist revolutionary. Why's he doing that?'

'Well, you see,' said the President, 'Conrad Hall believes that after a revolution Nyanga would still need him. With Nyanga running the country the WWM mines would all be nationalised, of course. But there would still be a need for skilled management to go on getting the copper and other minerals out of the ground. And Hall's belief is that in a nationalised WWM it would be a lot easier for him to feed his Swiss bank account than it is at present. . . . He may be right, of course. But my own belief is that he greatly underestimates the economic dislocation which would follow a coup – and I personally would not expect Mr Nyanga to keep a bargain for one moment. But, there we are – that's just my point of view. I expect it all looks different to Conrad Hall.'

For several miles the President's Rolls had been travelling along a dead straight road which was flanked on either side by monotonous scrub bush; this vegetation was made up of neither trees nor grassland, but of thick expanses of gnarled, level-topped bushes with a little grass beneath them.

At last hills appeared on the horizon, and on them Philip could see the deep scars of open-cast mining operations, on a truly massive scale; excavators and huge lorries littered the landscape for as far as one could see.

They had arrived at Tikiro.

Conrad Hall, the managing director of WWM Balembi, proved to be much as the President had described him. He was of average height, with a swelling midriff which he did his best to hide with an immaculately white but loosely-cut jacket. He had blonde hair, cut very short against his skull, and his face was pitted with acne scars.

The purpose of the President's trip was to see a new open-cast technique for mining copper, and Hall escorted the two visitors from hill-top to hill-top, spouting statistics at them in a constant stream. Ten-ton buckets on the enormous excavators were emptied into twenty-ton trucks. Productivity was thirty-two cubic yards per day per man. Half the copper ore was treated electrolytically and half refined by the blister method. And so on.

Philip was glad when it was time for lunch.

After lunch the President posed for publicity photographs with a beaming Mr Hall, and then departed for Digara.

On the way back he talked to Philip at length about his political colleagues in the Progressive party – their ambitions, their strengths and their weaknesses. And as the Rolls approached the outskirts of

Digara the President turned his attention to the National party, his opponents.

'You've never met Nyanga, have you?' he asked.

'Not yet,' said Philip.

'Well, we may as well complete your education,' said Kasaboru, and leaned forward to ask Bob Fuller to call in at the Parliament building. Fuller reached for the microphone to warn his police escorts of the change of plan, and a few minutes later the Balembi Parliament building came into view.

Governments with excessive powers tend to produce public buildings which are heavy and monumentally impressive. The Balembi Parliament building was not like that: it had been designed by an almost unknown English architect who had remained almost unknown after it was built – which certainly satisfied the Balembi government, if not the architect. They had not wanted a dramatic and architecturally outstanding structure, and they had not been given one. What they had wanted, and what had been built, was a graceful and attractive building which was in no way overpowering: even the white stone was restful rather than dazzling.

Once Fuller had brought the car to a halt, the President walked boldly up the steps to the Parliament building's main entrance. Not a good security practice, thought Philip, looking nervously around him; but no-one seemed to be paying any attention.

Kasaboru led the way briskly down a corridor until he found a door marked with the name of the leader of the National party. Then he knocked and put his head into the room.

'Ah, so you're in,' he said cheerfully, pushing the door wider open.

Joro Nyanga rose slowly to his feet from his desk. Somehow the action did not seem to be a sign of respect.

'We were just passing, so I thought I'd call in and introduce my new security adviser,' said the President, pushing Philip forward. 'Mr Morgan, Mr Nyanga.'

Philip stepped into the room and shook hands with Joro Nyanga.

He was immediately conscious of the other man's strength. There was no attempt to crush Philip's fingers – on the contrary, the grip was gentle – but there was an unmistakable sense of controlled power about Nyanga which Philip had rarely experienced. Only once before had he met such a man – an East End gang leader now serving thirty years in prison.

'Ah yes – Mr Philip Morgan,' said Nyanga with a wide smile. 'Yes, I have heard a great deal about you, Mr Morgan. I have read about your exploits with great interest. I believe that you managed to kill one of our citizens within half an hour of crossing the border. . . . That must be some kind of a record, even for a white man.'

The smile remained on Nyanga's face and Philip thought it best

57

to say nothing.

'But,' Nyanga continued after a pause, 'as the Coroner pointed out on Friday, perhaps you were acting to protect the lives of innocent women and children. And let us not forget that there was the son of an important politician present – and we must look after our politicians' interests. Is that not so, Mr President?'

'First rule of public life,' said the President, and Nyanga roared with laughter.

There were further good-humoured exchanges for the next five minutes, during which an outsider might have thought that all present were members of some closely-knit fraternity. Then the President brought the conversation to a close, and he and Philip returned to the waiting Rolls.

'A most interesting man, in many ways,' said the President thoughtfully as they climbed into the back seat of his car.

'Who, Nyanga?'

'Yes. Very well read, you know. I feel that in some ways we have a great deal in common. In fact sometimes I have to concentrate quite hard to remember that before long he will undoubtedly try to kill me.'

Ten

Yuri Semenov had been born in Batamay, on the edge of the central
Siberian plateau, in 1925; he was now forty years old.

At the turn of the century Semenov's paternal grandfather had
been banished to Yakutsk by the Czar. In those days the Yakuts
had still been tending reindeer, but Grandfather Semenov had made
the best of his fate: he had married and settled down. The result
was that his grandson was three-quarters Yakut, which meant that
in appearance he was very like an Eskimo; in fact some Russian
anthropologists believe that the Yakuts are ethnically related to the
Eskimos.

Semenov had straight black hair, cut in a fringe across his forehead, dark, slanted eyes, and a black moustache with the ends
turned down in the Mongolian manner.

Regardless of whether the Yakuts actually are related to the Eskimos, they certainly live in similar conditions, for in Batamay the
winter temperature often goes down to minus seventy degrees Fahrenheit. Why it was that a man who had grown up in such a climate
should have been sent to Balembi, Semenov could never quite
decide: sometimes he felt it was a punishment and sometimes a
reward. But whatever the reason, he had now spent ten years under
the African sun: first in Ghana, then in the Congo, and now in
Balembi.

Balembi was in many ways the least important country he had
worked in, but this was undoubtedly his most important assign-
ment. Balembi was not big enough to justify a huge investment of
men and money on the part of the Soviet Union. But it had been
made very clear to Semenov that the Kremlin expected to see a
take-over by the Nationalist party before the year was out. The
installation of a government which was sympathetic to the USSR
was considered a vital objective in a country adjoining Gabuti, and
Semenov had been ordered to supervise all stages of this process,
not just those relating to his own specialisation. Above all, he had
been told to succeed.

In all the countries Semenov had worked in he had officially been
a member of the staff at the Russian Embassy; unofficially he had
been an adviser and confidant to various key politicians. Even more
secretly still, he had been responsible for teaching and demonstrat-

ing a specific skill: the art of brainwashing. His Embassy colleagues had always found him an unsettling influence; he made people nervous because of what he could do.

Semenov had been a very bright child: his grandfather might have been politically unpopular but he had been no fool. After a highly impressive period of study at Yakutsk University, Semenov had been whisked off to Moscow, where he had consolidated his academic reputation as a Pavolovian psychologist; he had worked with rats, rather than dogs.

Not until he was twenty-five, however, had the authorities realised that Yuri Semenov was particularly well suited to working with humans rather than with animals in a laboratory. It had gradually dawned on his superiors that although Semenov displayed emotion – he could laugh and grow angry like anyone else – inflicting pain on other people did not distress him. Perhaps more important, it did not please him either: he was dispassionate.

The reason for this emotional detachment was simple, as far as Semenov was concerned. As a behaviourist he doubted whether any aspect of human life meant very much one way or the other. Certainly, as an individual, he hoped to avoid pain; but he had no great expectation of being able to do so in the long run. And in the meantime, he couldn't see that it mattered very much if others were made to suffer – particularly when something useful was achieved by it. Large numbers of people were always in agony, somewhere: what did it matter if small additions were made to that huge volume of pain?

In 1950, then, the Party had recognised Semenov's talents; in 1965 he was about to put them to use once again.

At seven-thirty on the evening of Tuesday 15 June, 1965, Yuri Semenov and Joro Nyanga arrived at the home of Conrad Hall for dinner.

Hall lived on the outskirts of Tikiro, in a huge mansion on to which he had already built two new wings. The house was set in fourteen acres of land, and the grounds were cared for by a European head gardener and four African assistants. With the exception of the President's palace, it was the most impressive residence in Balembi. Everything about the house, as about its owner, was immaculate: in the dry season the grounds were watered daily, and the surface of the lawns rivalled that of the average English bowling green.

Having greeted his guests, Conrad Hall showed them into his study, where they were to conduct some business before dinner. Hall saw to it that the three of them sat round a table for their meeting; he preferred formality. Semenov approved of that, though he did not care much for the opulence of the surroundings.

Hall opened the discussion by welcoming Semenov to Balembi; Semenov thanked him, speaking English with a thick Russian accent.

'And before we go any further,' Hall continued, 'perhaps I ought to outline the situation here as I see it myself. No doubt Mr Nyanga will have given you a briefing from his point of view – but I would like to explain how I see things developing. . . . Just so that there are no misunderstandings.' He smiled, but there was no response from anyone.

'Well now. . . . Basically, as you know, Balembi is still ruled under a form of democracy – based on British principles, for what they're worth. But there is in Balembi, as elsewhere, a strong trend towards the repossession by the African people of what is theirs by right. Now Mr Nyanga and I have agreed to support and develop this inevitable movement of history. Our immediate aim is to overthrow Kasaboru and his government. In their place we shall install Mr Nyanga as head of state, and we shall silence all opposition. In the classic manner, we shall nationalize all the means of the production and distribution of wealth. . . . In foreign affairs, the state will give support to, and will hope to receive support from, the Soviet Union.'

Semenov leaned forward. Rather to his surprise he was beginning to be impressed by Hall's crisp and efficient manner. He had already had extensive discussions with both Nyanga and with the staff of his Embassy; they had all given him long and rambling expositions of the glorious future which would be created after the revolution but no-one had yet shown any real grasp of the situation; now, he had met a man who appeared to know how to get things done.

'How precisely do you intend to depose Kasaboru?' asked Semenov.

'First,' said Hall, 'by undermining his political position, so that he will not be missed after he has gone. Second, by organising a military coup. . . . Kasaboru had a Mibambo father, and though he also had a Fanda mother, he draws his support mostly from the Mibambo tribe. Our policy has for some time been to persuade the Fanda people that Kasaboru is their mortal enemy. We do this by organising selected killings of Fanda villagers.'

'And who does these killings?'

'We use Mimbambo units of the army – one platoon in particular, which is officered by a man who approves of Mr Nyanga despite his tribal origins. The soldiers enjoy the work, and they are good at it. They also get paid.'

'And after the killings, the word goes out that they have been committed on Kasaboru's orders, I suppose.'

'That is correct.'

Semenov nodded and leaned back, his hands flat on the table. 'I see.'

61

'It has been a very successful policy,' Hall continued. 'There is widespread unrest among the Fanda tribesmen.'

'But the Fanda people remain in a minority – they are outnumbered two to one?'

'Yes.'

'Please go on.'

'We are also creating an unsettled atmosphere among the population as a whole. We do this by financing terrorism and random attacks by groups of unemployed youths – the so-called *jeunesse*. This is a field in which a small investment yields very big returns.'

'Good. And the details of the military coup?'

'We have them ready,' Hall declared confidently. 'Only a comparatively small force is needed, provided it is properly deployed. And after Kasaboru is captured, that, of course, is where your own talents are applied. That is why we asked for you, and that is why you have been sent – in order to work on Kasaboru so that he will admit to various crimes, and thus justify our getting rid of him. But of the coup itself, let me say this: there will be a minimum of disruption. I emphasise that,' he said, with a sharp glance at Nyanga. 'A minimum of disruption. Key points will be taken over by selected units of the army – Fanda units in this instance, of course. But as far as the general population is concerned – particularly the European population – the situation will remain just the same as before. There will be no loss of life, no damage to private property, nothing to cause an exodus. All that will change is the government. I will remain head of the newly nationalized mining operation, and all other essential personnel will also be retained. And under Mr Nyanga's leadership the profits which are generated by that mining operation will go to those who create them – namely the inhabitants of Balembi – rather than to shareholders and bankers abroad.'

'Yes,' said Semenov. 'I understand.'

A nice touch that, he thought. Hall had spoken of inhabitants of Balembi rather than citizens. Semenov also noticed that Hall's expression had remained entirely serious as he made his last statement. There had been no wink, no irrepressible smile of glee at the thought of all that loot. Semenov admired the man's command over his emotions, admired it all the more because he knew very well what Hall's motive was: he was inspired by material wealth. The belief in worldly possessions and the longing for them were thick in the air all around Conrad Hall. He was a greedy and fundamentally childish man: everything he wore, everything he surrounded himself with, screamed aloud with the declaration that it was what you owned that mattered. But Semenov knew that that was nonsense, of course.

Conrad Hall wanted to feel in control of his fate, in control of events and circumstances around him; and he sought to do that by buying things and buying people. But in the last analysis such an approach did not work, Semenov was convinced of that. Hall put his faith in money, but possessions could always be lost, stolen, or destroyed; and the people that money had bought could be tempted away by other men's money. No, Semenov thought, there was only one true source of control: fear combined with pain. If you made the fear and pain so intense that they altered the mind, then the subject could never give allegiance to anyone other than the source of his pain and fear.

'So much for a brief outline of our objectives,' said Hall after a pause. 'Now to specifics. . . . Yesterday afternoon I had a visit from Kasaboru. He brought with him his new security man, a certain Mr Morgan. This Morgan is no doubt someone who can be dealt with easily enough, but he needs watching.'

Nyanga stirred in his chair for the first time; his eyes were hooded as he glanced across at his companions. 'Yes,' he said, 'I know all about Mr Morgan. I have several men at the High Commission in London – in fact practically everybody there except the High Commissioner is a Nyanga informer – and they have given me a briefing on him. At first I thought it would be best to kill him, but now I have a better idea. Why don't we capture him, together with the President, and accuse MI6 of trying to assassinate me?' He looked from face to face. 'Is that agreed?'

'Agreed,' said the two others, after a moment.

'It will embarrass the British government,' said Semenov. 'Not much, but enough to be worth doing.'

'Now then,' said Nyanga, 'let us turn to the main business of the evening.' He obviously felt that Conrad Hall had been in the driving seat long enough. 'I can now confirm details of Thursday's attack. It is all fixed. The army unit mentioned earlier is briefed, and, I may say, bribed. Early on Thursday morning they will attack a Fanda village called Opana. It is some twenty miles from Digara, well off the main roads and suitably isolated – no water, no electricity, no telephone. It has a population of about one hundred, all told, but there will be fewer than that on a weekday. Most of the men work in Digara, returning only at the weekends.'

'This is bigger than anything we've tackled before,' said Hall, with an edge of doubt in his voice.

'Perhaps eighty women and children,' said Nyanga with a shrug. 'But we need to kill quite a number in order to make the necessary impact. Small-scale exercises are just no use at all.'

Hall accepted it. 'Very well. Any Europeans?'

'Only one – a lady doctor.'

'Good,' said Hall. 'We don't want to start a panic among the skilled personnel, but it will do no harm to weaken their confidence in Kasaboru's ability to protect them. . . . What about supervision – will you be there yourself?'

Nyanga looked up at him. 'No need. And it's best if I'm not seen in the vicinity. What about you?'

Hall twisted his hands together. 'Yes. . . . Yes, I think I will go. To make sure there are no slip-ups.' He glanced at Semenov almost shyly. 'Will you come too?'

Semenov smiled. 'Yes. Why not?'

'Good! Good!' Hall seemed immensely relieved. 'That's fine. I'll make all the necessary arrangements. Very discreet, of course!'

'Of course.' Semenov chuckled.

'And I'll send Bulu to help you,' said Nyanga.

'Ah yes, dear old Bulu. Things wouldn't be the same without him.'

Hall rose to his feet. 'And now my friends, let us eat.'

Semenov's slightly tubby figure bore evidence to the fact that he liked his food; he also had a very unproletarian taste in wine. Conrad Hall's appetite and love of fine food was, however, far greater than Semenov's, and dinner at Hall's house proved to be a rare culinary experience. The cuisine was essentially French, and the chef was evidently a man of great talents. The claret which accompanied the main course was a Chateau Margaux caught at just the right age.

Even more remarkable than the food and drink, however, was the manner of its serving. The service was supervised by a Mrs Schell, Hall's housekeeper. She was a tall, solidly built lady of about fifty; she had very cold, pale-blue eyes, and she was wearing a dark-blue belted dress and black stockings; her fair hair was cut very short and the set of her jaw was determined; Semenov guessed correctly that she was German; she and her husband had moved to South Africa in 1946, and she had been widowed soon afterwards.

Mrs Schell's sole function seemed to be to give sharp orders to the African waitresses. There were four waitresses in all, one for each man and one for the wine: they were all girls of the Fanda tribe, and Semenov estimated that none of them was aged more than twenty. Each girl wore white high-heeled shoes, a white cap, and a white frilly apron.

That was all.

They clip-clopped about the marble floor of Conrad Hall's dining room at a great pace, their pert young breasts jigging freely as they responded to Mrs Schell's abrupt commands. None of them smiled. Their black skin glistened in the candlelight, and as one of them leaned over to take Yuri Semenov's empty plate, he knew immediately what had generated the beads of sweat on her brow. It was not the heat; it was fear.

During the meal Conrad Hall was in great form. He told a long succession of racy anecdotes about Balembian businessmen and politicians, all of which Nyanga seemed to have heard before; at any rate he looked bored. And occasionally, almost absent-mindedly,

Hall would pass his hand up and down the legs of the Fanda girl standing beside his chair.

At the end of the meal there was coffee, brandy and liqueurs. There was also a disbursement, as Hall described it, of rewards and punishments.

One of the waitresses, who had pleased her employer, had a chocolate popped into her dark red mouth; she was then given the rest of the box to take away.

The waitress who had served the wine, however, was not so lucky. She was required to stand close to the table and to stretch forward so that the upper half of her body lay flat upon it. The starched white bow in the middle of her back stood up in strong contrast to the naked black skin of her rounded buttocks. The girl's eyes rolled upwards and she began to weep.

Mrs Schell was deputed to administer the punishment, which she did with the aid of a bamboo cane. The procedure, which was evidently a well-established one, was that there was a long gap between each stroke of the cane; during this pause the girl was not allowed to move, but she could beg and plead for the punishment to end, an opportunity which she naturally did not neglect. Eventually, after seven of Mrs Schell's vigorous and well-aimed strokes, the girl was allowed to be led away sobbing.

Nyanga watched this performance through half-closed eyes; he had seen similar beatings before, on his previous visits to Hall's house. And like the other two men present, in a few moments he would take one of the young waitresses into one of the many bedrooms in the house and use her for his own satisfaction. Fanda girl or not, it made no difference to him what indignity she was made to suffer.

But Nyanga had suddenly begun to appreciate something for the very first time – something which he had often thought about but which had never seemed quite real. Despite what Hall had said about the absence of disruption and the preservation of the safety of the European population, Nyanga knew very well that large numbers of his fellow Balembians were just waiting for an excuse to get their own back for decades of humiliation, both real and imagined.

Nyanga suddenly realised that in a very short time now it would be white women who would be begging and pleading for mercy in the streets of Digara. And it would be he, Nyanga, who would be making them scream.

The prospect was one which pleased him.

Eleven

On the Monday morning of that week, Jane Stuart hired a car to drive herself to Opana.

Jane's friend, Dr Enid Bracken, had given her detailed instructions on how to reach the village, but for the last five miles of the journey the road was marked by little more than a pair of deep ruts meandering through the bush. The hired car did not appreciate the lack of an asphalt surface one bit, and the heat didn't help, either: the temperature inside the car rose to almost unbearable heights, but eventually Jane arrived and was able to stagger into the shade.

Enid Bracken was delighted to see her visitor, and once Jane had recovered her strength the two women went for a walk round the village.

There was not in fact very much to see. Several dogs, goats, pigs and chickens roamed around at will, mingling with the children and scratching in the brown dirt. Here and there a young girl squatted on her haunches, pounding maize with a heavy pole.

There were about twenty huts in all, arranged roughly in a circle in the shelter of a steep bank. Each hut was made up of a framework of wooden piles driven into the ground; light branches and strips of bamboo had been fitted on to this skeleton, and the whole structure had then been covered with thick layers of grass. The result was primitive in the extreme.

Dr Bracken lived in the only brick-built house in the village – in fact the only such house for several miles around. It was a one-storey building with just four rooms under a corrugated-iron roof: a living-room, a bedroom, a kitchen, and a room where the doctor saw her patients; there was no bathroom. By normal European standards the house was very second-rate, but in these surroundings it took on the dimensions of a mansion.

In the evening Jane was treated to her first meal in the bush: elephant stew, with palm wine to wash it down. The elephant turned out to taste very much like beef, and the palm wine like lemonade.

Later still, Dr Bracken talked at length about her medical work in the village. Enid was fifty now, and had lived in Opana for twenty years. Her face was deeply tanned, but the lines on it were laugh-lines rather than signs of weariness. Her spare, angular frame was clothed in a strictly utilitarian khaki skirt, with pockets, and an ancient khaki bush jacket; both garments had been bought in an army surplus store in Digara. But despite a lack of interest in making more of her appearance, Enid Bracken was still an attractive woman; the attraction emanated naturally from her open and friendly personality, and Jane could see very easily why her father had been so fond of her.

'I first came out here in 1945,' Enid explained late that night. 'My fiancé was killed in the last weeks of the war, and I'd been working very hard myself, so inevitably I had a sort of breakdown. I worked in London hospitals all through the blitz, and I suppose that took its toll. . . . Anyway, I was advised to go somewhere warm to recuperate, and I had relations in Digara, so out I came. And I've stayed here ever since.' She smiled.

'Don't you ever feel lonely?' asked Jane.

'No, not really. Don't let appearances fool you, Jane. I don't have a life of great privation. You may have found it difficult to get here this morning, but that's because you're not used to it. Now me, I've got a Land-Rover, and I go to the theatre in Digara every weekend, regular as clockwork – except in the rainy season, when it's sometimes too muddy. When your father was alive I used to go in twice a week. I also attend more than my share of cocktail parties, read all the latest books from the library – and I have my radio to listen to. So one way and another I have a very full life.'

'What about the patients?' asked Jane. 'Are they interesting?'

'Yes, very. There are all the obvious medical problems which arise when people are living in circumstances like these, plus one or two rarer conditions.'

'Oh – what kind?'

'Well, we get a very high incidence of cancer of the jaw among African children in this part of the world. I've made a special study of it, together with a consultant at Digara General. Between us I suppose we're the world authorities on that particular problem, and there are other cases which are equally interesting. So it's never dull. I get patients coming to me from a very wide area with all sorts of aches and pains.'

'The people here clearly think the world of you,' said Jane. 'Have you entirely replaced the witch-doctor?'

Dr Bracken laughed. 'Not entirely, I'm afraid. The truth is, they use us both. As far as the locals are concerned, modern medicine deals with the symptoms of their illness, and it undoubtedly makes them feel better. But they believe that the traditional methods of magic and religion are still needed to remove the underlying causes – to dissipate whatever it was that was making them feel ill in the first place. And who knows? Perhaps they're right.'

For the next two days Jane was more than occupied in assisting Dr

Bracken in her work.

On the Thursday morning she awoke early, soon after dawn. She slipped quietly out of bed, trying not to wake her companion on the other side of the bedroom, and went into the living-room to look out on to the village through the Venetian blind which hung in the window. Just after awakening she had heard something un-usual at the very edge of her consciousness, and she wanted to know what it was.

The air was still and nothing was yet moving within the village itself. But gradually a rumbling was heard – a rumbling which grew steadily louder. Children awoke and peeped out of their huts; dogs barked and ran to and fro.

The rumbling resolved itself into a roaring cloud of dust sur-rounding a huge lorry with a green canvas tarpaulin top and military markings. The lorry ran right through the village, revealing as it passed a crowd of armed soldiers standing inside it. Fifty yards further on the lorry pulled to a halt.

A similar lorry stopped about fifty yards before the entrance to the village. And on a small rise two hundred yards away an open Land-Rover appeared: two white men were in it.

By this time Enid Bracken had also got up and was standing by Jane's side, still in her pyjamas. In the village everyone else was awake, milling about and shouting excitedly.

'What's happening?' asked Enid sharply.

'I don't know,' said Jane. 'But it looks as if the army has arrived.'

From the lorry on the far side of the village an African civilian in his mid-twenties stepped down to the ground. He was fat, and he waddled as he walked; he was dressed in blue slacks, sandals, and a brightly coloured shirt. He was immediately recognisable as a member of the Fanda tribe, like the villagers, and at first the children flocked towards him.

But then they saw that the man's face was hideously disfigured by a cleft palate which extended right through his nose and descend-ed in a double hare-lip. He shouted angrily to disperse the children and the cleft palate gave his voice a peculiar twang. Then he paused and gazed around, hands on hips; Jane noticed that he wore a gold watch on each wrist and several gold rings on his fingers. After a moment he pointed abruptly at a young girl and told her sharply in the local dialect to come with him.

The girl hesitated for a moment and looked at her mother. The man shouted angrily at her again, and immediately she did as she was told; she went up to the man's side. He walked away, past the lorry which had brought him into the village, pushing the girl ahead of him. He appeared to be making for the Land-Rover on the hill-top.

Enid Bracken, watching from the window of her home, shuddered involuntarily. Suddenly she understood, quite clearly, what was going to happen. Twenty years of life in the bush had given her an intimate knowledge of the love and affection which Africans could feel for each other. But she had also seen frequent and horrifying evidence of the evil side of Africa: the cruelty, the violence, and the callous disregard for the sufferings of others.

As the soldiers in the lorry which had driven through the village peered out from under their tarpaulin cover, she could see that they were Mibambos; and their faces were distorted by sneers and anger. Enid knew now that blood was going to be shed. She began to think very hard and very fast.

An officer appeared; he too was a Mibambo, and like his men he wore green jungle camouflage uniform. He ordered the soldiers down from their trucks, and following the officer's lead the men began to herd the villagers away from the circle of grass huts, back towards the steep bank to the north. Anyone who hesitated was kicked or prodded sharply with the business end of a Lee Enfield rifle. The villagers obeyed in sullen silence. They had no choice.

Enid Bracken had decided what she must do.

'Look, Jane, I think there's going to be trouble,' she said. 'I've got a gun in that cupboard over there – get it out while I keep watch.'

Jane turned and looked across the room. Then she went over to the built-in cupboard which Enid Bracken had indicated, opened the door, and peered in. But she could see nothing.

'Where?' she said desperately after a moment. 'I can't – '

Jane never finished her sentence. Before she could do so, Enid Bracken had struck her very hard on the back of the head, knocking her totally unconscious. As a weapon Dr Bracken had selected one of the two Indian clubs which she used for her morning exercises; it was not something she had enjoyed doing, but she felt it was infinitely preferable to allowing Jane to be killed.

Working frantically, Enid Bracken cleared out just enough jumble from her one and only store cupboard to allow her to push Jane's limp body into the narrow space remaining and close the door. She would just have to hope that there would be enough air in there. Of course there was still the evidence of a second bed which had been slept in, and the soldiers might wonder who had occupied it – but at least Jane herself was out of sight. And with a bit of luck, out of harm's way.

The shooting began while Enid was still heaving and pulling at Jane to manoeuvre her into the cupboard. She closed her ears to the staccato rattle of the rifles and concentrated on distributing the items she had taken out of the cupboard elsewhere in the room. Nothing must draw attention to the cupboard door.

When she had completed her task, she crossed again to the window. The screams and the shouts of agony and despair had become a blur in her own mind, and mercifully the worst was now over.

The officer in charge of the soldiers had found from bitter experience that the chief problem in an undertaking of this nature was the moronic eagerness of his men. Left to themselves they would probably have formed a circle with their victims at its centre, and would have shot at them from all sides, killing and wounding each other in the process; Balembian soldiers were unfortunately not very bright. But in this instance the officer had been lucky. There was a steep bank against which he could line up all those who were due to be executed; and much to his surprise his men had held their fire until he gave the order.

The result had been a reasonably efficient massacre.

Only one or two of the villagers were still trying to crawl away. One of them was a young woman clutching a wailing baby. The officer pointed her out to his corporal, who kicked the woman over on to her back. Despite her bleeding leg she spat at him defiantly as she lay there, and the corporal methodically clubbed her and the baby to death with the butt of his rifle. On the whole the soldiers were much happier using their rifles as clubs than as fire-arms; they understood how clubs worked, but triggers and safety catches and bolts were all a bit too complicated.

Enid Bracken had witnessed this last incident, and she cried aloud in horror and distress at each blow, her hands over her cheeks, the tears flowing. Afterwards she could hardly move, and she found herself wondering what that curious noise was, until she became aware that it was her own sobbing. Then she realised that she must move. To save Jane she must get right away from the house and convince the soldiers that no-one else was left alive.

Enid Bracken took several deep breaths and pulled herself together. She would have liked to have taken a last look round, to have thought of all the good times she had had in this house, to clear her mind of the scene she had just witnessed. But there wasn't time. Quickly she forced herself to walk down the three wooden steps of the house and across the bare expanse of red soil. The officer turned as he became aware of her at his side.

Enid cast a professional eye over the carnage which had been created in perhaps three or four minutes. About eighty villagers, mostly women and children, lay stretched out and silent; Enid herself had delivered many of them at birth. It was so easy to kill, she thought. So very, very easy. Perhaps it was also easy to die.

'Well,' she said to the officer, 'perhaps you ought to take me too. I'm the very last one.'

Enid Bracken knelt down in the dirt. With a great effort of will she cast her mind back to happier times, to moments spent with her fiancé, and with Jane's father, John Stuart. She had never been particularly religious, but perhaps, she thought, this is not a bad time to begin to pray.

'Our Father, which art in heaven, hallowed be thy name – '

The officer shot her through the back of her head with his pistol.

The man with a double hare-lip pushed the young girl ahead of him. Every second step she turned and looked back at her home in desperation, but the man angrily ordered her on.

Together the man and the girl reached the Land-Rover on the hill-top shortly before the shooting in the village began. In the Land-Rover Conrad Hall sat waiting impatiently; beside him was Yuri Semenov. And now that Hall could see how young and attractive the girl was, he was delighted.

'Well done, Bulu! Well done!' he said. 'You've really excelled yourself this time.'

Hall climbed down from the driving-seat, his blue eyes shining with pleasure. He unbuttoned a pocket of his expensive safari jacket and handed Bulu a bundle of five-pound notes; but his eyes remained on he girl.

'Now then,' said Hall. 'Let's have a look at her. Bulu – do the honours please.'

Hall indicated with a gesture what he wanted and Bulu seized the girl's shoulder. Then, with his other hand, he tore the ragged cotton dress off her body with one violent rip down the front; it was the only garment she was wearing.

Conrad Hall's beaming smile grew even wider. 'Ah, wonderful, wonderful!' he said.

Physically, the black girl was just on the point of passing from childhood to womanhood; there was no pubic hair on her body, but the breasts were beginning to swell. She was trembling from head to foot.

Totally ignoring his companions Hall reached for the girl and drew her closer to him; she was quite limp and unresisting. Hall fondled her vagina and buttocks for some time, muttering to himself with satisfaction. In the background the crackle of shooting began, and the girl gave a jump and an exclamation of fear. Hall ignored the noise entirely.

After a minute or two Hall sighed, almost sadly, and then stepped back. 'All right,' he said to Bulu reflectively. 'You can tell her to run now.'

Bulu issued a sharp command, but the girl stood quite still, her eyes glazed. Bulu repeated the order, and slapped her on the bottom for good measure. This time the girl moved away a few steps. Bulu shouted a third time, and at last the girl began to run for her life, running naked and headlong, haring through the undergrowth, her heels flashing.

'Beautiful. Beautiful!' said Hall as he watched her go. Then he reached into the back of the Land-Rover and produced an M.16 rifle.

71

The M.16 takes a .223 calibre bullet. When fired, the bullet travels with great speed and accuracy; it is very stable in flight, its centre of gravity well to the rear. The bullet is jacketed, and thus meets the requirements of the Hague convention; but when it strikes the human body it tends to turn sideways or shatter, causing a huge, shocking wound with a dumdum effect.

The girl ran like an antelope and she had gone perhaps a hundred yards before Hall picked her up in his sights. He fired once and missed.

The girl jinked from side to side.

He fired again, and this time the girl went down.

Hall watched her for a while through binoculars, but there was no movement. So he put the rifle away.

Semenov watched and said nothing. He felt no flicker of human sympathy, not a moment's doubt or disgust. He was immune to emotions of that nature. But he was very intrigued by Conrad Hall.

Semenov was fascinated by the practised facility with which Conrad Hall could kill. He doubted somehow that Hall had learnt that in South Africa, though it was always possible. What Semenov did know was that some time ago Nyanga had asked, through the Russian Embassy in Digara, for a report on Conrad Hall from whatever files were available in the Kremlin. And it would be very interesting indeed to see what they came up with; the report was due any day now.

After the young girl was killed, Bulu went back down into the village. Nyanga had told him that there was a white lady living there and that he could do what he liked with her. He was very disappointed to find that she was already dead, but he made the best of it by cutting off her ears to add to his growing collection.

Before they left Opana, the soldiers set fire to all the grass huts. Dr Bracken's house, being brick with a corrugated-iron roof, was obviously not going to burn as readily as the rest, so the officer in charge tossed a hand-grenade through the window instead. It blew the roof off and blew the windows out and generally caused a very pleasing amount of damage.

Twelve

A young man of the Fanda tribe had been half a mile away from Opana when he heard the shooting start. Knowing very well what the large number of shots meant, he had wisely put a much greater distance between himself and the village in a very short time. He ran over three miles to the nearest house with a telephone, and as a result news of the massacre reached the authorities relatively quickly.

Altogether there had now been five mass killings of Fanda villagers since the beginning of the year. After the first two incidents a standard procedure had been set up: a group of armed police was sent out, together with an ambulance; if necessary they radioed in for further assistance. In this case it was obvious that a whole fleet of ambulances would be needed, and the President was so informed.

Kasaboru was in conference with his Foreign Secretary, Richard Chokwe, when news of the fate of Opana first reached him. He sighed deeply and passed a hand wearily over his forehead: this was not a good way to start the day.

'Well,' he said when he had recovered a little, 'it won't be very pleasant – but I think it's my duty to go and see this one for myself.'

'May I come?' asked Chokwe.

'Certainly,' said the President. 'I'd be glad if you would.'

Pausing only to collect Philip Morgan on his way downstairs, the President ordered an army escort to accompany him to Opana. Bob Fuller, the President's transport officer and head chauffeur, selected a Land-Rover to cope with the dirt roads, and the President, Chokwe and Philip all clambered into the back. Before very long a convoy was under way; an army lorry full of soldiers travelled ahead of the President's vehicle, with a similar lorry behind; an armoured car tagged along at the rear for good measure.

As they travelled the President explained to Philip some of the background to the incident.

'I think I mentioned to you that one of the most serious internal problems we've had recently has been these random killings of Fanda women and children. Somebody – and we have our suspicions who it is, though we can't prove it – is spreading the word that the army is committing these murders on my orders. And in one or two cases we've had fairly reliable eye-witness reports that men in mil-

73

itary uniforms were involved in the crime. But – who knows? It's very difficult to separate truth from the wildest rumour. What is undeniably true is that as a result of these incidents, the ordinary Fanda tribesman, out in the bush, is not a Kasaboru admirer.'

Philip chose his words carefully. 'So Nyanga is making political capital out of these deaths,' he said. 'But do you think he is directly responsible for them?'

It was Chokwe who answered. 'We know that he is,' he said fiercely, striking his knee with his fist. 'We know it. We are absolutely certain of it.' He seemed incensed by the whole business and his jaw was clenched in anger.

The President gave a wry smile. 'Well, Philip, let's just say that we are morally certain that Nyanga is behind it all. I wouldn't like to put it any stronger than that.'

Up to the present Philip had been so busy bundling himself into the back of the Land-Rover and listening to what the President had to say that he hadn't really taken much notice of which way they were heading. But now he suddenly became uncomfortably aware that they were travelling north-east. And north-east was the direction in which Jane Stuart had gone on Monday.

The awareness that Jane might conceivably be at risk hit Philip like a physical blow. He winced and gave a slight exclamation of shock, causing Chokwe to turn and look at him.

Philip recovered after a second. 'This village,' he said, 'where the killings have taken place – what's it called?'

'Opana,' said the President. 'Why?'

Philip's face turned noticeably pale under his growing tan. And as soon as he could trust himself to speak he explained to the two politicans that Opana was where Jane Stuart had been staying with her friend, the doctor. As they listened, the President and Richard Chokwe became even more grim-faced than ever.

'Well,' said Kasaboru eventually, 'Miss Stuart is a very beautiful young woman – and a very able one too. So we must hope with all our hearts that she has not been harmed. But, until we see for ourselves, we cannot tell for certain what has happened.'

The village of Opana was totally devastated.

A doctor who had travelled on the first ambulance to arrive had checked the blood-stained bodies for any signs of life; he had found only one survivor, a young boy who was certain to die soon. The boy had been removed to hospital, but the police had decided to leave the rest of the villagers where they were until the President had seen the slaughter for himself.

As soon as they arrived Philip leapt out of the Land-Rover. He remembered very clearly that Jane had told him that the doctor's house was the only brick building in the village, and that made it very easy to identify. But first he searched anxiously among the dead.

'I'm looking for one person in particular,' he told the senior police officer in charge. 'A young white woman. Any sign of her?'

The officer took him by the arm. 'The only white woman we've found is over here,' he said, speaking with a strong Scottish burr. 'She was shot through the back of the head.'

Mercifully Philip could see at a glance that the body was not Jane's. 'No, that's not her. I think this must be the doctor who lived here.'

'Aye, it was,' said the policeman, his voice thickening with emotion. 'I knew her myself.'

In other circumstances Philip would have shared the police officer's distress at the truly appalling scene, but his mind was too full of the problem of finding Jane to feel any sense of shock; that would come later. He turned away and ran up the steps of the doctor's house.

The brick walls of the building were still standing, but the concussive effect of the hand-grenade had caused extensive damage: the corrugated-iron roof was largely displaced, the windows were blown out, and the front door was hanging by one hinge. Inside there was a hole in the floor about a yard in diameter.

Philip quickly searched the house, noting the two beds which had been slept in and the presence of some of Jane's belongings. As he did so the President joined him.

'Any luck?' asked Kasaboru.

'Not yet, no.' Philip frowned. 'I'm beginning to think she may not have been here when the shooting took place. Or perhaps she just ran for it.'

'In that case, maybe she's out in the bush,' said the President.

'Yes,' said Philip.

And both men thought of, but did not like to mention aloud, the possibility that Jane might be lying wounded, somewhere out in the dense undergrowth all around.

It was then that Philip heard the moan. If his senses had not been so acutely alert because of the need to find Jane, it was a sound he might not have heard. But at once he turned to its source.

'Over here,' he said urgently. 'Over here – there's a cupboard.'

Eagerly Philip pulled open the cupboard door, and the pyjama-clad figure of Jane Stuart rolled out on to the floor at his feet. She was conscious, but very dazed, and her eyes stared up at him without recognition.

After Jane was despatched to Digara in an ambulance, the President and Richard Chokwe conferred about what was to be done now.

Chokewe, who was seven years younger than Kasaboru and much

more impulsive, was determined to track down and punish the men responsible at whatever cost. He had been deeply shaken by the morning's experience, and he thumped the bonnet of the Land-Rover in his anger.

'They will *not* get away with it,' he said loudly. 'It is absolutely intolerable. What will the world think of us if we allow such appalling atrocities to occur? They will think that we are all nothing but savages. I will see Nyanga and Hall in jail for this if it's the last thing I do.'

The President answered sharply. He had fought in the Second World War, and the sight of dead bodies was nothing new to him, but he too was on edge.

'Aren't you rather jumping to conclusions?' he said. 'Until and unless any survivors of this massacre are able to give us some facts, we have no real knowledge of who committed this crime, much less of who ordered them to commit it.'

Chokwe was too tense to notice the cold edge in the President's voice.

'What proof do you want?' he shouted, and heads turned to look at the two men. 'I ask you, what more proof do you want? Who would do a thing like this? Answer, your worst enemy. And who is your worst enemy? Answer, Joro Nyanga. And who is behind him, urging him on, giving him the money to achieve these things? Conrad Hall. Hall and Nyanga, I tell you, they are the ones.'

In the face of this violent outburst the President remained calm, his arms folded across his chest. But Chokwe grew even more agitated, conscious that everyone present was listening and watching.

'I urge you now, Mr President – now, in the presence of all who are here, who can see and smell what Nyanga and Hall have done – I urge you to arrest those men and put them behind bars where they can do no more harm.'

'Arrest them on what charge?' said Kasaboru, his face stern.

'On no charge at all,' shouted Chokwe. 'Throw them in jail, as any African President but you would have done years ago. Or better still, kill them both – kill them so that they can commit no more crimes such as this.'

Chokwe's voice echoed back from the steep bank against which the villagers had been shot. Everyone present stood very still; suddenly there was complete silence.

The President's manner changed. He was at all times a man who conveyed to those in his presence a feeling of authority, a sense of controlled power and energy; but now, for the first time, Philip saw that power set to work. The President unfolded his arms, braced himself with his feet slightly apart, and raised his voice so that he was addressing not just Chokwe but everyone around him.

'There will be no more talk of killing,' he said. 'None. And so long as I am President of Balembi, there will be no imprisonment without trial, either – let me make myself plain about that.'

He stepped closer to Chokwe and gripped him by the arm like a father with a badly behaved child. 'You are not the only Minister who has urged me to use assassination as a means of solving our problems – don't think you are. But I say to you what I have said to the others – down that road lies anarchy and disaster. Not only will I not use such methods, I will not even have them discussed.'

Chokwe lowered his eyes. He realised that he had gone too far.

'We will observe the laws of the land,' said Kasaboru. 'Have faith. The system is sound, and we will use it. And in the course of time the men who committed this crime will be brought to justice and will pay the penalty. But there will be no more talk of killing, or unjust imprisonment – not now or at any time in the future.'

The President paused and searched the faces of those watching to ensure that the point was made. Then he turned and walked slowly away towards his Land-Rover.

Chokwe remained where he was for some moments, staring at the ground. He had been given a public rebuke, and as a proud man he was deeply embarrassed by it; yet he knew in his heart that Kasaboru was right.

After perhaps half a minute Chokwe recovered. He shook his head and sighed. Then he looked up at Philip with a sheepish grin.

'Well, Philip, I stand corrected. No doubt the President is right and I am wrong – that is usually the way. And on this occasion I suppose I allowed myself to get carried away by everything we have seen. But it is enough to unsettle the best of us.'

'It certainly is,' said Philip. 'I fully agree with you there.'

Chokwe fell in step with Philip as the two of them went to join the President. The Foreign Secretary looked very depressed.

'But the fact remains, you know,' he continued sadly, 'that the President is taking a very serious risk by not taking action. I am genuinely inclined to think that short of handing his enemies an open razor, he could scarcely do more to cut his own throat. But, try as I might, I simply cannot convince him.'

Thirteen

On the outskirts of Digara, in a run-down district known inappropriately as Peachville, there was an isolated church hall. The caretaker of the premises, a Mr Leopold, had authority to let out the committee room in the hall at a fee of one pound per evening (negotiable); and on the evening of Friday 18 June, 1965, that committee room was booked by Duncan Grey – or Major Grey, as he called himself when confirming the booking.

Major Grey had told Mr Leopald that he was booking the committee room for a meeting of a few businessmen who were considering setting up a charitable trust; but regrettably that was not quite true. In fact, the group of men who were meeting there that night were doing so in order to discuss something rather less than charitable – namely, the most effective means of taking over the government of Balembi by armed force.

By nine o'clock that evening Duncan Grey had been joined by four others: Joro Nyanga, Conrad Hall, Yuri Semenov, and General Juba; the latter was one of the three most senior officers in the Balembian army.

Nyanga arrived last. He was late and both Duncan Grey and General Juba were extremely nervous as they waited for him. Semenov and Hall, by contrast, were totally relaxed: Hall in particular seemed to give the impression that he was quite accustomed to high-level plotting, and he smoked a cigar with total aplomb. Perhaps part of his confidence stemmed from the fact that he had a chauffeur sitting nearby with a Thompson sub-machine gun within easy reach.

On his arrival, Nyanga seated himself at the head of the table; he gave no word of explanation or apology for keeping everyone waiting for fifteen minutes.

'Let us begin then,' he said, with a glance at those present. 'I think most of us know each other, except that Mr Semenov has not previously met Major Grey and General Juba. Mr Semenov is attached to the Russian Embassy. . . . Major Grey is the technical director of national radio network, and General Juba is, of course, with the army.'

Nyanga indicated each man with a wave of his hand as he spoke. Semenov smiled an oriental smile at the two others named, and they acknowledged him politely. General Juba wiped the sweat from his forehead with a large white handkerchief.

'Perhaps I should begin by reporting the outcome of the latest attack on a Fanda village,' Nyanga continued. 'And I think I can safely say that it was one hundred per cent successful. The Fanda people as a whole are highly incensed by this latest outrage – in fact if it were left to them, Kasaboru would have been deposed already. Is that not so, General?'

General Juba, a typical Fanda himself, nodded vigorously. The sweat continued to drip down his nose.

'Already,' said Nyanga, 'there have been reports of Fanda villagers making retaliatory attacks on neighbouring Mibambos – in the central province particularly. The idea that Kasaboru is planning to systematically eliminate the Fanda villages, one by one, has taken a deep hold – and my own belief is that we have brought the tension to as high a level as we can without taking the final step. But let me not anticipate – let us set that decision on one side for the moment, until we have heard reports from the rest of you. . . . General Juba?'

The General rolled his sodden handkerchief into a ball and stuffed it into his right-hand trouser pocket. Then, with his glance shifting anxiously from face to face, he began to speak.

The General was one of the very few native Balembians who had achieved high rank in the army. His origins were extremely humble, and he had spent his early childhood in a village. But gradually, through a combination of natural intelligence and extraordinary application, he had climbed the educational ladder to the frightening heights of an officer-training course at Sandhurst. And frightening that experience had been for Juba, because despite his intelligence and his education, he remained in his most basic beliefs a very primitive and unsophisticated man; at times, only his love affair with weaponry had kept him going.

Psychologically, the General was extremely insecure, and that, of course, was how Nyanga had recruited him. Juba had always suspected that his fellow officers – nearly all of them white – were secretly laughing at him; and it was only a short step from that nagging suspicion to outright paranoia. Nyanga had helped to bridge that gap by showing the General certain letters; the letters proved that Kasaboru intended to have the General demoted and later killed. Or rather, they would have proved it had they been genuine; the truth was that Nyanga had had them prepared at considerable expense by a retired civil servant who needed to supplement his pension. General Juba, however, had not been alert to the possibility of deception; he had accepted the letters at face value. And since his only interest in life was to become the sole commanding officer of the Balembian army, and since Nyanga offered to give him that post when he became President, Juba had been Nyanga's man from that day on.

Speaking with a pronounced Balembian accent which Conrad

Hall always found very amusing, the General described the present state of play among the units of the army manned by Fanda tribesmen.

'My latest calculation,' he said, 'is that two thirds of the army can be counted on to assist us. Traditionally, many young men from Fanda families have gone into the army, while the more intelligent Mibambo youths' – he spoke with the utmost contempt – 'have gone into banking, insurance and the civil service. Well, in that respect Kasaboru has sown the seeds of his own downfall. In any event, many of the officers in over half the units of the army have agreed to support us, and the men in the units they command will undoubtedly obey them. The officers who are not on our side are known and can quickly be imprisoned. Most of them are Europeans, of course.'

Nyanga looked pleased. 'Good,' he said.

'What about the units which are manned by Mibambos?' asked Hall.

'Most of them are stationed in the west,' said the General. 'Near Sungbarta. And should there be any difficulty, we can always count on receiving more than adequate help from our friends in Gabuti.'

'Are you satisfied with the assistance you are receiving from your counterparts in the Gabuti army?' asked Nyanga.

'Yes, completely. General Tchen is being most co-operative. As to our own army, I can give you a detailed written analysis of which units and which officers will be with us, and which against, if you wish.'

'I would like to have that later,' said Nyanga. 'But in the meantime, General, I am sure that we can count on you to have done a thorough job. Particularly since your life depends on it.'

Nyanga smiled, and the General gave a sickly laugh; his uneven teeth were yellow.

'Mr Hall,' Nyanga went on. 'What about our finances?'

Conrad Hall leaned forward, resting his arms on the table. 'Briefly, Mr Chairman, our finances are looking stretched. Like the General, I can supply details if required. . . . Over the past year or two we have derived most of our income from WWM, and a small part from the Gabuti government. We have had many kind words from Gabuti, but not much else, and it is important from my own point of view that we act within the next two months – that is to say before the end of my financial year. I have already survived one internal audit and I do not wish to have to ride out another. There are too many ghosts on the payroll for it to escape notice this time.'

Nyanga nodded. 'Very well. Mr Semenov – any questions?'

'None so far,' said Semenov.

'Good. In that case perhaps I can sum up. . . . I think that what we have heard confirms my view that we should move quickly.'

'How quickly?' asked Hall.

'Within the next few days. General Juba and I have discussed the military aspects of this operation many times – both in principle and in detail. Perhaps we ought now to examine the plans for one last time, particularly in view of Mr Semenov's presence – he is an expert in these matters and may be able to make useful suggestions.' Nyanga looked around the table. 'Agreed?'

Agreed it was. For the next half-hour the plans for seizing the key points in the capital and for arresting the President were reviewed and polished for the last time. The airport, the post office, the radio station, the newspaper offices, and all similar installations would be taken over by the army and Nyanga's authority would be imposed upon them.

Towards the end of the discussion Duncan Grey cleared his throat hesitantly. 'Um – just one thing?'

Nyanga gave him an amused glance. 'Yes, Major Grey?'

'I was wondering if I ought not to be – um – actually in the radio station at the appropriate time.'

'Yes, Major Grey, you should.'

'But how will I – um – '

'You will be told,' said Nyanga. 'You will receive a telephone call an hour or two in advance, and you will arrange for a breakdown of the facilities, so that if Kasaboru and his supporters wish to use the network they will be unable to do so. Is that clear?'

Duncan Grey's cheeks reddened. 'Yes, perfectly.'

'Good,' said Nyanga sharply. 'And if it is any comfort to you, let me say that key employees in the post office and on the staffs of the two Digara newspapers have also been recruited to assist in securing our control of communications. . . . Now – before I forget, General, the President is to be taken alive, as planned. But his security chief, a Mr Morgan, is also to be captured unharmed. Understood?'

The General nodded. 'Understood.'

'What about the other government Ministers?' asked Semenov. 'What are your plans for them?'

'They will all be arrested,' said Nyanga simply. 'And then they will be asked to assist us – the six most important, at any rate. After that it is up to them whether they live or die. We did make one or two attempts to recruit them to our side, but despite our generous offers they were incredibly obstinate and foolish. Chokwe even had our emissary thrown into jail for attempted bribery. Well, he himself is obviously beyond conversion, and his fate is clear. We will make use of his well-known weakness for women to disgrace him. Put him on trial for the rape of a little white girl – that will be the thing for him, I feel.'

Nyanga laughed heartily, and everyone joined in, some more convincingly than others. Nyanga then looked around the table. 'Any more questions?'

'Not a question,' said Hall blandly. 'Just a reminder. During the transfer of power there will be no greater disruption of services than is absolutely necessary. And there will be no harrassment of Europeans.'

For a moment an expression of anger crossed Nyanga's face; the emotion was so intense and violent that Duncan Grey and the General both flinched away from it. But then Nyanga regained control of himself. He bared his teeth in what might, at a distance, have been taken for a smile.

'Yes, Mr Hall,' said Nyanga. His voice was tight with menace. 'As you are so fond of reminding us, your fellow whites must be protected. At all costs.'

There was an appalling silence which no-one, not even Hall, dared break. Then Nyanga physically relaxed the tension in his shoulders and spoke again.

'Very well, then. That is enough for tonight. . . . You will be notified of the exact time and day, in advance, according to plan. Now let us leave this building one at a time.'

Hall left first, followed by the General. Then, as Duncan Grey made for the door, Nyanga called him back; he had now recovered his good humour.

'Major Grey,' said Nyanga. 'Aren't you forgetting something?'

'Oh – am I?'

'Yes – your fee.'

'Oh. . . . Oh, yes.' Grey smiled, as if the matter had entirely slipped his mind. He crossed the room to Nyanga's side and took the envelope which was offered. 'Thank you. . . . Thank you very much.'

'Don't spend it all at once,' said Nyanga, and winked.

After Grey had gone, Nyanga chuckled with genuine amusement. Only he and Semenov were now left in the room.

'Are you sure of him?' asked Semenov.

'Oh yes, absolutely sure. . . . He is a man with a very curious taste in women, is Major Grey, and some time ago I was able to secure some photographs of him in a very embarrassing position. But I throw him a little money from time to time because he is a useful errand boy. And because it amuses me.'

'And I suppose it's Hall's money, anyway?' asked Semenov with a grin.

'Precisely,' said Nyanga, and roared with laughter again. 'And speaking of our friend Mr Hall, what have you got for me?'

Semenov reached down into his briefcase and produced a blue foolscap folder which he placed on the table between them.

'I have received a very full report from Moscow,' he said. 'It is most interesting. You can digest it at your leisure later on, but briefly, Hall's real name is Konrad Höller.'

'German?' asked Nyanga.

'Yes. Much as you thought, in fact. He was born in 1920, and as soon as he was old enough he joined the Waffen SS. He was a member of the unit that provided the concentration-camp guards. They were known as the death's head battalion because of their skull and cross-bones insignia. He did very well in the military – exceptionally well. He was a full Colonel before he was twenty-five.'

'Which camp did he work in?'

'Dachau principally. He specialised in the torture and murder of young girls – as we might have guessed in view of yesterday's display. He killed one a day, personally, for many months.'

Nyanga was thoughtful. 'I see. . . . And after the war?'

'Well, many of his colleagues went to South America, as you know. But Hall had some relations in South Africa so he went there instead. He used the Jews' money to finance himself, and forged papers were no problem if you could pay enough. And then after a year or two, to protect his rear, he killed the people who'd sheltered him.'

Nyanga grunted. 'Hmm. A dangerous man, then?'

'Oh yes. Very. A very strong man, very experienced.'

'Yes. . . . This explains a good deal, Yuri. Hall is a fascist, but he's primarily interested in furthering his own ends, of course. . . . Well – what do you suggest we do with him?'

'Work with him for the time being,' said Semenov. 'Make use of his talents. Later on, when you are President, we can get in advisers from the USSR. Mining experts, management experts – they will do everything for you that Conrad Hall can do, and at that stage you can get rid of him.'

'How?' asked Nyanga. The problem seemed to worry him.

'Easy – just give him to the Israelis. Make yourself look like a responsible world citizen.'

Nyanga glanced at Semenov sharply. Then a weight seemed to lift from his mind, and his face lit up with a beaming smile. 'Ah yes,' he said. 'What a good idea.' He began to laugh once more, and Semenov joined in.

After leaving the church hall in Peachville, Duncan Grey did not go straight home. He knew that for once his wife Eileen would be at the house, waiting for him, but he couldn't bring himself to face her. Not tonight – not stone cold sober. He couldn't face the thought of being shown to be inadequate once again – the thought of being mocked, and jeered at. And being compared unfavourably, and in unsparing detail, with others.

He decided he would go and have a little drink. And then perhaps he might go home, after that.

But after one drink Duncan Grey decided he would have one or two more. And then after a while he counted the money that Nyanga had given him, and was amazed by how much was there. And that put the thought into his mind that for once he could afford a visit to Mama Pauline's.

At that point he began to cheer up a bit. Yes – he would go to Mama Pauline's.

The fat, handsome woman who was known as Mama Pauline had European blood in her veins – how much no-one really knew, not even her Mibambo mother. But while her features were pure Mibambo, her skin was as pale as most Europeans, and she was undoubtedly European in her dress and mannerisms. She was aged perhaps forty now – she didn't know her real age either – with straight black hair which she wore piled up on top of her head; her figure was delightful, generously proportioned in all the best places.

Mama Pauline had been discovered and broken in at the age of ten by a lecherous English schoolmaster. For six glorious months he had had her all to himself, and even after that he had guided and monitored her career as a high-class prostitute; now, at the age of seventy, he looked after the accounts of the multi-racial brothel which she ran with great success.

Mama Pauline greeted Duncan Grey at the door of her establishment: Nyanga had phoned her earlier that evening and had told her to expect 'the Major'. She was wearing an elegant grey satin evening-dress with a flower in her hair, and every other man who had come in through the door that night had stopped in his tracks to admire her.

But not Duncan Grey. He went straight past with scarcely a glance. The lady was not his type.

Mama Pauline trotted after the new arrival as he made for the reception area of her establishment. 'Take a seat,' she said firmly. 'Have a taste of rum. I've got just the thing for you, but it'll take a minute or two to arrange.'

Duncan Grey did as he was told and waited impatiently for a quarter of an hour. At the end of that time Mama Pauline escorted him down a corridor to the rear of the building; she pointed his nose at a small round window in a door.

Grey looked through the window.

Inside the room was the biggest, blackest Mibambo market-mammy he had ever seen in his life: her upper arms were the size of most men's thighs, and the rest of her was on a similar scale. Grey nearly fainted with pleasure on the spot.

'How much?' he croaked, when he could get his breath back.

Mama Pauline named her price, which was pitched as high as she dared. Duncan Grey's eyes remained firmly fixed on the window, so Mama Pauline hastily adjusted her quotation. 'Plus ten per cent service, of course,' she added.

'Does she know what to do?' the Major asked.

'Oh yes. Exactly.'

Duncan Grey took out the envelope which Nyanga had given him earlier and passed it over without a word. Mama Pauline noticed with satisfaction that his hand was trembling uncontrollably.

Fourteen

At the end of his first week as President Kasaboru's security adviser, Philip Morgan reported to the President on his review of the overall situation. Philip felt that he had only just begun to understand some of the problems involved, but that he had nevertheless made substantial progress in improving the existing arrangements.

He had started by trying to find out whether there really was a state of emergency in Balembi. To a newcomer like himself there appeared to be a risk of an immediate coup. But was that really so, or was it just that Philip was hearing of a long-standing possibility for the first time? Perhaps he was just being misled by the atmosphere of political and social instability which was to be found in many African countries.

Even the President himself found it difficult to make an objective judgement on this point. He explained to Philip that on the whole he felt that the tension was no worse now than at any time since independence. He hoped and believed that his intelligence organization would give him advance warning of any serious attempt to seize power, and he promised to let Philip see the intelligence reports from now on, so that he could form his own opinion. As far as the immediate future was concerned, Kasaboru felt that the most likely time for his enemies to attempt a take-over would be when he was out of the country at the beginning of July; at that time he was due to attend the Congress of Independent African States in Accra.

Philip, for his part, had concentrated on the problems of preserving the President's safety while he was still in Balembi rather than when he was abroad. The President's palace was defended by the army: Colonel Webb, the officer in charge, had clearly given much thought to his responsibilities. Webb was a professional soldier in his late forties, very able and very easy to get on with; Philip had every confidence in his plans and in his ability to carry them out. But the real problem was that it had to be assumed that the enemy would also have studied the palace defences, and would have equipped itself with the means to overcome them.

The Balembian army's equipment was ninety-nine per cent British; it was reliable but by no means up-to-date. Lee Enfield rifles and Sten guns were still the standard issue, while many other armies were using the Belgian FN or the Kalashnikov AK47. Philip was not yet sure what could be done about that; it would need more thought.

Outside the palace the police force was charged with the President's safety. The police were efficient in their methods but their equipment, like the army's, was again not the most modern available. However, as Kasaboru himself had pointed out, the example of President Kennedy had proved that even the most elaborate security arrangements were fallible; so this was another area in which much thinking needed to be done.

Two positive steps which Philip had so far taken were to practise using the Mark 5 Sten gun which was kept in the President's car, and to equip himself with a Smith and Wesson Model 39 automatic, which he carried as unobtrusively as possible.

One of the first questions Philip had asked the President had been where he would go if his base in the capital were no longer secure. The answer had been to Sungbarta, the second biggest city in Balembi. Sungbarta lay two hundred miles to the west, and was situated firmly in Mibambo territory; the Mayor of Sungbarta was a personal friend of Kasaboru's and the city's politics were strongly Progessive. In short, Sungbarta seemed likely to remain loyal in all foreseeable circumstances. The problem of maintaining the President's authority if Digara were held by the enemy consequently resolved itself into how to get him to Sungbarta as quickly as possible; and fortunately the President had no wife and children to worry about.

Philip decided early on in the planning exercise that if there was trouble in Digara while the President was elsewhere, it would be necessary to improvise. Much would depend on where the President was at the time, what transport was available, and so on. He made a note to review the police radio-communications system and to arrange for trained marksmen to be in the escort at all times, but there was not much else which could be decided in advance.

What had given Philip his biggest headache of the week was the question of how to preserve the President's life and liberty if he were actually in the palace when it was attacked. Philip's private opinion was that it would not take very long for a determined and suitably equipped force to break down the palace defences. The weakness lay not in the skill and courage of Colonel Webb's soldiers, but in the architecture of the building itself; it had simply not been designed to resist a full-scale attack.

The solution seemed to be to get the President away from the palace as soon as the first shot was fired. One possible means of escape was a helicopter, and Philip had already arranged for one to be on permanent standby within the palace grounds. He did not, however, intend that the President should ever use it. He had decided to assume that the attacking force would possess the capabilities of shooting the helicopter down; and even if the attackers could not do it, there was always the probability that the Gabuti air force would be called in to do the job from above. So the helicopter would never carry the President.

Instead of taking Kasaboru up, Philip had decided to take him down.

The use of the sewers as an escape route was a ploy which might well be predicted by a thoughtful opponent, but it was the best alternative Philip could come up with in his first week on the job. And no-one could say that he had not prepared this escape route thoroughly. He had discreetly obtained plans of the multitude of tunnels which ran under the city centre; most of them were comfortably big enough for a man to walk upright. He himself had been down into these dark, smelly passages and had signposted a way through the maze with paint; and in the palace itself he had set up a store of torches, wading boots and guns. Everything was ready.

The exit point from the sewers which Philip had selected was in a quiet cul-de-sac at the foot of a multi-storey car park. In the car park was an anonymous-looking Ford Anglia which would carry the President and himself beyond the city limits – provided they met no opposition. Once outside the city, there was just a remote possibility that the airport would still be accessible: if so, the President could fly his own plane – a Beagle B206S – to Sungbarta. But Philip doubted very much that the journey to Sungbarta could be completed in such comfort and with such speed. He was working on the assumption that the airport would be in enemy hands and that the President would have to travel overland – and by the back roads at that.

A couple of days after his arrival in Balembi the previous week, Philip's Uncle George had driven him ten miles south-east of Digara to Lake Kinley. There George Morgan owned an isolated cottage, with a garden running down to the shore of the small lake. It was this cottage that Philip had selected, with his uncle's permission, for use as a staging-post.

At Philip's request, Kasaboru had arranged for him to be able to purchase a second-hand Land-Rover. The transaction had been completed quietly and anonymously; as far as the garage which sold the Land-Rover knew, Philip was just an ordinary citizen in the market for a vehicle to take him out into the country at weekends. The Land-Rover was in excellent condition, and it was now locked in the garage behind George Morgan's lakeside cottage. Packed into the Land-Rover was everything Philip could think of to make a trip to Sungbarta as painless as possible, should it ever have to be undertaken. And so far only three people knew of this emergency arrangement: George Morgan, Philip himself, and the President.

Late on the Friday afternoon of his first week at the palace, Philip completed his verbal report on the steps he had so far taken.

Kasaboru was impressed, and said so openly. 'There's only one thing I can think of to make the plan complete,' he said.

'What's that?'

'More people. If we have to leave the capital, I mean. . . . You see, if it were simply a case of you and me driving to Sungbarta on the main road, there would be no difficulty. But we would not be able to do that. If there is an upheaval in the capital, then there will be even worse trouble in the country round about, you can depend on that. All the obvious roads would be blocked, of course, so you and I would have to go through the bush, as you rightly point out. Now the odds are that even a Land-Rover would not survive a journey like that. The country's unbelievably rough. And even if the vehicle did last out, three or four men would have to push it and pull it out of holes from time to time. And we would also need three or four pairs of eyes to protect ourselves on all sides, and to stand guard at night, all that sort of thing. Take my word for it as a native Balembian, Philip – you and I could not make it alone.'

'Very well,' said Philip. 'So who do you suggest to go with us?'

'Fuller and Thompson,' said the President without a moment's hesitation. 'Brief them accordingly.'

Philip nodded in acknowledgement.

'And I myself will make sure that the Mayor of Sungbarta knows in outline what our contingency plans are. The Mayor is an old friend of mine, and I can trust him to keep the information to himself. . . .' The President paused. 'There is, of course, one other aspect which occurs to me. . . .'

Philip looked at Kasaboru questioningly. 'What's that?'

'It sounds selfish perhaps – but if the object of the exercise is to get the head of state to Sungbarta in one piece, then ought we not to arrange to have a doctor with us? That's the first thought which crosses my mind. And the second point is this – if there were to be a revolution in Digara, would you wish to leave Dr Stuart in the capital to fend for herself?'

Philip smiled broadly. 'No,' he said. 'I must confess I wouldn't be too keen on that.'

Kasaboru nodded. 'I thought not. So perhaps she ought to come with us? Let me say straight away that the suggestion is not as considerate of your own feelings as it might appear. It's a practical matter really. You see, the greatest puzzle which faces me as President is knowing who to trust. I know beyond doubt that Nyanga has tried to bribe or threaten virtually all my colleagues. What I do not know is which of them he has succeeded in bribing or coercing into cooperation. A man will often do quite a lot for you if you threaten to blind his children or maim his wife. So that is why I lean so heavily on you, a total outsider. You have few relatives here who can be threatened as a means of turning you into a traitor –

and I have never disappointed you by offering a job that you wanted to someone else. And so on. . . . Much the same considerations apply to Miss Stuart. As a doctor she is no doubt fully competent, and she will look upon me much as on any other patient. But I could not be equally sure of the objectivity of virtually any other doctor in the nation. I do not wish to malign the medical profession by that statement – I merely point out that as they have wives and families, they are vulnerable. They might have been persuaded to harm me rather than help me.'

Philip's mind buzzed ahead, visualising the problems raised by the President's suggestion. 'Could a woman stand the strain of the journey to Sungbarta?' he asked.

'Not as well as a man could,' said Kasaboru frankly. 'But I have made some enquiries about Jane Stuart's father, and it appears he was an admirable man. If she has inherited even half his spirit then she would do very well – and her beauty would compensate us for any delay she caused. . . . So, see that she knows what to do if the need arises. That's an order.'

The following morning Philip went to Digara General Hospital. After being found semi-conscious in Opana, Jane Stuart had spent two nights in the Hospital, just to make sure that there were no after-effects from her head injury. Fortunately there were no complications, and by Saturday morning she felt perfectly well; the doctors were prepared to release her, so Philip took her out to lunch to celebrate her recovery.

Once he was sure that it would not upset her, Philip asked Jane how much she was able to remember of the events of Thursday morning.

'Not much,' said Jane. 'The police asked me an awful lot of questions, of course, but I don't think I was able to help them at all. I have a vague memory of seeing some soldiers driving up in a lorry, but that's about it. The next thing I remember is looking up at you, and even that memory is a bit fuzzy.'

Jane seemed upset that she could not remember more and Philip tried to comfort her. 'I think it's just as well that you didn't witness what happened,' he said. 'After all, the soldiers would undoubtedly have killed you with the others if they'd known you were there. And even if you had escaped alive, the sight of all the others being killed would have scarred you for life. It was a bad enough experience seeing them all lying there an hour or two later.'

Jane sighed deeply. 'Yes,' she said. 'I suppose you're right. You realise how I came to be in that cupboard, do you?'

Philip pursed his lips. 'Well, presumably your friend Enid knocked you out to keep you quiet, and then hid you away.'

Jane nodded. 'Yes, I'm sure you're right. It was absolutely typical of her. I suppose she guessed what would happen when the soldiers arrived, and she sacrificed her own life to save mine. And now all I can do to show my gratitude is go to her funeral on Monday. . . . It seems very inadequate somehow. I wish there was something else I could do.'

'There is,' said Philip. 'You can continue her work. Indirectly, I mean, not out in the bush. To work in a place like Opana would really be asking for trouble just at the moment.'

'Yes,' said Jane. 'I've sense enough to know you're right about that. But I've heard that there's a clinic here in Digara which specialises in helping the very poor. One of the directors came to see me in hospital and I've arranged to go and have a look at it next week.' Her expression became much more cheerful. 'Perhaps I can make myself useful in a place like that.'

'I'm quite certain you can,' said Philip.

After lunch Philip drove Jane back to the Greys' house in Victoria Vale. He himself returned to the President's palace where he still had plenty to do.

Duncan Grey was apparently out playing golf when Jane returned, but Eileen was at home; she was lounging by the swimming pool on an inflated air-bed, wearing the same tiny black bikini that she had worn on the evening of Jane's arrival in Balembi.

Duncan Grey had at least taken the trouble to visit his niece in Digara Hospital, but Eileen had not accompanied him, and that seemed to be fully indicative of her attitude. She greeted Jane with almost total indifference and barely looked up from the latest *Reader's Digest*. She enquired politely how Jane was feeling, but the question was obviously motivated more by a regard for correct social procedure than by any genuine interest. Jane got the feeling that if she had been found dead in Opana, Eileen Grey's reaction might have been a shrug of the shoulders at most. As for the massacre of the villagers – well, Eileen had read about it in the newspapers and it all sounded rather unpleasant. But the reports were exaggerated, of course, they always were. And anyway the natives were always cutting each other to pieces out in the bush; they had nothing else to do. And with that Eileen returned her attention to her magazine.

As soon as she decently could, Jane left Eileen to her sun-bathing and went upstairs to her room: she stayed there for the rest of the afternoon. After dinner she again excused herself as quickly as possible and went to bed early.

During the night she awoke. She looked at her watch and saw that it was nearly one a.m. Her mouth felt very dry – that was what had disturbed her sleep – so she slipped on a light dressing-gown and went out on to the landing to go to the bathroom.

The house was totally silent, but immediately after opening her bedroom door Jane became aware of a vaguely familiar smell. She stood for a moment and breathed deeply until she had placed it. Ah yes, of course – marijuana. Jane had been around enough to know the smell, though she had never smoked it herself. Well, what the Greys did in the privacy of their own home was, she supposed, their own business.

Further along the landing a light was on in the Greys' bedroom, and as Jane walked past on her way to the bathroom, she glanced curiously through the open doorway.

Inside the Greys' bedroom, sideways on to the door, stood Joro Nyanga. He was standing with his feet slightly apart, his hands on his hips; he was completely naked. Kneeling on the thick carpet in front of him was Eileen Grey; she too wore nothing at all and in the soft light from the bedside lamp her skin looked the colour of coffee with cream. Eileen's left hand was massaging Nyanga's groin; her right hand stroked the shaft of his hugely erect penis, and her mouth was closed firmly and greedily over the end of it; her eyes were tightly shut.

All this Jane took in with a second's glance. Despite herself she stopped in her tracks, and as she looked into the room, Joro Nyanga turned his gaze on her. He was not in the least surprised or dismayed by her presence – on the contrary he seemed pleased and amused. He smiled at Jane openly, and dreamily. Then he passed his red tongue slowly and lasciviously over his lips.

Jane moved rapidly onwards to the bathroom, and when she returned to her bedroom she kept her eyes fixed firmly on her destination.

Enough was enough.

Early the following morning Jane rang up Philip at the President's palace and asked him to come over and collect her. She wasn't sure where she was going to go, but she was quite certain that she was not going to stay with Duncan and Eileen Grey for one night longer; she clearly had nothing whatever in common with them.

Philip made one phone call before driving to Victoria Vale; as a result he was able to arrange for Jane to stay with his Uncle George. He explained to the old man that before long Jane would be getting a flat of her own, and that the arrangement would only be temporary. But his uncle said that he didn't mind how long Jane stayed. He had liked her enormously when he had first met her, the previous Saturday; and anyway, at his age it was no bad thing to have a doctor sharing a house with you.

Duncan Grey was still in bed when Jane left, and Eileen had gone to the golf club to have lunch with some friends, so there was no-one on hand to witness her departure. And as Philip drove her to King George VI Avenue Jane explained in more detail what had prompted her decision to leave.

'It's not that I'm a prude,' she said, able to smile about the incident now. 'But the way things were going it was only a matter of time before Nyanga made a pass at me – and that's something I can definitely do without.'

Jane was soon comfortably established at George Morgan's house; he had plenty of spare rooms, and Jane became noticeably more cheerful once she had arrived there.

After a light lunch prepared by Imbasa, the old man's servant, Philip took Jane out for a drive to Lake Kinley. He showed her his uncle's cottage on the edge of the lake, and explained the arrangements he had made to provide an escape route for the President in the event of political upheaval.

Philip was well aware that he was taking a considerable security risk in giving Jane the details of his plans; but he felt that unless she knew the reason why she had to make her way to the cottage in a time of trouble, she might not take his instructions seriously enough.

After he was satisfied that Jane knew exactly what to do and why, they went for a swim in the lake. Then they retired to the bedroom of the cottage, where they spent the rest of the afternoon very happily.

They returned to Digara late that evening.

George Morgan was feeling extremely unwell, and he went to bed soon after Jane came in; she noticed how pale and ill he looked.

George kept his health problems very much to himself, and he was not a man to complain about how he was feeling. But the fact was that cancer of the bladder had been diagnosed over a year ago. He had already had two spells in hospital for radiation treatment, and he had now been warned that not much else could be done for him. Some days he naturally felt worse than others, and tonight was a particularly bad night.

The old man lay awake in bed for some time, with the radio beside him playing one of his favourite symphonies. For several months now he had kept a loaded revolver close at hand, and he pondered for a while on the question of whether tonight might not be the right time to use it.

But after a few minutes he persuaded himself that the pain which he was experiencing was nothing serious really. Why, he'd had a toothache worse than that many a time. And anyway, there were lots of things worth living for. Lots of things he could still do: useful things, important things; various charities and good causes that he was interested in. When all was said and done, Balembi was not in such a marvellous state of peace and prosperity that he could afford to leave the country to its own devices – not by a long way.

So, for the time being at least, George Morgan put aside the thought of ending his own life. But he knew very well that his time on earth was now very limited; and the problem which exercised his mind before he eventually went to sleep was how he might use that time to the best advantage. To the advantage, that is to say, not of himself, but of the state of Balembi as a whole. He was not a conceited man, but he knew very well that in the past he had made important contributions to the welfare of the country; perhaps in the time that was left to him he could find some way to help to secure the future.

Fifteen

Joro Nyanga spent the latter part of Sunday morning in the gym at the Balembi Parliament building. He was a man with a well-developed appetite for food, women and a variety of stimulants; but he was also a man with a very well-developed sense of priorities, and he knew that today of all days he had to be completely fit and alert.

After lunch Nyanga went into an extended conference with his fellow conspirators, General Juba and Yuri Semenov. Late on the previous Friday night he had decided to launch his coup in the early hours of Monday morning, and he was determined now to make sure that every detail of the plan was sound.

Together the three men went through General Juba's analysis of the army officers and their loyalties. It took two hours to reach agreement, but at the end of that time they knew precisely which officers would be arrested and which would assume command in their place; they also knew which units could be left out of the reckoning entirely, either because they were solidly Mimbambo, or because they were based too far away to have any bearing on the situation.

Once the command of the various army units had been finally settled, it remained only to check General Juba's plans for capturing the key points of the city. These had been discussed and reviewed many times before, but the General was again subjected to a fierce cross-examination. On the whole he survived it well, and in the end Semenov and Nyanga were satisfied.

Nyanga then slept, from ten p.m. until two a.m. This pleased Semenov considerably: it demonstrated that the man's nerves were good. But at two in the morning Nyanga awoke, without being roused, and prepared himself for the most important day in his life.

Towards three o'clock Nyanga and Semenov made their way to the Windsor Barracks, where the army had its Digara HQ. There General Juba had called out his crack battalion of Fanda troops; this was the unit which had been selected to attack the President's palace. The battalion consisted of three companies of riflemen, with eighty men in each company, and a command group; two tanks and two armoured cars had also been added to provide the real punch.

As Nyanga arrived at the drill hall where the men were assembled, the soldiers were all standing easy. The air was buzzing with speculation and the faces of the troops were unusually animated, despite the time of day.

General Juba addressed the battalion first. He began by explaining that today the men were to see real action; they were to be offered a chance to make names for themselves by fighting a vital battle in their country's history. He was careful, however, to leave plenty of opportunity for Nyanga to fill in the details of the day's plans.

It was only when Nyanga began to address the troops himself that Semenov fully understood why the Kremlin had sent him to this country. On his arrival in Balembi, Semenov had been puzzled by what his lords and masters expected to gain from such a backwater. But now the Kremlin's purpose became clear to him: obviously they saw Nyanga as one of their key men in the process of turning Africa into a wholly communist continent. For Nyanga had class – there was no doubt about it. He was a natural mob orator, a rabble-rouser and a hypnotizer of the first order, with a resonant, powerful voice. If he could be brought to power in Balembi then he could gradually be built into a charismatic power-broker in Africa as a whole. Yes, Semenov could see it clearly now. He listened with increasing respect.

Nyanga's speech began on a low key. He emphasised first of all that all those present were tribal brothers. The troops only had to glance around to see that their white officers were totally absent; Nyanga explained that they were still in bed, and there was a roar of delight at this obvious lie.

Then Nyanga recalled the long history of persecution of the Fanda people by their enemies the Mibambos. According to Nyanga, the traitor Kasaboru had deliberately neglected the welfare of the Fanda people in every conceivable way; worst of all, he had used Mibambo soldiers to murder and maim innocent women and children in un-defended Fanda villages. It was, apparently, only Nyanga's heroic and unceasing efforts which had prevented the Fanda tribe from being totally annihilated.

For twenty minutes Nyanga had the battalion completely en-tranced; he played on their emotions with consummate skill. Fin-ally, in a powerful conclusion to the speech, he reminded the men of the need to restore liberty, justice and security in the state. In the next few hours, he said, if the assembled men acted with courage and determination, they could rid Balembi for ever of this monster Kasaboru. He, Nyanga, as the new head of state, would then guar-antee the safety of the Fanda people for ever. He would see that Fanda civil servants were appointed to those posts from which they had so far been unjustly excluded. He would see that Fanda busi-nessmen were given those government contracts which had so far been unfairly denied them. He would see that Fanda farmers were given back the land which the greedy Mibambos had seized from them. And he would, incidentally, see that the relevant units of the army were given a handsome pay rise to reward them for their bravery and initiative in putting things right.

In conclusion then, all those who wished to see justice, freedom and equality restored in Balembi were invited to come to attention and take three paces forward.

The battalion moved as one man.

For the next hour Nyanga relaxed and killed time as best he could; he was content to leave General Juba to see that his troops moved into the chosen positions at the right time. Then, at five a.m. precisely, Nyanga gave the word of command which unleashed the Balembi bloodbath.

Conrad Hall, out at his mansion in Tikiro, was waiting eagerly for news. He had received a telephone call from Yuri Semenov at four a.m.; he had been told that he could expect an early decision on the business proposition which they had discussed on Friday. Subsequently, of course, Hall had not been able to go back to sleep; there was far too much adrenalin flowing for that. Instead he had performed his early-morning exercises with his usual Teutonic thoroughness; and then, at five a.m., he rang his housekeeper on the internal telephone system and asked her if she would be kind enough to make breakfast for him. He apologised profusely for rousing her at such an unearthly hour – he was very conscious of the need to treat his servants with consideration – but he explained that he might shortly have to drive to the capital on urgent business.

Mrs Schell assured him that making breakfast would be no trouble at all. The truth was that she was very reluctant indeed to leave the comfortable bed which she shared nightly with a young black girl, but she obeyed her master instantly: she had not been born and brought up in Germany for nothing.

Duncan Grey first became aware that the coup had really begun when he heard the soldiers battering on the door of the Digara radio station. He looked at his watch: it was ten past five.

Like Conrad Hall, Grey had been woken by a telephone call from Semenov. He had immediately gone to his place of work, leaving his wife Eileen fast asleep at home. He was privately rather worried about her safety, but in fact he need not have been concerned: Joro Nyanga had arranged for a corporal and three soldiers to mount guard on his house while he was away.

Radio Digara would normally have begun broadcasting at seven a.m. with a news bulletin followed by a record-request programme. At five a.m., therefore, there was no-one else on the premises, apart from a sleepy night-watchman.

When he heard the soldiers' thunderous banging, Grey rushed out of his office and threw open the front door. But he realised immediately that this was not a good idea. The soldiers poured in, yelling and screaming, and two of them had him up against a wall at bayonet-point before he could even blink. The rest of the men pounded along the corridors in their heavy boots, banging open the doors and looking for action.

But there wasn't any.

Eventually a very sophisticated and effete Fanda officer wandered in and asked Grey to identify himself. Grey did so, and the officer then suggested to his men that they might release him. They were clearly very disappointed that they were not going to be allowed to disembowel the prisoner on the spot, but they obeyed. Grey then straightened his tie, combed his hair and generally tidied himself up. He was just congratulating himself on the coolness and self-control with which he had handled the whole incident when he became aware that the left leg of his trousers was soaked with urine. Apparently he hadn't been quite as calm and composed as he'd thought.

Thus the radio station was taken without difficulty. And from Nyanga's point of view, the attack on the President's palace also went well. Shortly before five a.m. the troops involved took up their positions in the surrounding side-streets. In theory at least, the noise made by the lorries and the tanks as they arrived ought to have alerted the palace guards, but in practice they noticed nothing unusual.

The two tanks were British Centurions, each weighing fifty tons, armed with 83.4 mm, 20–pounder guns. At five o'clock exactly, one of the two tanks lurched out of a side-street and moved into a position directly facing the main gate of the palace. It fired two rounds of tungsten-carbide-cored, armour-piercing ammunition. One shot was aimed at the main, outer gatehouse, and the second at the inner gates, which were made of solid mahogany and were closed. After the shots were fired nothing much remained of either target.

The first tank then moved straight ahead, crunching over the wrought-iron main gates and battering its way through the relatively narrow opening into the inner courtyard. The second tank followed, and two armoured cars took up positions where they could rake with fire the few soldiers who were left at the main gate. The result of this manoeuvre was that the defenders at the outer perimeter of the palace were cut down within minutes.

In the inner courtyard the fighting was more prolonged. The two tanks had insufficient room to move freely, and although they looked very dangerous and impressive, they could not in fact make full use of their strength. They rumbled around for some minutes, with rifle fire pinging off their armour-plating.

In the meantime, Colonel Webb, who slept in the palace, had leapt out of bed at the first shot and had begun to organize his men. Before long a spirited counter-attack was under way.

The helicopter pilot had also been woken by the gunfire. Following his orders to the letter, he pulled on his kit and raced out to the Westland Wessex HC. Mk. 2 on the pad. As quickly as he could he got the two Bristol Siddeley Gnome engines turning over, and shortly afterwards the machine began to climb steadily into the air. But the pilot had no sooner cleared the height of the palace railings than two machine-gun crews, which had been sitting there waiting for a clear view of him, poured fire into the body of his helicopter. The pilot was killed instantly, and in a screaming, jarring, juddering heap of whirling and disintegrating rotors, the Westland came down with a crunch. It exploded on impact with the ground; huge clouds of yellow and black smoke roared into the sky as the attackers jumped for joy at their achievement.

After twenty minutes the fighting was all over and the palace was taken. The defenders, under Colonel Webb, fought courageously, but they were heavily outnumbered; they were also completely outclassed in sheer fire-power.

Colonel Webb, despite having one leg shattered by a hand-grenade, fought to the very end and was the last to be captured. He was dragged out into the street by his heels, his head bumping on the ground, and was dumped at the feet of Nyanga and General Juba. Nyanga made a point of shooting him personally.

By six o'clock on the morning of Monday 21 June, 1965, every key point in Digara was held by Nyanga's supporters. The airport was closed until further notice; the post office was not allowing cables to be sent or international phone calls to be made; General Juba himself sat in the police headquarters control room; and one of his lieutenants had taken charge of the radio station. The owners and previous editors of the two leading newspapers were already in prison, and two deputy editors who were known to be friendly towards Nyanga were on their way to the office to take over editorial control; within hours they would produce special editions of their papers, reporting that the Balembian army had deposed Kasaboru and had asked Mr Nyanga to serve in his place. The new editors would make the point that on balance this action was fully justified. They would so so for two reasons: in the one case, to prevent his family from being blinded with acid, and in the other to prevent some embarrassing photographs of his activities at Mama Pauline's being sent to his wife.

The revolution did not go entirely unopposed. Apart from the resistance around the palace, a number of policemen and soldiers also opposed Nyanga's bid for power. But at five and six o'clock in the morning hardly anyone except the revolutionaries was awake and alert. The few who were sufficiently well organised and sufficiently courageous to launch a counter-attack at the appropriate time were unfortunately in a tiny minority; they were soon killed or captured.

By ten o'clock that morning the soldiers who had been involved in the coup knew for certain that they had overcome all resistance. There was no further need to remain alert, and they consequently began to relax.

The Fanda soldiers were for the most part country boys, the sons of poor farmers and half-successful traders. They had gone into the army because army training was free, and because their families could not afford to give them a better education. In many ways they had felt inferior to their Mibambo contemporaries, and in particular they had felt inferior to city dwellers.

But now it suddenly began to dawn on these young men that in spite of their tribal origin and in spite of their lack of a formal education, they had taken control of the capital. It was not the clever young Mibambos with their suits and ties who were running Digara – it was the Fanda units of the army. And it was not only the ordinary riflemen who felt this way – the Fanda officers also shared their elation, and began to experience a totally new and extraordinary sense of power.

The result of this mood was predictable, and indeed had been predicted, both by the President and by many others. Before long the windows and doors of liquor stores were smashed open and the men began to drink. In an hour or so they were completely drunk. The officers either lost control or lost interest in maintaining it, and the streets of Digara became desperately dangerous for anyone who was Mibambo, European, female, or wearing a tie.

Nyanga sent Bulu into the city with the specific instruction to 'go out and frighten people'. And for someone with Bulu's disfigured appearance and sadistic temperament, that was not difficult. Bulu took a platoon of soldiers and marched them down Piccadilly, one of the most select shopping areas in Digara. The plate-glass windows of every single shop in Piccadilly were smashed and the contents looted. Some of the managers and sales assistants had in fact come to work, despite the ominous silence of the radio and the sound of gunfire in the streets. But few of them ever went home again. The women were raped and then stabbed to death. The men, if they were lucky, were hanged from lamp-posts; if they were not lucky, like the owner of the city's premier jewellery store, Bulu cut off their legs above the knee and made them try to walk home if they could.

By noon the only live human beings visible in the streets of central Digara were either drunken soldiers or their Fanda hangers-on. Further out in the suburbs, bags were being packed in many European homes, and the heads of the households were worriedly cleaning and oiling whatever guns they possessed. Their children, by and large, didn't understand what was happening; the mothers tended to hope that it would all blow over soon; and the grim-faced fathers knew very well that before things got any better they were going to

100

get a damn sight worse.

In the city of Sungbarta, two hundred miles to the west, the Reuters correspondent discovered that it was still possible to dial a telephone call straight through to Balembi. As a result he was able to gain a very clear picture of what was happening, mostly from his colleagues on the Digara newspapers. And having been in the Congo in 1960 he could readily visualise the scene from the partial and disjointed descriptions of events that he was given.

Late on the afternoon of the coup, the Reuters man sent a despatch to London. He analysed the sides in the conflict as follows: on the one hand, President Kasaboru, the Progressive party and the Mibambo tribe, favouring the West and democracy; on the other hand, Joro Nyanga, the Fanda tribe and the National party, favouring socialism/communism, and looking towards the USSR and Gabuti. The situation was not, he emphasised, quite as simple as that – in Africa nothing ever was simple, but that was the gist of it.

'The key to what will happen next,' wrote the Reuters man, 'is undoubtedly President Kasaboru himself. Is he still alive? If so, can he muster his supporters and retrieve his position? Certainly the city of Sungbarta remains solidly loyal to him. And if Kasaboru can make his way here and assume command of those sections of the army which are in this area, then he might still be able to overcome Nyanga's bid for power. But for the moment Kasaboru's whereabouts are totally unknown. And, as the hours go by, the chances that he has escaped capture and reached safety must grow steadily more remote.'

Sixteen

In the President's palace, Philip Morgan was woken by the silence.

At least, that was what he thought as he first returned to consciousness. He came awake very suddenly, listening for what had roused him; but he could hear nothing.

Then, of course, he heard a massive *crump* as the Centurion tank at the palace gates fired its first shot; he was out of bed and half dressed before the echoes had died.

Philip's room was at the back of the palace, on the same floor as the President's. In thirty seconds he had pulled on the special clothes which he had left lying ready by his bed and had seized the Mark 5 Sten gun propped up against the wall; then he was off and running down the corridor.

He burst into Kasaboru's room without knocking and found the President pulling on a pair of khaki drill trousers.

'What's happening?' asked Kasaboru. A heavy volume of gunfire could be heard in the background.

'I don't know,' said Philip, 'but we're obviously under attack. I think we ought to get out as soon as we can.'

Kasaboru stepped into a pair of sturdy brown shoes and laced them up; his jaw was clenched and his expression grim. 'All right,' he said, once he was ready. 'Let's go.'

The two men raced down the main staircase, putting into effect the escape plan which the President had approved only three days earlier. All around them they could hear the repeated rattle of light-machine-gun fire as the battle for the palace gates continued; inside the palace there were occasional shouts and screams.

Philip was leading the way, and at first the President stayed hard on his heels; but once they reached the ground floor Philip became aware that the President had paused. He stopped and went back to where Kasaboru was standing; he found him looking through a window at the Centurion tank which had broken through into the inner courtyard.

Kasaboru's expression was deeply distressed. 'So,' he said. 'It has begun after all. Just as I feared.' A bullet ricocheted angrily through the window, spattering the President with broken glass. He remained standing exactly where he was and didn't even flinch; he turned to look at Philip. 'You know,' he said, 'Nyanga doesn't really care about the people. Only about himself. Perhaps we ought to stay and fight.'

'No,' said Philip firmly. 'Stick to the plan we made in calmer times. You must have a secure base. You can be far more use to your country somewhere else, as a free President, than you can be here as a dead hero.'

With a tremendous ear-shattering roar the Centurion tank fired its big gun straight into the body of the palace building. It blew a massive hole in the masonry on the far side of the courtyard, and the noise alone was enough to send Philip and the President staggering, their ears ringing; plaster from the ceiling showered down on to them.

Philip took the President's arm. 'It's time to go,' he said, and turned away.

The President followed.

Philip moved on into the palace kitchens; he unlocked the door into the cellars and locked it again after them. Then he went down two further flights of stairs, right down into the bilges of the building.

Kasaboru was totally lost. 'I hope you know where you're going,' he muttered. 'I certainly don't.'

One more door was unlocked, and then locked again behind them, and finally Philip was able to lift up a metal trap-door set in a concrete floor; beneath it was a steel ladder leading down to the sewers below.

Philip picked up a pair of waterproof leggings and tossed them to the President. 'Put these on,' he said. 'You'll need them.' He pulled on a pair himself. Then he handed the President one of the two powerful torches he had previously left in the cellar, and led the way down the ladder.

Kasaboru closed the trap-door after them and then the two men began to wade through the ankle-deep water. The tunnel itself was egg-shaped, rather rounder under-foot than at the top above their heads; it was of brick construction, about seven feet from floor to ceiling, and mercifully the smell was not too bad. But then, Philip reflected, Digara was a notably clean city in every way.

Down here they were insulated from the battle above, but once they had cleared the palace foundations an occasional explosion or burst of machine-gun fire echoed through the ventilation shafts. In some places fingers of dim light also penetrated through the grilles on the surface above.

Philip kept on at a good steady pace, following the paint marks he had dabbed on the walls the previous week. The President followed, too depressed by what he was leaving behind to make much comment.

After about half a mile they came to a straight stretch of tunnel; there was faint illumination from six patches of light shining through grilles at regular intervals on the surface above. This was a section of the sewer which ran below the surface of a road through a small park to the north of the palace; the bottom of the tunnel was dry at this point.

The two men had just passed the third of the six patches of light when there was a sudden clattering noise behind them; it was followed by a similar sound ahead.

'What was that?' said Philip sharply.

His answer came in the form of further clatterings both behind and ahead of them, as small, hissing canisters of gas were dropped through every grille.

'Run!' Philip shouted urgently. 'And hold your breath!' And he and the President took off as fast as they could.

But their waterproof leggings were not made for sprinting through an awkwardly shaped tunnel, and the distance to safety was just too great. Before they had realised what was happening, both men had already taken several lungfuls of the sweet-smelling gas which poured out into the narrow space of the tunnel in massive concentration.

Dimly Philip became aware of the repeated clattering of more and more canisters of gas dropping and bouncing into the tunnel. He found himself running as if through water. The shafts of light above his head wavered and shimmered. He kept going – he had to keep going – but he staggered and lurched, stumbled and fell, banging and grazing himself against the rough edges of the tunnel's cement.

Before long he could go no further. He gasped with exhaustion, and clawed at the wall to hold himself upright. But it was no good. He just . . . could not . . . keep going. He hit the ground very hard but felt nothing.

Richard Chokwe, the Foreign Secretary of Balembi, had spent most of Sunday night with an immensely beautiful lady diplomat from the Swedish Embassy. He had admired her on the cocktail circuit for some months, but not until tonight had he been able to persuade her to take him seriously. The waiting had, however, made the eventual conquest all the more satisfying; and if the lady's sighs and moans were any guide, she had no complaints about the experience either.

But eventually, as dawn approached, Chokwe began to feel that he ought to make some move for home; he had both his own and the diplomat's reputation to think about. So it was that shortly before five o'clock that Monday morning, Richard Chokwe was driving home through the streets of central Digara.

There were a few other cars about at that time of day, but Chokwe was the only driver who became seriously alarmed by the number of soldiers in the streets. He knew instinctively that something was wrong, and he immediately altered his route to avoid the area around the President's palace.

For two or three heart-stopping minutes he couldn't decide what to do. He knew that he was about to enter the most crucial period of his entire life, a time when making the wrong decision would bring him a very unpleasant death. And at first he couldn't decide whether to stop and raise the alarm from a call-box, or to keep going and ring the President from his home. In the end he kept going: he felt that the President was reasonably well protected, after all.

Fortunately for himself and for Balembi, Richard Chokwe was no fool, and once his immediate sweat of panic was over he recovered his judgement. He was certain that if someone was using the army to attempt a coup, then he himself would undoubtedly be scheduled for arrest, if not death. So he parked his car some distance from his home and completed the last few hundred yards on foot, going through gardens where necessary.

Just as he had feared, there were heavily armed soldiers at both the front and back of his house. And somehow Chokwe did not think they were there for his own protection. It grieved him bitterly to have to leave his wife and children alone – but, like the President, Chokwe decided that it would make more sense to stay alive, and try to retrieve the situation later, than to rush in and get himself killed.

He returned to his car and drove back towards central Digara, thinking hard. He had a bachelor friend who owed him a few favours: he would go to the friend's flat, turn on the radio, and lie low. He would see what developed as the day went on.

Among the many others who were woken by the five o'clock attack on the President's palace were Kelly Thompson and Bob Fuller. As soon as he heard the shooting, Kelly Thompson pulled a dressing-gown over his trim frame and went out of his bedroom into the living-room. He was of average build, with short brown hair which was retreating a bit at the temples; his skin was heavily tanned from his frequent swims in an outdoor pool.

Thompson could see smoke rising from the direction of the palace. The gunfire continued, intensifying if anything; Thompson swore under his breath. A few moments later he was joined at the window by his friend, Bob Fuller.

Fuller took one glance at the scene outside and then grunted. 'Right, then,' he said. 'This is it. . . . We'd better get moving.'

Before taking up their present posts, both men had been professional soldiers in the British army for the best part of twenty years. In the last few days they had been given contingency plans for just such an event as this by the President's security adviser; they had been fully briefed on what to do, and they now carried out their orders.

The two men dressed, picked up all the equipment which Philip Morgan had issued to them, and added a few items of their own; then they went downstairs (avoiding the lift) and entered the underground garage which was directly beneath the block of flats.

Fuller methodically checked over his car while Thompson stood guard with a Sten gun, but no-one disturbed them. Then they drove out of the garage and into the open street. Thompson kept the barrel of his Sten gun just below the bottom of the open near-side window, his finger on the trigger. Fortunately, by moving so soon after the trouble began they had managed to avoid all the chaos and disorder which filled the streets of Digara later on; they experienced no delays whatever, and they arrived at George Morgan's cottage beside Lake Kinley in a little over half an hour.

For the last three or four miles they made frequent checks to see that no-one was following them. And having arrived they mounted guard on the narrow road leading up to the cottage so that anyone who tried to approach would have to drive down the barrel of a gun. And that, of course, was about all they could do.

Except sit in the baking sun.

Sit. And wait.

Wait for the President.

Seventeen

Headache.

Nausea.

Philip was sick – repeatedly. Vomiting till there was nothing left to vomit and then going on retching and heaving for some time.

His head swam.

Vaguely he began to be aware of lights; he heard a roaring in his ears. But even as he lay there suffering, Philip's brain started to function again. Slowly and without focus at first, his mind began to mull things over.

He found himself wondering what the gas had been – the gas that had knocked them out in the sewer. Sweet-smelling, whatever it was. Nitrous oxide? Laughing gas. Nothing very funny about this lot. High concentration needed to produce anaesthesia, but a rapid loss of consciousness. Did it make you sick though? He couldn't remember.

More retching. Retching and coughing, the eyes and nose streaming. Perhaps a combination-gas – lacrimator, nauseator, anaesthetic. Bloody awful, anyway.

After a while Philip recovered his senses completely and became fully aware of his situation. He and the President both had their hands tied behind their backs; their ankles were also bound with rope. They were lying on the floor of a large, windowless room without much furniture in it: just a wooden table and three chairs. The walls were plain, with pipes traversing the ceiling; the lights were fluorescent. It was a basement somewhere, Philip decided – in a factory or a department-store. There was no noise, though – so perhaps they were in a hotel.

He turned his attention to the President. Kasaboru was also beginning to come round now, groaning between long spasms of vomiting.

Suddenly, as he watched the man struggling to regain consciousness, Philip was struck by a massive wave of depression. It seemed to him that he had failed utterly. He had been appointed to do a specific job – to keep the President safe from his enemies – and he had failed, absolutely and irretrievably. His heart went numb with despair.

But then, gradually, the rational part of Philip's mind took over.

When all was said and done, he wasn't dead yet, and neither was the President. And as long as they were alive there was still some remote chance of escape, some dim glimmer of hope. O.K., he thought, so you feel terrible. But fight it – kick back – struggle. Take deep breaths, work your hands loose. Do anything but give in.

With an effort Philip pulled himself up into a sitting position. As he did so, the door of the room opened and Joro Nyanga came in. He was followed by Yuri Semenov and two heavily built soldiers in uniform.

Nyanga approached Philip with an interested expression. 'Well now,' he said slowly, his voice deep and assured. 'Coming round, are we? Jolly good show, eh what?' He nudged Semenov with his elbow to indicate that he was playing the fool, and then roared with laughter. Semenov smiled faintly.

Nyanga pointed to the President. 'Bring him round,' he said to one of the soldiers. The man crossed to a sink on the far side of the room, filled a yellow plastic bucket with cold water, and threw it all over the President. After a moment or two to recover from the shock, Kasaboru also sat up; he blinked his eyes rapidly and looked around him.

Nyanga sat down on the table, letting his legs swing free. He seemed to be thoroughly enjoying himself.

'Well, gentlemen,' he said cheerfully, 'I don't intend to waste much time on you. Just called in to see how you were getting on.' He looked directly at Philip. 'Pretty dreadful hash you've made of things, Morgan. Supposed to be in charge of the President's escape, and you pick a route that even a child could have predicted. None of the other tunnels led anywhere useful – you simply had to go the way you did. . . . And then all that pathetic nonsense about the helicopter taking off as a diversion. Ridiculous! And you sacrificed the pilot in the process – that wasn't very ethical, was it? Sending a good man to certain death. Not exactly sporting, what?'

Philip said nothing. He knew very well what Nyanga was up to: he was trying to weaken whatever morale his prisoners might have left. With the rational part of his mind Philip ignored Nyanga's taunts; but try as he might, he found himself wincing as some of the barbs went home.

Nyanga grinned with satisfaction. 'Well, that's all in the past, anyway. . . . I'm going to leave you to Mr Semenov now. He's an expert, is Semenov – an expert in getting people to do whatever he wants them to do. A few days with him and you'll be barking like dogs whenever he rings a little bell. Isn't that the idea, Yuri?'

'Something like that,' said the Russian, his slanted, Eskimo eyes glinting with apparent good humour.

Nyanga slid off the table and stood up. 'Yes, that's the idea – soften you up a bit. Get our soldier friends here to beat your brains out every hour on the hour, and before long you'll be doing exactly what Yuri tells you. In fact you'll be begging him for instructions – positively yearning to know what he wants you to do next.'

Nyanga stepped up closer to the President. His manner suddenly turned vicious. 'It's called brainwashing,' he said. 'You hear that, Kasaboru? Brainwashing.'

Without warning Nyanga drew back his fist and smashed the President straight in the mouth. The President's head went back and struck the wall behind him, hard; blood spurted from a split lip.

'Brainwashing!' roared Nyanga, and again his fist battered into the President's face. 'But at least it's better than death – death – death!'

With every repeated word another blow pounded into the President's face. Kasaboru rolled with the punches as best he could, but already his face was swollen and bloody where Nyanga's ring had cut him.

Abruptly Nyanga tired of his bullying and straightened up. 'Well,' he said, 'we shall see how tough you are. I think you're pretty soft myself – both of you. We won't announce the fact that we've caught you for the moment – some misguided fool might try to rescue you. No, we'll just wait until the President is ready to stand up and resign of his own free will – confess to all his crimes. And then we'll say how clever we've been to poke you out of the corner where you've been skulking.'

Nyanga turned to look at Philip.

'As for you, Morgan, we've got papers to prove that you're a British secret agent, sent to assassinate an innocent Balembian civilian – namely me. . . . Interesting that, isn't it? Facts, names, places – all verifiable, and all on paper, courtesy of our local forgery expert. We'll release the details to the press in due course – when you're ready to testify.' He turned towards the door. 'And you will testify, believe me. Oh yes indeed, testify you surely will.'

After Nyanga had gone, Semenov remained behind with the soldiers. He pottered about the room for some minutes, setting out notebooks and some items of medical equipment; among the latter were a stethoscope and a sphygmomanometer. Then, with a gentle sigh, he nodded at the two soldiers.

Philip knew what to expect next, and he guessed that the President also knew the drill. The two large black men came over and began kicking Kasaboru and Philip with their heavy army boots. They kicked with some precision and care, starting at one end of the body and working their way up to the other, covering both the front and the back – legs, stomach, ribs and head. They kicked the two prisoners from one side of the room to the other and then back again. The two victims rolled and flinched away from the swinging boots as nimbly as they could, but they were manifestly handicapped by their tied hands and feet.

When the two soldiers had kicked themselves into a healthy sweat, they paused and had a can of beer. Then they started the exercise all over again. And after a while everything that was happening to Philip and the President became a numbed yet agonizing blur, as of course it was supposed to.

Some time later, for a little variation, the prisoners were dragged down the corridor to a room with two baths. Their clothes were cut off and one after the other they were plunged head first into a tub of iced water. They were held under until all bubbles had ceased; then they were pulled out and dumped into the other bath, which was full of steaming hot water, so hot that the guards themselves could hardly keep their hands in it.

And so on, and on, and on, until the guards grew weary and Semenov authorized a rest.

Eventually Philip and the President were returned to the original windowless room and were left alone. They were alive, and conscious, but only just.

Philip lay quietly on the floor and groaned every time he breathed. It would be nice to die, he decided. So nice . . . and peaceful . . . just to . . . slip . . . quietly . . . away.

He bit his lip hard, bit it until it hurt – until the pain cut through the overpowering, defeating pain of all his other hurts. He was *not* going to give in. He would fight and fight again.

Philip knew what was happening to him: the army had taught him what to expect, ten years earlier. The prisoners would be deprived of food, sleep and dignity; their sense of time would be shattered by being beaten and woken up at all hours of the night and day. They would be denied all hope of escape and they would be refused any kind of human comfort. Their life would consist of nothing but pain, hunger and fatigue, for however long it took – until the mind gave way under the strain and admitted defeat. Until the soul abandoned its identity and asked only for the privilege of being given a new name and a new number, new beliefs, new morals, new hopes, new fears.

The brainwashing process was very well documented; a lot of very thorough research had been done on it. No-one, even the strongest in mind and body, could ever resist this process; defeat was only a matter of time.

But Philip was determined not to give in just yet; he was determined to struggle for as long as he possibly could.

Out in the suburbs Jane Stuart knew of nothing at all amiss that morning until she came downstairs to breakfast. Then, one look at

110

George Morgan's face told her that something was seriously wrong.

She sat down at the dining-room table. 'What's happened?' she asked, her voice hoarse and anxious.

Her elderly host paused before answering; he turned up the volume of the portable radio beside him and then lowered it again.

'That's what's happening,' he said. 'Martial music on Radio Digara, when there ought to be a lunatic disc-jockey playing people's requests and talking about the traffic jams. And earlier this morning, there was gunfire around the President's palace. Imbasa went out to have a look. Isn't that so, Imbasa?'

'Oh yes, Mr Judge,' said the grey-headed African servant; he nodded emphatically several times. 'Much shooting earlier on. Many soldiers. Much trouble.' He waved his gnarled hands in the air to indicate activity; his eyes were heavy with distress.

Jane twisted her hands together; her face was pale. 'How can we find out what's going on?' she asked.

'We'll know soon enough,' George Morgan said grimly. 'Nyanga is going to make a speech over the radio at nine o'clock this morning.'

Jane tried to eat breakfast and failed. Then, at nine o'clock, she settled down with George Morgan and Imbasa to listen to the radio. After the time signal, Duncan Grey came on the air to announce that Mr Joro Nyanga, the leader of the National party, would address the nation. Jane was totally disgusted when she recognised her uncle's voice. At first she doubted the evidence of her own ears; but then she realised that it must be him. After all, she asked herself, what else could she expect from a man like that?

Nyanga's speech went on for some time. He spoke of the widespread and intense dissatisfaction with Kasaboru's government which had long been experienced by every right-thinking citizen. This dissatisfaction had stemmed from Kasaboru's frequent and blatant abuse of the principles of natural justice: imprisoning his political opponents without trial had been the least of his sins. His worst crimes involved the mass murder of civilian innocents, for no reason at all other than their tribal origin.

The army, said Nyanga, had put up with Kasaboru's tyranny for as long as it could. But now, prompted by the pleas of the persecuted, which could no longer be ignored, the army had acted. Kasaboru had been deposed in the early hours of this morning. Following this blow for freedom, the Military Revolutionary Council, headed by General Juba, had invited the leader of the National party to accept the post of head of state. This, Nyanga felt bound to say, was an honour which he had not sought, and which he would not have accepted but for the overriding need to preserve the stability of the nation. Accordingly, he, Joro Nyanga, etcetera, etcetera. Parliament would be dissolved and elections would be held in due course.

111

It was as much as Jane could do to remain listening to the man until he had finished. His hypocrisy was physically sickening to her; it left her stomach knotted into an aching ball and her hands clenched into tight, sweaty fists. Her voice was shaking when at last she felt able to speak.

'Well,' she said, 'there was no mention of where the President is now, much less of where Philip might be. What do you think's happened to them?'

George Morgan shook his head. He seemed deeply shaken. 'I don't know,' he said. 'But I think the fact that nothing was said about Kasaboru's whereabouts may be a good sign. I think – I hope – it means that he's escaped. And if he has, I expect Philip's with him.'

Jane sighed heavily. 'Well,' she said. 'I was given very clear instructions on what I was supposed to do if something like this ever happened. . . . So I suppose I'd better follow them.'

She wasn't sure what view Philip would have taken of the matter, but she decided to take George Morgan into her confidence. She explained quickly that she had to make her way to the cottage at Lake Kinley with as little delay as possible.

'Fine,' said the old man, rising to his feet. 'I'll help you get there. I won't stay at the cottage – it might draw attention to the place if I'm not here at home – but I'll see you arrive there safely.'

Fifteen minutes later, after Jane had changed and packed up the few essentials that she needed to take with her, the two of them set off. Jane was driving George Morgan's staid little Morris Minor 1000, while George himself rode shotgun: literally, in this case, because he clutched a loaded double-barrelled twelve-bore as they drove cautiously through the suburban streets.

All went well until they were forced to stop at some traffic lights. As the car drew to a halt, Jane saw a black youth on the opposite side of the road. He was struggling with a slightly built middle-aged white woman, trying to wrench away her handbag. The woman was resisting by hanging on to the bag and flailing away at the youth with her free hand; he for his part was cursing the woman loudly and punching her in the face at every opportunity.

If it were not for having to stop at the traffic lights, Jane might never have noticed this incident as she drove past. As it was, she could scarcely avoid seeing it; and there was something about this senseless, mindless piece of violence which made Jane lose all sense of reason and self-control.

She leapt out of the car and sprinted across the road towards the struggling couple. She kicked the black youth full in the testicles as hard as she could, poked her right thumb into his eye with all the force she could muster, and ripped the handbag out of his hand. The youth subsided on to the ground, howling and writhing with pain, one hand in his groin, the other over his eye.

Jane handed the handbag back to its owner. 'Run!' she yelled, and the woman did.

Jane then returned to the car, slammed the door, and drove off. The whole episode was over in about twenty seconds.

As the Morris Minor continued on its way, George Morgan glanced back over his shoulder at the black youth lying on the ground and at the white woman legging it away for all she was worth.

He raised a thoughtful eyebrow. 'Bloody hell,' he muttered.

Eighteen

Philip had either been asleep or unconscious, he didn't know which. All he did know was that he was coming round again – or waking up.

Almost as soon as he became conscious, his body cried out to go back to oblivion; he wanted to drift away into a peaceful, painless state where he could forget the intolerable reality. He ached from head to foot: his bones, his muscles, even his eyelids seemed to ache. Breathing was far more trouble than it was worth: the mere rise and fall of his chest sent nerve-jangling flashes of misery shooting up to his brain.

Once again, a large part of Philip wanted to do nothing more than lie still and capitulate – and once again the rational sector of his mind refused to let him.

Philip began to think. It was easier to think than to move, and in any case it was necessary. He began to think about time. It was important not to lose track of time, and already he had begun to do so.

Let's see now, he thought. We left the palace about ten past five. Gassed in the sewer – let's say quarter past five. Unconscious – well, perhaps an hour. Then Nyanga came in – perhaps six-thirty. After that the two soldiers started kicking us – and how long did that last? God knows . . . too long anyway. Call it half an hour. So where does that take us? Lost consciousness about seven a.m. And how long have I been unconscious? God knows again. Well *guess*. All right, say an hour. So now it might be eight o'clock in the morning.

God Almighty, thought Philip. Still morning, and to feel like this after only one beating. . . . But enough of that. Just think about how to get out of this mess.

Grunting and gasping and wincing, Philip manoeuvred himself into a sitting position and began to review the situation. He was still tied hand and foot and he still had no clothes on. He was alone, the President presumably being locked up somewhere else. This time the room he was in appeared to be a small cellar: Philip had a vague memory of being dumped in here, soaking wet, by the two soldiers. Well, he wasn't wet now, so perhaps more than an hour had gone by. Perhaps it was after eight o'clock.

The cellar was illuminated by a single bulb hanging from the

114

centre of the ceiling. The floor was concrete, and the walls were bare brick. The door was made of metal of some sort: solid, without a grille or a peep-hole. It was studded with the many rounded heads of bolts, and it was painted a dirty green; the paint was flaking off. It was a heavy door, Philip noticed. Strong. No way out of it.

There was something about that door, though. Something worth noticing. But he couldn't . . . quite see . . . what it was. Despite himself Philip drifted off into unconsciousness yet again.

Some time later the two soldiers came in and dragged him out into the larger room once more. They took it in turns to beat him with thick wooden truncheons, concentrating mainly on the arms and the legs. They hit him hard, but not hard enough to break any bones: Semenov had given them strict orders on that point.

The beating went on a long time, and Philip's mind began to wander as a result of the pain. Despite his best intentions he was forced to cry out. He remembered an army lecturer, many years ago, stating that in a situation like this you should pretend to be far more badly hurt than you actually were – in that way you could persuade your torturers to ease up on you. But how, Philip asked himself, could you pretend to be hurt any worse than this? He couldn't imagine anything worse than this – there *wasn't* anything worse. Being dead would be *much* nicer.

Yes, that was the thing. To be dead.

Although Philip didn't know it, the time was one p.m. After beating their prisoners for the second time, the two soldiers dumped Philip and the President back in the improvised cells in the basement of the warehouse building; then they went off for a meal. The soldiers were setting their own schedule now; Semenov had been called away by Nyanga.

The soldiers' meal lasted an hour, and by the end of it they had become aware of the huge sense of euphoria which had spread throughout the victorious units of the army. Some of their comrades came in off the street to the café where they were eating. The other soldiers told stories about white women being tortured and raped; they showed the watches, radios and clothes which they had looted from shops; and they brought bottles of whisky and gin as consolation prizes.

After the meal the two soldiers returned to their duties in the warehouse; but their minds were no longer on their work. They had been chosen to assist Semenov because they were reasonably intelligent, at least by the standards of Balembian soldiers. It had been thought that they could understand simple instructions, and that they were disciplined enough to follow them. But now that Semenov

115

had been called away to assist Nyanga in making other decisions, the soldiers were left alone; and in the event their reliability proved doubtful.

By four o'clock in the afternoon the two soldiers had each consumed the best part of a bottle of gin. They were feeling a little happier now, a bit less disgruntled and surly. They knew, however, that they were missing a great deal of fun out in the streets, and they decided that it was time to work out a few of their frustrations on the prisoners.

The larger of the two soldiers went down the corridor to drag Philip out of his cell for the next round of treatment. He aimed the key at the hole in the door.

He missed.

He aimed again, giggling drunkenly, and eventually managed to push the door halfway open. Then he began to step into the room.

But this time Philip was ready for him. Philip had taken advantage of the rest period granted by the soldiers' boozing, and he had made up his mind what to do. He had wriggled round until he was lying flat on his back behind the door. Then, as the door swung open, he bent his legs until his knees were over his stomach and the soles of his feet were pressed against the metal back of the door.

With every last ounce of his available strength and energy, Philip then straightened his legs as hard and as violently as he could. The outer edge of the door swung back in an arc with considerable force; it caught the drunken soldier sideways on as he was halfway through the opening. His head cracked painfully against the door jamb, making him gasp with shock. Then he fell forward in a daze.

As he fell, the soldier's shoulder pushed the door open again; it swung easily on its newly oiled hinges; and once again Philip slammed it shut with his feet, employing all the frantic power of a truly desperate man. This time the soldier's head was caught between the iron edge of the door and the corner of the brick wall. His skull was fractured instantly; the wound would kill him some hours later. A huge cut opened up in the vulnerable skin of his scalp, and dark red blood spurted wildly in all directions. The soldier slumped flat on the ground without even a groan.

Philip looked up to examine the damage he had caused. Then he listened carefully. But there were no shouts and no alarm bells ringing. Apparently the soldier must have been on his own.

Philip made the most of his opportunity. The success of his attack on the guard had lifted his morale tremendously: he was still a mass of aches and pains, but now he had the incentive to ignore them. And with the door open he could see a way to cut the rope which bound his hands together behind his back.

He stood up and hopped into a position where he could rub the rope binding his wrists against a rough upright edge of the brickwork, just outside the door. He worked frantically, ignoring the lacerations to his hands and lower arms, using the right-angle of bricks as a knife.

The operation took far longer than he would have liked but eventually the rope gave way. He then tried to untie his feet. At first he failed because his fingers were still too numb, but he tried and tried again, cursing obscenely under his breath; finally he succeeded. Next he dragged the clothes off the unconscious soldier and put them on, bloodstains and all; the boots were a little loose but everything else was an adequate fit.

Philip then walked cautiously along the corridor. He winced and limped at every step, but at least he was mobile, with no bones broken. There was another room next to his, with a similar door. Philip unlocked it with the guard's key and found the President lying on the floor within; he was conscious, but bewildered and in great pain.

The circulation in Philip's fingers was better now, and the knots on the ropes binding the President's wrists and ankles proved less of a problem. Before long Kasaboru too was up on his feet. He massaged his joints as the blood painfully returned to veins which had been starved for too long.

'Now what?' the President whispered.

'Wait here,' said Philip.

Moving quietly, he slipped cautiously along the corridor until he came to an open doorway. He looked through it and saw that the second soldier was dozing at a table; a half-empty bottle of gin stood in front of him.

Philip walked boldly into the room and picked up a truncheon from a chair near the door; he walked over towards the soldier. Blearily the soldier registered the uniform. That was all right. But then his eyes opened a little wider as he realised that the face above the uniform was white, not black. He opened his mouth to shout and began to lift his hands. But at that moment Philip hit him hard across the side of the head with the truncheon.

Then he hit him again, just to make sure. The man clattered off the chair and fell on to the floor, totally unconscious.

Philip knew that to cover his escape he really ought to kill the man in cold blood, together with his companion. But somehow he hadn't the necessary ruthlessness to throttle two unconscious men. Instead he contented himself with stripping off a second set of clothes for the President. Then he tied the two soldiers' hands and feet and gagged them while Kasaboru pulled on the uniform.

The soldier's rifles were leaning in a corner by the door. Philip picked up one for himself and tossed the other to the President. 'Remember how to use one of these?' he asked.

'Very well,' said Kasaboru. He rattled the bolt to put a round into the breech.

'How are you feeling?'

'Terrible,' said Kasaboru through swollen lips. 'But improving with every minute.'

Philip nodded. 'Me too. Now let's see if we can get out of this place. . . .'

Philip had noticed that further down the corridor there was a flight of steps, and also the gate of a lift. On the whole he thought it would be safer to use the stairs. He himself went up first, with the President keeping sufficiently far behind to avoid being hit by a burst of fire.

At the top of the stairs there was another corridor, and at the end of that was a door which evidently led to the outside world; beyond it was daylight.

Even the small exertion of climbing the stairs had left Philip feeling dizzy and faint. He leaned against the wall until his vision cleared, and then looked down the corridor again. Yes – it wasn't an illusion: there was a van parked outside. He motioned to the President to join him at the top of the stairs.

'Take a look at that,' he said when the President arrived. 'If the keys are in it we're made.'

'If,' said the President more realistically.

Philip accepted the point. 'All right – we'll have to see. . . . Well now, to state the obvious, you're black and I'm not. Consequently you're more likely to be accepted as a soldier than I am. Would you like to see if you can get that thing started?'

The President stared at the van; he too was wobbly on his feet. 'I'll certainly try,' he said.

Taking his time, the President walked down the corridor; he stepped out into the sunshine and then climbed unhesitatingly into the driving-seat of the van. He gave a thumbs-up sign to Philip to indicate that there was a key in the ignition. Then, belatedly, he realised that there were two other soldiers lolling in the sunshine a few yards away. With another glance at Philip he pointed ahead of him, pulled a face to indicate trouble, and gave a thumbs-down signal as well. Philip nodded in acknowledgement.

The van was parked in the yard of some sort of commercial building. Kasaboru didn't know exactly what it was, and he didn't care. All he was concerned about was that there were two soldiers sitting snoozing in the sun nearby, and a white man on the gate thirty yards away. The exit point to the street beyond was barred by a frontier-style post across the road.

Ah well, thought Kasaboru. It's all or nothing now.

He turned the key in the ignition. The starter motor whirred. And went on whirring. And on. And on. Kasaboru broke out into a sweat.

He tried again. Still nothing. More whirring, but that was all. One of the soldiers woke up and looked across at the van.

Choke, thought Kasaboru. But not too much!

He eased the choke out about half an inch, turned the key again, and this time the engine fired. Kasaboru could have cried with relief.

Without haste, Philip left his position at the top of the stairs; he walked quickly out of the door and got into the passenger-seat of the van. Kasaboru fiddled uncertainly with the unfamiliar gear lever, which was mounted below the steering-wheel. The gears grated noisily once, and then slipped properly into place. The van moved gently forward.

The soldier who had looked up relaxed again; he was too drunk to want to enquire into other men's business.

'What are we going to say to the gate-keeper?' asked the President thoughtfully.

'How about, "Open the gate or we'll blow your bloody head off"?' said Philip, and Kasaboru chuckled hugely.

Perhaps it was the sight of the President's white teeth flashing in a broad grin – or perhaps it was something else – but the gate-keeper didn't wait to be given any reason for the van's departure. He had noticed the vehicle approaching and he now swung the barrier arm up and out of the way without so much as a word. In fact he even waved in salute as they passed.

Nineteen

An hour after Philip and the President had escaped, Yuri Semenov returned to the warehouse. He was not pleased by what he found there.

Nyanga, when he heard the news, became speechless with rage; his face suffused with blood and he slammed the telephone down so hard that the receiver broke in two. Then he drove to the warehouse in his red MG, scattering pedestrians in all directions.

Nyanga took the fearsome Bulu with him. He was determined that someone should pay dearly for this disastrous mistake, and Bulu was an expert at inflicting punishment.

Fortunately for Semenov, it was Nyanga himself who had called him away from the prisoners some hours earlier, to give advice on some other matters; and it was also Nyanga who had approved General Juba's choice of the soldiers for the job. As a result there was no-one available to take the blame for what had happened except the two guards themselves.

One of the guards was still too deeply unconscious to be able to feel anything. Nyanga raged and cursed at his inability to kill the man more than once. The other soldier, however, had now recovered from his blow on the head; he could give no explanation for the prisoners' escape, and he was handed over to Bulu immediately. Later that night the other soldiers in his platoon were made to stand to attention on the parade-ground while Bulu tortured their comrade to death. It was a procedure which was designed to impress on the men the need to do exactly what their new President told them; and as the soldier took two hours to die, it was a lesson which sank in well.

Afterwards Nyanga felt a little more philosophical about the whole mis-handled episode; he even became quite cheerful.

'Well,' he said airily, 'it's not exactly what I planned. But let's face it, Kasaboru can't get very far. The main roads are blocked, he can't use the airport, and all his friends are under arrest. All he can do is run out and hide in the bush – and he can do no harm to us there.'

That diagnosis was not, in fact, one hundred per cent correct; but as Philip and the President soon found out, it contained a large element of truth. Their enormous sense of relief and achievement at escaping from the warehouse evaporated almost at once. The streets of Digara were filled with noisy, drunken soldiers, firing off their weapons at anything that moved, which included any passing vans. Philip's white face also attracted a few bullets, and both he and the President were slightly surprised when they found themselves on the outskirts of Digara and still in one piece.

Even then their troubles were not over. On the main road to Lake Kinley they came across a road block formed by two army lorries. Fortunately the soldiers manning it were sitting by the side of the road, making a meal on an open fire; they took no notice at all as the President guided the van through the chicane formed by the two lorries, and he was able to accelerate away without hindrance.

The rest of the journey proved completely straightforward; and having made one or two halts and detours to check that no-one was on their tail, the two fugitives arrived at George Morgan's lakeside cottage at five o'clock in the afternoon.

After their arrival there was quiet jubilation among the three friends who had been waiting for news of them for many hours. Jane flung herself into Philip's arms and hugged him tightly; at first she tried not to cry, but after a moment the tears and the sobs came anyway, and she just hung on tight until they subsided. Philip hugged her in return; relief that she had made her way here safely flooded through him.

As for the President, he was helped down from the driving-seat by Fuller and Thompson; they shook his hand warmly and patted him on the back as they half-carried him into the cottage. He was obviously extremely weak.

A few minutes later, when everyone had recovered a little, Kasaboru called a brief conference in the living-room. A few moments of relief and self-congratulation had now passed, and a sober awareness of the seriousness of the situation had returned. The President himself longed for sleep and rest, and he did not waste words.

'My friends,' he began. 'I cannot say how very pleased I am to see you all here. Of course, I had hoped against hope that we should never find ourselves in this particular difficulty – but, here we are, and we must make the best of it. . . . Now, as you can see, Philip and I are not in the best of health. We were captured, and badly beaten, but we escaped and no-one followed us. We must consider ourselves lucky to be still alive. I think we can safely stay the night here – in fact, speaking for myself, I shall have to stay here, because I can go no further without rest. . . . But tomorrow we will rise early and decide on a plan of action. All I will say now is that, as in normal times, I will be responsible for decisions on political strategy. Philip, again as in normal times, will be responsible for giving orders on all matters of security and safety.'

The President glanced at Philip, whose face was also grey with fatigue. Philip in turn looked at Bob Fuller and Kelly Thompson.

'Right,' Philip said wearily. 'Bob, and Kelly – tonight you're going to have to stand guard between you. What the President and I need now is medical attention, food, and sleep – in that order. The rest I'm going to have to leave to you, at least for tonight.'

Fuller and Thompson rose to their feet. 'Don't worry about a thing,' said Thompson. 'We're old hands at this game.' They both went outside.

Philip and the President then retired to one of the bedrooms, where Jane examined them carefully. Their bodies were inevitably covered in bruises, and she suspected that the President had cracked a couple of ribs; she bound up his chest accordingly. But, clearly, what the two men needed most of all was a good night's sleep; and after a light meal quickly prepared for them by Jane, they crawled gratefully into bed.

They slept for twelve solid hours.

The following morning Philip was so stiff he could hardly move.

He and the President were roused by Jane at six a.m.; it took both of them several minutes of careful exercise and massage to restore some degree of mobility. But at last they were up, and after the luxury of a warm shower they began to feel vaguely human again.

Philip was enormously thankful now that he had spent so much time and money in the previous week on equipping the cottage for just such an emergency as this. At the time he had felt a little doubtful and perhaps even foolish about laying in such items as stocks of clothing and assorted pairs of boots. But now he realised that his only mistake had been in not doubling up on the stocks of everything. However, as a result of his foresight, he and the President were at least able to put on clean underwear. They emerged from the bedroom wearing green jungle camouflage uniform (army issue), high leather boots, and forage caps. Fuller and Thompson were similarly dressed; Jane wore a khaki drill safari jacket and matching trousers, with a stout pair of walking boots to complete the outfit.

Jane cooked breakfast for the four men; they ate it in shifts to maintain a guard outside, but after the meal everyone assembled in the kitchen to discuss their next move. Jane had been deputed to listen to the early-morning radio bulletin, and she gave a succinct report of what she had heard.

'According to the BBC World Service, which I think we can assume is fairly accurate, the Military Revolutionary Council has appointed Nyanga as President. Apparently there was some resistance to the coup – a number of units in the army fought back, and also some of the police. But the BBC says that they were crushed in a matter of hours. There were a number of summary executions in Digara prison, and after that I suppose leadership was lacking. . . . All leading members of the Council of Ministers are reported to have been arrested, and public meetings have been banned. The BBC said that there was no news at present of President Kasaboru's whereabouts. But one piece of good news – the City Council of Sungbarta held an emergency session last night to consider the news from Digara – and it announced its full and unequivocal support for President Kasaboru.'

Fuller and Thompson cheered and clapped, and the President smiled wanly. He appreciated their good-humoured attempt to lighten his depression, though he had seldom felt less like cheering in his life.

'The Sungbarta Council,' Jane continued, 'totally rejects the appointment of Nyanga as head of state, which it says is illegal, and reaffirms its allegiance to the properly elected government and to the procedures laid down under the constitution.'

The President smiled again, but with a little more heart this time.

'So that's the good news,' he said. 'I always thought Sungbarta would stay loyal. But is there any news from the east?'

Jane pulled a face. 'Well, the bad news is that Nyanga has asked for military help from Gabuti. He says that he needs assistance from their armed forces to maintain peace and good order.'

'Which means,' said the President grimly, 'that he is going to use the Gabuti army and airforce to overcome resistance in Sungbarta. There may be a few loyal units of our own army regrouping there, and the Gabuti forces are undoubtedly much stronger than we are. They have Russian jets for a start.' He sighed and rubbed his eyes wearily. 'Well,' he said after a moment, 'the Gabuti authorities are notoriously inefficient, and it will take them a day or two to get organized. But only a day or two – so we haven't much time. . . .'

The President paused and appeared to gather his strength.

'Let me make my objectives clear to you,' he said, 'so that you are in no doubt about what we are trying to do. First, I must get to Sungbarta as quickly as possible. I did have some lingering hope that there might be pockets of resistance in Digara that we could build on – but what we saw yesterday, and what we have heard about the arrest of my Ministers puts paid to that. So, we must head for Sungbarta as fast as we can. Secondly, once I am in Sungbarta I must quash Nyanga's rebellion by force. That may be possible by using the loyal elements of the army, or it may not. I may have to call for assistance from the United Nations, particularly if Gabuti troops are involved. And thirdly, in nine days' time I must be in a strong enough position to attend the Congress of Independent African States as the acknowledged President of Balembi. Those are the key elements in our struggle.'

Philip felt unutterably weary. He felt sick and ill, and he didn't know where he was going to get the strength to walk out to the Land-Rover, much less travel to Sungbarta. But he forced himself to concentrate on the objectives which Kasaboru had set up.

'As you say,' he said, 'we'll have to take these things one at a time. But let's just look ahead a little bit. As far as the journey to Sungbarta is concerned, I think we're reasonably well equipped. But once we get there, what are your chances of being able to persuade the UN to intervene?'

The President linked his hands together on the table and pondered before answering. 'Quite good, I would say,' he said eventually. 'You see, the Gabuti involvement heightens the Cold War. It identifies Nyanga clearly as a communist, one who is receiving assistance from a communist state, which is in turn receiving assistance from the USSR. And the western powers won't like that. They will start to make aggressive noises, and that in turn will make many other African states feel nervous. They don't want to see the Cold War get any worse – far from it. The very last thing they want is an east-west confrontation on African soil, and consequently they will generate pressure on the UN for a return to the status quo. And if we *can* get the UN to intervene, then the Gabuti forces will have to withdraw – or be beaten.'

'What about the Congress of Independent African States?' asked Philip. 'What bearing does that have on the situation?'

'It has a very important bearing,' said Kasaboru. 'The point is this. If Nyanga can attend that Congress in the role of head of state – if he is secure enough at that time to go there and then come back to Balembi without losing his authority – then clearly he will have to be recognised by the world as the de facto President of this country. That, I suspect, is why he has timed his coup now. But the converse, of course, is also true. If I, in turn, can reach Sungbarta and overcome this armed revolt – and if I can then be strong enough and secure enough to attend the Congress myself – why then clearly I, and not Nyanga, will continue to be recognised as the President of Balembi. At least until I am defeated in a properly conducted election.'

'I see,' said Philip thoughtfully. It all sounded so simple when Kasaboru explained it – so simple and apparently so easy to achieve. And yet he knew from past experience that at every step on the way there would be problems and difficulties and disasters; and at the moment he didn't feel able to cope with any of them. But perhaps it was best not to think too much about the obstacles on the road ahead; perhaps the best plan was to live from minute to minute and to react to events as they occurred.

Philip took a deep breath; then he placed his hands flat on the table and stood up.

'Well,' he said, 'perhaps we'd better get started.'

PART TWO

The Journey

One

Bob Fuller went outside to check over the Land-Rover; his friend Kelly Thompson went up the lane to mount guard again.

There was an extensive waiting-list for new Land-Rovers in Balembi, and Philip had been lucky to find a two-year-old long-wheel-base model in good condition. Fuller was pleased with it: the all-aluminium body seemed completely sound and the 1977 cc petrol engine was well tuned. A bench-seat for three was fitted behind the driver's and the front passenger's seats, and the vehicle would carry five in fair comfort. The main gearbox and the transfer gearbox would between them supply a total of eight forward gears, which Fuller felt would cope with most conditions they were likely to encounter; but he knew better than most that the brutally hard Balembian terrain could pound the life out of anything less than a tank in no time at all. For the most part they would be travelling cross-country, deliberately avoiding roads and often going where there was not even a rudimentary track; Fuller privately felt that they would be fortunate if the Land-Rover lasted the course.

Behind the bench-seat the Land-Rover was packed with every item that Philip had been able to imagine they might need. There was ample petrol and oil, for a start; then there were first-aid and medical supplies, a radio, tinned food, maps, compasses, knives, pangas and cash; also spare boots, rope, explosives, rifles, Sten guns, pistols and ammunition. One item which Fuller particularly looked for, and found, was iodine tablets to purify water. He could think of nothing else which was missing from the collection that Philip had assembled.

While the Land-Rover was being checked, the President tried to use the cottage's telephone: rather to his surprise he found that it was working normally, and he was able to dial straight through to the home of the Mayor of Sungbarta.

Kasaboru kept his call extremely short: there was every possibility that the Mayor's phone was now being tapped, and once the listeners realised who was speaking the call would undoubtedly be traced.

The President made one statement and issued one order: first, he told the Mayor that he was now on his way to Sungbarta; and secondly he asked for a cable to be sent in his name to the Secretary General of the United Nations. The cable was to be signed by the

127

Mayor of Sungbarta, Daniel Levene, and it was to state that President Kasaboru had formally asked him to contact the Secretary General to request that United Nations troops be sent to Balembi to restore peace and political stability.

This order was perhaps the most crucial one that the President had ever given as head of state. He had had to make his decision in a matter of minutes, but the instruction had not been issued without careful thought. He realised that there was a possibility that he was doing something which might make him appear a nervous incompetent in the eyes of more experienced statesmen at the UN; some of them might feel that it was presuming too much to expect other nations to sort out his problems for him. But a number of considerations had helped him to make up his mind. First, if the situation deteriorated as badly over the next few days as he feared it would, then UN intervention was essential if Balembi was to survive as a democratic society. Second, if by any chance the situation did not prove to be as chaotic as he feared, then the UN could always turn down his request; it was better to do something which could be ignored than to leave men of goodwill without the justification for acting. And third, the President was by no means sure when he would next find himself in the fortunate position of being able to speak to an old and loyal friend, other than those with him at present; he was not even sure that a cable could be sent from Sungbarta now.

However, he had done all he could for the moment. The President put down the phone and went out to join the others.

Soon after seven a.m. Bob Fuller guided the Land-Rover down the narrow lane leading away from George Morgan's cottage. Philip sat in the front passenger-seat with a map on his knee; Kelly Thompson, rifle in hand, watched their rear. Behind them Lake Kinley glinted and flashed, bright blue in the morning sun; already the atmosphere was uncomfortably humid and hot.

The first stage of their two-hundred-mile journey west took them along dirt roads running through high-treed evergreen forest. They travelled as fast as the conditions would allow, which was ten or fifteen miles an hour at best. On either side of the narrow rutted track lay impenetrable mazes of knobbly tree roots and black mud; the forest was full of creepers and vines which reached out for the legs and head of anyone foolish enough to venture among them. In different circumstances Philip might have been interested in renewing his childhood acquaintance with some of the trees: the mohoboho, with their largish, spade-like leaves, and the brachystegia, climbing to ninety feet high; but as it was, his mind was on other things.

After three hours of painful lurching and banging from side to side, the Land-Rover had covered twenty-five miles. All five occupants already felt very travel-weary, and yet they knew that they would be incredibly lucky if the rest of the journey proved to be as straightforward as this first section.

A mile or two further on, they began to emerge from the forest. Clearings gradually appeared among the trees; then the trees gave way to scrub undergrowth; and finally they emerged onto bare, flatter land. There was still a track of sorts, twisting and turning its way westward; but if necessary they could now avoid the deeper gullies and the more formidable rock-hard ridges in its surface by driving carefully around them. The Land-Rover ground steadily onwards, its half-elliptic springs and telescopic hydraulic shock-absorbers taking the most appalling punishment without complaint.

They began to come across an occasional village; they drove through fast, the horn blaring to clear the way. Jane caught brief glimpses of houses with walls of mud and no windows, thatch roofs made from papyrus, and filthy wide-eyed children staring fearfully out at the monster roaring past.

After a further hour it was necessary to stop for a break. They pulled up in the badly needed shade of a mopani tree and climbed out to stretch their legs.

Philip felt numb all over: the rocking and the jerking and the pounding which had been transmitted from the corrugated surface of the dirt road had compounded with the bruises and muscle strains of the previous day to make him almost totally immobile. Both he and the President had to be helped out of their seats; then they were walked stiffly up and down until their circulation returned and they were at least able to stand unaided, if not walk very far. Philip gritted his teeth and did what he could to lubricate his seized-up joints: he had the feeling that he would need to be physically supple and responsive before very long.

The Land-Rover's engine was suffering from over-heating, as well it might. The temperature was above ninety degrees Fahrenheit, and the constant dehydration and the thick red dust had given everyone's throat and tongue the texture of ancient cardboard. A drink of water worked a miracle, but unfortunately the effect was purely temporary; in a matter of minutes the saliva had gone again. And if the heat, the humidity and the dust were not tiresome enough, the air was thick with flies.

'Tsetse flies, these, you know,' croaked the President conversationally. 'They sometimes carry sleeping sickness, but they're usually harmless.'

'Charming,' said Jane, spitting and pulling a face as one nearly flew into her mouth.

'They're deadly to cattle, of course,' the President continued. 'And oddly enough some people think it's just as well they are – it means that the cows can't go everywhere. If they could, there'd be no other wildlife left – the cattle would have taken over completely. And then we'd have a flourishing beef business but no tourist trade.'

After the Land-Rover had cooled down a little, together with everyone else, the party moved on. Bob Fuller was a highly skilled driver and no-one could get a better performance out of a Land-Rover, but already he could feel that the journey was taking its toll on the gears and the clutch. The conditions would have turned many other vehicles to scrap by now, and he was torn between the need for speed and the need to preserve the working life of their transport. After a while he stopped worrying and just negotiated each fresh obstacle as best he could.

Another hour went by, and they found themselves on what appeared to be a flat and grassy plain. But the flatness was unfortunately an illusion: lying just under the smooth green surface were innumerable bumps and holes; every few seconds these caused a hideous lurch and a crash as the suspension took yet another battering. The dirt road had now petered out completely.

After a particularly violent descent into the deepest pot-hole yet, Bob Fuller switched off the engine and paused for a moment, utterly weary. He glanced at the President.

'We can't go on like this much longer, sir,' he said. 'Something is bound to give.'

'We've got to go on,' said the President grimly. 'We've got to go on till we drop. Start the engine.'

Two

Joro Nyanga stood on the balcony of the control tower at Digara airport. It was late on Tuesday afternoon, and he was watching a succession of Ilyushin IL-18 Moskva turbo-prop transports coming in to land. Each one carried Gabuti troops and supplies which would enable him to strengthen his grip on Balembi. The last of the planes to land carried General Tchen, the Gabuti military commander. Nyanga went down onto the tarmac to greet him.

At Nyanga's side as he stood waiting for General Tchen to appear stood Eileen Grey. In the afternoon sunshine Eileen was a sensational figure of a woman; she had on a plain white dress under which she was clearly wearing nothing at all. The light breeze pressed the soft material against her body, emphasising her ample breasts with their large nipples, and showing up the roundness of her thighs. Nyanga looked at her and exchanged smiles. They understood each other, for they were two of a kind: totally self-centred, ruthless and strong-willed. And in some mysterious way everyone around them recognised that Eileen – a mature, desirable white woman, and someone else's wife – was a symbol of everything that Nyanga had achieved.

Eileen had known nothing whatever about the revolution before it took place. There was no need for her to know, and neither Nyanga nor her husband Duncan had felt the need to confide in her. Once the critical shooting was over, however, Nyanga had asked her to join him at his headquarters, and she had come at once.

As soon as she arrived Nyanga had stripped her naked, and they had celebrated his victory with the most violent act of sexual intercourse in which either of them had ever participated – which was saying a great deal. The members of Nyanga's immediate entourage had listened outside the door of the room where it was taking place with a mixture of awe, fear and vicarious lust.

During Monday night this victory ceremony had been repeated four more times. Early the next morning Eileen had been rewarded by a visit to one of Digara's leading jewellers. The jeweller later told his wife, with only a small degree of exaggeration, that she had left with half the shop; all of it had been charged to the new President's account, but the jeweller had an uneasy feeling that he would never

131

see a penny for any of it.

General Tchen's plane duly taxied to the control tower. After the official greeting, during which the General could hardly drag his eyes away from Eileen's breasts, Yuri Semenov hastily drove up in an army jeep. As soon as he decently could he pulled Nyanga to one side and explained that he had had a report from a village some forty miles away that Kasaboru and his companions had been sighted.

'He's in a party of about four or five,' said Semenov breathlessly. 'They're in a Land-Rover, travelling cross-country and heading west.'

Nyanga took it all very calmly. He shrugged without any apparent interest and said, 'Well, he won't get very far. He's obviously heading for Sungbarta, but in a few more hours Sungbarta will be surrounded, so he won't be able to get into the city anyway. . . . I don't think he's worth worrying about.'

Semenov was more cautious. 'Nevertheless, Mr President, I think it would be very much to our advantage to capture him if we can. If he is left alive and free there is always the chance that he might be able to rally some support. That could be a nuisance to us.'

Nyanga accepted the point with a sigh. 'Well, that's true,' he said. 'It would be best to have him under our control again. That was our original plan, when all is said and done – to brainwash him, have him acknowledge me publicly as his successor, and confess to various crimes. . . . Yes, you are quite right, Semenov – we should do something about him. What do you suggest?'

'I suggest a pursuit group,' said Semenov promptly. 'It need not be large – one officer and a few troops. Their mission will be to capture Kasaboru alive – and this man Morgan, too. The rest they can kill if they wish. And what is more, Mr President, I have just the right man in mind to lead that pursuit group – a man with some useful military experience, and a man whose absence I think you will not miss.'

'Oh?' said Nyanga. 'And who's that?'

'Major Duncan Grey,' said Semenov.

Nyanga turned sharply to look at him. For a second his expression was fierce, but then his face broke into a wide grin. He slapped his companion on the arm and chuckled.

'Semenov,' he said, 'you're a genius. . . . Set it up for me at once.'

An hour later Yuri Semenov summoned Duncan Grey to the office which he had allocated to himself in the police headquarters building.

Grey was sweating and ill at ease. The staff at the radio station had soon got wind of the part he had played in assisting Nyanga to

132

power, and it had not made him a popular man. And now this later summons worried him more than he would have cared to admit.

'Well now, Major Grey,' Semenov began silkily, 'President Nyanga has asked me to give you a very important job.'

'Oh?' said Grey. His throat had suddenly gone dry.

'Yes. A vital job. One which if completed successfully could bring you great benefits – the President would be very pleased with you. But the opposite, of course, is also true. If you fail to do this job properly you could find yourself in serious trouble – very serious trouble indeed. It would probably cost you your life.'

Duncan Grey said nothing, but his face went white and he suddenly felt an urgent need to use a lavatory. He had always known that co-operating with Nyanga was infinitely more trouble than it was worth. But then, he reminded himself, he had never had any choice, had he? Refusing to do what Nyanga asked would have got him crippled or killed in no time at all. Oh God, he thought, just let me get out of this in one piece and I'll leave this bloody awful country for ever.

He tried to concentrate on what the slant-eyed Semenov was saying to him.

'You're a military man,' Semenov continued. 'I've seen your record. Professional soldier for eight years, service in Korea – I don't hold that against you, by the way – and you might have gone a long way in the army but for that unfortunate misunderstanding over money. . . . Well, now's your opportunity to show what you're made of.'

Semenov spread out a map of Balembi on the desk.

'Now,' he said patiently, as if explaining matters to a small child, 'here's Digara and here's Sungbarta. Two hundred miles apart. The former President Kasaboru has escaped from Digara and is making his way to Sungbarta in a Land-Rover. From here, to here. Your job is to catch him.'

'Catch him?' echoed Grey.

'Yes, that's what I said. You can have two lorries, a sergeant, and fifteen men. Radios to keep in touch, supplies, ammunition, all that sort of thing. It shouldn't be very difficult. You can use the main roads, you see, and Kasaboru can't – he'd get caught if he did. So you can get ahead of him and cut him off long before he gets anywhere near Sungbarta. If you study the map I think you'll find that it's quite easy to predict the route he will take, and in fact he's already been sighted – over here, just a few hours ago.'

Duncan Grey swallowed hard. 'I – er – I'm to take him alive, am I?'

'Yes, that's right. Capture Kasaboru, and this man Morgan, his security adviser. Do you know him?'

'Yes. Yes, I've met him.'

'Good. . . . Any questions?'

Duncan Grey made a determined effort to gather his wits. He knew that this time he must succeed at all costs. Word about his involvement in the coup would soon spread among the European population, and while they might remain outwardly polite they would inwardly despise him totally. His only hope for the future was to prove himself in Nyanga's eyes – that, and a few kind words from his wife now and then, might just enable him to survive.

'Yes,' he said after a moment. 'Yes, I have a great many questions. Let's start at the beginning and go through it all again.'

For the next hour Duncan Grey and Yuri Semenov discussed in detail the mission which Grey had been selected to fulfil. And, as time went by, Grey's confidence increased. He had enjoyed his time in the British army, and in many respects he had been a capable and effective officer; if it had not been for the fact that his talents and strengths as a military man had been outweighed by his failings and weaknesses as a human being, he might have been in the army yet. But there had been nothing wrong with his basic training, and as the discussion with Semenov continued Grey began to feel his grasp of the situation becoming firmer. He was delighted in a way that he was being asked to do something he *could* do – something that was within his range.

At the end of their hour together, Semenov escorted Grey to the Windsor Barracks. Another hour saw Grey and his men fully equipped and ready to go; much to Grey's surprise, Semenov actually offered to shake hands as the lorries revved up their engines.

'Good luck, Major Grey,' he said.

Grey hesitated for a second and then accepted the offered hand. 'Thank you,' he said. Semenov nodded; then he turned and walked away.

The two lorries drove for thirty miles on the main road leading west. Then they turned off into the bush until they came to a small village which Sergeant Yakoma said was suitable for their purpose. It was dusk as they arrived.

The village headman proved almost comically eager to co-operate in every way possible. The reason for this was that he noticed immediately that all the soldiers were wearing heavy black boots, and he had no wish to be kicked by even one pair of such boots, let alone sixteen.

After Sergeant Yakoma had explained what was wanted, the headman personally led the way to the village drum. Like most such instruments, it was given pride of place beneath a neatly thatched roof. The body of the drum was formed from a section of hollow tree trunk, three feet thick with a slit in the top; it was quite possibly hundreds of years old. The drum was beaten with two rubber-ended mallets.

Duncan Grey had always been slightly sceptical about the efficacy of jungle drums, but in the next few minutes he had his mind changed in no uncertain manner. He gave his instructions to Sergeant Yakoma, who passed them on to the village headman in the local dialect. The headman in turn began to beat out the message with his mallets.

Before long there was an answering reverberating beat from the distance, and then another. And after perhaps twenty minutes the headman nodded his head in satisfaction and put down his mallets.

It was done, then. The word was out now and the message was clear. A party of four or five men in a Land-Rover were travelling west, avoiding the main roads. They were to be stopped as soon as possible and held until the authorities arrived. Any villager who failed to co-operate could expect torture and death from the army.

On Sergeant Yakoma's instructions, the village headman had made it very clear in his drum-beats that this was not an idle threat.

Three

The committee-room in which Sungbarta City Council regularly met was on the top floor of a fourteen-storey building which was known as City Hall. The police headquarters and the fire station were at ground level, and other council departments had offices on the floors above.

The Mayor of Sungbarta was a man called Dan Levene. The chief virtue of City Hall, as far as he was concerned, was that it enabled him to look out over the city and to visualise during the course of discussions the developments which he and his colleagues were planning. He stood now at a window in the council chamber and stared down at the busy streets below; beyond the city the surface of Lake Alberton shimmered blindingly in the sun. Levene found himself wondering how long it would be before Sungbarta's peaceful streets became the scene of bitter hand-to-hand fighting and violent death. Not long, he suspected. Much would depend on the decisions which the Council would make this morning; he only hoped that they would be the right ones.

Dan Levene was nearly sixty. He had inherited his name from a Jewish immigrant who had crossed the Channel to political safety in England in the mid-nineteenth century. Grandfather Levene had married an English girl, and their son had in turn married a girl whose mother and father had been Scottish and Irish respectively: the Mayor's family background was therefore cosmopolitan, to say the least. In religious terms he was an agnostic, but the name Levene suited him none the less. Despite being only a quarter Jewish, he looked one hundred per cent Jewish; an archetypal Jew was the way his wife described him. He had a handsome face, despite a prominent nose, and long wavy hair, parted on the left and brushed straight back; his hair had been dark brown originally but was now tinged with grey. Levene also talked a lot, which his wife said was a Jewish characteristic; he himself put it down to the Irish in him.

Dan Levene's parents had come to Balembi as part of the household staff of an early Governor-General; when the Governor retired he had moved to Sungbarta, taking the Levenes with him, and they had lived in the city ever since. By profession Levene was a lecturer at the Sungbarta College of Further Education; his subject was civics and politics. It was in this role that he had acted as mentor to many young Africans on their way to the top in politics, and it was this side of his life that had first earned him the friendship of the President, Paul Kasaboru.

Levene turned away from the window and glanced at the clock on the council-chamber wall: the time was eleven a.m. He crossed to his chair at the head of the table and sat down. Fourteen faces turned in his direction: eight were white, five were black, and one was Asian.

'Well, ladies and gentlemen,' said the Mayor, 'I think we should begin.'

With the Council's approval he signed the minutes of the previous day's meeting, and then turned to matters arising from them.

'I think I ought to report briefly on the action I took following our meeting yesterday,' he said. 'As most of you know, I made a broadcast over Sungbarta radio, reporting that the Council had rejected Nyanga's claim to be the new President, and reaffirming our support for the constitutionally elected government. I'm pleased to be able to tell you that this statement of our position was reported by both the BBC World Service and by the Voice of America in their news broadcasts later on yesterday. Let's just hope that those countries which care about the survival of democracy will take some active steps to support our stand. . . . Now – I have some more encouraging news for you. Early today I had a telephone call from President Kasaboru himself.'

His audience stirred excitedly; one or two of the councillors exchanged a brief word in whispers.

'The President told me that he intends to make his way to Sung-barta as quickly as possible. Now, for obvious reasons I must ask you to keep that information confidential and to yourselves for the time being – though goodness knows it's the only thing the President could do. Our enemies will almost certainly have predicted this move and will be doing everything possible to prevent it – nevertheless, we should not assist them by letting them know officially that he's on his way. When the President spoke to me he was still in the vicinity of Digara, so it won't be an easy journey for him. He'll have to avoid all the obvious routes, and the nature of the country he has to cross will make the journey very hazardous. It would tax even the toughest and best-equipped traveller, and what facilities the President will have been able to put together I don't know. Add to that the fact that he'll have a price on his head, plus part of the Balembian army and the whole of the Gabuti army and air force out looking for him, and – well, you can assess the odds for yourselves. Everything is against him and it'll be a miracle if the President can survive – but, a miracle is what we must pray for. . . .'

Levene paused and consulted the rough notes he had made before the meeting.

'One other thing I must tell you about my conversation with the

137

President is this. He asked me to send a cable in his name to the United Nations in New York, asking the Security Council to authorize the despatch of UN forces to restore the status quo. And that I've already done. Another piece of good news is that only a few minutes ago I had a telephone call from Richard Chokwe, the Foreign Secretary. He has also managed to escape capture, though goodness knows how, and he told me that he has every intention of trying to get out of the capital and fly to New York himself as soon as possible. His aim, of course, is to plead our case to the Security Council in person. Well, again, his chances of being able to leave Digara must be extremely limited. Every other leading Minister seems to have been arrested, and in my view Chokwe will be very lucky indeed if he manages to get away. But he left me in no doubt at all that he's absolutely determined to try.'

Levene glanced from face to face around the table. No councillor showed any sign of wanting to interrupt him, so he continued.

'There is one historical point which gives me some comfort. As many of you will remember, the United Nations response to the request for assistance from the government of the Congo in 1960 was extremely prompt. Once the Security Council had given the go-ahead, Tunisian and Ghanaian troops were on Congo soil within forty-eight hours. Let's just hope that the response will be equally fast in our case.'

'Can we attempt to quantify that, Mr Chairman?' came a voice from down the table. 'It looks as though we shall be attacked by the Gabuti army within the next few days – how long do you think we shall have to hold out before the UN arrives?'

Levene scratched his head. 'Well, I'm not sure I can answer that question. My own private guess is that we'll have to resist attack for about a week. But this raises the whole question of how best to defend the city in military terms, and that's why I've asked Colonel Smith to be with us this morning.'

The Mayor indicated the middle-aged man in army uniform sitting on his immediate right.

'I must apologise for not introducing Colonel Smith to you earlier,' he said, 'but my mind was on other things. As you all know, a large section of the army has thrown itself behind Joro Nyanga. But on the other hand an encouraging number of officers and men have remained loyal to President Kasaboru and to the properly elected government, and quite a number of them have assembled here in Sungbarta. Colonel Smith is the senior of the officers who have so far arrived, and that's why I asked him to come here today. I would like to formally propose to you that Colonel Smith be placed in command of the military aspects of the defence of the city from this moment on.'

The Mayor looked anxiously from face to face, but his suggestion was accepted without opposition and he nodded with satisfaction.

138

'Good. In that case, Colonel, perhaps I could hand over to you. I know you have some ideas on defence – perhaps you'd be kind enough to explain them to us.'

Colonel Smith thanked the Mayor and rose to his feet. The Colonel, an efficient-looking soldier with a typically military moustache, had seen active service in both the Second World War and in Korea, and although he would never have admitted it publicly he was quite looking forward to using his professional skills in earnest once again. At least fighting would enable him to forget, temporarily, his worries about the fate of his wife, who was living in Digara.

In the crisp, clipped manner typical of a British army officer, Colonel Smith gave a brief but admirably lucid account of the military situation as he saw it. The Mayor was delighted to note, after a very short time, that the Colonel was the sort of man who inspired confidence.

There were, said the Colonel, enough officers and men of the Balembian army now in the city of Sungbarta to form the nucleus of a defending force. There were not, of course, as many men as he would like, nor were they at all well equipped. But, thanks to Sungbarta's geographical location, they would be able to put up some sort of a show.

The Colonel turned to a blackboard and sketched a map of the city and its surrounding area. Then, brushing the chalk-dust off his fingers, he explained what he had drawn.

'It's easy for the citizens to forget,' he said, 'but Sungbarta is in fact an island. To the east lies Lake Alberton, and most of the city is built here, in a triangle on the delta of the River Sung. Fortunately for our purposes, the two branches of the river, which lie to the north and south, are both a hundred yards wide, and they form a major obstacle for any attacking force. The two branches meet, of course, up here in the north-west corner. . . .'

The Colonel picked up his chalk again and made three more marks on the board.

'Now – there are three routes into and out of the city. A north road bridge here, a south road bridge here, and a railway bridge to the south-west. My main recommendation for the defence of the city is that explosives should be laid around the foundations of these three bridges. We ought to be ready to destroy them if need be. Clearly we will not wish to blow them up if we can possibly avoid it. But – and we have to face this fact – we may be forced to.'

'What about the airport?' asked one of the councillors. 'That's on the south bank, across the river. And what about the residential districts on the south bank? Can they be defended?'

The Colonel shook his head. 'In my opinion, no – not with the troops at our disposal at the moment. We must block the runways and do our best to make the airfield unusable, and the people living to the south of the river will have to leave their homes and come across the bridge to safety.'

'The airport is already pretty well deserted anyway,' the Mayor commented. 'No planes have flown in for nearly twenty-four hours, and all but one or two small private planes have long since flown out. So the best thing to do is just dig a few holes in the runway and then abandon it.'

'Agreed,' said the Colonel.

An African lady councillor of formidable dimensions raised a hand. 'Will your soldiers need any civilian help?' she asked.

'We certainly will,' said the Colonel. 'Every able-bodied man will have to be prepared to fight, and some women too. That's going to take a bit of organizing. But we can use the radio to keep the people informed of what's happening, and that should reduce the risk of panic. The Mayor is absolutely right – we may have to hold out under severe attack for as long as a week. I'm absolutely confident that we can do it, but don't let anyone have any illusions – it's not going to be at all pleasant.'

The Council continued its discussions for another two hours, and the Mayor spent the rest of the day at his desk, trying to prepare for the worst. There was so much to do and so little time in which to do it; and if he had allowed himself time to think of the appalling possibilities ahead he would have become deeply depressed. But by keeping himself occupied he managed to remain reasonably cheerful.

One of Levene's main problems was getting people to acknowledge the seriousness of the situation. The citizens were all very uneasy, and yet they obviously did not believe that there was any real risk of the city being attacked. They didn't *want* to believe it, that was the trouble, and Dan Levene had the feeling that many of them were going to have to find out the hard way.

Late in the evening the Mayor went home to his wife, Jennifer. She embraced him warmly at the door, saddened by the fatigue and worry on his face; then she led him into the dining-room and sat him down to eat his dinner.

Dan Levene's home was on a small hill, near the shore of Lake Alberton, and as he ate he could see boats from the sailing club skimming along in the evening breeze. He sighed heavily: the message just wasn't getting through at all.

After dinner the Mayor's son, David, came over from his house two blocks away for a chat. At thirty-one, David was the father of two boys aged six and four. He was not by any stretch of imagination an intellectual and his interest in politics was nil – but two years working in South Africa had taught him how to smell trouble better than most, and he was deeply worried about the safety of his family.

He was a tall young man with light-brown hair, comfortably dressed in informal clothes.

David spent an hour with his father, discussing how he could protect his wife and children in the coming battle. But there was not a lot his father could tell him, except that before long he would certainly be called upon to use his target rifle in earnest.

After David had left Dan Levene went back to City Hall once more; he worked on into the night. When he came out again, long after midnight, he found a group of primitive Mibambo villagers wandering dazedly through the brightly lit streets. It was obviously the first time any of them had ever been to the city, and it was not at all easy for him to communicate with them. But he gathered that they had fled to Sungbarta because someone – he could not quite decipher who – had destroyed their village; the headman had been killed and the women and children had been terrorised.

The Mayor did the best he could for this forlorn group, and then went home to bed. But it was a long time before he could get to sleep. He suspected that anarchy and violence would spread rapidly through the surrounding countryside, and that the people he had helped that night would turn out to be the first of a long stream of refugees pouring into Sungbarta from all sides.

The following day proved this prediction to be absolutely correct.

Four

The time was eight p.m.

Conrad Hall was trying hard to persuade Joro Nyanga to see sense. Hall had always found Africans infuriating and Nyanga was no exception. Hall's private opinion was that without the help of the money which he had stolen from World-Wide Mining, Joro Nyanga would never have been anything more than a rather second-rate Member of Parliament; but he was definitely more than that now, so Hall had to be careful what he said. He kept his face a blank and repressed the anger he felt with all the self-control he could muster.

'Mr President,' he said calmly, 'I must repeat what I said to you last night – namely, that the anarchy which exists in the streets of Digara at the moment must be brought to an end. It simply will not do. . . . The coup is over – you are firmly established as the head of state, and there is no need whatever for gangs of thugs to be roaming the streets, frightening the life out of everyone.'

Nyanga looked bored. 'What gangs of thugs?' he asked innocently. 'I went out for a drive last night and I saw nothing unusual. Just a few soldiers out celebrating, that's all.'

Hall could not quite decide whether Nyanga knew very well what was happening outside the President's palace, or whether he was genuinely out of touch. He decided to describe the situation anyway.

'For your information, Mr President, there were dangerous gangs of civilians, as well as soldiers, out in the streets until the early hours of this morning. They were armed with shotguns, pangas, military weapons, car aerials – you name it, they had it. Any European who put his head outside was likely to be lynched on sight, and a good many native Balembians were also killed if their face didn't fit. Exactly the same kind of thing was happening as I drove here tonight. Now – what I am saying is this. . . .'

Hall leaned forward on the table to emphasize his points. Nyanga sat well back in his chair, very relaxed and still. Yuri Semenov and General Tchen, the Gabuti military commander, were also in the room; they listened with apparent respect.

'Before we launched this coup I emphasized very strongly that nothing whatever must be done which would unsettle the European population. Because they, of course, represent the only skilled manpower which this country possesses – and if they leave, then the production of wealth in this country will cease. At once. We shall be back to the Stone Age all over again.'

'Come to the point,' said Nyanga. He was beginning to sound impatient. 'What is it you're asking for?'

Hall moved back a little. He realised that he had almost over-stepped the mark. Nyanga looked somewhat sleepy, but he was not so sleepy that he would let an outright insult go unchallenged.

'I suggest that you issue a warning over Digara radio. Tell your people that they must get off the streets and stop the slaughter, or else. And after midnight, or one a.m., or whatever time you select, send out the troops to make sure that your word is obeyed.'

Nyanga stared into Hall's eyes. 'And the object of this exercise is to reassure the European population that everything is under control – to let them know that we are concerned about their welfare. Is that the idea?'

Hall nodded. 'Exactly.'

Nyanga uncurled himself from the back of his chair and rested his forearms on the table. He spoke with some precision and weight.

'Then let me make one thing clear, Mr Hall. One thing which you ought to understand. This is a black man's country – always has been and always will be. White men have come here from time to time because it suits them – because they think they can steal from us and get away with it. But they're wrong, you see. And if the crowds of Balembians thronging the streets choose to kill a few white people now and then, just to drive the point home, then I for one say good luck to them. In fact I'll give them a helping hand whenever I can. I'll string up a few myself if it makes the point any clearer. Do you know what Stalin said? He said you can't make a revolution with silk gloves – and he was right.'

Nyanga was an extremely powerful personality, and he had been known to reduce many political opponents to trembling incoherence by the sheer menace of his manner. But Hall had not risen to his present position by allowing himself to be intimidated easily. He smiled and spread his hands in a shrug, as if abdicating all responsibility.

'Very well then. If that's your attitude, Mr President, then all I can say is that pretty soon you'll have no country left to govern. Because everyone capable of adding two and two together will have left.'

'And I shall be glad to see the back of them,' said Nyanga sharply. 'We don't need the English and the French and the Dutch, and all the other parasites who have come here over the past eighty years. We don't need them. And why? Because we have been offered all the help we need from the Russians – is that not so, Semenov?'

Semenov nodded, making the light bounce off his silky black hair. Nyanga continued.

'The Russians have offered us technicians, teachers, administrators, engineers – even doctors. As far as I'm concerned, the sooner all the rest of your fellow Europeans depart, the better. Next week, when I go to the Congress of Independent African States, I shall be discussing all this in detail with high-level Russian representatives – possibly even with Gromyko himself – and once we have agreed on what I need, then the necessary personnel will be despatched overnight. I have received personal assurances on these points.'

'It will be as simple as that?' asked Hall with a questioning smile.

'It will be as simple as that,' confirmed Nyanga.

Hall gave a hollow laugh and shook his head. 'Last night, Mr President, to give just one example, I saw two white men being forced to eat their own testicles. Tell me, how do you think your fellow-countrymen will react to that, Semenov? How hard do you think they will work in that state of health?'

'Enough!' roared Nyanga, slamming the flat of his hand down onto the table. He had lost his temper at last. 'The situation will not arise, because the Russians are our friends, do you hear me? Our friends! And we will treat them as our friends. All other white men are our enemies – and all our enemies will die. Do you understand me? Die!'

Drops of white spittle emerged at the corners of Nyanga's mouth, and his eyes bulged in their sockets. For the moment even Hall was reduced to silence.

Conrad Hall appeared to have lost the argument. But as the Germans say: 'Der Klügere gibt nach' – the clever man always gives way. And Hall felt confident in his own mind that one day before long, when sufficient time had elapsed to make it look as though Nyanga was forming his own judgement, the suggested action would be taken: some sort of rudimentary order would return to the streets of Digara. In the meantime, Hall decided, he might as well take advantage of the situation and have a little fun.

He knew of a Jewish widow with two daughters, who lived out in Peachville. He had come across the widow at a cocktail party one day the previous summer, and he had made it his business to find out more about her. He had employed a private detective to look into the woman's affairs, and he now knew her address, her employer, the names and ages of her two daughters, the state of her bank account and her size in shoes.

During the course of the coup in Digara, and during the attacks on Fanda villages beforehand, Hall had become sufficiently well known for the army to accept him as one of their leaders. Consequently he had no difficulty at all in driving to the Windsor Barracks and collecting a section of soldiers to help him in what he was about to do.

He led the soldiers to the Jewish widow's house in Peachville. On arrival the soldiers kicked down the front door and dragged the screaming mother and the elder daughter upstairs into one of the bedrooms. Hall himself took the younger daughter into the living-room.

The younger girl was called Ruth. Hall tied her hands behind her back and settled her down on the settee. Then he sat back and admired her.

Ruth was a beautiful black-haired girl of fourteen, with a blossoming adolescent body. Hall talked to her softly and soothingly, stroking her arm as the girl shivered violently with fear. Her wide eyes were constantly glancing upwards towards the source of the hideous sounds from upstairs, but he kindly tried to distract her. Her breathing was panicky and shallow, her pulse fluttering under his fingers. Hall genuinely did his best to put her at ease.

Eventually, however, Hall became tired of that stage of the game; he rose to his feet and went round behind the settee. He had carefully positioned Ruth so that she was facing the mirror above the mantelpiece. Then he slipped a soft silk scarf around her neck. He tightened it, watching the girl's face in the mirror until she hovered right on the verge of unconsciousness. Her body arched in protest, the whites of the eyes rolling wildly, the feet kicking and jerking. Then he released the pressure until the girl came round again – until she became aware once more of what was happening to her.

Then he did it again. And again. And again.

Until at last Conrad Hall misjudged the moment of release and the girl gave a final violent spasm and died.

Hall unwound the scarf from her neck and sighed heavily. It had all happened much too quickly. But he was, after all, out of practice.

It had been a long time, he reminded himself, since he had refined his technique in Dachau.

After his meeting with Hall and the others had ended, Joro Nyanga had dinner.

Sitting opposite him at the table was Eileen Grey. She wore a glittering diamond necklace and a black cocktail dress with a startling depth of cleavage.

Nyanga ate ravenously: the acquisition of political power seemed to have increased his appetite. He drank the best part of two bottles of wine, and Eileen drank a third bottle; both of them laughed and joked a great deal. The meal was served by newly appointed staff: they were all European and they were all extremely nervous; Nyanga greatly enjoyed shouting at them, the waitresses in particular.

After dinner Nyanga drove to Digara prison in a newly acquired Rolls-Royce; Eileen accompanied him, wearing an equally new white mink stole. Bulu also went to the prison, but he travelled in a separate vehicle; he was incapable of learning to drive, but he was very proud of the fact that the new President had given him his own car, complete with chauffeur.

The prison authorities had been warned in advance of the President's visit, and six category A prisoners had been brought out of their cells and assembled in one room. The prisoners were all politicians, and until very recently they had all been leading members of Kasaboru's Council of Ministers. The six men had been taken to the prison some thirty-six hours earlier: since then they had been beaten up from time to time, and they had also been systematically deprived of food, water and toilet facilities; consequently their physical condition was poor. Their clothes, glasses, watches and all other personal possessions had been removed at an early stage.

In preparation for Nyanga's visit, the six men had been suspended by their wrists from some hastily assembled scaffolding; their feet had been tied to benches brought in from the prison gymnasium. The idea behind stringing them up in this way was to emphasise the hopelessness of their situation, their complete and absolute lack of control over their own fate.

On his arrival Nyanga walked round and round his captured enemies for some time. He regretted very much that Richard Chokwe, the Foreign Secretary, was not among the six, but all the other key figures of the government were present. Nyanga studied their reaction to his presence with interest. One of the men, the oldest and weakest, broke down and began to sob. He was clearly in great pain, and captivity had brought about a rapid deterioration in his health: he was suffering from acute diarrhoea, and his legs were streaked with faeces. His name was William Maiko.

The man next to Maiko spoke encouragingly to his colleague, urging him to try to summon up enough courage to die with dignity. But there was no apparent response.

Bulu and Eileen Grey stood in the background at first, not taking any active part in the proceedings. But when the man next to William Maiko was rash enough to show even this small degree of defiance, Bulu asked his master a question. To Eileen, Bulu's harelip made the question totally indecipherable, but Nyanga understood and he nodded in reply. Bulu then came forward and smashed the Minister who had dared to speak repeatedly in the mouth with his fist, until he almost choked on a mixture of blood and broken teeth. After that there was silence, broken only by Maiko's intermittent moans.

Nyanga continued to pace steadily round and round the six men, as if seeking some point of weakness at which to attack them – as if they were not totally at his mercy already. Eileen Grey's eyes remained fixed on the face of the man Bulu had beaten; she gnawed constantly on the thumb-nail of her left hand, biting it deep down into the quick, her eyes seldom blinking.

Something strange had happened to Eileen Grey during the past day and a half. She had begun to learn a few truths about herself; she had started to become aware of feelings and desires which had previously lain dormant within her, far below the surface. Having been exposed to the exercise of power at close quarters, Eileen had realised that above all else she adored seeing power used – and the more ruthlessly and savagely it was used the better.

The previous evening Nyanga had taken her out on a tour of the city. They had driven through the debris, heavily escorted by soldiers. On that drive Eileen had seen great numbers of dead and mutilated bodies in the streets – and after an initial disgust, she had acknowledged her own wish to see exactly what had been done to those bodies. Later on she had seen a white woman being beaten up and then raped in the gutter. Later still she had seen a man she knew slightly being hanged from a sign outside his shop. And at first she had thought that she was shocked and horrified by these sights. But then, quite quickly, she had accepted the fact that deep down inside herself she enjoyed them; and very soon she had come to terms with the knowledge that the sight of pain being inflicted on others gave her deep satisfaction. Quite why, she didn't know – but in some mysterious way it seemed to reassure her that she was in control of herself and of her destiny.

And now, in Digara prison, Eileen knew in her heart that the sight of the six helpless politicians was one which ought to have filled her with pity. But in reality it did not distress her at all. On the contrary: she liked it. It made her feel warm inside, made her feel happy and contented and secure.

Nyanga began to speak.

'Well, gentlemen,' he said cheerily, 'I thought I'd just call by to explain the situation to you. . . . The facts, you see, are these. Your homes have been taken over by my followers. Your wives, children and any other hangers-on have been kicked out into the street to fend for themselves as best they may. The contents of your bank accounts have been transferred to mine, and any investments you may have had are now held in my name. In short, everything you own has been taken away. . . . As for yourselves – well, very soon, of course, you will all be dead.'

He paused.

'Unless, that is . . . unless you decide to help me. It is just conceivable that if you agree to issue a statement, giving me your full and unequivocal support – well, it's just possible that I might allow you to live. It might do me a little good in the international community, and for help of that kind it might just be worth letting you survive.'

Nyanga ended his promenade by coming to a halt in front of the largest and perhaps the strongest of the six prisoners: Joseph Uvira.

Uvira was fifty-five years old, and weighed about sixteen stone; his huge belly and bald black head made him look slightly ridiculous, but there was nothing at all wrong with the man's spirit. In better times he had been one of the most able administrators in Kasaboru's government; he was a convinced Christian and he had absolute faith in the life eternal.

'Well, Uvira, what do you say?' Nyanga asked. 'Are you prepared publicly to give me your support?'

Uvira licked his badly swollen lips. 'No,' he said distinctly, and with surprising force. 'I say no. . . . Because everything you stand for is worthless and totally evil. You are no good, Nyanga, and none of us could ever say that you were. Just a typical Fanda thug.'

Nyanga nodded placidly and went down the line to William Maiko, the man at the end who was sobbing and moaning quietly.

'And what about you, my friend?' said Nyanga. 'What do you say?'

After a moment William Maiko opened his eyes, as if surprised to find that he was being addressed. Then, almost thoughtfully, he seemed to gather his strength. And he spat, suddenly and violently, straight into Nyanga's face.

The new President of Balembi stepped back sharply, reacting almost as if someone had shot at him. Then he wiped the spittle from his face with his fingers and examined it, as if he could scarcely believe what had happened.

There was a pause for perhaps two seconds, during which Nyanga remained immobile.

But after that his face creased into an animal snarl of rage. With a roar which was half a scream of fury and half a shouted curse, Nyanga began to pound his fist repeatedly into William Maiko's groin, punching the prisoner's genitals time and time again with all the strength he could muster.

Needless to say, after the first few blows, Maiko became deeply and permanently unconscious. But Nyanga wasn't satisfied. He paused for breath, his face grossly contorted, and turned about until his eye fell on a warder's truncheon. He seized it with a cry of triumph, gripped it with both hands, and approached the prisoner with murder glaring from his eyes.

Judging his distance carefully, Nyanga began to rain down blows from all angles onto the Minister's head and chest. Nyanga was a man of enormous strength and force, and the truncheon was heavy and stout; in a matter of moments the prisoner's face became totally unrecognisable. And long, long before Joro Nyanga became weary of taking revenge for the insult he felt he had suffered, William Maiko was dead.

Five

It was dark, and surprisingly cold.

Kelly Thompson put down his Sten gun for a second and rubbed his hands briskly together to restore some circulation. It was his turn to stand guard over his four companions, and for the moment, at least, they all appeared to be asleep. At first, the mosquitoes, the ants, the flies, and the hard ground had all combined to keep the President and his supporters awake; but eventually exhaustion had overtaken all of them. Philip and Jane lay with their sleeping-bags close together; the others had spread out for greater safety, and Thompson could barely see them in the surrounding gloom.

The previous day had not gone particularly well. For hour after endless hour they had driven painfully slowly across the grassy plain. Their progress had been hampered by the fact that the grass hid a number of treacherous obstacles. Every few minutes one of the Land-Rover's front wheels had dropped sickeningly into some unsuspected hole or gully, throwing the occupants heavily forward. Time after time they had to get out and dig the front wheel free; and after that it had been a matter of pushing and shoving and sweating and straining, until at last they were able to continue. In places the plain was totally impassable to wheeled transport, and they had had to make several long detours; and for the most part they had been reduced to walking pace, with the Land-Rover's suspension groaning and complaining bitterly about the battering it had received.

At dusk, when they pitched camp, they estimated that they had covered fifty miles at most; it was heartbreakingly slow progress. Even the President, who was privately the least optimistic of them, had hoped to complete the journey to Sungbarta in two days at the most, but it was now obvious that it would take a great deal longer. The map showed a main road some ten miles to the south, and it was galling to think how much easier and quicker the journey would be on a properly metalled surface; but using a major route was a risk they simply dare not take.

Their evening meal had been accompanied by the sound of drums in the distance. The President had no idea precisely what message the drums were carrying, but he had known well enough what they were talking about in general terms: they were talking about him;

the villagers were being asked to keep their eyes and ears open. The President had agreed with Philip that a guard would be needed during the night in case of attack, and that an early start would have to be made the next morning.

It was almost dawn now, and the level of light was beginning to creep up to the point where Kelly Thompson could discern objects perhaps twenty yards away: there were patches of mist here and there.

Thompson yawned. Bob Fuller had taken the first watch, so Kelly had had a few hours' sleep, and it was a yawn of boredom rather than of fatigue. But his boredom didn't last very long.

An arrow hissed out of the darkness and thwacked into the tree beside him. Then, before he could react, another arrow flashed over his head, passing so close that the flighting feathers brushed his cap.

Kelly Thompson let out a huge roar of a shout. It was a shout of alarm, outrage and surprise, and it was intended both to awaken his friends and to worry the enemy. He fired a quick burst of his Sten gun into the air to achieve the same ends. Then he turned to look all around him to see where the danger was coming from.

As he turned on his feet a third arrow winged out of the darkness and plunged into the fleshy part of his upper left arm. He gasped with pain, and clutched at the shaft with his free hand. fortunately there were no barbs on the arrow, and he wrenched it out just in time to fire two shots into a black and menacing figure hurtling through the mist towards him.

Suddenly the semi-darkness was filled with moving bodies: bodies running into Thompson's field of vision from the surrounding cloak of night, bodies leaping up from the ground to defend themselves, bodies colliding, falling, struggling, bodies desperate and dangerous, and bodies still half asleep. There were sounds too – the crunch and smack of fist on flesh, the crack of head meeting head, a cacophony of shouts and screams, warnings and curses.

Philip Morgan's sleep had been shallow and fitful, and several times he had been woken by minimal movements or by noises in the night. Now, in the presence of a full-scale emergency, he was instantly awake and on his feet, moving by sheer reflex rather than as the result of any rational thought.

A bare-chested, bare-legged tribesman swung at him with a spear, and Philip ducked under the blow and brought his jungle knife hard up into his assailant's ribs; he had slept with the sheathed knife looped to his wrist by a thong. The tribesman gave a violent, bubbling scream, jerked himself frenziedly off the end of a knife like a trout leaping free off the hook, and departed into the darkness.

Another tribesman took his place. Philip side-stepped away from the lunge of a spear and slashed hard at the man's face as he charged past. He felt the knife connect and slice its way down to the bone. The tribesman didn't come back.

150

Jane sat up, only half awake, and screamed in terror as the fighting swirled around her. She could see nothing but dark shapes running, figures wrestling, knives flashing, arms swinging, and all in total confusion.

In the end it was Kelly Thompson who saved them. Despite the arrow wound in his arm, he remained in firm control of himself. He was the only man present, apart from the attackers, who was fully awake and aware of what was going on, and he took his time about picking the right targets; then he put a single round into each of them, one by one.

The shots came regularly, loud and definitive, every one followed by a scream or a cry of pain and panic as the wounded tribesman was knocked over sideways, kicking and quivering in shock.

Thompson turned and fired, turned and fired, constantly protecting his rear. A gigantic, gangling Fanda tribesman six and a half feet tall towered above him, bringing down his panga in an enormous arc which would have chopped Thompson in two right down to his boots. But the ex-soldier swayed calmly to one side, fired a round up through the attacker's chin and out through the top of his head, and then bent his knees and turned his shoulder inwards to bounce the toppling corpse away from him and onto the ground.

After five of Thompson's shots had rung out, the message finally got home: the tribesmen realised that the men they were attacking were not going to be captured without numerous losses. And all at once the attackers melted away.

Two of them, more seriously wounded than the rest, limped slowly and painfully out of Thompson's view, presenting an easy target. He could have killed them both without difficulty – but like Philip two days before, he had no wish to end life unless it was absolutely unavoidable. He lowered his gun and allowed the men to stagger away.

In the next few minutes the five travellers regrouped and took stock of their position.

Everyone was very much on edge. Jane in particular was trembling violently; she was trying hard to put a stop to the humiliating sobs which welled out of her, but every time she tried to speak the words became choked and distorted by emotion.

Kelly Thompson, however, was more seriously hurt. At first he made light of the wound in his arm, saying it was only a pin-prick. But the President recognised the danger at once and forced Thompson to lie down. Then he sucked hard on the wound several times, hawking and spitting violently, and washing his mouth out with a mixture of TCP and water each time.

It took only a minute of two of witnessing this primitive medical treatment to calm Jane down to the point where she pushed the

President aside and took control. The previous day Kasaboru had given them all a stern lecture on the danger of poisoned arrows; at the time, Philip and Jane in particular had not taken the warning very seriously, and it was only now, when they saw the effect on Kelly Thompson, that they realised that the risk of paralysis or death was a very real one.

Thompson rapidly began to feel faint and ill. He had been very reluctant to lie down, but after a few minutes he would have found it hard to get up again. Jane hunted through the medical supplies in the Land-Rover and to her relief found some Coramine, a heart stimulant. She gave Thompson an injection of five millilitres, and after a while he began to feel a little stronger. He sat up and declared firmly that he was perfectly all right; but he had to be helped into the Land-Rover, none the less.

As soon as Thompson was safely installed in his seat, Jane took the President on to one side and questioned him closely about the types of poisons they were likely to encounter.

'If we're going to run the risk of being attacked again,' she commented, 'it looks as if I ought to get to know as much about these poisons as I can.'

The President scratched his head. 'Well,' he said, 'my father's the great expert on this kind of thing – he could tell you all the details, but I wouldn't claim to know very much. All I do remember is that the most common poison is made from the akokanthera tree. The bark and leaves are boiled up into a black gummy paste and then sometimes snake venom is added to give it a bit of punch. It's said to be pretty deadly, so much so that it's not usually put on the arrow points in case the owner of the arrows pricks himself accidentally – it's usually put on the shaft. The only good thing about it is that it soon dries, and the dryer it is, the less effective it is.'

'How does it act on the body?' asked Jane. 'Any idea?'

'Well,' said Kasaboru doubtfully, 'I believe it paralyses the heart, but I wouldn't know for sure. Strong men tend to recover, though it can weaken them pretty severely. Everything depends, as I say, on how old the mixture is. If it's brand new, then the heart damage is usually fatal. Of course there are lots of other poisons, and I believe they work in different ways – they cause blood cells to dissolve or coagulate, that kind of thing.'

Jane pulled a face. 'Charming,' she said disgustedly. 'And what are these other poisons made from?'

'Oh, putrefied crocodile livers and fish gonads, that sort of thing. And, of course, with any wound in this climate, even a scratch, you run the risk of gangrene and tetanus. I've seen the results of both on many occasions.'

'Do you know of any remedies for the poisons?' asked Jane. 'Any herbal antidotes, that kind of thing?'

Kasaboru sighed. 'No, not really,' he said. 'It's easier to kill than to cure, you know. Any of our attackers who gets wounded will be looked after by his own side, of course, but with pretty primitive treatment. And the enemy would show no mercy to us, I'm afraid. In fact in most African languages, such as Swahili and Lingala, there is no word for chivalry at all. So if we're captured, the best we can expect is ritual torture.'

Jane raised her eyebrows and made no comment out loud; she knew that the President was trying to educate her rather than frighten her. But inwardly she remarked to herself that this was all very different from the quiet medical practice she had been involved with in England. And occasionally – just occasionally – she found herself wishing that she were back in a relatively civilized environment.

Once they had tended to Kelly Thompson's immediate needs, the remaining four travellers ate a quick breakfast and listened to the news bulletins on their radio. The news was mostly about the valuable assistance being given to the nation by the armed forces of Gabuti. There was no encouragement in that, of course, so after breakfast they followed the President's advice and pressed on as fast as they could. Kasaboru knew that the word of their location would spread very quickly now.

Bob Fuller nursed the Land-Rover along at perhaps five miles an hour, doing his best to avoid the hidden pot-holes and projecting rocks, but inevitably not always succeeding. More than once there was a hideous crunch from beneath their feet as some part of the vehicle came into unexpected contact with the ground. On each occasion Fuller got out and peered underneath, but at no point could he see anything obviously amiss, so they just crossed their fingers and continued on their way.

Fuller's chief worry was the Land-Rover's clutch. All the men on board were prepared to get out and push if necessary, and they frequently did so. But the constant need to change gear in order to negotiate all the obstacles, and the repeated slipping of the clutch to keep them moving on inclines and to lift them over ridges and rocks, all these were making enormous claims on the clutch's account at the bank; in fact Fuller's view was that the clutch was already heavily overdrawn. There was, however, absolutely nothing he could do about the situation, except drive as carefully as possible, so he tried to put the problem out of his mind.

Towards mid-morning they saw in the distance a small farm-house; it was the first real building they had seen for many hours. As soon as he spotted it Fuller brought the Land-Rover to a halt and pointed it out to Philip.

'You know,' he said, 'Land-Rovers are legendary for their strength and durability, but even Land-Rovers don't last for ever – and by my estimation this one's life is about ten more miles at most. What do you say we call in at that farm-house and see if he's got a vehicle we can commandeer?'

Philip studied the farm-house through binoculars before answering. 'All right,' he said eventually. 'It looks pretty isolated. Let's go a bit closer before we decide one way or the other.'

They advanced on the farm-house by stages, stopping every few hundred yards to check for signs of movement; but there were none. The weakness of the clutch had suddenly intensified, and it was obvious now in the note of the engine. Philip was by no means sure that it would last as far as the farm-house, but it did.

They came to a halt in the front yard of the farm and looked about them. The house itself was a small two-storey building of wooden construction, with badly peeling paint. To one side was a decrepit barn with some quietly rusting farm machinery in one corner. But there was no sign of a car or lorry.

Philip went up to the front door and knocked. Almost immediately the door opened to reveal a white man who was perhaps sixty-five years old. He was a tough, wiry-looking fellow, badly in need of a shave. His shirt was torn and his ragged trousers were held up by an old tie knotted round his waist; his hair was long and grey. He looked Philip straight in the eye and nodded.

'Morning,' he said amicably, as though he were greeting the postman.

'Good morning,' said Philip.

'Seen you coming,' said the old man before Philip could utter another word. 'Know who you are too, so you don't need to tell no stories.'

Philip didn't quite know what to say to that.

'Still got a radio,' said the old man with a knowing grin, 'and I can still tell you how many beans make five. So I know who you are. . . . That's President Kasaboru over there, poking around the barn and hoping I won't notice him. And you're all on your way to Sungbarta. The name's Wicks, by the way, Ned Wicks.'

Mr Wicks held out his hand and Philip shook it; the old man came out on to the porch and looked around.

'Well,' he said, 'you're welcome to anything you can see that's useful to you. Not that there's much left. My wife died two years ago, and I've sort of lost interest since then – sold most of my cattle and just grow a little fruit now, out the back. And then Monday afternoon, when the boys that work for me heard what was happening over in Digara, they just threw everything on one side and left, and I ain't see one of 'em since. Took a nice little truck with them too, and I'll be surprised if I ever see that again.'

'I don't suppose you've got a spare clutch for a Land-Rover, have you?' asked Philip wearily.

'No,' said Wicks firmly. 'Ain't got no magic wand, neither. . . . Fresh water and a little food, that's the best I can do for you. Plus a little prayer, if that's any help.'

'Yes,' said Philip, 'I think we'd appreciate all of those.'

The travellers took advantage of Ned Wicks's offer and filled up all their water containers; their food supply was adequate for the moment. Then, once again, they moved on.

Just before they lurched out of the farmyard, Wicks suddenly chased after them and waved to them to stop. When he caught up with them he leaned through the Land-Rover's window and shook Kasaboru's hand.

'Good luck,' he said simply. 'That's all I wanted to say. 'And don't worry, I won't betray you. Now that my wife's gone there's no way anyone can hurt me.'

The clutch lasted for another two miles; then, as they were going up a steep incline, the transmission gave out completely. No amount of coaxing or skilled driving was going to squeeze even one more mile out of that particular Land-Rover, until it had been properly repaired in a well-equipped workshop.

For a moment everyone just sat there glumly, too tired to move. The red dust swirled around them, combining with the intense heat to make breathing an intensely uncomfortable experience.

'Well,' said Jane after a moment. 'What do we do now?'

'We walk,' said Philip flatly.

He got out, and with a sense of deep depression, almost despair, he prepared to unload a few essentials that they would be able to carry on their backs. As he did so, he looked back over the plain behind them; he saw a tall plume of smoke rising steeply into the sky.

Philip knew at once what it was, but he looked through the binoculars just to make sure. Yes – it was Ned Wicks's farm-house, and he could see the flames leaping urgently out of the windows, the gold fingers of fire turning to dirty black clouds as they climbed into the blue sky.

Philip could see a few half-naked tribesmen standing watching the fire, quivers of arrows slung round their shoulders; but of Wicks himself there was no sign at all. There was not much chance that he could have escaped, and Philip could only hope that his end had been a quick one.

The others also climbed out of the Land-Rover and stood looking in silence at the cloud of dark smoke below.

'Well,' said the President sadly, 'that's Mr Wicks's funeral pyre.'

His companions remained silent; there didn't seem to be anything to say.

155

'Do you think Wicks knew that that would be the price of helping us?' asked Philip after a moment.

Kasaboru answered immediately. 'Oh yes,' he said. 'I'm quite sure he did. And so, of course, did I.'

Six

Bob Fuller made one final and futile attempt to get the Land-Rover going again. The result was merely some expensive-sounding noises from the transmission, and in the end he simply shook his head sadly and abandoned his efforts. The President and his friends would just have to continue their journey to Sungbarta on foot.

Before they moved on, Philip sorted out the essential supplies which they would have to take with them: some food, water, maps, cash, compasses, Sten guns and ammunition; Bob Fuller insisted on taking some rope and Jane selected vital medical supplies. Then the three men who were still fairly fit split up the heavier items between them, and the party of five began to trudge wearily westward.

At first the going was largely uphill, the ground rocky and littered with loose stones. For the most part they walked in single file; they spread out to avoid presenting an easy target, Bob Fuller in the lead and Philip bringing up the rear.

This was a position from which Philip was well placed to review the physical condition of his companions. Bob Fuller seemed sprightly enough, and at the age of forty-one he would still have plenty of stamina. Kelly Thompson, in the number two position, was about the same age as Fuller, but he had clearly been badly weakened by the poison circulating in his bloodstream from his arrow-wound; he was carrying nothing, but he was staggering worse than anyone, and Philip suspected that he was being sustained mainly by sheer will-power.

Next in line came Jane, who was fully fit but who might not have as much staying-power as a man, and behind her strode the President. Kasaboru had never complained of feeling tired or ill, but Philip knew well enough what a savage beating he had taken two days earlier; Philip's own skin resembled a patchwork quilt of multi-coloured bruises, and his muscles ached fiercely, so he knew exactly how the President was feeling. All in all they were not the fittest group of travellers that had ever set out to walk a hundred and fifty miles, and Philip's main concern was to ensure that they found some wheeled transport as quickly as possible.

They walked for almost an hour, which brought them to the top of a high ridge: from here they were able to look down over the sand dunes which constituted the next major obstacle in their path; in the distance lay the Central Mountains.

'My God!' said Jane, panting heavily. 'That's a desert down there!' She brushed the sweat-soaked hair out of her eyes and slumped to the stony ground, exhausted.

The President sat down beside her. 'Actually,' he said when he had recovered his breath, 'it's not a desert at all. Technically it's known as a severely arid belt. But I agree with you that it would take a clever man to know the difference. It's difficult stuff to walk on, whatever it's called, and it's also very hot down there. Well over a hundred degrees at this time of day.'

Jane rested her head on her knees and groaned. 'Oh, God,' she said, 'don't tell me any more. I really don't want to know.'

Philip briskly set about organizing some food and drink to restore morale, and after they had all eaten and rested he discussed tactics with the President and Bob Fuller.

'From the point of view of time,' he said, 'I think we ought to press on as fast as we can.'

'Agreed,' said the President firmly. 'We must get to Sungbarta quickly – as soon as is humanly possible. I can't emphasize that too strongly.'

Philip nodded. 'Fair enough. Other things being equal, I wouldn't normally try to cross this arid belt, or whatever it's called, in the middle of the afternoon. But, other things aren't equal. Every hour counts. . . . Bob – what do you think?'

Fuller glanced at Jane and Kelly Thompson, who were sitting some distance away. 'It's going to be a hard slog,' he said. 'For those two particularly. But you're right, of course – we can't just sit here and wait for the sun to go down. We must get on.'

'It would be difficult crossing that sort of terrain in the dark, anyway,' said the President. 'The only hopeful factor is that when we get to the foot of the mountains there are a few outposts of civilisation – holiday cottages and the odd hotel, that sort of thing. With any luck at all we should be able to pinch a car or a lorry and ride on in relative comfort.'

Philip glanced at his watch. 'Right, then,' he said. 'Let's get started.'

Major Duncan Grey's pursuit group – consisting of himself, a sergeant, and fifteen soldiers – was having an altogether easier journey than the fugitives they were seeking.

After breakfast in the village where they had spent the night, the drum telegraph brought them news of the tribesmen's unsuccessful dawn attack. Duncan Grey was encouraged. The information confirmed his view that he was trailing the right people, and it didn't really matter that the President's party had survived the attack unscathed. On the contrary – his orders were to capture the President alive, and Philip Morgan with him, if possible; so it was better that the villagers should merely report the President's movements rather than succeed in cutting him into a thousand tiny pieces. Grey gathered his forces together and drove a few miles further west on a relatively smooth-surfaced main road.

Towards noon Grey heard further news. He called in at a small town on the edge of the grassy plain which the President and his friends had crossed with such difficulty. There the police told him that a group of five Europeans in a Land-Rover had called at the farm of a man named Wicks, asking for help. Wicks had given what help he could, and some of the 'local wild men', as the senior police officer called them, had killed Wicks and set fire to his house to make an example of him. Well, Grey was looking for a group which included at least one black Balembian – namely the President – rather than just Europeans, but again he had no doubt that allowing for a little distortion of the facts he was still on the right track.

Grey sat down and studied the map. He found it comparatively easy to decipher the general direction in which the President and his friends would be travelling, though with so many miles of open country it was impossible to predict exactly where they would be at any given time. His own next move was also fairly obvious: he should make his way to the top of the Central Mountains, and look out over the relatively flat desert to the east and see if he could spot anything moving.

This he duly did, and by late afternoon he was comfortably established five thousand feet above sea level; he gazed down on to the gently undulating sand dunes which rippled away into the distance.

Rather to his surprise, Grey saw what he was looking for almost as soon as he put the binoculars to his eyes: five tiny figures, plodding slowly across the sand in the full heat of the afternoon. He was too far away to see that one of the walkers was a woman, but he could see their exhaustion reflected in their movements and in their frequent pauses. He could hardly believe that anyone would be quite so foolish as to cross an area like that on foot, particularly at that time of day; but then, he thought, if the alternative was death, perhaps he could even have been persuaded to undertake such a walk himself.

Duncan Grey sat back and scratched his head and wondered what to do next. The figures were still a long way from the foot-hills, and there was no immediate hurry: there was nowhere for them to run to, even if they had the energy. In the end he decided that there was a danger that if the fugitives reached the foot-hills after dark, they might just get lost in some of the crevices and caves which scarred the sides of the mountains. So the first essential was to make radio contact with Digara and arrange for a helicopter to keep the group under observation. Before setting out he had been told that the Balembian army's one and only helicopter might be put at his disposal if he could produce a sufficiently strong justification; and his argument here was that the helicopter would be able to guide a group of soldiers into the desert to carry out the actual capture.

This was an argument which the authorities in Digara found convincing; they agreed to the use of the helicopter. Having made the necessary arrangements Major Grey sent Sergeant Yakoma and half his men down to the floor of the mountains in one of the lorries; he himself decided to stay where he was for the moment, to keep an eye on the overall picture.

It was Philip Morgan who noticed the helicopter first: everyone else was concentrating solely on putting one foot in front of the other.

The intense heat was totally unbearable, and yet it had to be borne. The sun blazed down mercilessly: its rays were reflected and their temperature magnified by the shifting sand beneath their feet. The air shimmered all around them, drying out their lips, tongues, throats and eyes. It seemed impossible to go on, and yet it would have been far worse to stop.

Kelly Thompson, sustained by a further injection of Coramine, was stumbling along, supported on either side by Philip Morgan and Bob Fuller; and Jane, who had long since ceased to be aware of which way she was going, was being led by the hand by the President.

When he first saw the helicopter Philip said nothing; he hoped it might go away.

But, of course, it didn't.

It hovered like a vulture waiting for them to die, keeping its distance and moving around them in enormous circles; from time to time it almost disappeared, but it never went away entirely.

After a few minutes Philip's mind began to clear, and he realised that he must do something about this threat. He pointed it out to Bob Fuller.

Fuller glanced upwards through eyes that were three-quarters closed and grunted. 'Yes,' he said thickly. 'I see what you mean.'

They trudged on in silence for some moments. Then Fuller spoke again.

'Looks as if they've got us spotted. But if we can just get into the mountains in the dark we should be able to give them the slip. There are lots of narrow passes and footpaths – lots of places we can hide. You'd need a whole army to cover them all.'

Philip thought about the situation for some minutes, panting heavily from the exertion of supporting much of Kelly Thompson's weight.

'All right,' he said eventually. 'Here's what we'll do.'

160

The helicopter pilot, a native Balembian, was a deeply worried man. As a result of the new President's policy of 'Balembianization' he had been allowed – or rather ordered – to fly the helicopter on his own, without the comforting presence of his European instructor beside him. The pilot's view was that Balembianization was all very well, but he was painfully aware that he was not really sufficiently skilled to fly the helicopter on his own; certainly he didn't *feel* very confident, and the observer sitting beside him, also a Balembian, was obviously scared stiff.

The pilot's peace of mind was even further undermined by the knowledge that he was flying the sole remaining helicopter in the possession of the Balembian army (the other one having been destroyed in the attack on the President's palace); it was a precious piece of equipment, not to be damaged or abused. It had also been made clear to him that the group of lunatics walking through the desert below contained no less a person than former President Kasaboru, and that it was the pilot's job to ensure that he was captured alive. The pilot had no doubt what would happen to him if he made a mess of *that* part of the operation. So, one way and another, the pilot was finding it extremely difficult to concentrate.

Suddenly he noticed that one of the figures below was falling further and further behind the others. First fifty yards, then a hundred yards. Finally, after a few minutes, two hundred yards.

Eventually the man below collapsed on to his knees.

Then he fell forward on his face.

Something would have to be done.

After two attempts the pilot managed to get through on his radio to Major Grey, who was sitting comfortably on the mountains some three miles to the west. The pilot explained the position and asked for instructions. Major Grey told him to wait until the remaining walkers were well out of the way, and then land and pick up the dead or dying straggler.

The pilot had absolutely no faith whatever in his ability to land the helicopter on the uncertain surface of the sand and then take off again, but – orders were orders. With a wave of his hand to his observer, to indicate what he was about to do, he began to manoeuvre the Westland helicopter downwards.

Philip Morgan didn't know that the helicopter was actually going to land, of course: he thought it might descend to within easy shooting range and then fire a few bursts to finish him off. What he was quite clear about was that if he and his friends were to escape capture, the helicopter must be immobilized.

Philip could both hear and feel, through the massive down-draught from the helicopter's blades, that it was coming closer and closer to him. He braced himself to receive the torrent of bullets which he feared might come his way once the gunship was close enough; but he dare not lift his head until the very last minute.

Then, when he sensed that the helicopter was perhaps fifty feet off the ground and some fifty yards to his left, he turned over. He had been lying on top of his Sten gun, and he offered up a silent prayer that its mechanism had not been clogged by sand. He pulled the trigger to find out.

A burst of bullets ripped into the body of the helicopter. Philip fired again, and again, watching the paintwork scar and the cockpit cover frost over as the shots went home. But the helicopter remained curiously stable: it neither rose nor fell, but hung there, apparently paralysed.

Philip emptied his magazine, hurled it away and slammed in another one. He fired three more bursts in rapid succession, and suddenly the helicopter heeled over. Fragments whirled off its blades, and the note of its engine changed in a frantic increase of power. Philip half expected to see the helicopter rise desperately into the air to escape from his gun.

But something had gone wrong with the controls: either the pilot could no longer operate them or they would not respond to his commands. Instead of lifting the helicopter free of danger, the increased revs merely carried it rapidly sideways; the machine howled and buzzed like a DDT-stricken fly, fluttering in panic as Philip emptied another magazine into it, firing and firing again and again – until at last, with a tremendous grinding crunch, the helicopter crashed violently into the side of a sand-dune.

The rotor blades struck first; they disintegrated into a melée of flying fragments of death, ripping apart the air all around Philip. Then the body of the machine pounded massively into the ground, smashing and crumpling the main frame and the tail. The engine screamed hideously for a few seconds; but finally, after a sickening staccato coughing and the grinding noise of revolving parts destroying themselves, it lapsed into silence.

A huge cloud of sand, splinters, dust and smoke, rose and spread all around; it was some time before Philip was able to see the helicopter clearly once more. When he did see it, he realised that it was a total wreck.

He pulled himself up to his feet; he clipped a fourth magazine into his gun and approached the helicopter warily from the rear. He listened carefully for any sound of movement or groans of pain, but there were none. And when he glanced quickly into the cockpit he could well understand why: the pilot and the observer had each been hit by several shots, and what the bullets had started the crash had certainly completed: they were both very dead indeed.

All at once Philip became aware of a figure running frantically across the sand towards him. It was Jane, calling his name repeatedly. He turned to meet her, and she flung herself hard into his arms, almost knocking him over.

She sobbed her heart out, clutching him tightly as if she never wanted to let go, and for a while at least Philip did not attempt to disentangle himself. He just leaned against the side of the helicopter and tried to come to terms with the fact that although he felt completely exhausted, they still had a long way to go.

Seven

After working in City Hall until one a.m., Dan Levene allowed himself five hours' sleep. Then he got up, ate his usual light breakfast, and prepared to leave for the office once more.

He kissed his wife Jennifer goodbye, and was just about to go out of the front door when Jennifer caught hold of his arm and restrained him. Her eyes were wide and worried.

'Dan,' she said anxiously, 'tell me the truth. Do you think this is the end?'

For a moment Levene pretended not to understand her. 'The end of what?' he said, his face blank.

'You know,' said Jennifer patiently. 'The end of everything. . . . I don't mind so much for ourselves – we've had a good life up to now, and we are getting on a bit.'

'Getting on?' echoed Levene. 'We're only in our fifties.'

Jennifer refused to argue with him. 'You know what I mean,' she insisted calmly. 'But it's David and Sally and the children that I'm worried about. Now tell me truthfully – how bad is it going to be?'

Levene sighed deeply and put down his briefcase so that he could embrace his wife and kiss her; he held her close until he felt able to speak.

'I'm sorry,' he said eventually. 'You asked me a serious question and I should have given you a proper answer. . . . The truth is, Jennifer, I just don't know how bad things are going to be. There's going to be trouble, and some people are undoubtedly going to be killed. But with a bit of luck I think we can probably survive.'

It wasn't a very reassuring statement, but at least it was frank, and Jennifer accepted it with a grateful nod. She kissed her husband goodbye and he made his way to City Hall, where there was work to do.

Later that morning Colonel Smith, the military commander of Sungbarta, reported to the Mayor in his office.

The Colonel's troops had now wired the three bridges into the city with explosives, so that if necessary they could be destroyed at a moment's notice. No-one was anxious to see the bridges blown – far from it. Massive inconvenience and expense would be incurred by their loss; but if it proved to be essential to turn the city into an island fortress, then at least it could now be done. All three bridges were manned with troops, and barriers had already been erected on the railway bridge; some traffic, carefully controlled, was still moving across the north and south road bridges, but arrangements had been made to ensure that they too could be blocked very quickly.

Other preparations for the defence of the city were also well advanced. The Colonel thought it unlikely that any attempt would be made to attack Sungbarta from the east, across Lake Alberton, but he had organised groups of civilians to keep an appropriate watch, just in case.

At the airport, landings by enemy planes had been discouraged by obstructing the runways with service vehicles, empty oil drums, and any other large and heavy objects which the troops had been able to lay hands on.

The Colonel reported that the city's supplies of water and food were being carefully conserved. But despite numerous appeals on Sungbarta radio, many citizens were still refusing to accept that there really was an emergency; they were complaining bitterly about restrictions on their movements or behaviour. A number of residents from south of the river had abandoned their homes and had moved into the city for safety, but many more were obstinately staying put.

The Mayor's only comment on that situation was that unfortunately it would not be long before the doubters had their noses rubbed in the truth. But on the whole he was pleased with the Colonel's efforts, and said so. He asked for details of any problems which required his immediate attention.

'Well,' said the Colonel. 'We've had reports that several hundred Fanda tribesmen are on their way here – led by a gang of witch-doctors.'

The Mayor laughed out loud with relief – it was the first time he had felt even remotely amused for several days. 'Well, Colonel,' he said with a grin, 'if that's the worst threat we ever have to face I shall be a very happy man. A few natives with bows and arrows are not going to be much of a problem – or are they?'

'Not in a military sense, no,' the Colonel agreed. 'But they're moving up steadily from the south, and there may be as many as a thousand of them by the time they get here. As you say, they haven't got any proper weapons and they're not trained or disciplined in any way. But don't underestimate the amount of havoc that a mob like that can cause. Once they get in among the residential districts south of the river they can do an awful lot of damage.'

'Well, yes, that's true,' the Mayor admitted. His attitude was much more sober now. 'You'd better put out a broadcast to warn those residents that this is their last chance to move into the city. As you say, these tribesmen will be a real menace to civilians. But you don't seriously think this gang are going to try to breach our defences, do you?'

'I don't know,' said the Colonel thoughtfully. 'We shall just have to wait and see.'

In the event, what became known as the witch-doctors' war took place late on that same Wednesday afternoon.

There was a good deal of speculation, both at the time and later, as to why the attack ever took place at all. One theory was that the witch-doctors organised it on their own initiative, misguidedly believing that they could achieve some success against an unprepared European population; certainly a successful looting and killing expedition would have strengthened their popularity and authority. The second theory, which the Mayor supported, was that Joro Nyanga had deliberately paid the witch-doctors to set up the attack on his behalf; Dan Levene was convinced that Nyanga's aim was to spread chaos and confusion while he prepared his orthodox military forces and co-ordinated them with those of the Gabuti commander, General Tchen.

Whatever the true explanation, the fact was that the witch-doctors' war was all over in little more than an hour. What happened was that a marauding crowd of over a thousand Fanda warriors appeared out of the bush at about four p.m. They rampaged through the residential district south of the river Sung, drinking anything that looked remotely alcoholic; they also killed or raped anyone who was stupid enough not to have sought refuge in Sungbarta. Then, towards five o'clock, the witch-doctors led several hundred of the drunker and braver warriors towards the south road bridge.

The tribesmen lined up in solid ranks, chanting and stamping and waving their spears; they made no attempt to seek cover. On the Sungbarta side of the bridge, a hundred yards away, they were faced by fully trained troops armed with modern rifles and machine guns.

To the European eye it looked as though the tribesmen were unshakeably determined to commit suicide. That was not, however, the way the tribesmen saw it. Before advancing on Sungbarta, the warriors had all taken part in a secret ceremony to protect them from harm; most important of all, they had drunk *dawa*, a magic medicine prepared by the witch-doctors. All Fanda tribesmen were utterly convinced that *dawa* made them immune to the white man's bullets. The origins of this belief lay in the fact that in colonial days the troops had often used blanks instead of live ammunition when firing on rioting crowds: the result was that the more intelligent witch-doctors had soon realised that they could claim to be able to make bullets pass clean through anyone who followed their instructions. The fact that every so often a warrior fell down dead with a bullet in him could always be attributed to the fact that he had not

fulfilled to the letter the witch-doctors' complicated and time-con-
suming instructions: and in any case it was believed that those who
had completed the necessary daily ritual were not really dead – they
were simply asleep and would rise again in three days. So strong is
the average African's belief in the power of witchcraft that even
trained black soldiers had often been known to throw down their
modern weapons and flee, if advanced on by tribesmen who were
said to be under the protection of this magic brew.

The witch-doctors themselves were an awe-inspiring sight. There
were a score of them in all, their bodies and faces brightly painted
in many colours. Tied to each witch-doctor's forehead were a pair
of antelope or goat horns, and egret feathers and ostrich plumes
waved in many of their head-dresses; others wore hats of leopard
skin. Some of the men had the mane of a lion strapped to their
chins, hanging down like a straggling beard. Often their only clothing was a strip of giraffe skin or a grass skirt round the middle, and
most legs and trunks were oiled with crocodile fat. Round the neck
of each witch-doctor was the fetish bag which contained the mysterious source of his power. The overall effect was enough to alarm
anyone, and even the watching European officers were impressed.

Eventually, with a sudden roar from every mouth, the first group
of tribesmen charged forward along the bridge. As they advanced
the warriors stretched out their hands and stared wide-eyed at the
enemy; their witch-doctors had convinced them that by doing this
they would render their opponents totally helpless. And had the
warriors been opposed only by black Balembian troops that might
even have been true – because all black Balembians acknowledged
the power of *dawa*, and all of them believed that men who had been
made insensible to pain and injury through *dawa* also had the power
to paralyse with their eyes.

But the defenders of the bridge were not only, or even mostly,
superstitious black Balembians: many of them were white, and they
were not at all impressed by the *dawa* idea, even if they had heard
of it. A few black soldiers actually did abandon their rifles and run
away in terror; but a much larger number, who showed signs of
uneasiness, were given the sharp edge of their white officers' tongues
and were ordered to stay where they were and open fire. After a
few hesitant shots to begin with, the defenders' reply to the attack
soon became a tremendous fusillade of gunfire, ripping huge holes
in the tribesmen's ranks.

The witch-doctors' response was to urge on a second group of
warriors. And almost incredibly their power over the tribesmen was
such that their command was instantly obeyed. The second group
stepped over and around the still-twitching bodies of their prede-
cessors and advanced steadfastly; they screamed death and defiance
and 'threw' their eyes at the enemy as hard as they could.

Again the defenders fired, and again there was massive slaughter

167

on the bridge. And now the rifle fire was augmented by a mortar, which put a dozen bombs high into the air, one after the other. The shells began to burst right in the middle of the witch-doctors and the reserve group of warriors on the far side of the river – and that, at last, was enough to cause total panic and rout.

The tribesmen broke and ran; they surged first into the neighbouring streets, and then headed back to the bush with all the speed they could muster. In a matter of minutes the far side of the bridge was deserted.

All that remained for the defenders to do was to cheer their victory, and to deal with the dead and the wounded. The civilian population proceeded to celebrate what they took to be a great victory.

David Levene, the Mayor's son, had been present among the defending forces. He was very anxious to do everything he could to protect his wife and young children, and he had come along with his target rifle, determined to play his part. Even he, a relatively level-headed young man, fell into the trap of thinking that in beating off the tribesmen, Sungbarta had somehow achieved something significant. But in fact nothing could have been further from the truth. The witch-doctors' war was a total irrelevance – a red herring which merely convinced the citizens that they had nothing at all to fear.

In that they were completely mistaken: the real attack was yet to come.

Eight

Duncan Grey watched the Balembian army helicopter crash into the desert with a feeling of complete incredulity. Surely, he thought, no-one – not even a Balembian pilot – could be incompetent enough to do *that*?

He was at least three miles away from the scene of the crash, and several thousand feet above it – too far away to be able to see or hear that the machine had been shot down by Philip Morgan. But Grey could see through the binoculars that the helicopter was never going to take off again, and there was no reply at all to his frantic radio messages to the pilot.

So in the end he just had to accept it: the helicopter was a write-off.

More to the point, Duncan Grey now had to report that fact to the military authorities in Digara. He was so nervous that he could hardly speak, but he finally managed to pass on the news; the radio operator at the other end curtly told him to wait.

Fifteen minutes passed, during which time the sun rapidly began to sink into the west; mile-long shadows from the Central Mountains started to creep out into the desert. The group of fugitives had now disappeared from sight, possibly behind a sand dune. But at least, Grey thought to himself, at least Sergeant Yakoma and his men were down there in the foot-hills to meet them.

After a quarter of an hour the radio operator in Digara told Grey that Nyanga himself wished to have a word with him. Duncan Grey's clothes were already wet with nervous sweat, and it was all he could do to stop himself whimpering with fear; he could hardly bear to think what Nyanga's reaction would be.

But curiously enough Nyanga seemed completely calm and controlled. He asked a number of straightforward questions and then issued his instructions. There had, he said, apparently been a bit of a balls-up. But never mind, the situation was basically very simple: Kasaboru was clearly heading for Sungbarta, and equally clearly he would not want to cross the mountains on foot: it would take far longer than Kasaboru could afford, and anyway it was far too exhausting and difficult a route. With any luck Sergeant Yakoma and his men would intercept the President's party at the edge of the desert. But if that did not work out, then Grey's next move almost determined itself. Nyanga pointed out that there were only two roads leading west across the mountains: with the aid of his two lorries and his sixteen men Grey would be able to block both of these with no trouble at all.

'Find a bottle-neck, Major Grey,' said Nyanga pleasantly, 'and man it. Do you think you can do that?'

'Oh yes, Sir,' said Duncan Grey earnestly. 'You just leave it to me.'

After a few further words of encouragement Nyanga ended the conversation; Grey sat down, greatly relieved, and began to work out a plan of action.

It was almost sunset now, and the soldiers who had stayed with him were lighting a fire. With a sigh of irritation Grey reminded himself that Africans were never very happy in the dark, and he had a nasty feeling that once the light faded Sergeant Yakoma and his men would not hang about in the foothills. And sure enough, as if to prove his point, Yakoma and the others came grinding back up the hill in their lorry just half an hour later.

No sir, they had not seized Mr President and his followers. No sir, they had not seen any sign of them. The sun had gone down long since – it was dark – how could anyone see anything? But it was not safe to linger on the edge of the desert after dark – there were too many spirits about, Major Grey sir. It was much more sensible to come back here and report and ask for further instructions.

Duncan Grey groaned with misery and swore. He felt ill. He had had a physically exhausting day and he was desperately weary – but above all he despaired of ever getting any sense out of Balembian soldiers. In theory, the capture of the President had been child's play. The man had been walking across the desert, in the full heat of the afternoon sun, for Christ's sake: how on earth could anyone have been more vulnerable? The Balembian army had provided a helicopter to watch the President staggering along, and a section of soldiers had been instructed to stand at the edge of the desert with their arms open to welcome him. Nothing could conceivably have been more straightforward. And yet what had happened in practice? The helicopter had crashed, and the soldiers had come hurrying home because it was getting dark and they were afraid of the ghosties.

Duncan Grey almost wept. His men had cooked a meal, but it was as much as he could do to bring himself to eat anything. However, an hour later, with a meal inside him, he began to feel a little more cheerful. He studied the map and located the two roads that Nyanga had told him about. Then he called Sergeant Yakoma over to him and explained everything in words of one syllable – twice.

He and the Sergeant would take a lorry and half the men each.

170

They would drive west along the two main roads and they would set up road blocks. The following morning they would then make contact by radio and see what had resulted; if radio contact was impossible they would rendezvous at a crossroads on the other side of the mountain range.

Grey asked whether Sergeant Yakoma could read a map.

'Oh yes, sir,' said the Sergeant confidently, looking at it upside down.

'There will be a big reward,' Grey told him, 'if you capture the President. Big reward? Understand?'

Yes sir, the Sergeant understood that. His mouth opened in a lewd grin, showing yellow and uneven teeth. Major Grey thanked the Lord for small mercies – at least the donkey knew what a carrot was.

Well, Grey decided, he had done the best he could with the men at his disposal. He despatched the Sergeant and half the men in one of the lorries and he himself drove off in the other one.

Ten miles further on into the Central Mountains Grey came across a narrow bridge over a stream; he had suspected from the map that this might be a suitable spot for his purposes, and it was. He blocked the road with the lorry and then briefed his men on what they should do. To keep them happy in the darkness he allowed lanterns to be lit, with strict orders that they were to be extinguished at the first sound of any approaching vehicle.

Then he settled down to wait.

And to worry.

He couldn't decide which was worse, to have the President come this way, or to have him travel along Sergeant Yakoma's route. This way almost certainly meant being involved in some shooting; Sergeant Yakoma's way almost certainly meant any and every kind of confusion and disaster.

Duncan Grey groaned yet again. He sat down with his shoulders against the wheel of the lorry; he looked back over his life and wondered where on earth he had gone wrong.

After the helicopter had crashed, the President and his friends had pulled themselves together as quickly as possible, and had then marched on towards the mountains.

They were very apprehensive now, because they knew that the enemy had located them precisely for the first time, and that it was very likely that news of their whereabouts had been passed on by radio before the helicopter was destroyed. However, there was nothing at all they could do about the situation except keep on walking and keep their eyes open.

Mercifully, they found that the shadows of the Central Mountains soon reached out to greet them, and once they were out of the direct sunlight the going seemed very much easier. The temperature dropped rapidly, and even the wounded Kelly Thompson perked up a little; he genuinely felt now as if the poison in his system from the morning's arrow wound was gradually beginning to disperse.

Dusk lasted only a few minutes, and before long visibility was limited to fifty yards or so. And just at that moment they suddenly found that there was no longer shifting sand beneath their feet, but sand sprinkled on rock – and after another hundred yards they were standing on the bare rock itself. At last they had reached the foot-hills.

The President, who was leading at the time, paused until the others caught up with him. He seemed greatly relieved by their successful crossing of the desert, and suggested that they should rest, eat, and consider their next move.

There was no opposition whatever to this proposal, and all five of the travellers sat down with their backs to one of the boulders which now littered the ground. They had carried with them from the Land-Rover only the most essential supplies, but basic army rations and water tasted better in their present state than the most elaborate banquet would have done in a more civilized context.

After eating they were all anxious to be off once more. It was not that they were exactly bursting with energy, but surprisingly enough, in view of the intense heat they had suffered all day, it was now too cold in the mountains for anyone to want to sit around for very long. They were also very conscious of the fact that they had taken many hours to cover a comparatively short distance – there was still a long way to go.

'I reckon we've covered about seventy-five miles all told,' said the President. 'And we've taken two days over it. The Central Mountains are about thirty miles wide, give or take a bit, and with a bit of luck we should be able to travel by boat after that – I wouldn't like to go through the lowlands any other way than by river. But at this rate it's going to take us at least another couple of days to get to Sungbarta.'

'And that's too long,' said Philip, sensing the President's concern.

The President sighed. 'Yes, it is really. If we're not very careful, time will go by and the control of events will escape us. I know we're all feeling very tired, and our chances seem very slim – it would be very tempting to just lie down and forget about everything. But we must never lose sight of our objectives. I must reach Sungbarta quickly – and if necessary I must take some risks to do so.'

'Well, motor transport is going to be a lot quicker than walking,' said Philip. 'Is there anywhere we can beg, borrow or steal something to ride in?'

'Yes,' said the President, 'there is. There's a tourist hotel not far from here – I think I can find it even in the dark. Let's make our way over there and see what turns up.'

172

One hour and forty minutes later the lights of the Mountain View Hotel appeared in the distance. After a further conference it was agreed that Jane, Kelly Thompson and the President would hide beside the long drive leading up to the hotel, while Philip and Bob Fuller reconnoitred to see what they could find. Philip gave Jane a warm hug and a kiss on the cheek and then disappeared into the darkness. He and Bob Fuller took with them an ample supply of cash.

One hour later a vehicle appeared round the side of the hotel. In the darkness the President could not see exactly what make it was, but it appeared to be a pick-up truck with a canvas top over the back. It drew to a halt at the agreed point on the hotel drive and Philip cheerfully helped everyone to climb in; Kelly Thompson rode in the cab beside Bob Fuller while the rest clambered into the back. They drove another half-mile for safety and then pulled off the road.

Philip explained what had happened. The news of events in Digara had turned the once-popular tourist hotel into a deserted shell. The hotelier had taken to drowning his sorrows in drink, but he had still been sober enough to know how to drive a hard bargain. He had obviously not believed the story that Philip and Bob had told him, but equally obviously he had not cared very much who they were or who was after them, provided they could pay for what they wanted. In the end they had handed over £1000 in cash for a truck which the owner would report as 'stolen' in a few days' time. Bob Fuller had carefully checked over the vehicle and had found it in good order: it had originally belonged to the Digara fire department, and had been well maintained. The hotelier had also been persuaded to throw in some hot soup and other fresh food, and after these had been consumed morale was noticeably higher.

After the meal Philip and the President conferred on how to proceed.

'Did you hear any news of the revolution?' asked Kasaboru.

'Yes,' said Philip. 'There are Gabuti troops in the capital, but Sungbarta is still secure. I gather that a handful of tribesmen looted the outskirts today, but so far there's been no serious attack by troops.'

The President nodded in relief. 'Good. . . . Well, I think we must now begin to live dangerously. Up to the present I have insisted that we should travel cross-country and avoid all genuine roads. But no vehicle can possibly go cross-country in the mountains, and we haven't time to do it on foot. I suggest that for tonight at least, under cover of darkness, we drive on as fast as we can. Had the man at the hotel seen any sign of soldiers round here?'

Philip shook his head. 'No. But the helicopter must surely have radioed in our position. There may be road blocks set up.'

'Well,' said the President grimly, 'in that case we shall either have to go round them or through them. I no longer have time to do otherwise.'

This policy was then put to the others, who accepted it immediately without question.

'There's no possibility of driving without lights,' said Bob Fuller. 'Not on these roads. So if there are any road blocks they're bound to see us coming before we see them. Now – this truck we've got is an old fire-department vehicle, and it's still got a siren on it. If we keep the siren going there is just a chance that anyone manning a road block will think we're an emergency vehicle of some kind and clear out of the way. What does anyone think?'

The general view was that this was a sound idea, and a few minutes later Bob Fuller drove off with the siren wailing. Those in the back of the truck made themselves as comfortable as possible on the pile of sacks thrown in by the hotelier, and tried to close their ears to the appalling racket of the siren, the blaring of which echoed back from the hills for miles around.

Sergeant Yakoma had been born in a Fanda village just over twenty-five years earlier. His schooling had been minimal, and he had been promoted more on the strength of his undoubted courage than as a result of any intellectual ability. He had what Balembians call 'the evil eye', that is to say a permanently truculent expression indicating a ready willingness to use violence. This impression was intensified by a jaw which jutted aggressively forward; and he was not a man whom his fellow soldiers would disobey lightly. He possessed great physical toughness and durability, with a streak of viciousness in him, and within strict limits he was a useful non-commissioned officer.

Sergeant Yakoma had travelled fifteen miles along the road Duncan Grey had indicated; once he got the map the right way up he had begun to decipher it quite well. Of course in the dark it was not at all easy to decide where to halt, but in the end he had chosen a satisfactory place for a road block, and had parked his lorry sideways on across the road. Legitimate traffic could bump its way slowly round the lorry to one side, after it had been checked and told to proceed.

Yakoma's men were restless and uneasy, terrified of the spirits which they were convinced were gathering out there in the darkness. As far as they were concerned there were only two safe places to be once the sun had disappeared: one was at home in their village and the other was back in the barracks. Unfortunately they were stuck out here in the middle of nowhere, with nothing between them and all kinds of evil ghosts and unmentionables except the one paraffin lamp which Sergeant Yakoma had grudgingly allowed them.

Time passed.

Then, after the Sergeant and his men had manned the road block for several hours, they suddenly became aware of a mysterious and frightening noise, far away in the distance. Those soldiers who had been dozing woke up rather quickly.

It was the sound of someone wailing and crying.

Someone long dead, obviously. Someone whose spirit could not rest, someone who was wandering for ever through the night, seeking victims on whom it could take some terrible revenge.

The sound grew louder. The spirit was approaching.

The soldiers' eyes widened and they stared at each other in horror. At last, one of them, even weaker-minded than the rest, let out a scream of pure terror and began to run. He ran, of course, straight out into the darkness, which was what he was afraid of most. There was no logic in that, but in some primitive way he felt that in running he was at least doing something, going somewhere rather than standing still and waiting for that dreadful wailing spirit to come and capture him. He ran blindly into the pitch blackness all around, ran screaming and shrieking in horror, haring along at a tremendous pace until after forty yards he ran headlong into the trunk of a tree and knocked himself totally unconscious.

This one man's panic was enough to set off the rest – all except Sergeant Yakoma. Six other men dropped their rifles and ran, yelling and screaming, hurtling into the surrounding gloom without the slightest idea of where they were going or why.

Even Sergeant Yakoma was temporarily paralysed with fear. He stood frozen and immobile, listening with horrified fascination to the ebb and flow of the spirit's misery.

But then, of course, he began to realize that he had heard that sound before. Never heard it coming at him out of darkness in the mountains before, but he had heard it none the less. It was the sound of a Digara police-car – or a fire engine – or an ambulance.

Sergeant Yakoma snarled in the darkness. Snarled at himself for being a weakling, snarled at his men for their unspeakable cowardice, snarled at the siren away in the distance. Well, he would see. He would see who or what it was coming down the road towards him, and if it looked in any way suspicious he would blow it to kingdom come.

The Sergeant ran to his lorry and hauled out the anti-tank weapon which Major Grey had thoughtfully provided for him. He fitted the two halves together, loaded it with a grapefruit-sized warhead, put on the eye-shield and turned out the paraffin lamp. Then he took up a position which would give him a clear field of fire as the approaching vehicle slowed to go round his lorry.

The siren screamed louder now, louder every second. And at last he could see the lights and hear the engine, which confirmed that this was no spirit. The note of the truck's engine altered as the driver saw the obstacle in the road ahead of him and changed down.

The driver turned the wheel to the right, and the truck lurched slowly, at walking-pace, over the rough ground to the right of Yakoma's improvised road block.

The Sergeant did not know who was driving this strange vehicle and he didn't care. All he did know was that this was the only form of transport which had passed along this road since he arrived. It was also a vehicle which had put the fear of death into all his men, and even, for a few seconds, into Sergeant Yakoma himself. And the driver of such a vehicle, whoever he was, deserved to be taught a lesson.

Sergeant Yakoma pressed the trigger. A twenty-foot long flame, yellow and red and gold, belched from the back of the bazooka; the warhead flew forward and struck the offending truck with a tremendous flash of light and a massive explosion. The projectile contained a hollow cone of high explosive with the open end towards the target; it detonated several inches from the rear near-side wheel of the lorry, and a jet of white-hot gas and molten steel totally disintegrated the metal and the rubber, carrying away the back axle as well.

The noise hurt Sergeant Yakoma's ears. He lay stunned and motionless as the lorry pitched over onto its side.

Nine

Dinner at the President's palace on Wednesday night was devoted exclusively to business. Present were Joro Nyanga, Eileen Grey, Conrad Hall, Yuri Semenov, and Generals Juba and Tchen.

The main topic of conversation was how best to overcome the tiresome resistance in Sungbarta, and there was much talk of military strategy and tactics which Eileen Grey found both incomprehensible and boring. In the end the military aspects of the matter were largely delegated to General Tchen, the Gabuti commander: it was agreed that the following day he would begin to move his troops into position to attack the recalcitrant city; he would also use the Gabuti air force to soften up the opposition in advance. No Balembian troops would be used in the attack, to avoid any possible problem over divided loyalties.

After dinner Conrad Hall announced his intention of going back to Tikiro to do some work; Nyanga made no comment, but inwardly he was very pleased. He found Hall's constant nagging on the subject of the welfare of his fellow Europeans distinctly wearying. This was largely because in his heart he knew that Hall was right; it was all very well to talk of obtaining Russian assistance, but if the present exodus of European managers and technicians continued, the country was shortly going to be in serious economic trouble. However, that was a problem which could wait till tomorrow.

With several brandies inside them, the two Generals also departed; they were returning to Windsor Barracks to put the final touches to their plans for the seizure of Sungbarta. The result was that by ten p.m. Nyanga, Semenov, and Eileen Grey were left to their own devices.

For a while Semenov held Eileen's attention with a fascinating and learned discourse on the effects of pain on the human body. But Nyanga had heard it all before, and in any case theory bored him: he was a practical man himself.

He got up and began to walk around the room, his hands in his pockets; from time to time he idly kicked the furniture, much of which was of an ornate design which irritated him greatly.

Nyanga felt restless and strangely disturbed. Here he was, at the height of his success, on top of the political pile at last, and yet somehow he wasn't enjoying it. There was nothing to stop him doing anything he liked: he could get drunk, go to bed with Eileen, drive his new Rolls, steal a few art treasures from the museums – do anything that took his fancy. And yet somehow none of it appealed.

Nyanga was far from being an introvert, and yet he knew enough about himself to recognise that this depression had afflicted him before. He knew from experience that there was only one way to change his mood, and that was to work his way through it. He had often expressed contempt for Conrad Hall's Germanic application to business matters, but he knew well enough why Hall chose to live that way: it was preferable to fill your hours with work than to be afflicted with debilitating ennui. He decided he would take some action; in that way he might lift himself out of his gloom.

'Semenov!' he barked suddenly.

The Russian looked up, startled, from his conversation with Eileen. 'Yes, Mr President?'

'The Ministers in Digara prison – the ones we saw last night. Are any of them still alive?'

'Some,' said Semenov, after a pause for thought.

'Good – in that case we will go and see them.'

Once again Bulu and his chauffeur led the white Rolls-Royce through the darkened streets of Digara. The only people out and about at this hour were black Balembians of Fanda origins, and they knew the President's car by now; they cheered it wildly, running out into the road to touch it and peer into the back as it slowed to turn corners. White eyes in black faces stared lustfully in at Eileen as she was swept almost silently past them. At Nyanga's specific request she was again wearing a dress with a deeply slashed front which exposed large areas of her breasts; she was wearing nothing underneath it, and even at speed she could see the men's expressions begin to change as they caught a glimpse of her figure.

When they arrived at the prison, preparations for their visit were not quite complete. The prison Governor, who had rushed over from his house nearby, was grovellingly apologetic. He was a man who had found himself barred from promotion in the British prison service by his inability to stand up to the tougher jail-birds, and he had emigrated to Balembi three years earlier in order to start afresh. But both the warders and the prisoners at Digara had quickly recognised him for the weakling he was; they had learnt to operate without him rather than under his command, and Nyanga also got the measure of the man very quickly. He sent him away and dealt with the head warder instead. The latter was a dour, hard-drinking Scotsman with an instinct for obeying orders, no matter where they came from; and it had only taken a glimpse of the summary executions in the prison on the day of the revolution to convince him

178

that Nyanga's word was law.

Five minutes after Nyanga arrived at the prison, the three remaining Ministers were ready for his attentions: as before, they were strung up naked by their wrists, suspended from a scaffolding frame; their feet were tied to benches.

Two of the Ministers appeared to be totally disorientated: their eyes were glazed and their expressions vacant. One of the two mumbled incoherently, his mind broken by some sixty hours of relentless physical abuse.

Only Joseph Uvira retained his senses, and even he was in a desperate state. His body was covered in bruises and dried blood from his endless beatings; his face was swollen and almost unrecognisable; many of his teeth were missing; and his scrotum was grotesquely enlarged with fluid as a result of repeated kicks in the groin.

Nyanga saw at a glance that he was wasting his time by talking to these three men, but already he felt a good deal less depressed. He had been right to get out of the palace, right to get out and actually do something instead of sitting at a table talking. He circled his three prisoners thoughtfully, examining their physical condition with a practised eye.

'Well, Joseph,' he said eventually, when he came to a halt in front of Uvira, 'you see what a lot of trouble you could have saved yourself if you'd done what I asked last night.'

Uvira said nothing, but he met Nyanga's gaze with steady eyes.

'Three of your colleagues are dead,' Nyanga continued. 'They didn't last long, did they? Pretty poor show, that. Still, you Mimbambos never did have much stamina or guts. Bunch of nancy boys if you ask me, all piss and wind. . . . However, it's not too late to do yourself a little bit of good, even now. I've got a proposal for you.'

Nyanga began to pace up and down again, his hands behind his back. Semenov and Bulu stood in the background, Semenov with his arms folded across his chest; Eileen Grey sat at ease in a chair which had been provided for her by the head warder. The warder stood behind her, trying hard not to be seen peering down the front of her dress. He was well aware that a lot of uncomplimentary things had been said about Joro Nyanga, but he found himself thinking that whatever else might be said, by God, that black boy could certainly pick women.

'How about a signed statement, Joseph?' Nyanga asked amiably. 'We could hardly parade you in front of the world's press looking like that, now could we? You wouldn't be very convincing when you said what a fine President I was, not with all those teeth missing. People might think you'd been coerced, or something like that. . . . No, that wouldn't do at all. But a signed statement of support for me – coupled with a lengthy dissertation on Kasaboru's sins and omissions – that might be useful. We'd write it for you, of course – you wouldn't have to put pen to paper or do any thinking. Just sign your name at the bottom, and try to make it look legible. What do you say, Joseph? Will you sign your name for me, hm?' He looked up at Uvira with a friendly, helpful expression on his face, his head tilted to one side.

Uvira mumbled something which no-one present understood.

'What's that?' said Nyanga. 'Speak up, old boy – can't hear you.'

Uvira ran his tongue round his cracked and bleeding lips and tried again. 'I said, what's in it for me?'

'Good man,' said Nyanga proudly. 'Good man – there speaks a true politician. A very right and proper question – what's in it for you. Well, I'll tell you. You sign your name on the right piece of paper and I'll let you go to hospital. I'll even let your friends and family come and see you. Bring you fruit and flowers and such. Now – how's that for a bargain? It's the best offer you'll get this year, Joseph. What do you say – will you sign?'

Uvira actually laughed. Not for long, it was true, because the effect of moving any part of his body was far too painful. But his lips curled up in a grin and he emitted a series of coughs which were clearly recognisable by those present as a dying man's version of a short laugh. After a moment he did it again.

Nyanga's own smile faded. 'Well?' he said sharply.

'Go to hell,' said Uvira quietly. 'That's where you belong, Nyanga, and that's where you'll end up.'

Nyanga's eyes narrowed. 'All right, my friend,' he said. 'If that's the way you want it.'

He opened the holster on his belt and took out a Russian Tokarev automatic pistol; it had been a gift from General Tchen. He put the barrel under Uvira's chin and forced his head upwards.

'Say your prayers, Uvira – because in a moment you're going to die.'

Nyanga went round behind the three politicians. He cocked the pistol with a brisk and well-oiled click. Then he reached up and pointed it at the back of the head of the Minister who had never ceased mumbling to himself. The deranged man knew nothing of what was going on and he continued talking right up to the moment when Nyanga pulled the trigger. Then, the front of the minister's forehead seemed to burst open: a fountain of blood, brain tissue and bone fragments spouted into the air and fell to the floor with a splattering noise like the sound of someone vomiting into a lavatory bowl. The man's body jerked convulsively as the bullet passed through him, contorting his features momentarily and making his genitals bounce obscenely. Then he hung limply from the rope which tied his wrists to the scaffolding above; his weight hung heavily, like a side of beef in a slaughter-house.

Nyanga moved calmly round to the front again, to observe the effect which the execution had had on the other two men. Uvira's eyes were closed, and his lips moved silently in prayer. The other man began to scream hopelessly and frantically, his voice hoarse and loud with desperation. The Minister ceased to be human and became a mindless lump of matter, reacting with blind terror to an event which had forced him right over the edge of insanity. He put back his head and howled and yelled with a hideous lack of all civilized control; he shook the ropes that bound him in a frenzied attempt to break free.

Nyanga disliked the noise and shot the man quickly to put an end to it – two shots through the heart in rapid succession. Then he turned to the head warder, whose face was ashen, and told him to find another piece of rope.

In a few moments the warder returned with a length of rope of the right specification.

Uvira continued to pray. He went on praying even while Nyanga was fixing the noose around his neck, and while his feet were being cut free from the gymnasium bench to which they had been bound. Then Nyanga hauled on the rope, making full use of his tremendous strength, until Uvira's toes could no longer touch the ground; he fixed the rope in position by taking a few turns round a horizontal bar on the scaffolding.

The noose had inevitably tightened under Uvira's left ear, and he gradually began to choke; his face went purple and his tongue came out. But it was just possible for Uvira to relieve the pressure on his throat by pulling himself upwards with his arms, because his hands were still tied to the scaffolding above. And the will to survive being what it is, this sixteen-stone man, who had been beaten countless times over the last few days, somehow found the strength to flex his biceps and give himself time to take in some gasping, rasping breaths. Then, as his arms quickly tired, the noose began to tighten once again, and his recently released legs began to twitch and thrash about in agonised reflex.

Nyanga stepped back to admire his handiwork: it was going to take a long time for Joseph Uvira to die. He glanced at Eileen Grey. Her legs were crossed and she was gnawing her lower lip; her face looked ravaged and her half-closed eyes burned with a fiery intensity as she stared fixedly at Uvira's contorted features.

Then Nyanga caught Semenov's eye. 'Out,' he said bluntly and Semenov immediately left, taking the head warder and Bulu with him; he closed the door after them. Only Nyanga, Eileen Grey, and the dying Joseph Uvira remained in the room.

Nyanga went over to Eileen with a smile on his face. As he pulled her to her feet her eyes never left the scene in front of her. He unzipped her dress at the back and she moaned softly; it slid to the floor and she stepped out of it, still in her high-heeled shoes. Nyanga put his hand over her right breast and squeezed it hard, digging his nails into her flesh, till Eileen cried out in pain and twisted under his grip. But still her eyes would not leave Uvira.

Then Nyanga took off his own clothes. He came up behind Eileen and ran his hands all over the front of her body, pressing himself fiercely against her back, clutching her so tightly that she felt her ribs would crack. Their bodies were running with sweat. He bit her neck and forced his fingers violently into her vagina, deliberately making her squirm with pain. Then, after a few moments, he bent her forward at the waist so that she supported herself with her hands on the seat of the chair in front of her; he entered her body hard from behind. His penis was exceptionally long and thick, and he pushed his way savagely into her, making her cry out. Then he seized her by the hips and rocked himself vigorously backwards and forwards, pounding his stomach against the deep, exciting cleft of her buttocks, pressing his legs against hers.

As Joseph Uvira died, Joro Nyanga attacked his mistress like a dog shaking a rag doll. He clawed and punched at her, grunting and panting and sweating and heaving, half throttling her, pinching and pulling at her flesh – until at last, with a series of gigantic thrusts which lifted Eileen clean off her feet, his orgasm pulsated massively within her. And then, suddenly, he slumped, exhausted and panting, resting his weight on her back, still with his flesh inside hers.

Eileen's body trembled violently beneath him and she groaned and sobbed alternately. But the sounds which emerged from deep within her were not, Nyanga knew, the result of pain or distress. On the contrary, the moans and sighs and gasps which shook her whole being were the outward and audible expressions of an overwhelming inner feeling: a feeling of warmth, of pleasure – above all a feeling of intense and lasting satisfaction.

Ten

The explosion caused by the warhead from Sergeant Yakoma's bazooka blew the former fire-department truck over onto its side.

Fortunately it was only moving slowly at the time, so the effect of the sideways blast was not compounded by forward speed: the canvas covering on the back of the truck was blown clean off, but the vehicle merely toppled over on to its side and stayed there, without rolling.

The three travellers who had been sitting in the back of the truck were all thrown out and landed on the hard stony ground with varying degrees of injury. Jane Stuart was thrown well clear, bouncing head over heels several times before she came to rest. She suffered enormous shock. One moment she was enduring a bumpy and noisy ride in the back of a very draughty truck, and the next she was tossed through the air, deafened and stunned and terrified by a totally unexpected and devastating explosion.

Jane picked herself up and ran. She realized dimly that behind her the truck was burning, and she could also hear rifle fire: several bullets ricocheted off the rocks nearby, whining away into the distance, and they were obviously aimed at her. Desperately, Jane scrambled and panicked her way up the steep hillside, completely without direction or purpose, frantically seeking to escape – where to, she had no idea. She was panting and gasping, cursing blindly as her feet skidded on the loose shale, sobbing and shaking with fear and exhaustion.

Eventually, after what seemed a very long time, Jane ran out of breath and stopped running. She slowed to a walk, and then, as some degree of calmness returned, she stopped completely.

All around her there was total darkness. She could see nothing, not even a glow in the sky from the flames over the horizon: perhaps there were trees in the way, she thought. Whatever the reason, she realized that she was now completely lost; she had no means of finding out where she was relative to the truck, to her friends, or anything else. She had no idea how far she had come, and she wasn't even sure that she had run in a straight line.

Jane swore loudly and sat down, utterly dejected. Her heart was not beating quite so fast now, and she was more in control of herself. She hugged her knees to try to keep warm: the night air in the mountains was cold, and she was trembling violently.

She wanted to call out and get someone to come and find her – but the problem was, who would answer her call? Whoever it was that had blown up the truck was clearly no friend, and the enemy were probably all around her – so perhaps it was best to keep quiet.

Jane put her hands over her eyes and had a good solid cry for at least ten minutes. After that she felt a little better. She was still extremely cold and she was still terrified of what might come at her out of the darkness – but at least the blind panic had passed. She was alive and relatively unharmed – and if she kept her head until morning she might just be able to stay alive.

Philip Morgan had also been thrown well clear of the pick-up truck. At first he lay stunned and winded, flat on his back. But he quickly became aware of the fact that he was lying in a patch of ground brightly illuminated by the flames from the burning truck. He also became conscious of someone firing a rifle: he could hear the shots and the sound of the bolt being operated – but fortunately whoever was doing the shooting did not appear to be shooting at him.

Philip pulled himself to his feet. As he did so he saw Bob Fuller assisting Kelly Thompson out of the crumpled cab. He went over to help, and the three of them then staggered and limped into the shadows as fast as they could. In the exposed circle lit up by the burning truck they were easy targets, and it seemed important to get under cover.

The three men put about a hundred and fifty yards and perhaps fifty feet in elevation between themselves and the furiously burning truck; then they paused and examined the extent of their injuries. They were all badly shaken: their ears were still ringing from the blast, and they had numerous cuts, grazes, sprains and bruises; but the injuries were by no means crippling.

'Well,' said Philip thoughtfully, 'the three of us seem to be reasonably O.K. But what's become of the others? Did either of you see Jane or the President?

Fuller and Thompson both shook their heads gloomily; neither of them had.

In fact, President Kasaboru was at that moment lying hidden in a ditch by the side of the road. Together with Philip and Jane he had been riding in the back of the truck, and the blast from the bazooka had tossed him high in the air; he had landed in a clump of bushes and had bounced out into the ditch, which was dry and lined with pebbles: it had not been a comfortable landing. In a dazed and semi-conscious condition he had crawled painfully along the ditch for a hundred yards or more, until at last the effort of going on had seemed far more trouble than it was worth. Now he slumped forward onto his face, his head whirling. He retched painfully for a few minutes; and then, succumbing to total exhaustion, he lapsed into a state which was half-sleep and half-unconsciousness. He remained in that condition for several hours.

The rest of that night proved to be as uncomfortable and miserable a time as any of the five travellers could remember. Jane Stuart dozed and shivered, and then dozed and shivered again, waking each time with a start and a fresh wave of fear.

The President also surfaced to consciousness occasionally – he was disturbed by the bed of sharp stones on which he was lying – but for most of the night he could not find the will-power to do more than shift his position to one which was temporarily at least a little less painful.

Only Philip and the two ex-army men were working to retrieve something from the wreckage of their plans. They had no idea whether their truck had run over a mine or whether they had been the victims of a hand-grenade or what; but while the flames from the pick-up truck lasted they could see that the road they had been travelling on was straddled by a lorry, so obviously they had run into some kind of road-block. And someone, soon after the crash, had been firing a rifle at them, all three were convinced of that; yet at the moment no-one was moving and no attempt had been made to follow them when they staggered away from the truck. It was all extremely puzzling.

After an hour and a half, when the flames died out, Philip crawled down to the remains of the pick-up truck and came back with a Sten gun, a Lee Enfield rifle, and some of their precious stock of ammunition; all these items had been thrown clear of the fire. He saw no signs of any kind of life down on the road, but the trip to the truck was not an easy one: it took him forty-five minutes to complete, most of the journey being made flat on his stomach. But at least they now had guns.

After that expedition, all the three men could do was lie still and wait for first light. They spoke little, but all of them shared the same concerns: what had happened to Jane, and where in the world was the President?

Sergeant Yakoma was also waiting – and strangely enough he too was a frightened and worried man. He had bazooka'd the truck with the siren, yes – fired at it in a moment of anger and successfully blown it apart. But what if it turned out to be a perfectly legitimate vehicle after all? What if it contained some important white man? Or even, God forbid, an army general or an influential politician?

The very thought of all these possibilities brought Yakoma out into a sweat, despite the cold night air. But after a while he decided that if the worst came to the worst he could always kill one of the men under his command, and blame the luckless private for the rash and hasty shot with the bazooka.

Another possibility, of course, was that the truck actually had contained the fleeing President Kasaboru – and that presented a whole new set of problems. Major Grey had told him to capture the President *alive*, not blown into numerous pieces. The Major had also said that there were four other men with the President – and at present there was only one of Sergeant Yakoma; he couldn't see any dead bodies lying about, so if the men from the truck came looking for him he was almost certainly heavily outnumbered.

Sergeant Yakoma was also frightened of the dark: but his was not an irrational fear of spirits, of the kind which had caused his men to run away. His fear was generated by a vivid awareness of the risks which were run by anyone sleeping out in the wilds without suitable protection. The best defence against the animals of the night was a fence of thorn bushes, five feet high at least; without such a barrier, sleeping men had been known to lose a hand or a foot to bold and savage packs of hungry hyenas. The Sergeant didn't know whether there actually were any hyenas up here in the mountains, but he was damn sure he didn't want to find out the hard way.

Once the flames from the pick-up truck had died down Sergeant Yakoma also, like Philip Morgan, performed an act of considerable courage and initiative. He had seen one person running away from the scene of the crash, an outline illuminated by the flames – and he had known instinctively that the figure was that of a white woman. He had fired at her several times and missed. Well, either she was a companion of the President, or else she was an innocent civilian. In either case she ought to be accounted for and, if necessary, silenced.

Sergeant Yakoma made a careful mental note of the direction in which the woman had been running when he last saw her. Then, for the next four hours, he crawled through the mountain darkness. He crawled for a while and then paused to listen; and he repeated this process over and over again.

It was painful, agonizingly slow work, and it was an activity filled with danger – danger from his enemies, danger from snakes and animals, danger in the sense that he might easily crawl over the edge of a cliff. But Sergeant Yakoma was patient and very, very careful.

After four hours Yakoma heard a mewing sound. He moved closer to it. And after a further ten minutes he identified the sound as that of a woman; she was whimpering while she slept.

Yakoma waited, totally motionless, until the first thin rays of light appeared in the sky. Then he could see the woman, and very soon he could see that she was entirely alone.

Sergean Yakoma grabbed her. He twisted one of her arms up

186

behind her back, kept his other hand firmly over her mouth, and marched her cautiously back to his lorry. He was very strong and she presented no problem at all.

Once back at the army lorry, Yakoma warned the woman that if she made the slightest sound he would slit her throat; then he tied her hands and feet and dumped her in the back of his lorry. He wasn't sure who she was or where she came from, but he had decided that before questioning her it would be best to get her away from here as quickly as possible. He climbed into the driving-seat of the lorry, turned on the lights and the engine, and pushed the gear-lever backwards into reverse.

As soon as Jane heard the engine start up, she let out a piercing scream from her position on the floor of the lorry. 'Philip!' she yelled. 'Philip! Help! Help!'

As soon as he heard the lorry engine turn over, Philip Morgan sat up with a jerk. Now, when he heard Jane scream, he knew that he had to do something about it, and fast.

Yakoma began to reverse and then turn the lorry to get it back onto the road: during the night it had been parked sideways across the highway.

Jane continued screaming.

Philip wondered where the hell she was. In the army lorry somewhere, presumably – but was she in the cab? He couldn't be sure. Well, one thing was certain – she wasn't likely to be in the driving-seat.

Philip thumbed off the safety catch on the Lee Enfield rifle which he had rescued from the fire-department truck; he operated the bolt to put a round into the breech.

The lorry began to move forward along the road: another few seconds and it would be gone. He fired and the windscreen starred; he flicked the bolt backwards and forwards and fired again.

The lorry's engine howled as the driver's foot pressed down on the accelerator, and for a second the lorry's speed increased. But then it swerved violently to the right. Its lights slewed across the highway, bounced up high and then dropped. The front wheels of the lorry plunged into the roadside ditch and the engine stalled; after a judder of protest from the suspension there was suddenly complete silence.

Philip and Bob Fuller raced recklessly down the mountainside to the stricken lorry; Kelly Thompson followed as fast as he could. Philip heaved open the door on the driver's side and the dead body of Sergeant Yakoma flopped out sideways and slid to the ground: Yakoma had been shot through the left eye and also through the chest.

In the back of the lorry Jane was trying to manoeuvre herself into a sitting position; she was also trying hard to stop crying. But within a matter of moments her tears of frustration and fear became tears

187

of relief and happiness, as Philip climbed in to untie her.

With the coming of dawn the President had also started to take more interest in his surroundings. And now, hearing the noise of the lorry, followed by two rifle shots, he cautiously peered over the edge of the ditch and tried to find out what the hell was going on.

At first, in the half-light, he could see nothing at all enlightening, but after a minute or two he made out the shape of Philip and the three others standing round the stationary army lorry; he could also hear them talking and recognized their friendly voices, so he pulled himself slowly to his feet and staggered down the road to join them.

Once he got moving the President felt much less ill. He was still a mass of tender bruises from the heavy beating he had received three days earlier, and his experiences since then had hardly been a rest cure: his night in the ditch had left him stiff with cold and he had a thick layer of dried blood on his forehead from a cut. But, despite all his aches and pains, he was at least mobile and able to think clearly. He felt weak and a little dizzy, but he convinced himself that he was far from done for yet.

Kasaboru's companions were all enormously relieved and pleased to see him again, and Jane gave the President an impulsive kiss on the cheek. His arrival took her mind off her own condition, and she gave him a quick medical check to ensure that he had come to no serious harm.

The President had obviously been badly shaken by the bazooka explosion, and ideally, like all of them, he should have spent a few days in bed to recover; but there was no chance of that, of course, and Jane gave him an encouraging pat on his back instead.

'Well,' said Philip, after he had pulled Sergeant Yakoma's body into the ditch, 'we can be quite certain that this soldier here wasn't out in the mountains on his own. The rest of his platoon are probably around here somewhere, so I suggest we get moving as fast as we can.'

No-one disagreed.

Fuller and Thompson rescued what little of their gear they could find in the wreckage of the fire-department truck, while Philip familiarized himself with the controls of the army lorry. He had to knock out the broken windscreen, but apart from that everything seemed in working order. Once everyone was ready they backed the lorry out of the ditch and then drove on for two miles; then they stopped, both for food and for a conference.

It was daylight now, though the sky was heavily clouded over and rain seemed likely at any moment.

While they were all working their way through the soldiers' rations from the back of the lorry, Philip and the President looked at a map which the Sergeant had left in his cab. They could see clearly enough that the road they were on came to a junction with a road from the north some ten miles further on.

'It's my guess,' said Philip, 'that there'll be an army check-point at that crossroads. It's a very strategic spot.'

Kasaboru nodded. 'Yes, I'm sure you're right. But if we drive another seven miles or so – to this point here – the contours show that we can look down onto the junction and see what awaits us. And if it's obviously an unfriendly welcome, then we must set off on foot again, cross-country. We're heading for this river over here – it will carry us a long way west with very little effort, and it's wide enough to be fairly safe, even in daylight. Obviously I'd like to drive all the way to the river if we can – but it may not be possible.'

'Well, let's not anticipate trouble before it finds us,' said Philip. 'We'll carry on and keep our eyes skinned.'

As the President had suggested, they drove for nearly another eight miles, until they came to a high ridge overlooking a valley. And sure enough, at the junction of the two roads, several thousand feet below, they could see an army lorry similar to their own; it gave every appearance of waiting patiently for its mate, and there were soldiers standing around it.

The President sighed with regret. 'Ah well,' he said. 'It was a pleasant ride while it lasted. But we can't go any further by road. For the present it's back to Shanks's pony, I'm afraid.'

They parked the lorry below the top of the ridge, out of sight from the valley, and began to prepare to travel on foot once more.

A mood of depression settled on all five of them as they did so. Each of them was feeling overwhelmingly weary, and to compound their misery the rain which had been threatening for some time now began to fall. Within a matter of moments they were in the midst of a fierce tropical downpour such as Philip and Jane had not seen for many years, and before long they were all completely soaked. The huge raindrops bounced up from the road to a height of about two feet, and in five minutes visibility had closed down to perhaps a hundred yards.

The four men cannibalized the soldiers' equipment from the lorry, taking such guns, food and other supplies as they felt were essential and which they could carry without crippling themselves; Bob Fuller insisted on adding a coil of nylon rope, which he said might prove very useful in the mountains. Then they prepared to march off.

But at the last moment, when the three others had turned away and were already trudging through the rain, Philip noticed that Jane was lingering by the lorry, her face turned away from him. When he touched her shoulder to indicate that it was time to go, he realised that her features were ravaged with despair. He pulled her round to face him and she leaned against his chest and sobbed bitterly, her arms limply looped around his waist.

Philip realised that, temporarily at least, Jane was at the end of her mental and physical resources. He let her cry quietly for a while, conscious of the fact that the other three men had stopped and were waiting. After the worst of Jane's sobs had subsided he pulled her chin up and kissed her.

'Come on, love,' he said. 'It's time to go.' He did his best to sound cheerful, though in the circumstances there was nothing at all to be cheerful about.

Jane shook her head; her eyes were blurred with tears, and when she spoke her voice was tight with emotion. 'It's no good,' she said. 'I simply can't go on. I'm completely and utterly exhausted. I can hardly put one foot in front of the other, and now you're expecting me to walk miles and miles across the open mountains. In the rain as well. But it's no good, I just can't make it. You'll have to leave me behind.'

Jane's breath was coming in fits and starts and she began to hiccup through trying to talk while crying. So she stopped trying to talk for a while and just went on leaning against Philip while he gently patted her back.

After another pause, he held her away from him and looked down into her face. 'Now then,' he said calmly. 'Let's get one thing clear. I'm certainly not going to leave you behind. And you're not the only one who's tired. We're all very weary and we're all just going to have to keep going as best we can, for a few more miles at least. After that we should be able to find a boat, and you'll be able to sit back and relax while we all sail down the river.'

The rain spattered constantly down on to the tops of their heads, plastering their hair to their scalps: they both looked slightly ridiculous. Philip kissed her again.

'I'll help you,' he said. 'Come on – we're keeping the others waiting.'

He took Jane firmly by the hand, and then they set off together, across the loose and crumbling surface of the mountain. Jane slipped and stumbled at first, but after a few hundred yards she got into the rhythm of it. And after a mile or so she and Philip had caught up with the leaders, and all five of them were together in a group once more.

Major Duncan Grey looked up at the storm clouds from the valley below. It wasn't raining where he was, but in a way he wished it were: the thick clouds above were holding down and intensifying the heat, and the atmosphere was unbearably heavy and humid. The Major's head ached and his eyes throbbed, and he longed for a glass of something long and cool. But there was not the slightest chance of that.

Grey sighed and scratched his head; he wondered what on earth had happened to the other half of his men. During the night no traffic whatever had approached his own road block, and he had therefore made his way to the agreed rendezvous point at dawn. But Sergeant Yakoma had not yet appeared – nor was he answering Grey's repeated radio calls. Any number of factors could have delayed him, from a puncture to a full-scale mutiny. It was the uncertainty which was so worrying.

In the end Grey decided that as usual he would just have to do everything himself. He climbed into the driving-seat of his lorry and made his way slowly to the top of the ridge. There, in the rain, he found the twin lorry which Yakoma had taken, with the windscreen missing and with blood on the front seat. None of the eight soldiers who had been with the lorry were anywhere to be found, so somewhere along the line they had obviously met trouble.

Grey drove further in the same direction, and eventually he found two of his lost sheep dragging their tired feet unhappily down the road towards him. He questioned them closely and began to gain some inkling of what had happened during the night. Further on still, he came across the burnt-out wreckage of the fire-department truck, together with the dead body of Sergeant Yakoma, and the picture became almost complete.

After studying the map, Duncan Grey made an educated guess as to which way the President and his friends were now heading. He also worked out his own best route for cutting them off before they reached the river which would carry them west. His group of sixteen men was now reduced to ten: one dead and five lost. But he still outnumbered his quarry two to one, and he still had every advantage: he had transport, they were on foot; he could obtain supplies, they had to live off the land.

Grey considered the odds carefully, looking at the problem from every angle. Then he put away his map and smiled happily to himself. He felt that he had every justification for believing that before long he would complete his mission successfully.

Eleven

Dan Levene, the Mayor of Sungbarta, was awake by half past six that morning. He padded downstairs in his slippers and tuned in to the BBC World Service to see if there were any developments affecting the fate of his country.

According to the BBC, Sungbarta was now the last outpost of support for President Kasaboru, of whom there was still no positive news. The Gabuti government was making no secret of its intention to assist the Nyanga regime in overcoming resistance in Sungbarta. And meanwhile, Richard Chokwe, who prior to the coup had been Foreign Secretary of Balembi, was reported last night to be in Cairo; he was apparently making his way to New York to seek United Nations intervention to restore peace.

Dan Levene was both depressed and relieved. Depressed because the BBC confirmed his own predictions of what would happen – he had anticipated that Gabuti troops would attack his city – and relieved because Richard Chokwe had apparently succeeded in escaping from Digara as he had intended. Levene had heard from Chokwe very briefly two days earlier, and he had often wondered since whether the Foreign Secretary was alive or dead.

Levene switched off his radio and went back upstairs to have a shower. Today was probably going to be one of the most crucial days in his entire life, and yet somehow it didn't feel very special; it just felt ordinary and dull, and he was still going to have to shave just the same as usual.

The day did not remain dull for very long. At seven-thirty, Russian-built MIG-19s of the Gabuti air force came screaming in low over the airport and the residential district south of the river Sung; these planes were single-seater fighters armed with cannon and carrying thirty-two 55mm rockets.

The airport had been abandoned by the city authorities the day before, and the 'witch-doctors' war' of the previous afternoon had finally convinced most residents that it would be safer to cross the river into the city proper. As a result Sungbarta now had a great influx of refugees, and the MIGs were left without targets in the area south of the Sung. However, the pilots of the planes warmed up by shooting at a few of the larger houses, and then they moved a mile or two north and began to strafe the city itself.

The MIGs came in from the east, across the lake. They swooped down out of the sun from about five thousand feet, machine-gunning with their 23mm cannons whichever buildings caught the pilots' fancy; they did not appear to be working to any particular plan. Used cartridge cases rained down from the skies as the planes skimmed over the rooftops.

There were six jets in all, and they made several runs each, firing rockets during their last attack. The rockets swooshed down to explode with a massive *didoom* in the streets, pock-marking the buildings with shrapnel. Then, after twenty minutes, the jets disappeared into the east, back towards Digara and the Gabuti border.

The damage they left behind them was more psychological than physical. Of course some citizens were hit by the machine-gun bullets and were killed; others lost limbs ripped off by jagged fragments of shrapnel. But the casualties could be numbered on the fingers of two hands, and Sungbarta General Hospital could cope with them easily. The jets' real achievement was to bring home to the inhabitants of Sungbarta that their lives were genuinely at risk. The city had never before suffered any sort of aerial bombardment, and for many Sungbartans war was something they read about in books or watched on film: it was distant, exciting, and harmful only to other people. Now, for the first time, they realised that war was close at hand: it was terrifying, dangerous and painful.

An hour later the planes reconnoitred the airport again, checking that it was still undefended. Then seven stately helicopters rattled in from Digara and landed on the airport perimeter; they were Russian-built MI-4s, and they each carried fourteen soldiers.

The Gabuti troops fanned out quickly and took up defensive positions; but they soon realized that no-one was remotely equipped to repulse them and they promptly got on with their job of clearing the runways and making the airport operational for larger troop-carriers.

The soldiers worked steadily but without any sense of haste. Their commanders did not expect the isolated city of Sungbarta to give them any real trouble: it was just a matter of flying in enough men, battering a brisk hole in the defences, and then walking in to take the place.

By four o'clock in the afternoon the runways were cleared of obstacles and a steady succession of transport planes began to ferry in troops and supplies. Four Ilyushin IL-18 Moskvas brought in soldiers, each plane making several trips, and two brand-new Antonov An-12 freight transporters brought in the guns, jeeps and armoured cars to back them up.

After the first attack by the MIGs, Dan Levene rang up his son to check that David and his family had not been hurt; then he made his way to City Hall.

Business life had almost come to a halt, and the jacaranda-lined streets in the city centre were almost deserted. Levene called in briefly at his office, where he learned to his relief that communications were unimpaired by the jets' attack. He also looked out of his window onto Lake Alberton, and noted with a certain amount of satisfaction that no-one was out sailing this morning. Then he decided to pay a visit to the hospital to see how the staff were coping with what he feared were the first of many casualties soon to be admitted.

Sungbarta General Hospital was situated in the north-west corner of the city, near the point where the River Sung divided to form the delta on which most of the city stood. The hospital was surrounded by green parkland which had been put there deliberately to insulate the patients from the noise and the bustle of their fellow citizens; acacia trees provided shade.

Levene avoided bothering any of the medics at the hospital; he suspected that they would have plenty to do without him talking to them. Instead he called on the chief administrative officer, and obtained from him an assessment of the hospital's capacity to deal with any major emergency.

The answers Levene received to his questions were not altogether reassuring; the administrator was also concerned that the MIGs had shot up one of the hospital's outlying buildings – what could be done about that? Planes weren't supposed to attack hospitals, were they? Wasn't there a Geneva convention or something?

'Yes,' said the Mayor, 'there is. And for a start we might try identifying the hospital in some way so that it's visible from the air. As far as I can see, the jets weren't shooting at anything particular this morning – they were just letting fly at anyone who was silly enough to show themselves. Why not put some large red crosses on your roof? I'm sure you've got plenty of flat roofs.'

'Good idea,' said the administrator – he would get the painters on to it straight away.

Before leaving the hospital Levene walked through some of the wards. He knew very well that he ought not to do so, for he was far too soft-hearted for it to do him any good; but he did it anyway.

Sure enough he found himself deeply moved by some of the sights he saw. He glimpsed briefly a white man whose leg had been shattered by shrapnel, and a woman who had lost an eye. But most pathetic of all were the primitive Mibambo villagers, all of them refugees from the upheavals in the surrounding bush, who had made their way into the city over the last few days.

In one ward Levene saw a small six-year-old Mibambo boy whose parents had apparently been killed in some sort of ambush. The boy had carried his wounded baby sister into the hospital and now refused to be parted from her.

In another ward the male head of a family was recovering from the amputation of his left arm, which had been almost severed in a fight with a Fanda tribesman. This man had been accompanied to the hospital by his wife and two children. The wife had carried all the family's possessions in a bundle on her head; the bundle also included food for the duration of her husband's stay in hospital. She had intended to cook the food on a fire on the floor of the ward, but she had been gently directed elsewhere; the meal she had planned consisted of a number of hairy caterpillars, three inches long, and three dead rats.

Levene left the hospital with tears in his eyes, shaking his head in dismay. He was upset by what he had seen, and perhaps that was no help in keeping a cool head; but at least he was quite clear now about what he was trying to achieve, and what he was trying to prevent.

On a normal day, David Levene, the Mayor's son, would have gone to work at the garage which he had bought with the help of a loan from his father-in-law, and which he ran with great success. He was car-mad, which motivated his expertise, and he was well liked by a wide circle of acquaintances, which provided him with plenty of customers. But today was not a normal day, and instead of going to work he answered the city's call for able-bodied volunteers to make their way to the south road bridge. Once there, he offered his services to the officer in charge, and was asked to return in the afternoon to help man the defences. All three bridges into the city had been wired with explosives the previous day, and they could be blown up immediately if need be; but for the moment there were still refugees limping into the city, and no-one wanted to take over-hasty action, even if a full-scale attack were to start. The bridges would be destroyed only in the direst emergency; and in the mean-time, with only a very limited number of regular soldiers available, young men like David Levene were likely to be extremely useful.

David said very little over lunch with his family, though it was an excellent meal, as usual. It was left to his attractive thirty-year-old wife Sally to ensure that their two children remained cheerful and unworried. David and Sally had a son who was six and a daughter who was four; fortunately the children were not quite old enough to understand what was going on.

Over the washing-up Sally declared firmly that if her husband was going to take an active part in the defence of the city, then she was certainly not going to be left out. Sally was a qualified nurse, with five years' experience behind her, and the hospital had also put out a call for assistance.

195

'Your mother rang me this morning and said she'd be only too pleased to look after the kids if I wanted to help,' said Sally. 'So I thought I'd take her up on it.'

David's immediate response was to curse his mother inwardly for not minding her own business. But then he realised that the arrangement would give both Sally and his mother something to do instead of sitting around worrying – so after some discussion he agreed to the proposal. A little later he drove his two children to his mother's home and then dropped Sally off at the hospital.

Sally gripped his hand hard as she was about to get out of the car. Her serious blue eyes stared at him brightly. 'Look after yourself,' she said with a forced smile.

David grinned in return. 'You too,' he said, and kissed her.

Back at the bridge there was a total absence of developments, but during the afternoon there was a brief sound of gunfire within the city. A group of Nyanga supporters broke into a gunsmith's shop; and armed with half a dozen shotguns they made a thoroughly botched attempt to take over the police station; this mini-coup was soon firmly squashed, and the offenders, who were Fanda workers from a local brewery, were dumped in the city's jail to cool off.

And apart from that, nothing significant happened all day. The MIGs came back in the evening and indulged in further target practice – but as the officer in charge of the bridge remarked, the Gabuti forces had obviously decided to wait until dawn the following morning before launching anything that could properly be called an attack.

In the meantime the defenders could only wait.

Twelve

The President and his friends walked steadily across the mountains for three hours. The rain poured down incessantly out of a solid grey sky, and for much of the time visibility was limited to fifty yards. Fortunately they had found a compass in the soldiers' lorry, otherwise they might well have wandered in circles.

In the circumstances it was not surprising that morale in the group was low. Bob Fuller was the fittest of the five travellers and he tried his hardest to raise the others' spirits; but for the most part his attempts at humour met with a stony silence. In the end he decided that he could make a better contribution to their progress by leading the way and setting a pace for the others – which he did. His friends followed on behind as best they could.

After three hours Fuller spotted a cave in the mountainside, and once he had checked it for safety the five of them took shelter. They were all bone-weary and also very hungry, and the food they had brought with them from the soldiers' lorry soon disappeared.

The President found the interior of the cave very interesting: it was lined with belts of schist, which is a coarse-grained rock formed by heat and pressure. Kasaboru knew that in all probability there were veins of gold and silver nearby, and in better times he might have commented on this to his companions; but he could see by their exhausted expressions that at this stage of their journey they would not be too enthusiastic about a lecture on geology, so he let it pass.

If anything, the travellers felt even more miserable in the cave, without the rain constantly spattering down on them, than they had done out in the open. Sitting around in soaking wet clothes was highly uncomfortable, and the dirt and grit on the cave floor seemed to get into the food. Their depression was relieved only by the presence of two beautiful Colobus monkeys, who overcame their normal shyness of man to come forward and pick up a few crumbs. The monkeys were about half the size of a chimpanzee, with white bushy tails longer than their bodies; their colouring made them look like little old men in black skull caps. The President explained that the monkeys preferred the tall trees and the cool air of the mountains, which was why they were to be found in these parts; they were becoming increasingly rare now, large numbers of them having been killed over the past few years for the fur market.

After they had rested, Philip and the President again looked at the map. The contours suggested that their route was now mostly downhill, but as the President pointed out, much of the country had not been properly surveyed for fifty years or more; the map might not be one hundred per cent accurate. In any case, they still had at least another ten miles to go to the river Jarnoko in the plain below, and there was no knowing what kind of natural obstacles might lie in their way.

'You can expect anything except a glacier,' said the President as they set off once more. 'And I wouldn't even rule that out completely.'

Bob Fuller again led the way; he had been carrying the heaviest load all day, but he remained cheerful and optimistic. Kelly Thompson followed, still moving sluggishly as a result of his arrow-wound of the previous day, and the President came third. Jane was next in line: she was even wearier now than at the start of their trek across the mountains, and as usual she was concentrating solely on putting one foot in front of the other, over and over again. Philip Morgan brought up the rear, doing his best to stay alert.

Another two hours passed, without even the slightest pause in the constant heavy rain. Then, in the mists ahead, Bob Fuller began to hear a roaring sound; and after a few more yards they could all hear it.

They advanced cautiously, and a hundred yards further on they came across the raging torrent of a swollen mountain stream. It was pouring down over a waterfall and pounding mightily onto the rocks below, causing the noise they had heard in the distance. Upstream they could see nothing except an ugly and dangerous-looking body of water swirling swiftly out of the clouds; and downstream there was nothing but rocks and rapids, also disappearing very quickly into a hazy white mist.

'Is this the famous river we've been looking for?' asked Jane, shouting to make herself heard.

The President shook his head. 'Nothing like it,' he said. 'This must be a tributary. In normal times you could probably paddle across it, but today, after all this rain. . .' He shrugged and waved his hands to indicate the hopelessness of it all.

Philip and the President looked at the map yet again, and found a wavery blue line which might, once upon a time, have been the stream which now blocked their way. Ideally, they should cross it immediately and continue due west until they struck the river they were heading for; but obviously they were not going to get across at this point for several days. The alternatives were therefore to follow the tributary downstream until it joined the main river, or to go upstream in the hope that higher up the force of the flood would reduce to the point where they could somehow wade through it.

The four men put their heads together over the map and decided that going downstream would probably add some twenty miles to their journey. The alternative route was not so easy to assess: no-one could be quite certain how far they would have to travel upstream before they could cross this torrent, but the general consensus was that it could scarcely be more than ten miles at the most.

Agreement was therefore reached, and they began to walk upstream.

It was now quite cool, or any rate it was when they stopped walking, and the fog was thicker than ever. They plodded steadily uphill, keeping well within sight or earshot of the stream, and continued walking for a further two hours. At the end of that time they climbed a particularly steep stretch of mountainside, over which the stream crashed in a waterfall, and walked on for another hundred yards beside a series of pools and rapids.

It was then that they found the bridge.

Or rather, what had once been a bridge.

In its heyday it had been nothing more than three planks in line, spanning the width of the water. There was a stout post at each end of the bridge, and two more tree trunks had been driven into the bed of the stream at one third and two thirds of the way across; it was at these points that the first plank was joined to the second, and so on. Someone had added a rudimentary handrail, made from a branch of the nearest tree, and that was that.

In good weather the bridge was no doubt a perfectly sound way of crossing the water without getting your feet wet. But in the present downpour the situation was rather different: only the handrail and the two upright posts in midstream were visible, together with the ends of the planks on the rocks at either side. The central part of the bridge, some thirty feet of it, was well under water, and fast-moving, swirling and treacherous water at that.

The travellers stood on the rocky outcrop which formed the eastern bank and stared across. The noise of the rushing water was still considerable, even though they had travelled some distance upstream; and below the bridge the water creamed and rippled over jagged boulders, reminding them that anyone who fell into this particular mill-race would have to be a very good swimmer, and very lucky, to survive.

They looked at each other, none of them wanting to have to take the necessary decision. In the end it was Philip who spoke.

'We aren't going to do any better than this,' he said firmly. 'Let's get across it while we can.'

It was agreed that Philip would go over first, taking with him the nylon rope which Bob Fuller had insisted on bringing with him from the army lorry. One end of the rope was fixed to the post at the near end of the bridge, which they tested and found firm enough, and Philip was to tie the other end either to the far post or to one of the trees which dotted the opposite bank.

Philip went across quickly. He had never been over-fond of fast-moving water, and this particular piece of it seemed even more unfriendly than most.

He had expected a tremendous pressure of water on his legs, once he got onto the submerged part of the planking, but even so the enormous force of it took him by surprise. The surface of the planks was slippery and insecure, and several times he almost lost his footing; but in the end he managed to reach the other side safely. He took a couple of turns of rope around the trunk of the nearest tree, and still had more than enough left to tie the end of the rope firmly round his own waist. Now, if anyone got into trouble, he could wade out into the water to help them without any fear that he would also be swept away.

It had been agreed before they started the operation that the travellers would cross one at a time; there was no way of telling how much weight the planks and the handrail would take. An order of precedence had also been agreed: Jane would go second and the President third; he would be followed by Kelly Thompson and finally Bob Fuller.

Jane's mind was numb as she stood waiting for her turn. She had passed through the stage of being frightened by new developments, and she had entered instead a state of permanently horrified equilibrium. She knew that she had to go across the bridge, but the thought of exposing herself to the weight of that roaring, dirty water was absolutely terrifying.

Unfortunately there was no alternative. So, when Philip signalled from the far side that he was ready, and Bob Fuller beckoned to her with an encouraging grin, Jane stepped up calmly and approached the bridge as if this were the kind of thing she did every day.

'Put your left hand on the handrail,' Fuller shouted into her ear, 'and your right hand on the rope. Don't pull on either of them unless you have to, but use them as a guide. And lean to the left in the water – lean into the current like leaning into the wind.'

Jane nodded dumbly. She looked up, and Philip smiled at her. Somehow she managed to smile back.

Jane succeeded in getting two thirds of the way across. She had just lifted her right foot to take another step forward, when suddenly her left foot skidded out from under her and she fell sideways onto the handrail, her feet trailing out behind her.

For perhaps two seconds the handrail held while Jane scrambled desperately to regain her footing. Then it broke, and she was dropped feet first into the torrent.

As soon as he had seen Jane's feet slipping, Philip had started out across the bridge to help her; and when she fell he was near enough to dive head first after her and grab her by the arm.

For a few moments both of them were sucked completely beneath the surface of the water, and they were carried with tremendous speed a few yards downstream. Then the rope around Philip's waist reached its limit with a tremendous jerk, which almost wrenched Jane's arm out of his fingers, and the force of the current began to swing them round towards the western bank.

It was at this point that the weight of water pouring down from the upper heights of the mountains, after many hours of continuous heavy rain, proved to be just too much. Philip was battered and winded, forced under water and left desperate for breath – but most important of all, his head was slammed against a jagged piece of rock. The blow stunned him for a moment, loosening his grip on Jane's arm. Then, mercilessly, the current seized him once again; it pounded him against another submerged boulder and he lost consciousness completely. His fingers opened, and Jane was carried away.

From then on, Philip knew nothing of what was happening for several minutes.

In fact, a great deal was happening.

Jane's head appeared only periodically above the surface of the water, and she disappeared from sight with amazing speed. At first Bob Fuller tried to go running after her along the eastern bank, but the ground they had just covered to reach the bridge was far too difficult to cover quickly, even going downhill. Within seconds he could no longer see Jane, and although he carried on for a hundred yards or so, he soon realized that he had no chance whatever of catching her up. He came back slowly, checking that she was not trapped in any pool or eddy, but feeling quite certain in his own mind that she had already been swept a very long way downstream – whether dead or alive he had no way of knowing.

Kelly Thompson and the President, meanwhile, took enormous risks in crossing the bridge together in a far shorter time than they would have taken in other circumstances. But they could see very plainly that Philip was being battered unconscious on the rocks at the end of his rope, and that unless they reached him fast he would surely drown.

Fortunately they managed to cross the bridge without falling off it themselves, and they hauled Philip in and laid him flat on his back as quickly as they could. Kelly Thompson, who had been trained in life-saving, pumped the water out of Philip's lungs and eventually got him breathing again; but it took a minute or two to achieve that result, and Thompson had never been more relieved in his life than when he saw Philip's chest begin to rise and fall unaided once more.

The rain continued relentlessly.

Bob Fuller returned empty-handed, his face white and strained. He and his two companions made Philip as comfortable as they could, and then they waited for him to recover consciousness.

After five minutes Philip opened his eyes. After a further ten minutes he seemed to understand what they said to him. And after half an hour he was able to sit up and discuss the situation rationally.

The four men were all stunned by the loss of Jane. They had known from the outset that there was every chance that some of them would not complete the journey, but the first real casualty was still a major shock.

Never the less, they were all professionals, and their objectives remained the same as before. Their mission was to get the President to Sungbarta, safely, and in the shortest time possible. There was to be no deflection from that purpose. The only exception to this rule was proposed by Kelly Thompson and accepted by the other three.

Thompson pointed out, with some justice, that since being wounded by an arrow the previous day he had been by far the weakest member of the party, and at times he had slowed down the overall rate of progress. He was now feeling a good deal better than he had, but his stamina was definitely limited. He therefore proposed that the other three should continue the journey west on their own; in the meantime he would follow the mountain stream downhill to try to find out what had become of Jane.

There was no denying the overwhelming probability that she had already been drowned: they all recognized that likelihood. But there was a chance that she might have survived; she might have managed to pull herself out of the water some distance downstream. If so, Thompson would try to link up with her and find somewhere for the two of them to shelter for the next few days.

'If you do reach Sungbarta,' Thompson told the others, 'and if you do manage to get things back to normal, then in a few days' time you can send out troops to look for us. But if you don't get there, or if for some reason the President is not able to get back in power, then in a week or so we're all going to be dead anyway.'

Everyone present agreed that this was a realistic if somewhat brutal assessment of the situation. As a result, Thompson's proposal was accepted unanimously; he himself began to follow the course of the stream downhill and Philip, Bob Fuller, and the President began to continue their weary march to the west.

Thirteen

As soon as she felt Philip's grip on her arm give way, Jane abandoned all hope of surviving.

The current swept her away at a tremendous pace. It threw her body into rocks, hurling her from side to side. She opened her mouth in shock, and dirty water flooded in. She spluttered and coughed and gasped for air. She was sucked under the surface: her eyes saw only a glimpse of brown light above. Then her head struck a boulder and her vision was blurred with blood.

Jane surfaced temporarily and took a huge despairing breath. Then she was tossed and flung about, all over again. The stream roared and hissed at her: its noise was truly appalling. The rain fell unceasingly, blending the sky into the surface of the water, slapping and stinging her face in those rare moments when it was exposed to the air.

Then the stream narrowed as it approached the waterfall which Jane and the others had only recently passed. She was carried along even faster – and as she was propelled out into space over the edge of the rock, Jane closed her eyes and screamed despairingly as she fell.

The force of the falling water carried her deep down into the dark of the pool below. She was whirled hopelessly and helplessly about in total blackness. She lost consciousness – or at any rate she ceased to be fully aware of what was happening to her.

From time to time, when she felt the water drain away from her face, Jane took huge, rasping, red-hot lungfuls of air, her body twisting in torment from the shortage of oxygen. She had long since ceased trying to swim: swimming was impossible in a flood of this order. Her body reacted solely by reflex, the instinct for survival taking over completely from any semblance of clear thinking.

A long, long time later the stream seemed to quieten and calm. Jane opened her eyes.

The rain had eased off now, though the sky was still dark and gloomy, brooding low overhead. She was in midstream of a river some thirty yards wide; the river was still rushing along with the force of the flood draining off the mountains, but it was running through flatter country at this point, and no longer tearing headlong down the rapids and waterfalls higher upstream. Somehow or other Jane had found a piece of driftwood, a branch of a tree, and her arms were looped over it; the wood was just buoyant enough to support her head above water, and she had just enough strength left to hang on to it.

The river was dark, muddy and powerful; it whirled her along for a while, giving her no choice but to submit to its will. Sometimes she came close to the banks, and once her feet even touched the bottom; but she could never quite manage the effort needed to take advantage of these chances. The stream snatched her away again, and carried her on still further.

Still more time passed, and several miles with it; and then she saw an African in soldier's uniform standing on the right-hand bank, some fifty yards ahead. The most she could do to help herself was to raise an arm and wave.

The man saw her. He gave a great yell. He pointed and jabbered in his native dialect. Other African heads appeared on the bank, and further excited words were exchanged.

The rain had stopped now. The river was still moving swiftly, but it had ended its angry roaring and was contenting itself with occasional ripples and splashes.

By this time Jane was level with the first soldier, but he ran along the bank to keep pace with her, calling back instructions to his companions. A few moments later another soldier sprinted ahead of the first. This man was carrying a rope, which he whirled round his head and threw out into the stream in Jane's path.

Jane reached out for it – and missed.

The man pulled in the rope, ran ahead again, and threw it once more. This time Jane managed to grab it.

Her fingers were cold and weak, but she let go of the driftwood and held fast to the rope with both hands. The soldiers on the bank, amid enormous excitement, began to pull her in to the shore, until at last she felt the bed of the stream under her feet; the weight of the current fell away, and she was able to stagger, dripping and gasping, out of the water completely.

Five Balembian soldiers, with more running up every second, reached out to help her along. There was much flashing of white teeth and loud, high-pitched conversation: it was not every day that the soldiers fished a beautiful white woman out of the river; and this woman undeniably was beautiful, even if she was temporarily a little bedraggled.

The soldiers half-carried and half-pulled Jane back to their camp. For her part, she was far too exhausted to care where they were going. But when they arrived she was pleased to see that the soldiers had a fire going; there was also a tent pitched beside their two lorries.

The men deposited Jane on to the ground beside the fire. Once they ceased to support her she simply crumpled into a heap and fell. She lay face-down in an awkward position, but she had no energy or will to move. The world swung around her until she closed her eyes, and even then the giddiness continued.

She felt sick and worn out, numb with cold and fatigue. She had no wish to do anything except drift away peacefully into sleep, unconsciousness or death; she made little distinction between them, and at that point any one of the three would have been entirely acceptable.

'Well now,' said a man's voice suddenly. 'What's all this?' It was a voice which Jane felt she ought to know – a voice which was somehow familiar.

'It's a white woman, sir,' said one of the soldiers, speaking in English for the first time.

'I can see that, you fool. But where'd she come from, out of the river?'

'Yes, sir.'

There was more noisy jabbering in a Fanda dialect, a dozen voices at once.

'Quiet!' roared the officer.

He bent down to examine the woman whom his men had rescued. He turned her over on to her back.

'Good God!' he said after a moment. 'It – it's Jane, isn't it?'

Jane opened her eyes. The face of the man leaning over her swam hazily into focus. The tanned skin, the military moustache, the brown hair and eyes – she knew them, of course. The features were those of her uncle, Major Duncan Grey.

'Hello,' she said softly. And then she fainted.

Duncan Grey stood up and looked down at his niece in amazement. Balembi was a very small country by any standards, and the European element in its population was smaller still; he was well accustomed to running across the same faces at dinner parties, and being introduced to strangers who turned out to be friends of friends. But even so, meeting Jane out here in the mountains was totally unexpected, and at first he couldn't imagine how she came to be here.

Explanations, however, would obviously have to come later. The first essential was to get her warm and dry.

'Right,' he said briskly to his men. 'Carry this woman into my tent.'

The senior non-commissioned officer in the group was now Corporal Avakubi. The Corporal was twenty-five; he was slim and slightly built, but he was extremely tough, with mean, bloodshot eyes which blinked frequently; he did not like white men, and those who had experienced his violent temper thought twice before crossing him.

It was Corporal Avakubi who had thrown the rope to Jane, and Corporal Avakubi who had answered the Major's questions. And it was now Corporal Avakubi who spoke up on behalf of the other soldiers; the smile had suddenly disappeared from his face.

'Why carry her into your tent, Major Grey sir? This woman our prisoner.'

There were heavy nods of agreement from the assembled soldiers: they had a number of interesting ideas about what could be done with an attractive white woman who unfortunately happened to have fainted.

'Prisoner?' said Grey. 'What the hell are you talking about, man? She's just fallen into the river, that's all.'

'Our prisoner,' repeated Avakubi stubbornly. 'We look after her.'

Duncan Grey looked thoughtfully at the faces all around him and then made a sudden decision. He pulled out the .38 Enfield revolver from a holster at his waist and pointed it straight at the Corporal.

'Carry her into my tent, Corporal, or by God I'll shoot you where you stand.'

He stared at the Corporal without blinking, and the Corporal stared back.

But then, after a moment, Avakubi decided that he didn't want to argue with the business end of a .38 Enfield after all. He gave a curt order in his own tongue – and with many a surly look the soldiers carried Jane into Duncan Grey's tent and laid her flat on a camp bed.

Grey came into the tent with her. He was privately very relieved that the men had accepted his authority – for a moment he had feared that they wouldn't. So when he got out the bottle of brandy which he had slipped into his kitbag just before leaving Digara, he took a hefty swig at it himself before administering some to Jane.

After a few minutes Jane felt well enough to sit up and take off all her wet clothes, while the Major tactfully waited outside. Then she towelled herself down, wrapped herself in two army blankets, and passed her clothes out to Grey to be dried by the blazing fire.

Fortunately the men now seemed to have resumed obeying orders without protest. There were numerous lewd comments made as the soldier who had been given the job pinned up Jane's underwear on a line near the fire, but at least the mood of rebellion had passed. And once he was sure that all was well outside the tent, Duncan Grey came back inside to talk to his niece; he sat down in a canvas chair opposite her.

'Well, my dear,' he said, 'perhaps you'd better tell me how you come to be out here in the middle of nowhere.'

Jane glanced at him. He seemed to be genuinely puzzled. 'I fell off a bridge,' she said after a pause. 'A few miles upstream.'

'Yes, but how did you come to be out here in the first place?'

206

Grey repeated. He really couldn't understand it.

Jane hesitated. 'I was out walking with some friends,' she said at last.

Very belatedly, Duncan Grey added two and two together and came up with four. 'Oh,' he said gravely. 'Oh – I see. . . .' He rubbed his chin as he realized what must have happened. 'Yes, yes, it's all beginning to make sense now. You and that fellow Philip Morgan were as thick as thieves, of course. And he was appointed as Kasaboru's security adviser – and so when it came to getting the President out of Digara, he took you along for the ride. Both because he was keen on you and because it made sense to have a doctor in the party. . . . Yes, I can understand it all now. Well, well – how very interesting.'

'What about you?' said Jane, determined to give as good as she got. 'I wasn't exactly expecting to meet you out here, either. What brings you to this part of the world?'

The Major suddenly began to look distinctly sheepish and defensive. 'Ah, well, yes, that's a different matter,' he mumbled, turning rather red.

'Why aren't you back in Digara?' said Jane sharply. 'Looking after the radio station. I should have thought that was rather an important job, in the circumstances.'

Grey swallowed hard before answering. 'Well – you see – the thing is this. Nyanga's taken over completely in Digara, as you probably know. Rules the roost, as it were. And, well, to cut a long story short, he's rather a ruthless bastard one way and another – and he made it pretty clear to me that if I wanted Eileen to be kept safe and well, I'd better do exactly what he told me.'

'I see – and what did he tell you to do?'

'Well – to, er, to take a few men and come out and pick up Kasaboru. The former President is obviously not going to get very far – he's got nowhere to go to, quite frankly – and, as I say, it was made pretty plain to me that Eileen's safety was at stake if I didn't do what he said. So, naturally, being concerned about her, I decided I'd better do what I was told.'

Jane almost spat at him. She felt nothing but the deepest contempt for the man. 'I don't believe you,' she said bluntly. 'I don't think Eileen's in the slightest danger. I think you're doing this just to save your own skin, and for no other reason at all. And I think it's totally despicable. Any man with an ounce of courage would have told Nyanga what he could do with himself.'

Grey winced and then looked down at his feet. 'That's all very well, my girl,' he said after a moment. 'It's all very fine to talk. But if you had to choose between being shot at dawn and doing as you're told, you might possibly take a different view. . . . Anyway, this is getting us nowhere.'

He got up, took another pull at the open brandy bottle, and then sat down again. The alcohol seemed to restore some of his confidence.

'Well, I'll say this for your friend Morgan and the President,' he continued. 'They've led me a fine old dance so far. They shot down the helicopter – that didn't please the authorities back in Digara, I can assure you of that – and they even got round my road block. They also shot my sergeant, which wasn't very friendly. It took me ages to pick up the pieces after that, and even now I haven't got all my men back. So your beloved President is certainly not giving up without a struggle. How far upstream were you when you fell off this bridge?'

Jane shook her head. 'I don't know. And I wouldn't tell you if I did. A long way, anyhow. Too far away for you to catch them.'

Grey scratched his chin again. 'Hmm. I suppose they're trying to cut across country now, to join the River Jarnoko – that's the only viable route there is through the lowlands. I was making for the river myself until we came across this flash flood blocking the way. Did the rest of your party manage to get across the stream?'

Jane shook her head, refusing to answer.

'You don't know. . . . Well, I don't suppose it's worth sending any men to look for them at this stage. But at least it's stopped raining now, and with a bit of luck we should be able to ford this stream ourselves tomorrow. . . . The President and his friends won't get very far you know – I don't know why they're bothering. Even if they reach the river they'll find no-one willing to help them – everyone's been warned not to, and they're all too scared. The best they'll be able to do is pinch a little dinghy, or a dug-out. And when I get there I'll just commandeer a nice big ferry boat and then chug down the river till we catch up with them. It'll be no contest – they can't possibly win. And in any case, Sungbarta is already surrounded by Gabuti troops – don't they know that?'

Jane pulled the blankets closer around her and said nothing.

'Ah well, be like that if you must. But there's nothing to be gained by sulking.'

Jane turned her back on him, and after a few minutes, and several more gulps of brandy, the Major went back outside to join his men.

The soldiers had been busy cooking a meal, and Grey sat down to eat it with them. As he ate he tried to work out what to do.

He felt some degree of responsibility for Jane, but not much. It was true that she was his sister's child, but she had been born in America and he had never even met her until a couple of weeks ago. And she was twenty-five years old, when all was said and done; she was a mature woman, a qualified doctor no less, and fully responsible for her own actions. And she certainly hadn't shown any signs of wanting to be helped – she'd been positively insulting, in fact. No, damn it, he was not going to feel in any way guilty or at fault if the stupid girl got herself into a mess; she must answer for her own actions.

After he had drunk a cup of coffee to finish off his meal, Grey went over to one of the lorries and reported to Digara by radio. He spoke to General Juba on this occasion, and he explained the circumstances as best he could. At the end of this discussion it was agreed that it was too late to do anything this evening – it was already almost dark – but that early tomorrow morning a Gabuti helicopter would fly in and airlift Dr Jane Stuart back to Digara. No doubt, said the General, with a smile which Duncan Grey could almost hear, President Nyanga would be very interested to hear her story.

Kelly Thompson made his way down the western side of the grossly swollen stream as fast as he could. He stopped frequently to check likely pools and eddies for any signs of Jane's body, though he knew very well that if she had drowned her body might quite possibly never come to the surface at all.

It took him three hours to cover perhaps five miles, and it was already beginning to grow dark when he spotted the soldiers' camp on the far bank. He proceeded very cautiously until he came level with the tent and the lorries, which he observed from behind some bushes.

Kelly Thompson might never have connected the soldiers' presence with Jane at all, had it not been for the sight of her brassière hanging on the line near the fire. Corporal Avakubi rammed the point home by picking up the bra and prancing around with it held over his chest, much to the amusement of his fellow soldiers. Kelly now had no doubt that Jane had been picked out of the water by the soldiers, and the fact that her clothes had been put out to dry suggested that she was still alive. He was also certain, because he recognized the lorry with the shattered windscreen, that these were the soldiers who had been chasing the President; Jane was not, therefore, a guest who was free to leave at her own discretion.

Kelly settled down to wait until darkness. Then he hid his rucksack and Sten gun, and taking only a knife with him he went downstream and swam across to the opposite bank. The force of the current carried him a good half-mile out of his way, and the swim left him wet and shivering. As he crawled through the undergrowth back towards the camp, every different kind of insect and its brother made a meal of his flesh, but he stuck it without complaint. He had been given a job to do, and he intended to see it through, come what may.

Two hours after sunset, Kelly found himself on the outskirts of the camp. Everyone seemed to have retired for the night, with the exception of one man standing guard by the tent. The guard only had the fire to protect him from all the evil in the surrounding darkness, and he poked it nervously from time to time to encourage the flames; he peered about him anxiously.

Kelly Thompson crawled stealthily round to the back of the tent. He listened. There was steady breathing from within – two people, he thought.

Very gently and quietly, taking several minutes over it, he slit the back of the tent with his knife until he could easily get through the opening. Then he crawled inside.

The light from the fire provided just enough illumination for him to see that the two camp beds were occupied by Jane on the one side, and by a white man on the other. Kelly Thompson supposed, correctly, that the white man was the officer commanding the soldiers. For a second he debated whether to kill the man with his knife. But he was not certain that he could do it absolutely silently, and he decided that it was better to let the man sleep on.

Kelly approached Jane on all fours. He woke her as gently as he could, putting a finger to her lips. Very slowly she turned to face him, and he realised that she was tied by both hands and feet to the bed. He cut her free. He noticed as he did so that Jane was wearing a pair of men's pyjamas: this was because her uncle, like the true gentleman he was, had insisted that she should accept them, while he himself slept in his underclothes.

Finally, with a nod of his head, Kelly indicated that Jane should leave first through the slit he had cut in the back of the tent. Ideally she would have taken her clothes and boots with her, but there was going to be no opportunity for such refinements.

Jane followed his mimed instructions: she slipped silently down to the floor from her camp bed and crawled out of the tent ahead of him.

Kelly followed close behind. He was just about to lift aside the canvas wall of the tent when Duncan Grey, who had been lying awake all the time, sat up in bed and shot him four times through the spine with his .38 Enfield revolver.

Fourteen

During dinner at the President's palace on Thursday evening, Joro Nyanga monopolized the conversation. He talked mainly about his attendance at the Congress of Independent African States in Accra in one week's time. He rehearsed in some detail the speech he would make to the assembled African leaders on the first day, and he boasted repeatedly about how fascinated the world's press would be by his performance.

His fellow diners concentrated hard on trying to look suitably impressed: as usual since he had taken over the palace, Nyanga had been joined for dinner by Conrad Hall, Yuri Semenov and Eileen Grey.

After finishing his meal Nyanga belched loudly, cheerfully begged everyone's pardon, and poured himself a glass of vintage port. Then he rubbed his hands together with gleeful anticipation.

'Well, Conrad,' he said, beaming with good humour, 'coming to the stadium tonight?'

Conrad Hall, who knew all about the public executions which were to take place in Digara's main sports stadium that night, shook his head with a polite smile. 'No, thanks,' he said. 'I've been over at Tikiro most of today and I've still got a lot of work to catch up with. If you don't mind I'll stay behind and get on with it.'

Nyanga seemed disappointed, almost hurt. 'No? Not coming? I should have thought tonight's show was right up your street, Conrad.'

'Some other time,' said Hall, refusing to be anything other than calm and unruffled. 'I'm sure there will be other, similar, opportunities within the next few weeks.'

Nyanga roared with laughter. 'My dear chap,' he said when he had finished chuckling, 'how right you are. How very right you are!'

Nyanga and Hall parted on good terms, but Nyanga knew very well why his partner in revolution had decided to absent himself from the fun and games. It was because Hall felt that the public torture and execution of a large number of Europeans was no encouragement to the remaining whites to stay in Balembi and look after the mines. Well, he was quite right about that, thought Nyanga. Tonight's demonstration would scare the shit out of the Euro-

211

peans – but it would also show them, in no uncertain terms, exactly who was boss.

Nyanga and Eileen Grey went upstairs to change for the evening's entertainment. As he watched Eileen slipping into a white satin knee-length dress, Nyanga wondered whether to tell her that her juicy young niece, Jane Stuart, had been caught by her husband Duncan out in the mountains. But no, he thought – she would find out soon enough the next day. Instead he gave Eileen's ample bosom a playful squeeze and encouraged her to be generous with the very expensive perfume which she was dabbing onto her neck.

Ten minutes later Nyanga came downstairs in a pale cream military uniform with black calf-length boots. On Eileen's advice he had reduced the number of medals on his chest, and as a result he looked truly magnificent. Together they set out in the white Rolls-Royce, with armoured cars provided by the army accompanying them fore and aft. Bulu and Yuri Semenov travelled separately.

As they approached the sports stadium the crowds in the streets grew thicker. Almost everyone carried a drum or a tin can or a whistle or a horn; they beat or blew or honked on anything they could find which would make a loud noise: the result was cacophony. Most of those in the streets were drunk or high on marijuana; without exception they were all members of the Fanda tribe, and the lowest-paid, least-educated members of the tribe at that. Nyanga was their god, and they worshipped him by creating as loud a din as they could.

A platoon of soldiers used their rifle butts and boots to batter and kick a way through the crowd for the Rolls to enter the stadium. And when the audience which was assembled inside the arena first saw Nyanga, he was greeted with a roar of hysterical applause which could be heard literally miles away. Fortunately the crowd was held back by barbed-wire fences seven feet high, with a row of trigger-happy soldiers standing beyond that, or they would undoubtedly have rushed forward to greet their saviour personally.

General Juba was in charge of arrangements inside the stadium, and a long platform had been built in the centre of the field; it was lit by four banks of floodlights high in each corner of the stands. Prior to Nyanga's arrival the crowd had been being entertained by a group of energetic dancers, mostly female, accompanied by more than a dozen drummers. The performers now hastily left the platform.

Joro Nyanga and Eileen Grey stepped forward and stood together in the focus of the spotlights, looking out into the darkness of the stands; they wallowed in the overwhelming roar of sound which came at them with an almost physical force from all sides. Nyanga waved and saluted in all directions, smiling broadly. As for Eileen – well, she almost writhed in the throes of the ecstasy which this adulation induced in her. With each outward breath she was making

212

small sounds of deep satisfaction. Her eyes blazed intensely; her jaw hung open, and she all but drooled as the saliva filled her mouth. Nearly one hundred men and women were to be killed in public tonight, and never in her life had Eileen Grey looked forward to anything quite so much.

But first there had to be a speech.

Nyanga understood that. If people were to appreciate anything properly, they had to be made to wait for it; they had to have time in which to recognize how badly they wanted to see it, time in which to understand exactly who it was that was providing this feast of revenge.

So there had to be a speech.

General Juba, sweating profusely, stepped forward to the microphone and checked to see if it was working. It wasn't, because naturally no European technician had come within two miles of the stadium all day. But after a moment or two, and some very nervous work on the part of a Fanda officer from the Regiment of Signallers, everything was ready. General Juba called for silence, and rather to his surprise obtained it fairly quickly. He then announced that the President would address the people.

Nyanga began to speak.

He announced first of all that tonight, as everyone knew, they had assembled here to see a hundred enemies of the state brought to justice – to see them meet the fate which all traitors richly deserved. Less than a week ago Balembi had been ruled by a tyrant, but now . . . etcetera, etcetera.

It was much the same speech as Nyanga had made on the previous Sunday night to the battalion which had attacked the palace, and it went down equally well. And while the speech was being delivered, officers of the army moved among the crowd handing out free bottles of whisky: this strengthened the already widely held view that Nyanga was a wise and capable leader who held the interests of his people close to his heart.

After ten minutes Nyanga was well into his stride, and the contents of forty-four cases of good-quality Scotch whisky were lining the stomachs of several thousand spectators. Nyanga was just at the point where he was singing the praises of those who had stood up against the tyrant Kasaboru, particularly those who had taken part in the never-to-be-forgotten attack on the palace, when out of the corner of his eye he saw someone walking across the open field towards him. A lone figure, brightly illuminated in the floodlights, easily visible from all sides.

It was someone in a lightweight suit.

A man with silvery-grey hair.

A white man, by God!

Nyanga nearly choked on his own eloquence. But he regained his concentration just in time, and carried on speaking, pretending not to notice.

In the meantime, the crowd buzzed with excitement.

The elderly white man reached the central dais. He came and stood directly in front of Nyanga, staring up at him without the slightest sign of fear. One or two of the soldiers looked towards General Juba for instructions. The General, in his turn, licked his lips and looked at Nyanga for a sign: was the white man a part of the act, or was he not? Should he be seized or shot down, or had Nyanga, for reasons best known to himself, arranged for him to be there? The General didn't know, and in the absence of clear orders, he sat still, paralysed by nervous indecision.

Now that the white man was standing directly in front of him, Nyanga could see who it was. It was the former Lord Chief Justice, George Morgan.

By God, thought Nyanga, someone is going to pay for this.

He went on speaking without missing a syllable, but his mind was no longer on the speech. How had George Morgan got in here? And what did he want? Someone's head was going to roll, Nyanga decided. Those god-damned soldiers had been too bloody busy chatting up the dancing girls to pay any attention to what was happening in the centre of the field. Why, thought Nyanga, this old man could have walked up and shot me without any trouble at all – and her; certainly looks as if he'd like to.

Nyanga cut short the rest of his speech and then stepped back to an enormous roar of appreciation. Once out of range of the microphone he gave orders for George Morgan to be arrested, and for the dancers to be brought back again to keep the crowd happy. Both orders were obeyed with the kind of speed which is generated by the knowledge that failure to obey instantly will lead to a slow and painful death.

Nyanga retreated into an area of shadow while the crowd devoted its attention to the glistening bodies of the near-naked dancing girls. Then he ordered George Morgan to be brought over to him.

The whistling, the yelling and the hooting of the crowd, coupled with the frantic amplified rhythms of the drums, were so loud that Nyanga could barely make himself heard. In the end he climbed into the back seat of his Rolls and signalled for George Morgan to be put into the car with him, held at gunpoint by an officer.

When at last the doors of the Rolls-Royce were shut and he could hear his own voice again, Nyanga sighed. 'Now then,' he said. 'What, precisely, is a former Lord Chief Justice of Balembi doing here tonight? This is no place for you, Morgan. And why did you come and stand in front of me like that? Staring at me like an angry schoolmaster.'

George Morgan licked his dry lips. 'I came to protest,' he said firmly. 'You said at the beginning of your speech that the crowd had come here tonight to see enemies of the people brought to justice. But what sort of justice are you talking about? Which laws of the land have been broken by the prisoners you have here tonight? And which court of law has found them guilty? Which judge has ruled that their penalty is death?'

Nyanga sighed again. 'Don't try your rhetoric on me, old man,' he said wearily. 'You're not addressing a church garden party now, you know. . . . The answer to your question is that the prisoners who are going to be executed tonight were found guilty in the court of rough justice – you know it and I know it, and that's the end of the matter.'

George Morgan's frame seemed to crumple. He suddenly looked a very old and exhausted man; his face was lined with weariness, and sweat stood out on his forehead. His journey through the streets to the stadium had been a terrifying nightmare, and he had escaped being pulled out of his car and torn to pieces only by saying that he had been invited to the executions by the President himself. That lie, together with sheer force of character, had carried him a long way tonight, but the strain was beginning to tell.

'But these executions are totally unjustified,' he continued. 'They are absolutely and unquestionably wrong. They should not be allowed to happen.'

Nyanga shrugged. 'Well, they are going to happen, and there is no way you can stop them. But, if it eases your conscience, at least you have made a protest. It makes not the slightest difference, but you have certainly had your say.'

Nyanga stared at the old man opposite him with something close to admiration. He knew better than most what a risk George Morgan had taken in coming to the stadium, what nerve and authority of manner it must have taken to bluff his way past the guards. Nyanga had always admired courage, and he could not help feeling impressed by this demonstration of it.

'By rights,' he said thoughtfully, 'I ought to have you shot, Mr Morgan. But because you are an old man, and no danger to anybody, I will send you home to bed instead. But let me tell you this. If you try to meddle in Balembian politics once more – just once more, that's all – I will have you killed without the slightest hesitation. Do you understand me?'

George Morgan nodded.

'Good.' Nyanga then looked directly at the officer holding a gun at the old man's head. 'Now – you. Take this gentleman away – and see that he arrives home safely.'

Half an hour later, after the dancers had thrashed themselves into an unparalleled state of frenzy bordering on trance, the ninety-seven prisoners were brought out and were paraded round the perimeter of the stadium, close to the barbed-wire fence. The crowd screamed and gestured obscenely at them, leaving them in no doubt at all about what their fate would be.

Most of the prisoners were Europeans, of whom about thirty were women. Their 'crimes' consisted mostly of having worked on President Kasaboru's staff, but some of them had done nothing worse than allow themselves to be caught out on the street at the wrong time. Several of the African prisoners had made their basic mistake many years earlier, by being born into the wrong tribe: while others were guilty of the sin of looking well-dressed and prosperous. Their offences, or lack of them, were scarcely relevant; the issue of whether they lived or died had been decided when they were arrested – decided, that is, entirely at random and on impulsive whim, as would be the manner of their dying.

Each prisoner was brought up on to the stage and was prodded into the limelight. His or her name was read out, together with details of the alleged offence. In a surprising number of cases, that seemed to consist of unspecified 'crimes against the state'; the officer in charge of this part of the proceedings did not have much imagination.

After that Bulu took control for the main business of the night; it was by then eleven p.m. Nyanga had put Bulu in charge of the killings because he had observed, over the years, that this hare-lipped moronic monster had a grisly talent for the job.

As an hors d'oeuvre Bulu stripped naked twelve white women. He had them chased round the track by men with bamboo canes; the crowd found this very entertaining. Eventually the women fell, panting and bleeding, unable to run any further, their throats raw from endless screaming. Then they were lifted and thrown bodily over the barbed-wire fence and into the crowd beyond. None of them lived for more than three minutes after that.

As a main course, between thirty and forty prisoners were beheaded one at a time. Bulu selected those who were to die in this way, picking a woman here, a man there. Two soldiers wielded axes on an improvised block, and the severed heads were impaled on spikes and paraded round the stadium; the following day they were exhibited in central Digara.

A few special prisoners were shot by Nyanga with his Tokarev pistol, after a little speech on their wickedness. Many others were beaten to death with iron bars, close to the perimeter fences, so that the crowd could get a better view. And one man, who made the mistake of cursing Bulu, was given the full treatment. Bulu cut off his hands, ears and tongue, and then hammered a wooden stake into his rectum. This took all of half an hour.

In the end there were only ten prisoners left, and after a whispered conference between Eileen Grey and Nyanga, it was announced that 'the President's Lady', as she was now known, would personally despatch the remainder; this information was greeted with rapturous applause. The prisoners were then forced to kneel down, facing the main stand.

Over the past few days, Eileen Grey had been having lessons in the use of the Tokarev pistol. She took it now from Nyanga, holding it with both hands to control the trembling of her fingers. Her dress was soaked with sweat in the pulsating, steamy heat; her body ran with rivulets of perspiration from the top of her scalp down to the soles of her feet. Her heart pounded fiercely – and yet she felt somehow fully integrated, entirely complete as a person. It was as if all her life had been a preparation for this moment, as if this were the natural culmination of everything she had ever wanted and worked for.

She shot each of the remaining victims through the back of the head, pausing once to reload the eight-shot magazine. And so appalled were the prisoners by the events of the night so far that none of them made the slightest attempt to escape, or even to move out of the way. They just waited patiently, glad that their end was to be quick.

Eileen killed them one by one, spattering their brains out onto the already blood-stained platform, leaving the bodies lying in forlorn and untidy heaps. And every time a shot rang out the crowd would cheer deliriously, and Eileen would wave to acknowledge her acclamation.

The roars of the crowd convinced Eileen that everyone assembled in the stadium worshipped her.

She loved it. She felt safe and secure at last. She felt as if she could go on killing people all night.

Fifteen

The President, together with Philip Morgan and Bob Fuller, spent Thursday night in a cave. They had made some progress towards the river Jarnoko on the latter part of Thursday afternoon and evening, but Philip had naturally been very slow to recover from his submersion in the flooded mountain stream; as a result they had stopped well before dark.

Now, after nine solid hours' sleep, Philip felt very much stronger. He constantly found himself thinking about Jane, and his facial expression reflected his deep concern for her safety. But he tried his hardest to put her out of his mind for the moment: Kelly Thompson would do the best he could for her, and in any case Philip's main task remained that of getting the President to Sungbarta.

The three men ate the last of the food they had brought with them from the army lorry the day before; then they picked up their guns and rucksacks and resumed their journey west.

They still had a hundred miles to go, which Philip found acutely depressing. Bob Fuller pointed out that every step they took reduced the distance a little, but unfortunately the other two did not seem very uplifted by that piece of information.

Philip's gloom was understandable in view of the loss of Jane, and the President was obviously deeply worried not only about that problem but also about the length of time it was taking them to cover relatively short distances. It was not until they had been walking for some time that the two of them recovered their normal spirits and could look at their situation objectively once again.

By nine o'clock they were well into the foot-hills on the western side of the Central Mountains, and there were plenty of trees about, which sheltered them pleasantly from the full heat of the sun; the atmosphere was clear and not too oppressive. Then, as they reached the brow of a hill, they suddenly saw the River Jarnoko in the distance for the first time. The view stretched for many miles from this point, but there wasn't a house or another human being to be seen anywhere.

As they approached the river Philip was reminded that in many ways the landscape of Balembi was exceptionally beautiful. The banks of the Jarnoko were lined with euphorbia trees, and the ground beneath them was a mass of brilliantly coloured flowers. Magnificent crested cranes rose up from the water's edge and flapped lazily away as they approached.

Once they reached the eastern bank of the river, after walking for several hours, they sat down with relief for a rest.

'Well,' said the President, 'in different circumstances this would be a very nice place to come for a picnic. It reminds me of the River Thames.'

'They don't have insects like this on the banks of the Thames,' said Philip grimly, as he was bitten for the umpteenth time. 'And it's not going to be as easy to hire a boat, either. Just what are we going to do about finding a vessel to sail in?'

The President smiled. 'Let's just sit here and wait,' he said calmly. 'There are plenty of people living around here – I know we can't see them, but they're not so very far away for all that. And in a quiet, primitive sort of way they're very astute businessmen. Here we are, sitting on the river bank, and it's obvious that we're looking for some sort of transport. And where there's a demand, eventually you get a supply. Let's just wait and see what turns up.'

They rested and waited for an hour – then an hour and a half. And by that time Philip and Bob were beginning to wonder whether the President's analysis of the situation was correct. But then, quite suddenly, a dug-out canoe appeared round a bend upstream. In it were two men dressed only in loin-cloths.

The canoeists drew level with the three travellers and paused; then the President addressed them in their own tongue. The others could not understand what he was saying, but the tone of his voice was obviously encouraging.

In a minute or two, after exchanging a few words with each other, the two men in the canoe brought their craft into the bank, pushing its nose through the pale blue water hyacinths. The President produced some money from the pocket of his jacket, and the two locals took it and walked quickly away. It was clear from their excited chatter that they felt they had done a damn good deal.

'There you are,' said the President triumphantly. 'One dug-out canoe, with paddles, tired travellers for the use of.'

'It doesn't look very stable,' said Bob Fuller doubtfully. 'Will it take all of us?'

'Of course,' said the President. 'Provided you sit still. Some of these dug-outs are sixty feet long, and they carry fifty men, so this one will take the three of us and our very limited baggage with no trouble at all.'

Wasting no time, they climbed gingerly into the canoe. Bob Fuller sat in the bow, the President in the centre, and Philip in the stern. The craft had been fashioned from a single heavy log, and its gunwale was only four inches above the surface of the water, so it needed careful balancing.

They had little idea how to get the best out of the canoe, and they found that if they tried to paddle at all hard they came close to turning it over; so for the most part they let the current carry them forward, using the paddles only to keep them in the faster-moving part of the stream. The river broadened out to half a mile wide in places, with thick forest on either side.

They floated down the river in this manner for nearly two hours. Apart from their nervousness about falling into the murky water, they felt as relaxed and comfortable as they had for a very long time. They kept their eyes open for settlements, as it was probably going to be advisable to go past such places on the far side, but for a long time they saw no signs of human habitation at all.

After about two hours, however, they spotted a landing-stage jutting out from the bank; tied up to it was a fair-sized ferry-boat. As soon as they saw it they pushed the canoe into the shelter of a tree overhanging the water to consider what they should do.

'Any idea what this place is?' Philip asked the President.

Kasaboru pored over the map. 'Well, it's probably a small village called Melonville. The ferry-boats stop here – or at least they do when they're running normally. I imagine the service is somewhat dislocated at present.'

'What do you think?' said Philip. 'Is it safe to go past? Or dare we try to find some food and try to get news of what's happening in the outside world?'

The President thought about it. 'Well,' he said eventually, 'Melonville is a smallish place even in normal times, or so I believe. I've never been here before. Just a few houses and a school, as far as I know. We could do worse than reconnoitre the place. I don't know about you, but my stomach is rumbling.'

Philip nodded. 'I'll go take a look then.'

The President raised an eyebrow at him. 'Are you sure you're feeling up to it?' he asked.

'Yes, I'm all right,' Philip insisted. 'I'd rather be on the move than sitting here, anyway. . . .' That part at least was true. 'I won't be long,' he added.

Philip scrambled up the bank and made his way cautiously through the forest towards Melonville. He went almost all the way round the village, keeping well under cover, and as far as he could see the place was completely deserted; not even a dog was moving. As the President had suggested, there were very few houses: only half a dozen wooden bungalows, one shop with living accommodation above it, and a larger one-storey building which was presumably a school serving the surrounding villages.

So, as there seemed to be no obvious dangers, Philip stepped out of the forest and advanced down the dusty main street. There was still no sign of life.

The shop had the name 'K. Whittaker' painted above its two display windows, and Philip went up the steps and pushed open the door.

A bell rang.

After a moment a curtain at the back of the shop was pushed aside and a white man moved forward; he had a revolver in his hand. The man was aged about thirty; he was fair-haired, with a beard to match, and he looked as if he knew how to take care of himself.

'Come forward slowly,' he said. 'And put your hands on the counter.'

Philip did as he was told.

In the next few minutes he also answered a large number of questions about who he was and what he wanted. He explained that he was on his way to Sungbarta with two companions; Digara had definitely got a bit too hot for them. He wanted food chiefly, and he could pay for it.

The questions went on for some time, but eventually the shop-keeper, who introduced himself as Keith Whittaker, was satisfied that Philip represented no threat to him.

'Sorry about the gun,' he said as he put it away, 'but you can't be too careful these days.'

'That's O.K.,' said Philip. 'I'd do the same myself in your shoes.'

With the preliminaries out of the way, Philip wasted no time in stocking up with as much tinned food as he thought they could reasonably carry. To be on the safe side, he also bought two can-openers and several knives. Whittaker explained that in more settled times his shop provided the surrounding villages with many basic items, such as pangas and other ironmongery, but that he did his most lucrative trade with tourists; the visitors came up-river on the ferry boat and then transferred to a bus to take them to a nearby hotel in a game park.

'But,' said Whittaker regretfully, 'when the shit hit the fan last Monday, all that came to a sudden halt. Not only the tourists left, but all the other Europeans as well. My wife and I are the only ones left.'

'What about the tribesmen round about?'

Whittaker shrugged. 'God knows what they're up to. There's been a lot of drumming these last few nights, but no-one's called on me for two days. The teacher's left, so the kids don't come to school. And when the ferry boat tied up yesterday the crew just disappeared into the bush.'

'Wasn't there a European in charge of it?'

'Was is the right word,' said Whittaker gravely. 'I've a feeling he's floating belly-up in the river right now.'

Philip spent another twenty minutes talking to Keith Whittaker.

221

He soon decided that the man had a great deal of guts and determination. Whittaker had been born and bred in Balembi, and he had built up his business in Melonville from virtually nothing; he was very reluctant to give it all up now, at the first hint of trouble. In any case, Whittaker's view was that Digara was undoubtedly ruled by Nyanga, and Sungbarta would very soon be attacked by Gabuti troops; so short of leaving the country entirely, there was nowhere to run to anyway. It was better, he felt, just to sit tight and wait for some degree of normality to return.

Philip tried to buy a radio, but unfortunately Whittaker only had one portable, which he was quite unwilling to sell. And there were none lying unwanted in the bungalows in the village either, Whittaker added; he'd had a look himself. The Europeans who had driven away in panic earlier in the week had taken their sources of information with them.

Philip did obtain one piece of good news, however: he learnt that Richard Chokwe, Kasaboru's Foreign Minister, had reached New York, and that the Balembi situation was due to be debated by the United Nations Security Council sometime within the next few days; Whittaker had heard that reported on the Voice of America news.

Eventually Philip got around to talking of boats. By that time he trusted Whittaker completely, though on the need-to-know principle he didn't mention the fact that one of his companions was President Kasaboru. He explained that at present he and his two friends were using a native dugout – was there anything a bit faster that Whittaker could sell him? A dinghy with an outboard motor would be ideal.

Whittaker scratched his head. Well, yes, he had a little boat – he had three as a matter of fact, he was keen on sailing. He named a price for a dinghy with an outboard fitted which was high, but Philip told him that if the craft passed an inspection he had a deal.

Together they went down to the jetty and Philip checked out the boat which Whittaker showed him. It was about ten feet long and ideal for their purposes: it was far from new, but it was well maintained. The outboard motor was a Seagull, which Philip knew to be a good make, though he was no sailor himself; the motor started with no trouble at all. What about fuel? Philip knew that the boat would need to go about fifty miles on the river, and together he and Whittaker worked out the amount of two-stroke mixture needed. Then the shopkeeper provided it in cans. He was not short of fuel at the moment: he sold petrol and paraffin from tanks at the back of his shop, and there was another petrol pump on the jetty for the ferry-boat.

Altogether Whittaker wanted five hundred pounds for the goods he was supplying; it was a high price, but since what he was selling might very well mean the difference between life and death, Philip did not haggle. He paid him in cash.

'What about guns?' said Whittaker as he folded the money and put it away in his pocket.

'Guns?' echoed Philip in surprise. 'You mean you've got some?'

'Sure. Come and look.'

Whittaker led the way back to his shop and took Philip to a curtained-off room at the rear. There, set out on the floor, was a small armoury: three Bren guns, four Stens, and a number of rifles and revolvers. Philip whistled.

'Guns are another interest of mine,' said Whittaker modestly. 'I was in the army for three years, and I used to be a Boy Scout, too – be prepared, you know? And after what happened in the Congo five years ago I decided I would be. I had friends living in the Congo in 1960, and they told me stories you wouldn't believe – so I made up my mind to be ready for any kind of trouble. And I am ready. My wife tends to keep out of the way of strangers these days – she spends most of her time upstairs. But I can look after her all right – and that's why I'm not afraid to stay.'

Philip was getting a bit worried about the time – his friends would be wondering what had happened to him – but he quickly selected some ammunition for the Sten guns and the Lee Enfield rifle which they already possessed. Then, at last, he had finished trading for one day.

With Whittaker's help Philip loaded up his new boat with the various items he had bought and then headed back upstream to collect his companions. They transferred from the dug-out with pleasure.

The news Philip brought back with him, about Richard Chokwe arriving in New York and the prospect of a United Nations debate on Balembi, gave them all a tremendous surge of hope. They realized, of course, that United Nations intervention would mean nothing if Nyanga were firmly in power; but if the President could reach Sungbarta, and if the UN were there to help, well, anything seemed possible. After that news, the cans of beer and the corned beef tasted better than ever.

When they were all well fed they started up the outboard motor and headed downstream again at a much improved rate. For safety's sake they passed the Melonville jetty on the far side, but Keith Whittaker watched them go through 8 × 30 binoculars. He was very curious to know what his customer's fellow travellers looked like; he wondered why they had not come into the village themselves. But when he saw the profile of the handsome African who was sitting in the bow of the boat, he understood the situation immediately – and he felt a tremendous surge of excitement and pride.

So President Kasaboru was still alive! In spite of everything. . . . And he was on his way to Sungbarta. Well, Keith Whittaker for one wished him well.

Whittaker turned away from the jetty and made his way back towards his shop. As he did so he looked down the long straight road which was the only route into the village; and in the distance he could see a growing cloud of dust. He put his binoculars to his eyes once more and saw that the dust was being raised by two army lorries, advancing along the road towards him.

Keith Whittaker's mouth set into a hard thin line. He knew perfectly well who was controlling the army these days, and he knew that they were no friends of Kasaboru's. Well, he decided, as far as he was concerned, he hadn't seen a soul all day.

Sixteen

On the morning of the day which found the President in Melonville, Dan Levene was awake soon after dawn.

His wife, Jennifer, had disturbed him by her restless movements in bed: she was never a good sleeper at the best of times, and this morning she claimed that she had been having a bad dream about the hospital fund-raising committee. Well, Jennifer Levene was on every second committee in the city, and it was always possible that some of them were giving her nightmares – but the Mayor doubted whether that was the true cause of this particular sleepless night. He thought it more likely that she was worrying about the future of her two young grandchildren, who were staying with the older Levenes while their parents helped to defend the city.

Whatever the cause, Dan Levene and his wife were both irreversibly awake long before their usual hour, so the Mayor decided to make the best of it. He shaved and dressed quickly and made his way downstairs for breakfast. Fortunately he managed to complete all this without waking his grandchildren.

As his wife served him a fried egg on toast, Levene slipped his arm round her comfortably plump hips and smiled at her reassuringly. But try as she might, Jennifer couldn't seem to smile back: somehow it just wasn't a smiling day.

Shortly afterwards Levene drove his Volkswagen to City Hall and surveyed the scene from his office on the fourteenth floor: the lake was completely deserted this morning, without so much as a ripple on its surface, but to the south there was a flurry of activity at the airport. Through binoculars Levene could see lines of troops filing out of the Gabuti transport planes; and standing on the runways there were already several tanks, numerous jeeps and some heavy artillery.

Levene sighed; he didn't feel much like smiling himself, now.

The Mayor's son, David Levene, woke up at about half past six. He reached over what he thought was the still sleeping body of his wife, to check the time by the alarm-clock on her side of the bed, only to find that in fact Sally was wide awake. She embraced her husband fiercely, pulling his body down on to hers, and for a moment she took him by surprise. He was startled by the strength of her kiss, and in contrast to their usual situation he found himself lagging behind her in sexual readiness.

However, David had never needed very much stimulation to prepare him for intercourse with his wife, and within a matter of moments they were locked firmly together. With no children about who might come in at an awkward moment there was nothing to inhibit them, and their love-making was prolonged and exceptionally passionate; afterwards they both felt exhilarated rather than exhausted.

They breakfasted normally, listening to the latest news on the radio, and it was not until they were clearing the table that they began to hear the whistle and crunch of mortars in the distance. The Gabuti troops were shelling the southern edge of the city.

David and Sally exchanged glances without speaking. They didn't need to say anything: they both knew that this time the attack on Sungbarta was in earnest.

A few minutes later they set off on their bicycles towards their respective destinations: David was going to the south road bridge, which was likely to be the centre of the day's fighting, and Sally was heading for the hospital again, to help nurse the wounded.

They cycled part of the way together and paused when they reached the crossroads where they were to go their separate ways. The sound of the shelling from the other side of the river was louder now, and smoke could be seen in the distance.

David kissed his wife goodbye. He noticed, not for the first time, what a good figure she had: she looked at least five years younger than her actual age, which was thirty. A slight breeze ruffled her long blonde hair, and he told her on impulse how much he loved her.

Sally smiled back, and paused before leaving him. 'David,' she said thoughtfully.

'Yes?'

Sally hesitated. 'Promise me something.'

'I will if I can,' he said with a grin.

'If anything happens to me, you will marry again, won't you?'

David Levene laughed. 'Well, what a thing to say!' he said in surprise. 'Nothing's going to happen to you – or to me, either.'

Sally's face was serious. 'No, well, perhaps not. We hope not, of course. But if anything did happen, just remember what I said.'

She looked so serious that David couldn't help being amused. But then, seeing how important it was to her, he nodded. 'All right,' he said. 'I'll remember.'

And with that, Sally Levene pushed down on her pedals and cycled rapidly away.

Her husband waited for a while before moving, watching her until she rounded a bend in the road. And for some strange reason, which he couldn't quite understand, he found that his vision was suddenly blurred with tears.

General Tchen, the commander-in-chief of the Gabuti army, was what the Belgians in the Congo called an évolué – an African who had made rapid progress up the social ladder from the most poverty-stricken background imaginable.

Tchen was thirty-six. After a minimal formal education he had joined the army at eighteen, and had eventually been promoted to the rank of sergeant, which at that time was as high as he could go without changing the colour of his skin. After five years as a sergeant, during which time he had continued to educate himself, Tchen had left the army and become a journalist; by that point he was a recognized expert on African history and on African politics generally.

Once out of the army, Tchen had joined the Gabuti Liberation Movement, and in due course he had become personal secretary to its leader. And when Gabuti was given independence, and the leader of the Movement became head of state, the former sergeant was overnight made Chief of Staff of the Gabuti army. This appointment had, needless to say, aroused the deepest scorn among the outgoing European bureaucrats, but in fact Tchen had proved himself fully capable of running the army at least as well as his white predecessor.

It was well known that Tchen now had considerable behind-the-scenes influence in the political life of Gabuti; it was rather less well known, because Tchen preferred it that way, that he had powerful political ambitions of his own. He was a communist, like all those in power in Gabuti, but he was not doctrinaire: he was a pragmatist and a realist, and there were some African observers who saw him as one of the truly great leaders of the future. And unlike most of his kind, Tchen was prepared to wait.

Physically, General Tchen was tall and heavily built; like many tall men he tended to slouch a little, despite his military training, but he was still an imposing figure in his immaculately neat uniform. He was short-sighted, and wore glasses with metal frames; they did not fit very well on his nose. He had prominent lips and was unusually black-skinned. He had a healthy appetite for women, and a number of beautiful 'personal assistants' invariably travelled with him wherever he went.

Towards eight a.m. Tchen decided it was time to apply some psychological pressure in addition to the mortar barrage. Consequently he telephoned the Mayor of the besieged city, and after a few preliminaries made what he felt were some sensible suggestions.

'Tell me, Mr Mayor,' he said 'You can see the airport from City Hall, I assume?'

'Yes,' said Levene.

'Well then, you will have observed that we have already brought in large numbers of troops and equipment, with more arriving hourly.'

'Yes, I can see that,' Levene admitted.

'While you, for your part, have only a handful of Balembi soldiers and a few old men and boys to man your barricades.'

'That is not the situation,' said Levene firmly. 'But go on.'

'Well then,' said the General amiably, 'it's very much a case of amateurs against professionals, and the result is a foregone conclusion. So what I want to suggest is this. You can go on defending your city for an hour or two – possibly even for a day or two – but there will be a tremendous amount of damage caused and no doubt a lot of casualties. And for what purpose? No purpose at all, because the outcome will be the same in the end, whether you resist or not – the city will fall to us. Don't you think that in the circumstances it would be a lot more sensible to come to terms with me now, before any great harm is done?'

'What sort of terms?' asked Levene warily.

'Oh, very simple. You just open the south road bridge to us, and I for my part will guarantee that when my troops enter the city there will be no violence, no looting or raping, no harm done to anyone. Just a peaceful transfer of power.'

'Sorry,' said Levene. 'But I can't accept that.'

'I think you ought to consider the consequences,' insisted Tchen politely. 'You see, if you resist, then inevitably a few of my soldiers are going to be wounded – possibly even killed. And that will annoy the rest of them, you see. And then when we finally do capture the city, as we're bound to before very long, there will obviously be some repercussions. I mean my men are bound to want a bit of their own back, aren't they? I will do my best to control them, of course. But you know what soldiers are.'

Yes, thought Levene, he knew what soldiers were, all right. He knew exactly what to expect when the Gabuti troops entered the city, and that was why he was not about to let them in without a fierce struggle.

'Sorry,' he said. 'No deal.' And he broke the connection.

General Tchen sighed as he put down the telephone; he genuinely felt rather sad. 'Such a nice city,' he said regretfully. 'Such a shame to have to spoil it. . . . Still, there we are. What will be, will be. Get me Nyanga now, please.'

A few minutes later the General was in telephone conversation with Joro Nyanga, who was still in Digara. He explained the latest position.

'The railway bridge has been blown,' said Tchen. 'It was destroyed by the Sungbartans late last night to prevent us attacking across it. That leaves the two road bridges. The north road bridge is on the far side of the river and is inaccessible without a great deal of trouble, so we're leaving that alone for the moment, and concentrating our forces on the south road bridge.'

'Do you think you can take that bridge without destroying it?' asked Nyanga. 'I'd prefer it not to be breached if possible.'

'We can take it in time, yes,' said Tchen. 'But it may be a little tricky. The Sungbartans will certainly have mined it, so that it can be destroyed if need be, though they too will try to avoid that if they possibly can – and they're certainly not ready to surrender yet. They seem to be prepared to defend with some determination.'

'Well then demoralise them,' said Nyanga promptly. 'Shell the European residential districts. Knock out the radio station to hamper their communications. Hit the schools and kill a few children. Is there a hospital?'

'Yes,' said Tchen. 'They've marked its roof with large red crosses.'

'That's thoughtful of them,' said Nyanga with a short laugh. 'Well, they're obviously going to need that hospital. So destroy it. Wipe it out completely – now.'

General Tchen gave the necessary orders; he was not a man to let a little thing like a hospital stand in the way of a victory. Half an hour later six MIG 19s took off from the airport; they were armed with napalm.

The six planes made one dummy run over the hospital, to get the feel of its location. Then they came in to attack. Again and again they swooped down to drop their deadly loads onto the totally undefended target, and time after time the great bursts of yellow flame and black smoke engulfed the hospital buildings. In twenty minutes the Sungbartans' only important medical centre was completely destroyed, and ninety-five per cent of the occupants of the buildings were killed; most of those who escaped were badly burnt.

David Levene, on duty at the south road bridge, saw what was happening, though to begin with he could not believe it. He noticed the planes' dummy run and assumed that they were just practising. Then, when he saw the first smoke go up, he thought that the pilot must have made a mistake – but eventually, when the planes came in time after time, he realised at last that the attack was both deliberate and merciless.

Once he accepted what was happening, David leapt onto his bicycle and pedalled frantically through the deserted streets; but by the time he arrived at the hospital, some distance away in the north-west corner of the city, the attack was all over.

The buildings, or what was left of them, continued to burn, the flames crackling and roaring in the stillness of the morning. There was little movement – only one or two survivors staggered about, unable to describe coherently what had happened to them.

It took David Levene two hours to find his wife's body. In the end he could only recognise her by the shoes on her feet, which by some fluke had escaped being enfolded in that particular gobbet of napalm. David knew the shoes well: he had repaired the heel of one of them only two days earlier, so he was in no doubt about Sally's identity.

For a long time after he discovered that Sally was dead, David Levene sat in the shade of an acacia tree in the hospital grounds, too stunned to move. The world suddenly seemed very unreal and distant. But gradually he recovered his senses.

Towards mid-day he cycled slowly back to his post at the south road bridge. When he arrived he found that a Russian-built T55 tank was parked on the opposite bank of the river. Its 100mm gun was pounding the defence positions on the Sungbarta side, smashing great holes in the nearby buildings. It was obviously going to be very difficult for the defenders to hold out much longer, but David made up his mind to play his own part to the full: after all, he still had two children to fight for.

Seventeen

Duncan Grey climbed down from the driver's seat of the army lorry into the main street of Melonville and wearily stretched his legs.

He was feeling extremely tired and depressed. The experience of Kelly Thompson crawling into his tent the previous night had scared him half to death, and he had not been able to sleep afterwards. Grey was not a courageous man by any standards, and he never took any risk which could conceivably be avoided. On this occasion it had only been his well-developed sense of self-preservation which had saved him: it was that which had ensured that he went to bed with a loaded revolver under his pillow, and it was sheer terror which had ensured that he lay completely still, and apparently asleep, while Kelly Thompson was cutting Jane free. And again, it had only been his strong instinct for survival, not coolness and nerve, which had caused him to shoot Thompson dead as he crawled out through the back of the tent. Grey's first impulse had been to let the dangerous intruder go, and good luck to him. But then he had realised that if Jane got away, and Nyanga ever found out about it, the new President was going to be very angry indeed; and it was that thought alone which had forced Grey, at the very last moment, to sit up in bed and fire the four fatal shots.

Even then, of course, Grey had been panic-stricken by the thought that the rest of the President's gang were all around the camp, armed to the teeth. And for several minutes after those four pistol shots had rung out, there had been total pandemonium. The soldier on guard had abruptly become aware that someone, some-where, was shooting – possibly at him – and he had begun to fire back at random into the darkness. Other soldiers had followed suit, and in the general chaos Jane had almost escaped. Almost, but not quite. She had tripped over a tree root on the edge of the camp, and a startled soldier had grabbed her as she fell on top of him. And once having felt how nice and warm and soft she was, he had not let go, and that had been that.

In the end, after about ten minutes, a sort of normality had returned to the camp. The shooting had ceased; Grey had decided, quite rightly, that the man he had shot in his tent had been making a rescue attempt on his own; and after an hour of recriminations and voluble discussion, everyone had finally settled down for the night once more. But by then, of course, so much adrenalin had been flowing that no-one had been able to relax at all, much less go to sleep – so Grey had had an exhausting night.

In the morning the promised helicopter had flown in, and Jane had been air-lifted out. Grey still felt a little bit upset about that decision: Jane had spat in his face as she was being dragged away, which didn't help. But he told himself that she would be no worse off in Digara than she would have been out here in the wilderness with the President and his friends – safer if anything. And once the helicopter had whirled away into the distance he had soon managed to put her out of his mind and had begun to concentrate on more important matters.

The soldiers had been forced to wait until nearly mid-day before the level of the flooded mountain stream had dropped to the point where his two lorries could just inch their way across; and then they had continued on their way to the river Jarnoko. The tribes living along the river bank, when suitably persuaded, had yielded the information that two white men and a Balembian had been seen going down-river in a dug-out canoe; this was highly encouraging. The tribesmen had also told Grey that a ferry-boat was tied up at the Melonville landing-stage; and sure enough, here it was.

Grey stretched his arms and yawned as he looked about him. Well, Melonville seemed to be a really creepy little hole: right in the middle of nowhere, and not a sign of life anywhere; a real dead-end of a dump.

Without wasting time Grey advanced single-mindedly on the ferry-boat and gingerly stepped on board. He knew that his delivery of Jane Stuart to Digara would please Nyanga enormously, but he was still under no illusions whatever about his own role: it was to capture the President, alive if possible. And if he failed to achieve that, then his own future would undoubtedly be seriously at risk. The best he could hope for would be to be found with a bullet in his head; the worst didn't even bear thinking about. And as the ferry-boat now seemed likely to be the key to the success of his mission, he examined it eagerly to see whether it was in working order.

Grey had never been any sort of a sailor, but some twenty years earlier he had had a week's holiday on a cruiser on the Norfolk Broads. The ferry-boat was about twice the size of a Broads boat, but probably, he thought, it wouldn't be much more difficult to handle. So far as he could remember, controlling a cruiser was much the same as driving a car, except that there weren't any brakes. Yes, he thought as he looked around, this shouldn't be any trouble at all.

He wondered idly what had become of the crew. They seemed to have disappeared into the bush – done a bunk, no doubt, like the rest of the inhabitants of Melonville. Well, he would just have to manage without them.

Grey spent twenty minutes checking over the ferry-boat, which was named *Miranda*. The keys were still in the ignition switch, and the controls seemed admirably simple. The engine worked when he switched it on, and the fuel gauge showed half-full. Grey went out on to the jetty and filled up the tank from the nearby pump, which he unlocked with another key on the ring he had found on board.

Towards the end of his survey of the *Miranda*, Grey's attention was momentarily distracted by the sound of angry voices raised from nearby. He couldn't see what the cause of the disturbance was, but there were shouts from what sounded like a European, and a series of screams in a shrill voice which was probably that of a woman. Then there was also a hubbub of babble in Balembian dialect, which undoubtedly came from the soldiers under his command, and after that there was silence once more.

Grey cursed under his breath. You couldn't leave those idle bloody soldiers on their own for two minutes without them getting into some sort of a scrape. Anyway, whatever the cause of it, the noise subsided fairly quickly, and Grey went on with his work without troubling himself any further. Corporal Avakubi was there, after all – and it was his job to see that the men behaved themselves.

Eventually, when he was satisfied that the *Miranda* was ready to pursue the President, Grey walked back into the main street to collect his men.

At first he couldn't find anyone. Then he noticed that the door of the village's one and only shop was ajar. He pushed it further open and went in; he could do with a drink himself.

The shop was empty, so he helped himself to a can of beer, opened it, and followed his nose into a store at the rear. Then, in the garden behind the shop, Grey found three of his men.

Like their superior officer, they were drinking beer, with a pile of replacement cans on the ground beside them. Grey watched them for a minute from a window. Every so often, when they had nothing better to do, the soldiers would kick the semi-conscious and badly beaten white man who was lying tied up at their feet; then they would have another drink of beer.

Grey sighed heavily. Over the last few days his shock threshold had risen considerably, and he was no longer the least bit surprised or put out by scenes such as this. However, he wandered out into the garden and enquired what was going on.

Sheepishly, with much waving of hands and multiple assurances that none of it had anything to do with them, the soldiers explained that Corporal Avakubi and a number of others had gone into the shop to buy food. The shopkeeper had accused them of stealing, which was, of course, a complete misunderstanding. And then, horror of horrors, the shopkeeper had tried to order them out with a gun. Well, naturally, Corporal Avakubi, in the interests of peace and good order, had been forced to disarm and subdue this aggressive and violent individual. The good name of the army had been impugned, and obviously that could not be tolerated. That was the gist of the story, anyway.

Grey listened to this unlikely tale without comment, patiently drinking his beer. At the end of it he asked where Corporal Avakubi was now – and where were the rest of the men?

The three soldiers in the garden exchanged leers and salacious grins. Well, actually, they thought Corporal Avakubi was probably upstairs, above the shop, taking care of the shopkeeper's wife. She had become hysterical and abusive, and Corporal Avakubi had been forced to calm her down, etcetera, etcetera.

Oh, thought Grey.

He glanced at the upstairs windows of the house; the windows were all shut, but for a moment he saw a black face at one of them, looking down at him. The expression on that face was so filled with lust and cruelty that when he first saw it Grey's mouth opened a fraction and he took a sudden step backwards; the man above broke into a smile when he saw the Major's reaction.

Grey swallowed hard. Shit, he thought. That's really going to slow things up.

He went back into the shop and found himself a tin of ham. He was hungry. He opened the tin and ate greedily with trembling fingers, making crumbly sandwiches with a packet of cream crackers.

After the ham he had a tin of fruit; the syrup was unusually sweet. Upstairs, above him, he could hear boots clumping around on the floor and the sound of bedsprings squeaking, but he pretended not to notice.

Eventually, after he had satisfied his hunger, Grey could think of no further justification for delay. He realised that he was going to have to go upstairs and get his men onto the boat. He had a vague nagging feeling that he ought to have taken this step earlier, but he was, he told himself, a realist in these matters. Balembi was at war, and in wars people got hurt. And soldiers, who lived under constant stress, needed relaxation. All that was natural, and inevitable, and a good officer had to take these things into account. But there were limits, after all, and enough was enough.

With his heart pounding furiously against his ribs, Grey went slowly up the stairs to talk to his men.

In one of the bedrooms he found the shopkeeper's wife stretched out naked on the bed. Her flesh seemed unusually pale and she was fat, with heavy white thighs. Four soldiers were holding her down, one at each limb. A fifth soldier lay on top of her, his hips moving briskly; three others stood waiting their turn.

None of the men paid much attention to Duncan Grey when he entered the room, and certainly none of them showed any sign of abandoning their activity. Only Brenda Whittaker's eyes moved. A pair of her husband's socks had been stuffed into her mouth to prevent her screaming, but her eyes said everything for her: they bulged with pain and horror, shining intensely at Duncan Grey out of her sweat-soaked face.

Major Grey took in the scene with one glance. It was appalling, and yet, in some mysterious way, quite acceptable.

'Avakubi,' he said.

The Corporal condescended to raise his eyes from the far side of the bed.

'Yes, Major?'

'I want you and your men out on the ferry-boat in ten minutes' time,' said Grey, in a tone of voice which brooked no disagreement. Then he turned on his heel and went back down the stairs. Behind him he could hear the active soldier grunting and snorting as he came to the end of his efforts.

Not ten minutes later, but three-quarters of an hour later, Duncan Grey had managed to load one of his two lorries onto the ferry-boat. He had also transferred all the essential gear from the other lorry, which he was abandoning to its fate in Melonville. And finally he had managed to assemble on board Corporal Avakubi, who was looking very pleased with life, and four of the other nine men.

That left five men unaccounted for, but neither Grey nor Avakubi could find them. Grey suspected that they were hiding somewhere in the surrounding forest, waiting for him to depart so that they could renew their attentions to Mrs Whittaker. But damn it, there was nothing he could do about that. He couldn't force the men to come out of the forest, and he couldn't afford to wait any longer – the need to catch up with the President was far too urgent for that. So in the end he cut his losses and cast off from the landing-stage.

The Major was aware, in the back of his mind, that by taking this action he was quite probably sentencing the Whittakers to death. He hadn't even bothered to see that Keith Whittaker was untied. But he decided that he simply didn't care. He was constantly having to decide between priorities, and his chief priority now was to run down the President and his two companions. That was the overriding aim, and the fate of a couple of civilians was not going to distract him from that, not for one moment.

Grey guided the *Miranda* out into midstream, taking his time over getting the feel of the controls. He performed a few turns and other manoeuvres, and then, when he felt certain that he knew how the craft responded, he opened up the engine and went full ahead downstream.

So far as Grey could estimate, from what he had been told earlier that morning by the riverside villagers, the President had about a two-hour lead. But Grey now felt fairly confident that before night-fall he would succeed in catching him up. And who could tell what that might mean? If he succeeded in capturing Kasaboru, Nyanga might even promote him. Major Grey began to whistle.

The President and his companions, for their part, were also feeling a great deal more confident than they had been for some time.

At long last they were moving really quickly. They were not thrashing the outboard motor to death – they wanted it to carry them fifty miles – but they were skimming comfortably over the water with the breeze cooling their faces, and they felt well fed and relaxed from the beer. They had guns, ammunition, maps, and compasses. They knew where they were, and where they were going. They had heard from Keith Whittaker that the situation in Balembi was going to be debated in the United Nations, and they were blissfully unaware that their pursuers had taken over the ferry-boat and were following quickly in their wake. The only major problem in their minds was what had happened to Jane, but they knew that Kelly Thompson was a disciplined and tough profession-al, and they were quite convinced that if anyone could save her, he would.

The President turned and smiled at his two companions. 'You know,' he said, 'in spite of all we have been through, and in spite of the fact that we still have a long way to go, I am beginning to think that we shall be successful after all.'

Eighteen

The MI-4 helicopter carrying Jane Stuart to Digara took an hour to complete the journey. Jane lay on the floor, tied hand and foot, shivering in the bitter draughts from the half-open door.

On arrival at a military aerodrome just outside Digara, Jane was transferred to a police van which carried her to Digara prison. There she was delivered into the care of two heavily built black policewomen; these two untied her feet and frog-marched her unceremoniously downstairs, into a room with no natural light. This was the room in which Joseph Uvira and several colleagues had been killed earlier in the week; Jane did not know that, but she could see that there were bloodstains on the stone walls and floor, and the room had an unmistakable aura of death about it.

Once they were all inside the room, the two Fanda policewomen sat Jane firmly down on a wooden straight-backed chair and tied her arms and legs to it. Then they stepped back and passively awaited developments; neither of them had so far said a word.

Both the policewomen were in their early twenties; they had an abundance of frizzy hair, brushed out in all directions, and their caps were perched rather ridiculously and insecurely on top. Both women were wearing markedly ill-fitting uniforms and they seemed very unsure of themselves and ill at ease. Jane wondered if they had been appointed since Nyanga's take-over; if so they had presumably been chosen for their race and muscular development rather than for their intelligence.

Half an hour passed, and then Yuri Semenov came into the room, accompanied by the hare-lipped Bulu. Jane had never seen either of these men before, but she could not help shuddering as soon as they arrived. Bulu, with his deformed mouth, was a stomach-turning sight in any circumstances; and Semenov, with his expressionless Oriental features, seemed cold and unfeeling. It was unlikely, Jane felt, that either of them was going to help her in any way. The two policewomen sensed what kind of men they were too: they glanced at each other apprehensively, and almost immediately shuffled over to a far corner of the room, well out of the way.

Bulu grinned widely when he saw Jane. He made some gleeful remark to Semenov which Jane could not catch. Then he advanced towards her and immediately began to fondle her breasts. He leaned over her, breathing heavily and noisily, his tongue flicking in and out with pleasure; his hands were large and brutal.

After a few moments Bulu grew tired of feeling Jane's flesh through the material of her khaki blouse, and he began to fumble with her buttons to undo them. But Semenov spoke to him sharply, and Bulu, very reluctantly, abandoned that particular activity. He moved away, grumbling angrily, and turned his attentions to the better-looking of the two policewomen: for the next few minutes the girl stood petrified on the spot, her eyes glazed with fear, while Bulu groped clumsily inside her uniform.

Five minutes passed.

Semenov smoked a cigarette, ignoring his companion's activities; occasionally he glanced at Jane, as if observing her reactions, but for most of the time his thoughts seemed to be elsewhere.

After another five minutes the door opened again, and Conrad Hall and Joro Nyanga came in. Nyanga took one look at what Bulu was doing and ordered him to behave himself; Bulu did as he was told, looking distinctly crestfallen. Then Nyanga came round in front of Jane and sat down on a table to have a look at her. In spite of staying up until the early hours of the morning supervising the executions at the sports stadium, he looked rested and completely relaxed, as if he had achieved everything he could possibly desire.

'Well now, Miss Stuart,' he said amiably, 'or Doctor Stuart, I suppose I should call you. How very nice to see you again. How are you feeling this morning?'

Jane didn't answer; she kept her eyes on the floor.

'You look a bit tired, if I may say so,' Nyanga continued. 'Well, that's understandable. You'll have walked quite a long way these last few days – all to no purpose of course – so you're bound to feel a bit footsore and depressed. Anyway, that's all over now – you're back here in civilization, with us.'

Nyanga paused and glanced briefly at Conrad Hall, who was staring at Jane with a more than fatherly interest, his eyes gleaming. Nyanga seemed slightly amused by Hall's attitude, but he carried on without reference to it. He slid off the table and began to pace restlessly around the room.

'I had a word with your uncle, Duncan Grey, earlier on this morning. He was most concerned that we should treat you properly – didn't want you to be molested, he said. And naturally I'm going to give his views the unlimited respect they deserve – so let me tell you exactly what the alternatives are. . . . Now then – if you show that you're willing to help us, we might just let you stay in prison for a week or two and then deport you as an undesirable alien. On the other hand, if you're stubborn and stupid, then I shall feel inclined to hand you over to that handsome fellow over there by the wall – Bulu his name is. . . . You ought to know about Bulu, Doctor Stuart. Bulu has had a white woman for breakfast every day since the revolution began. Yesterday he had one who lasted for all of ten hours – he cut out her tongue, shaved her head, sliced off her ears, and generally amused himself no end. And I'm quite certain that he would just love to get his hands on you. Isn't that so, Bulu?'

Bulu nodded vigorously and sniggered with an obscenely ugly grin.

Nyanga came and stood directly in front of Jane, his feet about eighteen inches apart, his arms folded across his chest.

'Now – we know that there were five of you in Kasaboru's party, because you were observed and counted when you were crossing the desert. However, you yourself have been captured, the man Thompson has been shot dead, and so that leaves only three. Kasaboru, Morgan, and presumably Fuller. Is he the third one?'

Jane again said nothing.

'Well, it really doesn't matter. But there are three of them, anyway. And what I want to know is, where exactly do they think they're going?'

He paused, giving Jane an opportunity to speak, but for the third time she remained silent.

'No? Well, it's pretty obvious what they're up to – they're heading west, towards the River Jarnoko. And when they get there they're going to make their way downstream as far as they can, and then they're going to cut across country again to Sungbarta.'

Nyanga waved his hands in the air to indicate what he felt to be the futility of it all.

'What a waste of time and effort! It's really quite extraordinary. There are a lot of very angry tribesmen in that area, and your friends will probably get cut to pieces long before they reach Sungbarta. Even if they survive they won't be able to do anything except surrender when they get there. . . . However, let's not worry about that – that's strictly their problem. All I want from you is confirmation that my diagnosis is correct. Now surely that's not much to ask for in return for your life?'

He paused again. 'Well, Dr Stuart, what do you say? Am I right, or have your friends got some other plan?'

Jane made an effort of will and looked up at the man. He frightened her by his very presence in the room, and to look him in the eye was almost more than she could manage – but she knew that she had to do it.

'I haven't got anything to say to you, Nyanga,' she told him. 'Not now, or at any time in the future.'

Nyanga seemed genuinely disappointed, but he made a game of it. 'Oh dear,' he said, pulling a long face. 'I am sorry to hear that.' He sighed and turned to Conrad Hall, who was standing beside him. 'Well, Conrad – what do you think we should do with this unco-operative little bitch?'

Hall's expression was vicious; his eyes narrowed. 'Chop her up and feed her to the pigs,' he said callously. 'That's all she's fit for.'

Nyanga grinned. 'Well, maybe we will,' he said thoughtfully. 'Maybe we will at that.' Then he addressed Hall and Semenov together. 'I tell you what, you two go back to the car, and take Bulu with you. I'll join you in a moment.'

Hall and Semenov, with a quick glance at each other, immediately left the room; Bulu followed them. Nyanga then went over to the two policewomen and whispered to them for some time, glancing occasionally at his watch. Finally he too went out of the room and closed the door behind him.

After Nyanga left, the two policewomen locked Jane into a cell. She was given water and two slices of hard bread; they were far from appetizing, but she ate them thankfully.

The cell itself was filthy: the mattress on the narrow iron bedstead was stained and smelly, and there were insects crawling all over the floor. Normally Jane would have found it all completely repellent, but for the moment she was just too exhausted to care. She lay down on the bed and tried to think.

She wondered what had happened to Philip and the others. The night before, when Kelly Thompson had crawled into her tent, she had assumed for one delirious moment that Philip would be there with him, ready to rescue her. But obviously, in view of what had happened afterwards, he had not been there at all. Presumably he and the President and Bob Fuller had pressed on quickly towards Sungbarta – well, in the circumstances that was the right thing to do, and she felt no bitterness or sense of betrayal. The problem was, what could she do now – both to help herself and the President? She closed her eyes to help herself to think, but almost immediately she fell into a deep sleep which was close to unconsciousness.

Jane lost track of time. She slept or dozed for many hours, over-whelmed by total exhaustion. Later in the day the policewomen brought her another meal, and then she slept again.

Later still, the policewomen returned once more. This time they took Jane along the corridor to a shower-room. They watched her warily, with truncheons in their hands, while she stood under the almost painfully hot stream of water; they seemed to be worried that she was going to attack them, but for the present at least Jane hadn't the energy even to think of trying to escape.

When Jane came out of the shower the policewomen gave her an enormous blue towel and a comb, and after she had finished drying herself and tidying her hair they seemed pleased with the overall effect. They handed her a coarse prison dressing-gown in place of her clothes, and then took her back along the corridor.

This time they put her in a different cell, larger and much cleaner than the first, though still without any natural light. Inside the room, two iron bedsteads had been pushed together, and a brand-new double mattress had been placed on top of them. Jane's heart sank when she saw this arrangement: she doubted somehow that the mattress had been provided entirely for her own benefit.

At this stage the two policewomen demanded the return of the dressing-gown, and one of them gave Jane a painful crack on the elbow with her truncheon when she was slow in removing it. Then they ordered her to lie down naked on the bed, flat on her back, and they handcuffed her wrists together to the frame of the bedstead above her head. The position was uncomfortable but not intolerable: she could turn on either side or onto her stomach, and at least the temperature in the room was such that she wasn't at all cold.

With their work apparently complete, the policewomen went away, and Jane fell asleep once more.

She was awakened some time later by the sound of a key in the cell door. She tried to sit up, but immediately realized that she was still handcuffed to the bed.

After a moment the door swung open and Joro Nyanga entered; he immediately closed the door behind him and locked it again. Then he walked forward in a leisurely, relaxed manner and stood at the end of the bed, his hands on his hips. He stared down at Jane's naked body, an amused expression on his face.

To her great dismay Jane blushed crimson: she simply couldn't help herself. The trouble was, there was nothing at all she could do to cover her nudity: her hands were restrained, there wasn't an inch of covering anywhere on the bed, and the best she could manage was to bend her knees and bring her heels up into her groin. Then she turned her head and hid her face in the crook of her arm; the light in the ceiling above suddenly seemed intensely bright, and she closed her eyes against it.

Nyanga laughed quietly at her discomfiture. He was wearing a khaki military uniform tonight, and he carried a short sergeant-major's swagger-stick under his arm. He took hold of the stick and struck Jane smartly across the tops of her thighs, leaving deep red weals; he struck her several times, until with a gasp of pain she gave in and lowered her knees.

'That's better,' said Nyanga happily. 'That's much better.'

Nyanga then proceeded to take off his own clothes; he laid them carefully on a chair beside the bed. He seemed well pleased with himself and hummed loudly as he undressed.

Jane bit her lip to stop herself groaning. She knew exactly what was going to happen next and she also knew that there was nothing whatever she could do to prevent it. Her feet were not tied up, and in theory she could try to kick out and protect herself – but what would happen if she did? Nyanga would merely have her roped to the bed, or else he would beat her unconscious, and either way he would succeed in satisfying his obvious desires. Jane certainly wasn't going to give Nyanga any encouragement, but there didn't seem to be much point in getting herself beaten up for no good purpose; so she decided to simply lie still and do nothing.

Nyanga finished undressing and turned around. Despite herself, Jane could not help looking at him. He had a heavily muscled torso and powerfully built thighs, and he obviously kept himself fit. Strangely enough, there seemed to be no hair on his body anywhere: the black skin was perfectly smooth, even around the unusually large genitals.

No doubt anticipating that Jane was not going to be a very co-operative partner, Nyanga had brought his own sexual lubricant with him; he now came and stood very close to the bed, massaging the colourless jelly on to his enormous erect penis. Jane turned her head away.

Without further ado Nyanga climbed on top of her. He put a knee in between her legs and forced them apart; then he entered her body roughly and made a series of violent strokes. Despite the lubricant, he was so big, and Jane was so unprepared for him, that she cried out with pain, her face contorted in distress. Nyanga took not the slightest notice.

His weight came down heavily on top of her and he began to ram himself deeper and deeper into her, setting up a powerful and regular rhythm. He went on and on thrusting for a very long time, until Jane felt that she couldn't possibly stand it for even another second – and then, at last, after a succession of even more rapid and painful thrusts, Nyanga seemed to collapse in a panting and sweating heap. His body crushed her so that she could hardly breathe.

Nyanga slept for a while, without withdrawing from her. Then he roused himself and began to repeat the process; all Jane could do was try to minimize the discomfort as much as possible, but she was so sore by now that he hurt her however she lay. The second climax seemed to take even longer than the first, and they both began to run with sweat – but eventually, when it was all over, Nyanga lay down on his back beside her and drifted off to sleep again. Jane hoped that this time he would stay asleep for some hours.

But it was not to be. After a few minutes Nyanga began pawing at her yet again, and almost immediately he turned her over and began to mount her from behind.

When she was first captured Jane had made up her mind that whatever happened she would not beg for mercy – but the thought of the agony involved in what Nyanga intended to do to her now was so appalling that she almost broke her own rule. However, instead of breaking down and pleading with him she used her intelligence instead – and when she felt Nyanga begin his urgent proddings around her buttocks she lifted her hips and manoeuvred herself so that he slipped easily and immediately into her vagina. This was still very uncomfortable, but it could have been a great deal worse.

Fortunately Nyanga didn't seem to care one way or the other: he just grunted and shoved and heaved in his usual boorish manner. He cupped his hands over her breasts and slammed her around the bed so hard that at times he almost knocked the breath out of her. And as he approached his third and apparently most intense orgasm, Nyanga's teeth closed around the flesh between Jane's right shoulder and her neck; he bit her long and hard, until Jane screamed and twisted in agony, and Nyanga shuddered and groaned as the gouts of sperm gushed out of him. She could feel him violently throbbing within her.

In the morning, or what Jane took to be the morning, Nyanga dressed and left the cell without so much as a word.

Nineteen

The Gabuti army's attack on the south road bridge into Sungbarta had ended at dusk on Friday.

It began again at dawn the following morning.

David Levene spent the entire night behind the barricades. It was an uneventful few hours and he got plenty of opportunity to sleep, but he thought he might as well be there as at home. His wife had been killed, and his two young children were being well looked after by their grandmother, so there was no reason for him to be anywhere else but here.

For the time being David felt calm and fully in control of himself – but he knew that this feeling would not last for ever. He was aware that sooner or later an appalling sense of shock would catch up with him: he would feel anger, bitterness and despair; the world would suddenly seem totally unjust and cruel, and life would begin to seem empty and meaningless; he would probably want to die himself. But for the present he felt none of those things: he knew that he was not the only one to have suffered grievously in yesterday's bombing, and while that was no real comfort it did at least help him to see the situation in perspective. Mourning could wait, and in the meantime there was a job to do.

At dawn on Saturday the MIG 19s returned and strafed the Sungbartan defence positions around the south road bridge. By that time, however, the defenders were well bedded down, and the attack hardly disturbed them at all. Under the skilled guidance of Colonel Smith, the most senior of the Balembian army officers who were within the city limits, the defenders had set up a series of barricades; they had also made good use of the many commercial buildings placed strategically around the north end of the bridge. As a result their machine guns could now rake the full length of the bridge without hindrance, and one burnt-out T55 tank was already testimony to the effectiveness of their anti-tank weapons. The tank had been knocked out in the middle of Friday morning, and the Gabutis had not tried to cross the bridge since then; they were afraid of blocking it with their own dead armour. For the moment they simply contented themselves with shelling the Sungbartan positions, non-stop.

Half an hour after dawn, the MIGs climbed away into the sky to return to base, and David Levene helped to attend to the casualties who were inevitably left behind them. Now that the hospital had been destroyed, the wounded had to be despatched to the city's new medical centre, which had been set up in a small private nursing-home.

A few minutes later there was an outbreak of heavy rifle and submachine-gun fire from behind the Sungbartan lines, and after a short period of confusion it became clear that the defenders were being attacked from the rear by a small force of Gabuti troops; there appeared to be about a dozen of these men, and they had apparently crossed the river under cover of darkness. Fortunately their attack had been badly timed, as the cannon-fire from the MIGs had already put everyone very much on the alert; but even so, the invaders were able to cause far more trouble than their numbers justified because the defenders were not very well protected in their rear; they had assumed that that sector at least was secure.

At first David Levene was pinned down by the Gabuti rifle fire, but after five minutes there was a lull in the shooting; he took advantage of it to scuttle ten yards into the doorway of a nearby block of offices. David smashed a pane of glass in the door to get in, and then made his way rapidly up the stairs to the sixth floor; the building was deserted.

Once he had reached the height he wanted, he peered carefully out of a window. Sure enough, he now had an excellent view of the Gabuti attacking force; they were spread out in their camouflaged uniforms behind whatever cover they could find at ground level. Quietly he slid open the window; he poked the barrel of his rifle through, and before the attackers realized what was happening he had picked off two of them and was aiming at a third.

Then he was spotted, and a burst of automatic-rifle fire thudded into the outside wall, shattering his window into a million fragments. David moved along the corridor to another room; there he repeated his earlier tactic, this time shooting straight through the glass. As a result one more Gabuti soldier sprawled motionless in the street, and again there was an answering burst of angry fire from below. But this time, from the shouts and the sound of two hand-grenade explosions, David knew that his fellow defenders at street-level were gaining the upper hand.

Sure enough, when he sneaked a look out of a third window, on the fifth floor this time, he saw that at least six of the enemy were now lying dead or wounded and a number of others had their hands in the air. That particular emergency was clearly over.

David Levene went slowly back downstairs. He felt no emotion at all: no exhilaration, no distress. He had simply been doing a job.

He left the office building by a rear door, thus putting the whole width of the block between him and the Gabuti army: this area was comparatively safe, as the troops on the other side of the river could not fire directly into it.

As he came out of the building David discovered that two of the surviving Gabuti troops had been dragged into this street by some of the more hot-blooded Sungbartan 'irregulars'. One soldier had been battered unconscious and another was spread-eagled on his back on the pavement: four hefty young men were holding him down, and a fifth was unfolding a clasp knife.

As David approached, the fifth man knelt down and unzipped the black soldier's trousers. It was obvious to everyone present that he intended to return with interest some of the brutality which had been inflicted on the European population of Balembi during the last few days. It was particularly obvious to the soldier on the ground, who let out a shrill scream of terror and began heaving and kicking frantically in his attempts to get away.

Whether the white man really did intend to carry out his proposed mutilation of the soldier David didn't know – and he didn't wait to find out. He just stepped forward and kicked the knife swiftly out of the young man's hand. The boy yelped with pain.

'That's enough,' said David sharply. 'Let him up.'

The five young men looked up at David Levene in surprise, and he took stock of them. He guessed that they were probably sixth-formers from the local grammar school; they were perhaps eighteen years old, but fully grown and heavily built. To them war still had a certain amount of glamour.

'That's enough,' David repeated. 'He's a prisoner now, so treat him correctly. There's a procedure laid down for dealing with pris-oners – don't you know what it is?'

The young men glanced at each other. 'Yes,' said one of them sheepishly. 'They're to be taken to the city jail.'

'Right then,' said David curtly. 'Two of you do it – and the rest of you get back to your posts.'

There was a moment's pause while they thought about it; and then, slowly, the young men pulled the prisoner to his feet.

The Sungbarta City Council convened at eight a.m.

The Councillors had decided to meet daily during the emergency to review the latest situation. Each Councillor had been made re-sponsible for one aspect of the city's welfare and each reported in turn on the latest developments in his field. The news was not at all good.

The previous day had seen a ceaseless bombardment of the area around the south road bridge; other parts of the city had also suffered, and something very close to panic had been created among large numbers of the population. Food was short and there had been some looting and hoarding. The city's water-pumping plant had been bombed and supplies of drinking water were now very limited; the lake, of course, offered an inexhaustible source of fresh water, but distributing it was not an easy matter.

The deteriorating situation had prompted a number of citizens to try to escape across the lake by boat, but a company of Gabuti troops seemed to have been deputed to block that particular bolt-hole: any craft rash enough to set out from the shore had rapidly been machine-gunned into matchwood, and a number of bodies had been recovered.

During the night the random bombardment of the residential districts had continued; this had severely damaged morale, as Nyanga had predicted it would. Already many of the Councillors had had neighbours or members of their own families killed or wounded by shrapnel. And the Mayor himself, of course, had lost a daughter-in-law in the merciless bombing of the hospital.

Dan Levene winced with distress as he thought once more about the death of his son's wife. He had not yet been able to bring himself to break the news to his two grandchildren, but they would have to be told today. It was not a task he was looking forward to, and he found himself wondering how best to tackle it. But then he realised that one of the Councillors had asked him a question, and with an effort of will he dragged his mind back to the discussion in hand.

For twenty minutes or so it had been clear that what the Council was really discussing was whether or not the city should surrender; and it was time now to bring that discussion to a close.

Levene glanced around, looking for two speakers to summarize the opposing points of view, and his eye was caught by Councillor Gregg, halfway down the table on the right. Levene nodded. 'Mr Gregg,' he said, and the Councillor began to explain what he thought should be done.

John Gregg was in his early fifties. He was a printer by trade, and a prominent churchman in his spare time. Today he was grey-faced; he looked emotionally shattered, as well he might, because on the previous day his wife had been killed and his young daughter had had both her legs blown off; she was not expected to live.

Gregg spoke quietly and rationally. He had always had the respect of the other Councillors, and today he impressed them more than ever. He started by summarizing briefly the disasters which had already befallen the city. He estimated the total casualties to date, and the number of people likely to be killed or wounded as the struggle went on, together with the city's capacity for giving them appropriate care. The two numbers did not match up: before long the wounded would be getting no professional medical help at all. Gregg argued that on the basis of these figures, there was every reason for seeking a negotiated peace immediately. Whether the Sungbartans liked it or not, Nyanga was now the de facto President of Balembi – and they would have to come to terms with him sooner or later. The city could not, on the most optimistic estimate, hold out for more than a week; and since the final outcome was inevitable, surely it made sense to acknowledge Nyanga's rule now, while there were still some buildings left standing and some citizens left alive to inhabit them.

Despite himself, Levene had to admit that Gregg had put forward a powerful case; it was all the more impressive because he had avoided all reference to the tragedies he had experienced himself.

Levene's eyes now sought a speaker to put forward an opposing view, and he found the city's best dentist, Tom Jardine, ready and waiting. Levene nodded his permission to speak.

'Mr Chairman,' said Jardine, 'I would like to congratulate Mr Gregg on the restraint he has shown in stating his opinion. The sacrifices which will have to be made if we fight on are undeniable, and if anything Mr Gregg has understated them.'

There were nods of agreement from around the table. 'The cost of continuing to fight will be great,' Jardine went on, 'and the prospect of negotiating a ceasefire – of surrendering, in other words – therefore has certain attractions. But let us be clear about one thing, ladies and gentlemen. If we surrender, we allow the Gabuti troops into this city without let or hindrance. In effect, we give them the freedom of the city. And let us not have any doubt what that means. It means anarchy – it means looting, rape and murder on a very wide scale, because no-one can control those soldiers – not their officers, not Nyanga, and certainly not any of us here. In the days immediately following a surrender no-one would be safe, whatever the colour of their skin, because we have already fought back – and they will not easily forgive us for that.'

Jardine paused and extracted some notes from a folder in front of him.

'Now – let me refer you to events in the Congo some five years ago. . . . On 11 July 1960, the Congolese government asked for United Nations assistance. On 14 July the Security Council met and agreed to send in a UN force, and the first troops arrived as early as the following day! And by 28 July there were 10,000 UN troops in the Congo, and their presence was a major stabilizing force.' Jardine looked up from his papers. 'The point I am making, ladies and gentlemen, is that once the UN decides to act, it acts quickly – and we already know that the Foreign Secretary, Mr Chokwe, has managed to make his way to New York to address the Security Council on our behalf within the next few days. I submit, Mr Chairman, that this city should not consider any form of negotiation with Nyanga until the outcome of that Security Council debate is known.'

The Mayor glanced around the table, but no-one else wanted to speak and he put the matter to a vote: the result was fifteen to three in favour of continuing to fight.

The Councillors rose and went out to defend their city for one more day at least.

Twenty

On Friday afternoon the President and his two friends travelled fifty miles down the River Jarnoko. Needless to say, they were delighted with their progress.

Throughout the afternoon they treated the Seagull outboard motor with the greatest respect: they wanted to avoid working the engine to death, and they also wanted to be able to avoid any sunken logs and other obstacles which they might spot in the water ahead of them. The Seagull gave them only one nervous moment: after two hours it suddenly cut out for no obvious reason. However, Bob Fuller quickly made a few simple adjustments to it and they were on their way once more after only a few minutes' delay.

Towards dusk the river began to turn away to the north, and on checking the map they realised that the Jarnoko had now taken them as far west as it could; unfortunately it was time for them to take to the land again.

At this point the areas on either side of the main stream of the river were largely swamp, and it took the three travellers some time to find a suitable piece of firm ground on which to disembark. But at last they came to a bend where the western bank sloped gradually upwards from the edge of the water, and they guided the boat into the shallows and stepped out. It was here that they spent the night, during which sheer exhaustion ensured that they were only occasionally disturbed by the teeming hordes of mosquitoes.

In the morning they began to stir with the first light.

As soon as he woke up Philip found himself wondering what might have happened to Jane and to Kelly Thompson. It was now some thirty-six hours since Jane had been swept away and Philip would have given a great deal to know precisely where she and Kelly were at that moment. But there was, of course, no way in which he could resolve that doubt except by reaching Sungbarta and sending out a search party – so he put the question out of his mind entirely and concentrated on the main objective, which was to make progress westward.

All three men felt thoroughly filthy and uncomfortable, and they made an attempt to wash in the river. Their clothes were caked with mud and their feet were swollen tight inside their boots, which they did not dare remove for fear of not being able to get them back on again. Those areas of their skin which had been exposed to the elements over the last few days were covered with scratches, bruises and bites, but they still had a few basic medical supplies left, and they started the day by anointing themselves with antiseptic cream.

Their next thought was breakfast, which was another need they were happily able to satisfy. They ate hugely, working on the principle that the food they had bought from Keith Whittaker's shop was far more use to them inside their stomachs than as a weight to carry on their backs. And while they were giving their meal a few minutes to settle they again examined the map.

They now had approximately another thirty-five miles to cover before they reached Sungbarta: twenty miles of the journey was across a grassy plain and ten miles of the ground was largely covered by forest; after that they would strike the eastern end of Lake Alberton, and Sungbarta itself was another five miles further on, at the opposite end of the lake.

Apart from the fact that they were without a radio to bring them up to date on the latest developments, the three men felt tolerably well equipped. They had food, guns, ammunition, maps and compasses; they also had rucksacks in which to carry their equipment. Not surprisingly in these circumstances their mood remained optimistic. They thought that with a bit of luck they might even reach Sungbarta that night; and although they were tired and physically the worse for wear, they felt that a successful completion of their journey was now within their grasp. For the moment they weren't thinking any further ahead than that.

An hour after dawn the three men finally abandoned their boat and set off on foot once more.

At first their progress was slow. The land around the river was heavily waterlogged, and although they had tried hard to find dry ground on which to disembark, they soon found themselves getting their feet wet.

That in itself was not a serious problem, but a few steps further on they found themselves trying to wade knee-deep through heavy mud. The President had already warned his friends that this part of Balembi was notorious for a sort of quick-mud, which had even been known to swallow elephants, and there was nothing for it but to take a long detour to avoid the soft black bog which blocked their most direct route. Eventually, however, after two frustrating hours of back-tracking and circling, they emerged at last onto a dry and level plain which stretched in front of them as far as the distant horizon.

The grassland, or savanna as it was known locally, proved to be deceptively difficult going. It appeared to be perfectly flat and smooth, a wide expanse of tall tawny grass waving attractively in the breeze; and the only interruptions to the flatness seemed to be occasional bushes and termite hills a few feet high. But they soon

251

found out that, as on the plain which they had crossed on the first day of their journey, the grass served to conceal countless holes and ruts, which frequently made them stumble and sometimes fall; the risk of a seriously sprained ankle was never far from their minds.

The sun blazed down out of a sky which was dotted sparsely with small white clouds like balls of fluffy wool. In the distance they sometimes saw herds of deer: the dignified eland, the streamlined impala and the ungainly wildebeest; there were also others which even the President could not name.

They walked steadily across this featureless plain for some three hours, covering perhaps nine or ten miles at most. And it was then that they first saw the planes.

There were about half a dozen of them, the sun glinting off their silver wings in the distance. At first the aircraft were too far away to be identified, but as they were flying westwards the President suggested that they were probably part of the Gabuti air force, and that they were on their way to attack Sungbarta.

Half an hour later, when the planes returned to the east, this opinion was confirmed in unmistakable terms.

One of the planes passed them a mile or so to the north, heading east. They could see clearly now that it was a MIG fighter, carrying Gabuti markings on its tail. But the pilot must have seen the walkers too, because a few moments later he banked left in a wide circle. Eventually he came hurtling back towards them, flying directly over their heads.

The MIG's engine screamed hideously as it passed barely thirty feet above them; the sound violently assaulted their ears and all three men instinctively dropped to the ground; the long grass was flattened and cowed by the sheer force of the MIG's passing. In a split second the MIG was gone, and they were able to look up into the twin exits of its turbojet engines as it curled away into the sky.

'Spread out!' shouted the President. 'He may come back!' The three of them hastily separated, seeking what little cover they could find in hollows among the grass.

The MIG did exactly what the President had predicted. Whether the Gabuti pilot had any real idea who the travellers were, they never knew; what did become painfully clear was that he had made up his mind to kill them, whoever they were, and he took appropriate action.

The MIG banked in a long, low curve, several miles to the north. Then, taking plenty of time to get things right, the pilot lined himself up on some distant landmark and came at them low over the landscape, from west to east. The three men, fifty yards apart by now, simply hugged the ground hard and hoped that the grass was long enough to hide them.

The MIG's cannons opened up when it was still about a mile away, and great plumes of turf and stones flew into the air in quick succession as the bullets ploughed up the ground. Philip ducked his head and covered his ears; through the earth beneath him he felt a rapid series of seismic shocks as the cannon-fire hammered into the rock-hard soil nearby, and the screaming violence of the noise was almost wounding in itself. But then, suddenly, the plane was gone.

Philip turned over and watched the MIG continuing on its way eastward. The pilot was either short of fuel or ammunition, or else he simply couldn't be bothered to come back and check whether he had hit his targets or not; whatever the reason, he just flew steadily onward, heading back to his base.

Philip sat up with relief; at least that was over. 'Everyone O.K.?' he called.

The President's head appeared over the waving grass to Philip's left. 'I'm all right,' he said. 'What about you?'

'Yes, I'm all right,' said Philip.

But then, simultaneously, both men realised that they had not heard from Bob Fuller. They leapt to their feet and began to search for him, over to their right where they had last seen him.

They found Bob Fuller a few moments later. He was lying on his back, trying hard to pick himself up with his elbows into a sitting position. The reason why he was finding it so difficult to sit up was that one of the MIG's bullets had shattered his left leg. The bullet had gone in through the back of his thigh and had emerged messily at the front; blood was pulsing regularly out of the wound, and Fuller himself looked stunned with shock. The force of the impact had left him dazed and disorientated.

Philip and the President knelt down beside their friend and began to give him first aid. But after a moment a brief and careful glance passed between them.

They both knew at once what a serious wound this was: ideally it would have called for immediate hospitalization and careful treatment, probably surgery, and plenty of antibiotics. But out here, with no medical facilities at all, there was an enormous risk of sepsis and gangrene, and an injury of this magnitude was an almost certain sentence of death. Both men felt absolutely appalled and sickened.

They persuaded Bob Fuller to lie back while they examined his leg more closely. Bob winced and drew in a sudden breath as the pain began to hit him.

'Well,' he said shortly, 'that's finished me all right. You two will just have to press on without me.'

The President didn't answer immediately; he was thinking through the implications. Bob would clearly be unable to walk; they would have to carry him, and that would delay them enormously, at a time when further delay was the very last thing they could afford. With every passing hour Nyanga's grip on the presidency grew more secure, and long-term communist control of the country became more and more certain. It was vitally important that they should move fast. And yet, what was the alternative to slowing themselves down by carrying the wounded man? The only possibility was to leave Bob here, to fend for himself against the wild dogs which ruthlessly attacked any living creature which was bleeding. And that was unthinkable.

'No,' said Kasaboru, with the utmost determination. 'We are not going to leave you behind, Bob, not out here. . . . What sort of people do you think we are? We'll carry you until we find some form of transport – or until we find someone to look after you. We can't be all that far from civilization.'

And with that issue settled, Kasaboru slipped out of his rucksack and began to wonder what he could use for a tourniquet.

Twenty-one

Philip's uncle, George Morgan, did not sleep at all well on Friday night, and he breakfasted early the following morning; he had a cereal followed by two eggs and bacon, which was a menu he had enjoyed daily for at least fifty of his seventy-five years; the meal was cooked for him, as always, by his Mibambo servant, Imbasa.

After serving his master's breakfast Imbasa went out into the road at the front of the house and shooed away a large crowd of bare-footed Fanda children and a number of superstitious adults. The news of George Morgan's appearance at the mass executions on Thursday night had spread through the poorer sections of Digara almost before the former Lord Chief Justice had arrived back at his home. The fact that he had emerged unscathed from that appalling slaughter-house – the only European to do so – had greatly impressed many of the less well-educated citizens. They assumed that he must be a very powerful magician indeed to be able to avoid being killed by Nyanga, who was himself thought to possess great supernatural powers. As a result, Friday morning had seen the first of a steady procession of sightseers; Imbasa had regularly driven them off, but each group had been replaced by another, usually even more awe-struck than the last.

After breakfast George Morgan looked briefly through the morning paper, which to his disgust was daily proclaiming its support of Nyanga, and then retired to his study.

He sat down at his desk and wrote a short letter to his nephew, explaining what he was about to do, and why; he offered up a silent prayer as he did so that Philip was still alive and would one day be able to read it. Having completed the letter, the old man sealed it in an envelope, wrote Philip's name on the front, and dropped it into a drawer of his desk. Then he went out to his car and drove round to see Hector Black, a friend of many years' standing.

Hector Black was an elderly widower. In appearance he and George Morgan could almost have been brothers: they had the same white hair, neatly trimmed, and the same white moustache on a tanned face. But if anything Hector was carrying his age rather less well than George: his shoulders were bowed when he stood up, and his clothes were beginning to look a bit too big for him. He was rapidly becoming a doddery old man.

When his friend arrived, Hector had barely started his own breakfast, but the early visit did not disturb him; on the contrary, he welcomed it: since the death of his wife, two years earlier, loneliness had been his biggest problem.

'Well, George,' he said cheerfully, as soon as his visitor was seated opposite him, 'what brings you round to see me so soon on a Saturday morning?'

George Morgan pulled his chair up closer to the table. 'I've got a proposal to put to you,' he said forthrightly.

'Oh?' Hector's expression brightened. Three years ago he had been eased out of the retail food business which he had built up from next to nothing by a number of younger and much more aggressive directors; and since that time he had greatly missed the wheeling and dealing of his former life. At present he seldom did anything more exciting than play bridge; but now, from George's demeanour, he guessed that something very unusual was in the air. 'What kind of a proposal?' he asked eagerly.

'How old are you?' said George, without answering Hector's question.

'Sixty-eight. Why?'

'I'm seventy-five,' said George. 'Tell me – what do you think of life, now that you're a widower and a pensioner?'

Hector Black stopped buttering his toast and glanced out of the window at his immaculate garden; nowadays he spent most of his time just sitting in it. 'George,' he said, 'life these days is absolutely, completely and utterly, one hundred per cent bloody awful. I'm so bored you wouldn't believe it. . . . Lonely, too. My wife's dead and the children have gone back to England – I never see them.'

George Morgan grunted. 'Hmm. That's what I thought. Now listen, Hector – I'm going to tell you something about myself. Not because I want your sympathy, but because it's important in connection with my proposal. Understand?'

'Yes.'

'Good. Well the point is this. The doctors tell me I've got cancer of the bladder. Nasty place to get it, and I'll live for about a year at the most, and then that'll be that. What about you – how long do you expect to live?'

Hector paused thoughtfully. 'I don't know. I'm sorry to hear what you say, George – very sorry indeed. As for me, well, I haven't got cancer, but I'm certainly not getting any fitter. . . . I suppose I've nearly done my three score years and ten, so I could go at any time. And all my pals seem to be pushin' off at a great rate of knots.'

'Yes, precisely my point,' said George gruffly. 'You can't expect to live long anyway, so you might as well risk your life helping

256

me. . . . Now then, let me tell you another thing. My nephew Philip came out from England recently and got a job as Kasaboru's security man.'

Hector nodded, his toast forgotten altogether. 'Yes, I heard about that.'

'He's my only close relative, and to tell you the truth I invited him out here mainly to see whether he was worth leaving some money to. Well, he is. I've left some to charity and some to him. Now then, as soon as this revolution business started, Philip and the President set out to make their way to Sungbarta – though whether they'll ever get there is anyone's guess, and they certainly don't seem to have got there yet. And naturally I want to do all I can to help them, so I've been up most of the night wondering if there was anything I could do to improve the situation.'

'And is there?'

'Well, not directly, no. But indirectly, yes. . . . Tell me, what do you think of Nyanga?'

Hector Black stared at his friend. 'I think he's a bloody crook, of course, like everyone else I know. He's an expert at leading people astray, and the Balembians are a very easily led people. As as for those executions in the sports stadium the other night – well, words fail me. It's back to the dark ages with a vengeance.'

'Agreed. I was there, and I know. What about Conrad Hall – what do you make of him?'

'Ten times worse in my view,' said Hector stoutly. 'He's got the breeding and the education to know better – a lot better.'

'All right. So we see eye to eye. Now then – the key question is this.' George Morgan looked directly into his friend's eyes. 'Do you feel sufficiently strongly about Nyanga to be willing to kill him yourself?'

Hector Black sat back in his chair. 'Oh, so that's the way your mind's working, is it?' he said slowly. 'Yes, I begin to see what you're getting at. . . .'

'Do you want time to think about it?' asked George.

'No, no, I don't need time. Not long, anyway. . . . The answer, in a nutshell, is yes. . . . As far as I'm concerned, Nyanga is just a mad dog. And like any other rabid animal, he has to be got rid of for the good of the rest of us. Perhaps if we can achieve that, we may have some peace in this country once again.'

Hector Black stirred his coffee pensively for a few moments.

'You know,' he continued shortly, 'I often think back to the time we spent in the trenches, back in the first world war. We didn't know each other then, you and I, but we both fought, and we were both wounded – isn't that right?'

'Three times,' said the former Lord Chief Justice. 'I was on the Somme, and I've got metal in me to prove it. I've no business to be alive at all.'

'I agree. By rights I shouldn't be here either – but we survived somehow or other, when so many others didn't. And after that war was over, you and I couldn't get away from Europe fast enough – right?'

George Morgan nodded.

'I killed my share of the enemy in that war,' Hector continued, 'as I'm sure you did too, George, and Nyanga is a far worse villain than any of them. . . . So the answer to your question is yes – I am willing to assassinate Nyanga. I personally have got nothing to lose, and Balembi has everything to gain. . . . Tell me, though – how do you propose to do it?'

George Morgan leaned forward and rested his elbows on the table in a business-like manner. 'Well,' he said, 'I've been thinking about that.'

Towards noon a chauffeur-driven hired Rolls-Royce cruised through central Digara towards the President's palace. In the back seat, immaculately dressed, sat George Morgan and Hector Black.

Each one carried a loaded .455 inch Webley Mark 6 revolver; George carried his in his jacket pocket, and Hector's was in a slim document-case. These guns were both souvenirs from the 1914–1918 war.

The design of the .455 Webley had been based on the experience of the British army in the nineteenth-century native wars; the heavy bullet was intended to be fully capable of stopping a charging warrior. The revolvers were difficult to handle but absolutely deadly in the right hands.

It was now many years since either of the two old men had fired these weapons in anger, but a quick practice earlier that morning had convinced them that they could still command a fair degree of marksmanship; enough, at any rate, to enable them to complete their mission if they could somehow get close to the target. And that was the purpose of the Rolls-Royce.

Shortly before twelve o'clock the Rolls arrived at the palace gates – or to be precise at the temporary barrier which had replaced the gates; the originals had been destroyed in Monday's attack on the palace. A worried-looking Balembian sergeant approached the car, scratching his head anxiously; no-one had told him that these people would be coming and he didn't quite know what to do about them.

George Morgan wound down his window as the Rolls came to a halt. 'Lord Chief Justice Morgan,' he barked imperiously, 'to see President Nyanga by appointment. Open the gate.' And he wound the window up again.

The Sergeant was totally nonplussed now, and looked it. But George Morgan helped him to make up his mind by ordering the chauffeur to move the car slowly forward, and after a moment the

258

Sergeant gave way to this display of confidence. He ordered the barrier arm to be swung upwards, and the Rolls passed silently through. The Sergeant comforted himself with the thought that there were, after all, other guards on duty at the entrance of the palace itself – let them decide what to do about these important, but unexpected, visitors.

Inside the inner courtyard, which had been severely battered by the tanks five days earlier, the Rolls halted by the steps leading to the main door. George Morgan and Hector Black stepped out.

There was a soldier standing guard on each side of the tall, open entrance doors, and George swallowed hard as he prepared to bluff his way through for a second time. But in the event he didn't have to do anything. The soldiers snapped smartly to attention as the two old men came up the steps towards them, and they then proceeded to present arms in honour of these distinguished arrivals; the two would-be assassins were able to walk straight in, no questions asked.

'So far so good,' said Hector out of the corner of his mouth.

In the entrance hall they met their next obstacle in the shape of a Fanda civil servant at a reception desk. He rose to his feet to meet them. A plaque on his desk proclaimed that he was a Mr T'kolo, the President's first secretary.

T'kolo was a handsome and intelligent-looking man, beautifully dressed in a crisp cream suit. Unfortunately he turned out to be hopelessly drunk, or high on marijuana. Whatever the cause, he was quite incapable of distinguishing between friend and foe, and it seemed almost unkind to take advantage of his condition.

Without stating their names or their business, George Morgan declared firmly that they had an urgent appointment with President Nyanga. The President had sent for them; he would be very angry if they were not taken to him at once.

Mr T'kolo smiled dreamily. Of course, of course. They must proceed up the stairs at once and then turn left along the corridor. He waved them cheerfully by and weaved his way back to his seat.

George and Hector went slowly up the stairs. Slowly because if they went up quickly they were going to be in no condition to kill anyone when they finally reached the top.

Having negotiated the stairs, they turned left, as instructed, and made their way towards another desk at the far end of the corridor, which then branched off to the left and the right.

This desk was manned by a much more formidable official, too important to need a name plaque on his desk. He was very large, very black, and clearly not easily fooled. The man watched them coming with narrowed, suspicious eyes, and when they arrived at his desk he gave them no help whatever.

'We have an appointment with the President,' said George calmly. He looked about him to see if there was any indication of where Nyanga's office was; he knew where Kasaboru's office had been in the past, but apparently there had been some changes since his last visit.

'What names?' said the official coldly.

'Mr Morgan and Mr Black.'

The official didn't even check his list. 'You have no appointment,' he said flatly.

'The President has sent for us,' George Morgan insisted. 'He probably forgot to mention it to you, but it's vital that we should see him at once.'

'If the President did not mention it to me, then you have no appointment,' said the official, as if that settled the matter. 'I will arrange to have you shown out.' His hand moved towards the telephone.

Just then a door opened down the corridor to the left. Nyanga stepped out, some papers in his hand; he was about thirty feet away. After a couple of steps he glanced up and noticed the two elderly men ahead of him; he paused in his tracks.

Hector Black unzipped his document-case and reached inside it.

'What are you doing here, Morgan?' asked Nyanga.

'They say they have an appointment, sir,' the official began.

Hector Black dropped his document case and took aim with his Webley revolver.

After that everything happened very rapidly – far too rapidly for two old men to be able to keep up with events.

Hector Black aimed – fired – and aimed and fired again. Both shots missed, but not by far. Nyanga, thoroughly shaken, dropped his papers in alarm and bolted back into the room he had just emerged from.

The official sitting at the desk immediately reached for his own gun, which was an automatic pistol in a shoulder holster. In two seconds he had put three shots into Hector Black at point-blank range, sending the old man reeling and staggering backwards into the opposite wall, spouting blood from his chest. In the meantime George Morgan had brought out his own revolver. He now fired two rounds into the official, killing him instantly; the impact knocked the man violently off his chair.

George Morgan then turned in horror to look at his friend. Hector lay on the floor in a sitting position, his back against the wall; he stared up in shock, his eyes wide open.

'Get him!' he said hoarsely. 'Go and kill Nyanga!' And then blood came out of his mouth, his eyes closed and his head fell heavily forward.

George Morgan wasted no more time: he went down the corridor at a trot, his heart pounding, and threw open the door Nyanga had closed after him.

In the meantime Joro Nyanga was not distinguishing himself with clear thinking and calm unhurried action. He was not a coward, but equally he had not expected to have to fight for his life in his own office – or at least, not without a little warning. As soon as the shooting began he had dashed back to his desk and started searching for the spare Tokarev pistol which he was sure he had left in there somewhere. He opened drawers frantically, but without success. He thought of locking the office door, but then he couldn't think where the key was, so he abandoned that idea. Next he turned to the window; he threw it open and bellowed for the guards to get up here at the double. But in fact he needn't have bothered taking the time to do that: every soldier within earshot had been alerted by the gunfire and was already heading for the President's office as fast as he possibly could; their own lives depended on it.

Nyanga turned back to his desk. He heaved the bottom drawer right out and emptied it on to the floor – and there, at last, was the Tokarev.

George Morgan swung open the office door. He saw the pistol in Nyanga's hand and he knew at once that he must shoot now, although he was too far away – if he didn't take this opportunity he would never get a chance to shoot at all. He aimed and fired.

The recoil from the heavy .455 was considerable, particularly for an old man, and he could not get the rounds off in rapid succession. He aimed carefully and fired again.

Nyanga ducked down behind his desk. George Morgan's first shot blew great chunks of wood in all directions, but Nyanga was not hit.

Nyanga fired back, three times, fast, and saw George Morgan buckle. A final shot from the Webley went hopelessly wild, somewhere up into the ceiling.

Nyanga fired again and again, and George Morgan's eyes closed as he fell back into the corridor. He folded up in slow motion and slumped to the floor.

At that point George felt no pain or distress, but he could no longer function: his finger would not tighten on the trigger, and his legs would no longer hold him up. He felt dizzy and unco-ordinated.

He toppled down on to his back, and his legs slowly stretched out flat on the floor. He began to feel an appalling, unbearable agony in his belly; but almost immediately that feeling passed, and a huge numbness began to sweep over him.

But for the moment he was still conscious. Still able to think.

He had failed, he realised that, and it was the sense of failure that had hurt him for a moment. But it was an honest failure, and nothing to be ashamed of: he had done his best. He lay quietly and peacefully, aware that these were his last moments of life.

A little later the former Lord Chief Justice opened his eyes again. Above him he could see Nyanga, breathing heavily, with a pistol in his hand. Soldiers were clumping along the corridor from all directions, and officers were shouting loudly.

A face appeared beside Nyanga's shoulder, a curious, Oriental face: it belonged to Yuri Semenov. The Russian looked down at the seventy-five-year-old man with a detached and professional interest.

'Is he dead?' he asked.

'Not yet,' said Nyanga curtly. He knelt down on the carpet and looked into George Morgan's eyes. 'Can you hear me?' he asked.

The old man nodded; his mouth was beginning to fall open.

Nyanga paused and then chuckled. 'If you had been on my side,' he said, 'we would have been a formidable team. We really would. . . . I admire your courage, damn you.'

He lifted his pistol and brought it up towards George Morgan's forehead, but he saw at once that there was no need to fire. The old man's eyes flickered shut, and his head slowly turned to one side.

Twenty-two

Major Duncan Grey, like the President and his companions, spent Friday afternoon on the River Jarnoko. On the few occasions when the ferry-boat passed a village or some outpost of civilization, the Major brought his commandeered craft into shore and asked if a party of three men had been seen heading downstream. The answer was always affirmative, and he soon learnt that the President had now found himself a boat with an outboard motor. Well, that was unfortunate, because he would not be so easy to catch, but it was not perhaps the end of the world.

The Major continued down the Jarnoko until at seven p.m. he reached a small settlement called Monkstown. He was unhappy that he had not been able to overtake the President on the river, but he knew that he now had an opportunity to jump ahead of him. The President and company would have to beach their boat within the next few miles and then walk across open country towards Lake Alberton. At Monkstown, however, the Major could unload his lorry and use the highway to reach the southern shore of Lake Alberton first; and once he was there he could again use the tribal drum communications system to mobilize the people of the forest to assist him. So while Duncan Grey was still worried, he was not yet panic-stricken by the thought of failure.

In the event, off-loading the army lorry from the ferry-boat took much longer than Grey had anticipated, because the landing-stage was two feet higher than the deck of the ferry. When at last the job was done he decided to spend the night in Monkstown; there he could at least sleep in a proper bed at a small hotel, and he could be on his way first thing in the morning.

The Major's men also liked this idea: it enabled them to get amazingly drunk at no cost at all, because the proprietor of the hotel was too frightened of them to charge anything for their booze. In fact one of the men liked Monkstown so much that he decided to stay there permanently; at about ten p.m. he went off to spend the night with a little servant girl who cleaned out the hotel kitchens, and that was the last Grey ever saw of him.

The following morning Duncan Grey roused himself reluctantly – he too had had a great deal to drink – and persuaded Corporal Avakubi to round up the remaining soldiers. The Major noticed as the men clambered onto the lorry that he seemed to be losing manpower at an alarming rate – the original complement of sixteen men had now been reduced to four. But never mind – he was certain that if he captured Kasaboru all would be forgiven.

The lorry then made its way westward, into the forest area south of Lake Alberton. There the mere sight of guns and soldiers was enough to secure from the local population the co-operation which Grey wanted. The drums were soon at work, and towards mid-day the Major was able to sit back and simply wait for something to happen. The forest people had been warned to look out for the travellers; and if they knew what was good for them they would seize the three men and hold them until the army arrived.

For the President and Philip Morgan, the problem of carrying the wounded Bob Fuller across the grassy plain proved to be far more difficult than they had anticipated.

They started by carrying Bob between them, his arms round their shoulders. Bob did his best to help by carrying part of his weight on his one good leg, and they proceeded in this manner for about an hour. But then they had to give up. Bob himself had soon become exhausted and faint, and the ground was so uneven that his two helpers often found themselves stumbling in different directions. They had to stop frequently to give Bob a chance to recover his breath, and after an hour it was quite clear that he could not go on in this way any longer; his strength had simply given out.

From then on Philip and the President took it in turns to carry their wounded companion individually, usually in a fireman's lift. This was also very far from satisfactory. In the first place, carrying a full-grown man over this terrain demanded enormous stamina in itself. Add to that the complication caused by the fact that the man's left leg had been shattered by a heavy bullet, so that the slightest movement caused him great agony, and the task of transporting the patient without hurting him became impossible; being carried with his head hanging down for long periods was doing Bob no good either. However, unsatisfactory and exhausting though it was, it was the best arrangement they could think of, so they kept at it with all the determination they could muster.

The President and Philip carried Bob Fuller for the whole of that Saturday afternoon and well into the evening.

At first they were able to walk about a quarter of a mile each, but as time went on the distance they could cover with Bob over their shoulder shrank to a hundred yards or less. At the end of that distance they found they were trembling with fatigue and soaked with sweat from head to foot; every breath they took of the oven-hot afternoon air was like breathing in molten lead. At that time of day and in those conditions all sensible creatures were resting quietly in the shade. But there was no shade on the plain – and if there had been any they would not have been able to stop, because if they did not find some skilled medical assistance soon, Bob Fuller would surely die.

As the hours went by, Bob's condition swiftly deteriorated. The tourniquet on his leg needed to be loosened periodically, and this involved a constant and serious loss of blood. Before long Bob's mind began to cloud over with the pain and the shock of his injury. Despite his undoubted courage he began to groan aloud with every step his carrier took, until after three or four hours he drifted into unconsciousness. It was quite clear that moving Bob in this way, and in the intense heat, was aggravating his injury. But they had no choice in the matter: the only alternative was to leave him in the grass to die, and they were not prepared to contemplate that.

Philip and the President walked and walked, their minds over-ruling their bodies' urgent demands that no further energy should be expended for many hours. Towards evening they ran out of water; they abandoned all but the most essential equipment; and their resting periods extended until they were spending more time in recovery than they were in carrying. In short, they had reached the very limit of their endurance – and that limit had in itself already been extended further than either of them would have thought possible.

At last they saw the forest in the far distance, and although they knew they would never reach it today it gave them a target to aim for. And gradually the land lost its monotonous flatness and began to roll into hills and valleys.

Just before dusk, as they reached the top of one of these hills, they came unexpectedly on a house nestling in the valley below. It was a small wooden-built bungalow, about a quarter of a mile away, set amidst a copse of tall silver gum trees; a dusty approach road curled away behind it.

As soon as they saw this house Philip and the President rested again, too weary even to make much comment at first. But after a few minutes it was decided that Philip would go forward to investigate, while the President remained behind to care for Bob Fuller. Bob's face was an ugly colour now, and his breathing was hoarse and rasping, with pauses between each intake of air. Philip did not like the look of him, and he had spent a long time wondering how they could get him into hospital without surrendering themselves; perhaps the people in this house would provide the answer.

Philip hurried away.

He kept well below the brow of the hill in order to get as near as possible to the house without being observed, because there was no knowing who might be living there: in all probability they would be Europeans, and willing to help, but it was best to be ultra-cautious.

In a minute or two he had manoeuvred himself into a position where he could see that the front door of the house was wide open. But there was no movement within, and no sound of any activity; the owners seemed to have gone.

Once he was sure that the place was completely silent, Philip simply came forward and went directly up the path to the front door. He knocked and called out, but there was no reply, so he went inside.

Very soon he realised why there was no-one about. From the clothes in the one and only bedroom it seemed probable that the residents were a man and a woman, and there were signs that they had not left willingly. There was broken crockery in the kitchen, and bloodstains on the floor, with a trail of drips leading out of the house at the back.

Wearily Philip stepped outside at the rear of the house, half-expecting to find a corpse or two in the garden. But as it happened he could find no-one, either alive or dead.

What he did find was a car, an elderly Morris 1000. There was no ignition key in it, but perhaps, he thought, if they searched the house they would find one; alternatively they might well be able to start it some other way.

In a cabinet in the bathroom there were also some liquid antiseptic, some penicillin tablets, and plenty of bandages. With these Philip and the President would at least be able to make a start on giving Bob Fuller the medical treatment he so urgently needed.

In the thickening dusk Philip hurried back towards his two friends. The house offered transport, food, water, and two comfortable beds; they could scarcely ask for anything more. He jogged the last hundred yards through the thick grass, arriving at Kasaboru's side decidedly out of breath, but feeling a bit more cheerful.

'It looks promising,' he panted. 'No-one there – but there are some of the things we need. And there's a car, too. Let's get him over there as fast as we can.'

The President turned his face towards Philip; his eyes were very white in the half-light of late evening.

'There is no longer any great rush,' he said quietly. 'I'm afraid Bob died about five minutes ago. . . . You'd better have a look at him yourself, but I am in no doubt that he has gone.'

Death was unmistakable, and irreversible. Bob Fuller was now beyond their help.

The two men carried his body down to the house in the valley. There, in a patch of ground at the end of the rudimentary garden, they buried him as best they could. They would have liked to have gone down six feet, because there was the risk of a shallow grave being disturbed by wild dogs and hyenas, but the ground was brutally hard and they could not manage more than about eighteen inches. However, they covered the top of the grave with some large stones from the rockery, which they felt would give it adequate protection.

With the burial completed the President spoke a short prayer. Then the two survivors went back into the house for the night.

They lay down, fully clothed, on the two single beds in the bedroom, and within five minutes they were both deeply asleep.

Twenty-three

Joro Nyanga had been badly shaken by the attempt on his life which the two old men had made on Saturday morning. Apparently not even the palace was safe any longer; he seemed to be surrounded by idiots and incompetents. His biggest worry, however, was that Sungbarta remained uncaptured. Sungbarta! A grubby little city in the middle of nowhere – a child could take it with one hand tied behind his back, but the Gabuti army evidently couldn't. It was only a matter of time, of course, but with the United Nations about to debate the Balembi situation it was important that he should be seen to be in complete control of the whole country.

By five o'clock on Saturday Nyanga had decided that he would fly to Sungbarta himself to investigate the delay. As far as he could see, all that was needed was a little leadership from the top.

At five twenty-five p.m. Nyanga left Digara in a Russian-built helicopter of the Gabuti air force. He took Semenov and Bulu with him.

Towards six o'clock Eileen Grey noticed that the corridors of the President's palace were no longer buzzing with activity. Her beloved Joro was not in his office, and his aides were not in theirs. Eileen began to search the premises, plaintively asking anyone she met where the President had gone. But no-one knew – or if they did, they weren't telling her.

In the course of her wanderings Eileen came across Conrad Hall, who had just returned from another visit to the mines at Tikiro. Hall had guessed almost immediately that Nyanga had gone to Sungbarta – that, after all, was where the principal problem lay – but, like Eileen, he was wondering anxiously why Nyanga had not bothered to tell him about his plans. The fact that he was no longer being consulted about important decisions made him distinctly nervous.

Thus it was that both Eileen Grey and Conrad Hall, for quite different reasons, found themselves needing an ally in the constant struggle for the President's favour; and both of them were painfully aware that from now on it was going to be a struggle. They decided to have dinner together, both to pool their information and to find out tactfully what use each could make of the other in the future.

They dined at the city's leading hotel, where business had continued entirely as usual throughout the civil disturbances; it was going to take more than a mere military coup to change anything at the Hotel Imperial.

After a few preliminaries, both gastronomic and conversational, Eileen complained bitterly that Nyanga had ignored her all day; what was much more important, however, was that he had not slept in her bed last night. Where the hell had he been?

Conrad Hall could supply the answer to that question if not to others. He explained about the American-born doctor, Jane Stuart, who had been accompanying Kasaboru on his pointless trek across Balembi, and who had now been captured.

'Have you met this Dr Stuart?' he asked innocently, knowing full well that the girl was in fact Eileen Grey's niece by marriage.

'Oh, I've had some contact with her,' said Eileen vaguely.

'Your husband was the one who caught her,' Hall continued. 'Fished her out of a river, so I understand, and sent her back by helicopter.'

Eileen's eyebrows rose almost to her hairline. 'Really?' she said. 'Well, I am surprised.' And she was, too – surprised that at last her husband was letting his head rule his heart. For far too long, in Eileen's opinion, Duncan Grey had been held back in life by all sorts of childish notions about doing the decent thing and playing the game. But now, apparently, he was learning. Well, perhaps it was not too late for the stupid bastard to save himself even at this stage.

But then, of course, Eileen realised what Conrad Hall had been getting at. Jane Stuart – Nyanga – a night away from the palace. Her jaw dropped.

'You don't mean – ' she began in outrage.

Hall nodded, trying to hide his amusement. 'Yes, I'm afraid so. My information is that Nyanga spent all night with Jane Stuart in Digara prison. A very vigorous night too, by all accounts.'

Eileen Grey put down her knife and fork with a clatter and clenched her fists till the nails nearly drew blood from her palms. 'God damn and blast that dirty little bitch,' she said vehemently. 'I'll scratch her eyes out the next time I get near her.' And she went on in that vein for some time.

Eventually Hall managed to calm Eileen down. Not to worry, he told her. You want to get rid of Jane Stuart – well, these things can be arranged, no problem at all. He, Conrad Hall, could fix it. But in the meantime, Eileen, there were just a few little pieces of information which he would like to have himself. Perhaps she could help him. What, for instance, were Joro's views on. . . . And so on.

Their discussions lasted well into the small hours of the next day.

The helicopter carrying Joro Nyanga and his associates to Sungbarta landed two miles south of the firing line. General Tchen then escorted his visitors to his operational headquarters, where he outlined the latest position to Nyanga and Semenov.

Rather to his surprise, Tchen found that both men were knowledgeable and entirely reasonable; they wanted action, but they were not expecting miracles.

'So,' said Nyanga, when he had fully absorbed the map in front of him, 'the only accessible route into the city is across the south road bridge. The bridge has been mined with TNT, correct?'

Tchen nodded.

'I see. And we know that they can destroy the bridge if driven to that extreme because they have already successfully blown the railway bridge. Yes. . . . Now tell me, could you if necessary replace the road bridge with a temporary one – what do the British call them, a Bailey bridge?'

'No,' said Tchen. 'We could not do that. We haven't the capability.' He didn't like to mention that the last time his army had tried to build a Bailey bridge it had collapsed, involving the loss of three tanks and fourteen men in a relatively narrow and slow-moving river.

Nyanga accepted Tchen's answer without question. 'Well, if that is the case, then it seems to me that what we ought to do is send a small force of men across the river in darkness so that they can prevent the bridge being blown. While they're doing that we rush across a few tanks and men and secure a strong foothold on the other side. What do you think of that idea?'

'We tried that this morning,' said Tchen. 'Unfortunately it didn't work.'

'Did you use your own men?' asked Nyanga.

'Yes. Of course.'

'Ah.' Nyanga smiled. 'But you see, I have other ideas. . . . Don't misunderstand me, General, but I am in a hurry – there isn't much time left. Tomorrow morning, at about three a.m. our time, the United Nations Security Council will debate the Balembian situation at length. I am hopeful that the Russians will do the sensible thing and veto any suggestion of sending a peace-keeping force here – but, with all due respect to Mr Semenov, one can never be quite sure what the Russians will do. And of course, even if the UN do decide to send in a few troops it will be some time before they can set up the operation. Nevertheless, General, I want this Sungbarta business settled, and I want it settled tomorrow.'

Nyanga turned back to look at the map. 'These explosives on the bridge – they will presumably be set off by one of those blasting machines, in which a handle is pushed down to generate electrical current – am I not right?'

'Perfectly.'

270

'Good. And you know where this plunger is located?'

General Tchen pointed to the map. 'All the indications are that it is in this block here. Round the back, out of sight of our guns.'

Nyanga was pleased. 'Good. Then the matter becomes very simple, General. We need about six good men – men with skill, courage and initiative. We will send them across the river first thing tomorrow morning.'

'But I regret to say, Mr President, that we lost our best men last night in just such an attempt.'

'Well actually, old boy,' said Nyanga in his best Oxford accent, 'I wasn't thinking about using *your* men. Not this time. I took the precaution of bringing my own troops instead. I had them flown in from Elisabethville earlier today. There are six of them – and they're the best white mercenaries that money can buy.'

In the next few hours detailed arrangements were made for the six mercenaries to establish a bridgehead on the north bank of the river Sung. Their job was to prevent the bridge being blown for a few precious minutes, during which time Gabuti troops would storm across and sweep through the heavily defended area on the Sungbarta side. After that it was felt that the battle would be all over. Taking the bridge would solve nine-tenths of the problem: once that was secured, Sungbarta would fall.

The mercenaries' fee for this operation was agreed at five thousand pounds per man, half to be paid in cash in advance. The leader of the mercenaries, who negotiated the price, was a thirty-year-old Englishman called Jack Thorpe; his accent betrayed the fact that he had originally come from Manchester.

Thorpe was six feet two inches tall and weighed fifteen stone, very little of which was fat. At the age of eighteen he had joined the British army, rising eventually to the rank of sergeant. In his view this rank did not fully reflect his talents as a leader of men, and unfortunately he became convinced that there was still no room in the army for an officer of working-class origins, particularly one who came from the north. As a result of this disenchantment with his country's official fighting force, Thorpe had gone back into civilian life, only to find that it bored him stiff. And when a South African in a London pub had offered to recruit him into Mike Hoare's Fifth Commando in the Congo, Thorpe had been only too delighted to accept. Since then he had made a good living as a soldier of fortune, and he saw himself continuing in that role for some time.

The mercenaries were given everything they asked for by way of military equipment. They were also given a detailed and highly professional briefing by General Tchen himself on the known and inferred positions of the Sungbartan defenders. Once it grew dark

271

they went out and reconnoitred personally a number of possible crossing-points on the river.

By three a.m. the six white men were ready; they now had blackened faces and were wearing light–weight camouflaged uniforms.

They swam across the river in pairs, pushing their weapons and other gear ahead of them, wrapped in groundsheets. The sky was cloudy and the night was dark, without much wind. They crossed at a point where there were very few buildings on the Sungbarta side, and they assumed, correctly, that the Sungbartans would not be able to watch every inch of waterfront; in fact, the defenders could not find the men to monitor even half of the riverside effectively.

Once on the Sungbarta shore, the mercenaries flitted silently through the dark and deserted streets. By four a.m. they were close to the bridge itself; Jack Thorpe could actually see into the brightly lit room where the explosives plunger was located.

The north end of the bridge was manned by a mixed group, consisting of professionals from the Balembian army and a handful of local volunteers. At that time of the morning all their energies were at a very low ebb, and most of the men were quietly dozing, or else listening to the radio in the hope of hearing some news of the United Nations debate, which had begun at three a.m. Although they should certainly have known better, the fact that the debate was taking place at all had lulled them into thinking that their problems were over. And in the meantime Jack Thorpe moved quietly among the defence positions, either unseen or else unsuspected as an enemy.

In ten minutes Thorpe had successfully cut the wires leading from the electrical blaster to the explosives on the bridge. He had also positioned his men so that they could fight off any attempt to reconnect the wires or to detonate the explosives by some other means. He then flashed a message across the river by morse code, using a simple pocket torch.

The result was almost a walk-over. Almost, but not quite: there were a few casualties.

It was the roar of the T-54 tanks which first alerted the defenders to what was happening. The tanks began to race across the bridge, one after another, filling the air with the sound of their engines. Six of them crunched through the crude barricades and were on the north shore before any attempts to use anti-tank weapons were made, and even then the shooting was very amateurish and ineffectual.

The man responsible for blowing up the bridge in just such an emergency as this panicked; he wondered whether he should or should not do it, eventually decided that he should, and finally tried to. He pressed the plunger, found it didn't work, and ran out of his post, shouting hoarsely. He was shot through the head by Jack Thorpe.

Gabuti troops in lorries now began pouring across the river in large numbers, but they met very little resistance. Only two men on the Sungbartan side fought with real determination and heroism: one was Colonel Smith, the officer in charge of the defence of the city; the other was David Levene. Both of them were killed in the first five minutes.

By four-thirty a.m. the south road bridge and all the buildings nearby were firmly in the hands of the Gabuti army. General Tchen seemed determined to send over the whole of his force, right down to the cooks and the clerks, and the bridge was clogged with military vehicles. Elsewhere in the city there were occasionally sporadic outbreaks of shooting, particularly around City Hall, but after five a.m. even that died out. Resistance came to an end.

At five-thirty a.m. the Voice of America announced that the Security Council had agreed to the British Government's proposal for a UN peace-keeping force to be sent to Balembi as soon as possible. The Russians, who had been receiving detailed daily reports from their embassy in Digara, had decided that Nyanga was in a strong enough position to make it unnecessary for them to veto the British plan; instead they had merely abstained, thus allowing the UN to act. The Sungbarta radio station had been intending to relay this news, if and when it was received, but unfortunately the station was by then in the hands of the enemy. Nyanga was not worried by the UN's decision, but he saw no reason to trouble the heads of the citizens by letting them know of it.

At six a.m., and again every hour on the hour throughout the rest of the day, Radio Sungbarta broadcast a message which Nyanga had recorded the previous day. He advised the citizens that the city had now been relieved by units of the friendly Gabuti army. Everyone should stay at home for the time being and behave themselves; life would return to normal the next day.

Life was not very normal at present, however, as the Gabuti soldiers soon began celebrating their famous victory. Liquor and jewellery stores were rapidly looted; a few fires sprang up and were largely ignored; and the officers turned a blind eye to the usual instances of light-hearted rape and murder.

By nine a.m. it was felt that the city was sufficiently secure for Joro Nyanga to enter it. Under heavy military escort he was driven to the Mayor's house, close to the shore of Lake Alberton.

Jack Thorpe was sent inside to check out the residence for possible threats to Nyanga's health, and his first action was to send the Levenes' grandchildren upstairs with the least psychopathic of his fellow mercenaries to keep them company. Then he searched the house carefully, and in due course pronounced it safe for Nyanga to enter.

Nyanga immediately despatched the Mayor's wife, Jennifer Levene, to look after her grandchildren; they needed, he said, the presence of an affectionate grandmother. Then he turned his attention to Dan Levene, who not surprisingly looked physically ill and utterly depressed. At five-twenty a.m. Levene had received a telephone call from a man whose word he trusted completely; the caller told the Mayor that his son, David, was undoubtedly dead; he had seen his body himself. After that the Mayor functioned as if in a trance.

'Well, Mr Mayor,' Nyanga began briskly, 'I won't waste very much of your time. . . . All Balembi is now under my control and will remain so. There is only one remaining problem, and it is this – the whereabouts of Paul Kasaboru.'

The Mayor looked up at Nyanga sharply. His thoughts had been far, far away, but that name roused his attention.

'Kasaboru,' Nyanga continued, 'has spent most of the last week making his way towards Sungbarta on foot. Why he has chosen to do so, heaven alone knows – a sensible man would have headed for the border. But no, Kasaboru has to come here. Well that, as they say, is his funeral.'

Nyanga came and sat down in a chair beside Levene.

'Now you, Mr Mayor, are an old and valued friend of Kasaboru's. Is that not so?'

Dan Levene nodded.

'Yes. I thought so. Now it's my belief, Mr Mayor, that in the circumstances Paul Kasaboru will have found some means to let you know that he is coming. He will also know that until this morning the city has been under seige, and he will have made some sort of an arrangement with you. He will have agreed some sort of signal to let you know that he is about to enter the city. And you, for your part, will have agreed to give some sort of a reply to confirm that it is safe for him to come in. I am assuming, of course, that since he knows the city is under attack on the land, Kasaboru will come to you across the lake.'

The Mayor sighed. 'I don't know what you're talking about,' he said. 'I'm afraid I can't help you at all.'

'Oh yes you can,' said Nyanga roughly. 'And you will. . . . It is possible, of course, that Kasaboru might even have arrived already, and you might be sheltering him somewhere. But I doubt that, or he would have made a speech over Radio Sungbarta – he would have contacted the world's press and made all kinds of a fuss. So I don't think he is here yet. But let me tell you what is going to happen, Mr Mayor. You have a very simple choice. . . . Either you will tell me exactly what your arrangements with Kasaboru are, or else I am going to get my soldiers to start work on your wife, and on your two young grandchildren.'

Dan Levene's face turned white.

In order not to leave any doubt in the Mayor's mind, Nyanga went on to describe in detail and at length what he would do to Jennifer Levene and to the two children. And that, of course, was more than Dan Levene could bear, particularly coming so soon after the death of his son. He broke down and wept uncontrollably.

Later, when he was at last able to speak, Levene haltingly explained to Joro Nyanga precisely what signals had been agreed between himself and his old friend Paul Kasaboru. Nyanga had caught him at precisely the right psychological moment, when he was at his most vulnerable; and faced with the choice of explaining what the arrangements were or seeing his wife and grandchildren tortured, he felt that he had little choice in the matter.

When the Mayor had finished, Nyanga put a hand on his shoulder. 'Mr Mayor,' he said, 'I know how hard this has been for you. Believe me, I understand these things. . . . I will keep my side of the bargain, and your wife and grandchildren will not be harmed. As for you, well, you will have to go off to prison, I'm afraid. But don't worry, you will not be mistreated – not if you continue to co-operate.'

Nyanga walked to the door. Then he turned and looked back.

'Co-operation,' he said sternly. 'That's the word to remember. Co-operate with me, Mr Mayor, and I think you'll find that I'm not as black as I've sometimes been painted.'

Nyanga laughed hugely as he went out of the door and made his way to his car.

Twenty-four

It was broad daylight when Philip and the President awoke – they had slept for longer than they intended.

They made themselves a large breakfast from the selection of tinned food in the house and then had a quick look around. Like most houses which lay beyond the outskirts of towns, this one had no electricity, and the water supply was a large rain-water tank on the roof. The house seemed to be about ten or twenty years old, and they guessed that it had originally been built as some city-dweller's week-end cottage.

During their tour of the house they successfully located the keys to the car in a kitchen drawer. They also came across papers and letters which indicated that the two people who had been living in the house until recently were an American couple. They appeared to be anthropologists from the University of Chicago, and they seemed to have been studying the life-style of the Nula tribe, which was located nearby.

Philip's next move was to check over the car. Its petrol tank was three-quarters full and it seemed in good working order.

Philip and the President felt slightly guilty about using this car without permission – it might after all mean the difference between life and death to its owners. But although they had seen no bodies the two men felt quite certain in their own minds that the American couple were already dead. If the Americans had been in any fit state to make a break for it, they would surely have taken the car themselves some days ago; and from the evidence Philip and the President had seen, it seemed more than probable that the anthropologists had been killed by members of the very tribe they had been studying. However, to be on the safe side the President left a note to explain what he and Philip were doing, together with a sum of money equal to the value of the car. The President also made a mental note that if life in Balembi ever returned to anything like normal, he would send troops or the police out to this area later, to find out what had really happened.

The car was soon loaded with the few essential items which they felt they would need on this last stage of their journey; and after checking that Bob Fuller's grave had not been disturbed during the night, they finally set off.

It had not needed much discussion to convince the pair of them that the need to reach Sungbarta quickly was now so great that they had to take a few risks. They would stick to country roads as far as possible, but they would use the main highways if they had to. This was the sixth day of their travels, and every passing hour meant that the likelihood of Kasaboru being able to re-establish himself as President was growing more and more remote.

They drove along dusty, pot-holed roads, nursing the car's engine and suspension; they travelled about fifteen miles in all, which was the equivalent of perhaps ten miles as the crow flies, because the road meandered in all directions, touching every landmark and village on the map, plus a few which were not on the map at all.

Eventually they came upon a village which was rather larger than the others they had passed, though still nothing more than a collection of twenty-odd mud huts. The road passed to one side of the village, and following their usual practice they drove through at speed, causing considerable panic among a crowd of chickens as they did so.

As they bounced and lurched past, they noticed a crowd of fifty or sixty excited villagers gathered in the open space in front of the huts. The villagers were talking animatedly, prodding each other with their fingers and waving their arms in the air. In fact the subject under discussion was so enthralling that hardly anyone paid any attention to the passing car, which was most unusual.

Philip was driving and he kept his eyes mostly on the road, but as soon as they were over the brow of the hill just beyond the village, the President tapped him on the shoulder.

'I think you'd better stop,' he said quietly.

Philip brought the car to a halt and turned to look at his companion. 'Why's that?' he asked.

'Did you see that crowd of villagers back there?'

'Yes, more or less.'

'Did you see why they were all so worked up?'

'No – what were they on about?'

'I only just saw it myself – but in the middle of that crowd of locals there were two young white children. A boy and a girl – both of them under ten, I should say.'

'Oh,' said Philip heavily. 'I wonder where they came from.'

The President looked back towards the top of the hill. 'I don't know,' he said. 'But somehow I don't think we ought to leave them there. . . . It grieves me to say this, but sometimes my fellow countrymen do not show the level of respect for human life that I would wish. Especially these past few days.'

Philip nodded. 'I know what you mean,' he said with feeling. 'Well, the position is quite clear. Your main aim is to get to Sungbarta quickly, no question about that. So I'm not going to have *you* going back there to investigate. If anyone's going, it's me. I'll go back and see what all the fuss is about, and unless there's a very good explanation for those two children being in the village I'll bring them back to the car with me. In the meantime you just sit here with the engine running and ignore anything you hear. If I'm not back in twenty minutes you're to go ahead without me – O.K.?'

The President sighed. 'Well, yes. I suppose so. I don't like it, but I suppose you're right. At any rate I don't want to go on unless I know that those children are not in any danger. So we'll do as you suggest – you go and take a look and I'll stay here like a good boy.'

Philip grinned. He took a Sten gun from the back seat of the car and then walked back a hundred yards to the ridge they had just crossed. As he approached the brow of the hill he took to the trees, which were thick on either side of the road, and from this more than adequate cover he was able to look down on to the village below without being observed.

The huts were grouped in a circle, with the village drum to the left as Philip viewed the scene, and the road running well to the right. The carcase of a young antelope was drying on the roof of one of the huts, and in the centre of the circle the villagers were still busily arguing with each other.

One man, probably the village headman, was engaged in fierce argument with several other men; the women and children looked on, occasionally adding their own shrill comments to the discussion. Philip noticed that many of the village children had the pinkish hair which is a sign of kwashiorkor, the debilitating illness which results from malnutrition. In the centre of it all, and clearly the subject of this whole heated debate, were the two white children whom the President had spotted as he passed.

The children were both fair-haired and were obviously brother and sister; the boy was perhaps ten, a couple of years older than the girl. They were both dressed in blue jeans and white tee-shirts, and the girl's blonde hair hung down well below her shoulders.

Philip watched for a minute or two in the hope of finding out what was going on. As far as he could see, a few of the hotter heads in the tribe wanted to do the children some sort of harm; he didn't like the look of some of the more violent gestures they were making. But the village headman seemed to be resisting this idea, and the rest of the villagers were more or less evenly divided.

Philip wondered what on earth to do, and in the end he decided that he had no choice but to go down among the villagers and ask a few questions. Ten days earlier he wouldn't have hesitated to do this for a moment, but his more recent experiences had made him very wary. However, he decided that even now it would be wrong to assume that the villagers would necessarily leap on him without warning; they were probably just ordinary, peaceful people having an everyday argument about something.

Well, he hoped so, anyway.

Holding his Sten gun in what he felt was the least aggressive position possible, Philip walked down the road and entered the village.

At first no-one noticed him, but as he came closer to the chattering group, the women and children on the fringe fell silent and moved aside. Gradually the men also became aware of his presence: they too stopped their discussion and stepped back a little, so that eventually Philip was face to face with the headman.

Keeping a very careful eye on the handful of men who were carrying spears and other weapons, Philip ignored the headman and addressed his first remarks to the two children.

'Hello there,' he said kindly. 'Are you here on your own?'

'Yes, sir,' said the boy rather hesitantly.

'Where are your Mum and Dad?'

'At home, sir.'

'And would you like to go home too?' asked Philip.

The children looked at each other with immense relief. 'Oh, yes please, sir,' said the boy.

Philip nodded. 'Good. Come and stand by me then.'

With a nervous glance at the village headman the two children did as they were told. Philip then looked at the faces all around him, but he found very few eyes which would meet his own. Finally his gaze settled on the headman.

'I'm taking these children with me,' he said evenly. 'I'll take them back to their parents.'

The village headman nodded; he at least was obviously pleased by this information, though one or two of the other men muttered under their breath. 'Good,' said the headman, with a grin which revealed only three teeth. 'That is good. You take.' He grinned again.

Philip turned, and then, with the little girl's hand in his own, he walked swiftly away. He was sorely tempted to glance behind him from time to time to see that no-one was aiming a spear at his back, but he noticed that the boy was keeping watch for him, so he refrained; it was best not to show any sign of weakness.

However, once the three of them were safely over the brow of the hill, and could see the Morris 1000 just ahead of them, Philip abandoned the pretence that he was immune to danger and broke into a trot.

'Come on, kids,' he said. 'Let's run.'

And they did.

The children were soon happily installed in the back seat of the car and the President drove off, leaving a large cloud of dust behind them. Philip then began to talk to the children to establish who they were and where they were from.

279

Their names were Colin and Susan Carlow, and their parents were apparently teachers at a little mission school a few miles to the south. The previous evening the two children had been out playing near their home when a group of tribesmen had suddenly appeared out of the forest and had carried them away; they had prevented them from crying out to warn their parents. After a mile or so the children had been forced to walk under their own steam, and they had eventually been brought to this village, where they had spent the night.

It seemed clear to Philip and the President that the children had been abducted by a few younger men from the village who had been caught up in the general hysteria which had followed Nyanga's coup. Once they had got the children as far as the village, however, the young tribesmen had discovered that they were not at all popular with the headman and some of the older men; the wiser heads had soon realised that this action would bring nothing but trouble to the village, and a long debate had ensued on what should be done next.

Fortunately the children did not seem to be too upset by their adventure. They had been badly frightened at first, of course, but they had not been physically hurt in any way, and they had been given a good breakfast by the headman's wife. Although they had not previously been familiar with this particular village, they knew the ways of the forest people as a whole, and they even knew a little of their language, so it had not been too traumatic an experience for them. Their main worry at the moment seemed to be what their parents would say when they returned.

'Do you think Mummy will be cross?' asked the little girl.

'No, I don't think she'll be cross,' said Philip with a grin. 'I think your Mum and Dad will be very glad to see you.'

The children's home lay a few miles further to the south than Philip and the President would otherwise have gone, but it was a detour which they were pleased to make. And in due course, by following the children's directions, they arrived at the Carlows' home.

Home turned out to be an extremely isolated villa; beside it stood a school-hut made of wood, with a corrugated iron roof. From the sign outside this primitive school-house it was clear that the Carlows were members of one of the many Protestant missionary groups which had given decades of selfless service to Balembi and to many other parts of Africa. The President knew better than anyone what a debt his country owed to such people; many of the mission-school teachers lived and worked in the most remote of country areas, far from their friends and relations and cut off from all but the most occasional contacts with the comforts of civilized life. The President could not have been more pleased to be able to repay just a very small part of that huge debt by bringing these children back home.

The Carlows turned out to be a young couple in their mid-thirties,

English by origin. But it was a long time before either of them could say anything to the two men who had arrived with their children so completely unexpectedly.

Martin Carlow and his wife had almost given up hope of seeing Colin and Susan again, and their joy at being reunited was touching to see. They both hugged and kissed the youngsters alternately, with tears streaming down their faces, and the President and Philip stood back, feeling thoroughly out of place. They would have preferred to drive quietly away, leaving the family to celebrate in private, but they badly needed information on the developments in Sungbarta; and in any case, Martin Carlow begged them not to go until he had had a chance to thank them properly.

Eventually Mrs Carlow took the two children inside the house to clean them up, and her husband made cups of thick black coffee for everyone. They drank it on a shaded veranda at the back of the house, where Philip and the President explained how it was pure chance that they had spotted the children from their car. Martin Carlow gave no sign that he recognized the President, and Kasaboru felt that this reaction was not a pretence; missionaries of this kind were traditionally quite uninterested in politics.

'Well,' said Martin when they had finished their story, 'this has certainly been a real test of faith!' And he laughed for the first time, changing the whole aspect of his face; he began to look more relaxed and at ease. 'But our prayers have been answered,' he continued, 'as we should have known they would be. . . . Now tell me – I think you said you were on your way to Sungbarta.'

Philip nodded. 'Yes. And we were wondering if you had heard any recent news. We understand that the city may be under attack.'

'So I believe,' said Martin Carlow. 'So I believe. There are rumours about Gabuti troops.' He took off his glasses and polished them on a handkerchief. 'Unfortunately, as you will appreciate, we are very much out of touch here. We do have a small portable radio, but the batteries gave out two days ago.'

'How far is Sungbarta from here?' asked the President.

'Oh – about ten miles. The road is quite reasonable once you strike the main highway.'

'Ah,' said the President. 'But that's just the point. We weren't thinking of going by road – at least, not all the way. With Gabuti troops all around that would be much too dangerous. What we want to do is to approach the city across the lake.'

'Oh,' said Martin Carlow in surprise. 'You mean by boat?'

'Yes.'

'Do you have a boat at your disposal?'

'Not yet,' said the President. 'But sailing is a popular pastime round here – there must be a boat somewhere that we can beg, borrow or steal.'

'Praise the Lord!' said the missionary suddenly. He put his hands

281

together in an attitude of prayer. 'Praise the Lord,' he repeated.
'God is good – I knew that He would show us some way in which
we could repay you, and indeed He has. You need a boat – and I,
thank God, can give you one.'

The Carlows invited Philip and the President to stay for a meal with
them, but they quite accepted the point that the travellers were
anxious to be away, and shortly afterwards Philip and the President
drove off once more.

They took with them detailed instructions for reaching another
mission school, some five miles away on the shores of Lake Alberton. This school was a rather bigger and better-equipped one than
the Carlows' and it was run by a group of six nuns. The nuns were
good friends of the Carlows, despite the fact that, as Martin explained with a shy smile, they were of a different branch of the
Christian faith. And it was there, at the lakeside mission, that the
Carlows kept a small sailing dinghy which constituted their only
concession to frivolous amusement. They offered the boat as a gift
without any qualification, and for the moment Philip and the President had accepted; later, if all went well, they would be able to
return the gift with interest.

Following the route along the dust-track roads which Martin
Carlow had sketched out for them, they reached the nuns' school
in about twenty minutes. The Carlows had advised them that as it
was a Sunday the nuns would not wish to receive visitors, particularly men, but Martin Carlow had written a long letter which he
suggested they should hand to Sister Mary on their arrival.

At first the mission school seemed totally deserted. There were
four main school buildings: these were prefabricated wooden classrooms set in a square on the side of a small hill which sloped down
to the lake about fifty yards away. The nuns' residence was set
further back in the trees: it was an older wooden building with three
storeys culminating in a bell tower. The setting was exceptionally
beautiful, with the sun reflecting dazzlingly off the ripples of the
blue lake; the trees all around provided shade and a relatively cool
atmosphere.

The two visitors made no attempt to knock on any doors because
the Carlows had told them that it would be sufficient just to arrive
and to wait: their presence would not go unnoticed for long. And
after ten minutes Sister Mary, the senior of the six nuns, came out
of the main house to greet them.

At first the Sister was polite, but distant. However, when she had
read and digested the Carlows' letter her attitude became very much
warmer.

'Well now,' she said, 'you've done a great service to the Carlows,
I see.'

Her accent was still very Irish, despite ten years in Africa. 'They've asked me to help you in every way I can, and of course I surely will. And you're to take their boat whenever you wish, they say.'

'That's right,' said Philip. 'They've offered us the loan of it for the time being.'

'Good – well then let me show you where things are.'

Sister Mary led the way through the trees to a small banda or summer-house with a thatched roof, about sixty yards from the main buildings. Beside the banda, on a launching trolley, was the Carlows' small dinghy.

'Here's the boat,' said Sister Mary. 'And forgive me for asking, but will you be leaving soon?'

'Not until dusk,' the President answered.

Sister Mary looked at him sharply. She was somewhere in her late forties, small and slim and dressed in a white knee-length habit with a white hood. She held her hands folded comfortably in front of her at waist level; her expression was lively and alert, but her face was pale compared with that of most people who lived in the Balembian climate.

'Oh,' she said with wry smile. 'I see. That seems a little odd – but no doubt you know best, and I'll not be asking you any awkward questions. You've proved beyond doubt that you're good men at heart, though you certainly look like villains.'

Philip and the President glanced at each other and then burst out laughing. A dirtier, scruffier, more shop-soiled pair could hardly ever have called on the nuns.

'Well, we'll keep out of the way and try not to be any trouble until we go,' said Philip.

'Sure and you'll not be any trouble at all,' said Sister Mary. 'But I'd be glad if you'd stay out here in the banda – that would be more discreet, I think. I'll bring you food and drink in a little while.'

'Thank you very much,' said the President. 'That would be very kind.'

'What about your car? Will you be leaving it here?'

Philip hesitated. 'Well, yes,' he said. 'For the moment.'

'Well park it deep in among the trees,' said the Sister. 'It'll come to no harm there if it's right out of sight – and we prefer not to advertise the fact that we have gentlemen callers.'

With a smile Sister Mary then left them, and Philip and the President began to prepare for the last stage of their long journey.

They moved their car as requested and checked out the dinghy, which was a Heron; they put up the mast, got out the sails from a cupboard in the banda, and generally prepared it for the coming five-mile trip. The equipment all seemed to be there, and they were well pleased with the craft; Philip was the more experienced sailor, but Kasaboru had also done a little in his time.

Shortly afterwards Sister Mary returned with a lunch of bread, cheese and milk, for which she refused all payment.

They began to ask her some questions about recent events in Sungbarta, and she stayed with them for a while, obviously anxious to help if she could. Like Martin Carlow before her, she evidently had no idea that one of her two guests was President Kasaboru.

The nuns had no radio, but Sister Mary had heard through the children who came to her school about the so-called 'witch-doctors' war'. The nuns had also seen Gabuti planes flying in across the lake on many occasions, and smoke had afterwards been seen rising from the city; gunfire had often been heard, particularly on the previous two days. A fair number of boats had reportedly tried to sail out of Sungbarta, but very few had succeeded; most had been shot up from the shore and sunk. Sister Mary confessed that she had not heard of anyone else trying to sail *into* the city; but then, she added, no doubt the two of them had their reasons.

After the two men had finished their lunch Sister Mary removed the empty plates and left them to their own devices. Cooled by a soft breeze off the lake, they settled down in easy chairs inside the banda and began to make plans for the coming night.

'Presumably you're going to head for a particular point on the Sungbarta shore,' suggested Philip.

'Yes.' Kasaboru nodded. 'Many months ago, when the situation first began to look serious, Dan Levene and I made plans for just such an eventuality as this. It was decided then that I would approach the city across the water, tying up at a jetty near where he lives. We land there, all being well, and then move on up towards the house. At midnight precisely I then make a pre-arranged signal with my torch, and if I get the correct answer it means that all is safe and we can go in.'

'And what if we don't get the right answer?' asked Philip.

The President sighed. 'Well, I will deal with that particular problem when I have to. But basically I suppose that if Sungbarta has been taken and the Mayor captured, the only sensible thing to do would be to head for the nearest friendly country. . . . Still, let us hope it does not come to that.'

'As far as I can see,' Philip continued, 'this is only the third day on which Sungbarta has been under really serious attack. I should have thought they could hold out for at least that long, wouldn't you?'

The President hesitated. 'Well, it's always difficult to predict,' he said eventually. 'I would have said that a week was the limit of endurance myself. It all depends on what sort of defences the Sungbartans have been able to put together. But if I can just get into the city, even if it is under siege, I can get the chance that I'm looking for. All I need is an opportunity to speak to the Balembian people over the radio, and an opportunity to ask the UN formally to help us. That's all – and if I can't pull the situation round, given the facilities to do those few things, then Nyanga deserves to win.'

The President then fell silent, occupied by his own thoughts, and after a while he began to doze.

Philip also relaxed in his chair, watching the lizards in the thatched roof of the summer-house making short work of the flies. Then his mind began to work back over the events which had occurred in the few short days since Nyanga's coup; above all, he worried and wondered about what might have happened to Jane Stuart.

He was well aware that in all probability Jane was long since dead, drowned in the grossly flooded mountain stream which had swept her away. But you could never be quite sure what had happened in a situation like that – there was always just a chance that she might have kept her head above water. Just a chance. . . .

He too began to fall gently asleep.

The peace and quiet of that Sunday afternoon lasted for all of half an hour.

Then, faintly at first, but growing steadily louder, Philip woke up to the sound of an approaching vehicle. It was a heavy lorry of some kind, grinding its way in low gear down the hill towards the mission school. The President heard it too, and woke up with a jerk.

Cautiously the two men peered through the trees to see what was happening – and to their dismay they saw that the noisy engine belonged to an army lorry, which now pulled to a halt on the edge of the children's play area. A number of soldiers climbed down from the back of the lorry and began to look around them with interest; they were obviously here to search for something – or someone.

Philip and the President glanced at each other in dismay. Then, keeping low to remain out of sight, they hurried towards their car.

Twenty-five

Duncan Grey had a splitting headache, which had not been improved by the half-bottle of whisky which he had drunk since dawn. So far he had had a terrible day, and the only prospect of improvement seemed to lie in the other half of the whisky bottle.

Grey had spent most of the previous afternoon sitting around in a primitive dirty hut, waiting for the tribal drums to tell him that the President had been captured in one of the villages in the forest around Lake Alberton. But the message had never come through, and towards midnight he had decided that as usual he would just have to do everything himself.

This morning therefore he had set off with his four remaining men and had begun to quarter the ground on the southern shore of Lake Alberton. He had covered as many of the small settlements occupied by Europeans as he could. He had warned the few residents who were still there to be on the lookout for three dangerous men, one black and two white (he didn't yet know that Bob Fuller was dead); if seen, these men were to be detained and the authorities notified. Up to now, however, Grey had not met with much success: certainly no-one would admit to having seen any such men passing by, and all he had received for his pains so far had been a number of half-hearted promises to keep an eye open, and a great number of undisguised insults – and these had been offered despite the risk of offending his soldiers.

So Duncan Grey was not a happy man. To cap it all, his radio had ceased working and he could no longer communicate with anyone except in face-to-face conversation. He had reluctantly been forced to the conclusion that unless he could somehow pull off something miraculous this afternoon, he was going to have to link up with the Gabuti forces at Sungbarta tonight and openly admit that he had failed. He took another swig of whisky and wiped his mouth with the back of his hand – which reminded him that he hadn't shaved this morning, either.

As soon as they saw the soldiers arriving, Philip and the President rapidly left the banda where they had been resting and made their way unseen to their car, hidden deep in the forest. There Philip

286

collected a .303 rifle and some ammunition, and the President picked up a Sten gun. Then they came back in a wide circle to the south, which placed them among trees on the hill behind the nuns' residence. From here they could comfortably see down into the square of ground flanked by the four classroom buildings, and they could observe what the soldiers were doing without being seen themselves.

There seemed to be a white officer in charge of the four Balembian soldiers, and something about the way the man was standing looked familiar to Philip. Then the officer turned so that Philip could see his profile. Of course! Philip recognised him at once: it was Duncan Grey, Jane's uncle.

At first Philip found it very hard to understand what the technical director of Radio Digara was doing out here in the wilds. But then he remembered that Eileen Grey had been having a flagrant affair with Joro Nyanga, and it all began to fit. Nyanga would naturally have been interested in getting Grey out of Digara, so that he and Eileen could carry on their affair without the awkward problem of her husband hovering in the background – and in all probability Nyanga had also been short of reliable European helpers. Yes, it made sense all right.

Duncan Grey was now talking to Sister Mary. Philip and the President were too far away to hear what was being said, but Sister Mary could be seen shaking her head. And despite the inherent danger of the situation Philip could not help being slightly amused. He could not imagine Sister Mary telling a lie, not for one moment, but he could not see her betraying them either – and he guessed that the fluency of her Irish tongue had enabled her to put together some convincing answers to Duncan Grey's questions without actually endangering her immortal soul; he would have loved to be able to hear what the Sister said.

In any event Duncan Grey soon dismissed her. Sister Mary then stood on one side while the soldiers lethargically searched the buildings; Grey himself sat down and concentrated on his bottle of whisky.

After a few minutes the soldiers abandoned their search and the Corporal spoke to his officer. Grey nodded, and Corporal Avakubi began shouting and clapping his hands: it became apparent that he was demanding food and drink for the men.

During the next half-hour a table and five chairs were set out in a patch of shade, and the nuns provided the soldiers with a simple meal, similar to the one Philip and the President had already enjoyed. Corporal Avakubi took charge of the arrangements, and to the great amusement of his men he insisted that every detail should be just right. Duncan Grey pretended not to notice. The six nuns were kept running and fetching non-stop, and one or two of the older ones became very harrassed and upset. Not Sister Mary, however: she remained calm and self-possessed, and she often spoke words of encouragement to the others.

After the meal was over the soldiers relaxed in their chairs, laughing and joking. Philip, however, kept a careful watch on the Corporal; he felt that the man had a nasty gleam in his eye. And sure enough, it was not long before Avakubi decided to amuse himself.

The Corporal began shouting at the nuns once more, pushing and shoving them until they were all assembled in a line by the table. Duncan Grey occasionally uttered a word of protest, but he was clearly pretty well drunk by now, and Avakubi ignored him completely.

Avakubi then walked proudly up and down the line of white-cloaked nuns, a bayonet swinging in his long fingers. He obviously enjoyed playing the part of a general inspecting his men, particularly when most of the 'men' were clearly terrified of him.

Having inspected the Sisters closely, Avakubi then selected the youngest and most attractive of them. His choice was a nun aged about thirty; she was short and stocky, but with a pleasing bloom to her cheeks.

Avakubi now indicated unmistakably that the nun should take off her clothes. Naturally she refused, shaking her head violently. The other nuns protested, but Avakubi threatened them with his bayonet and they stepped reluctantly back into line. The pattern was quite clear: Avakubi was going to cause trouble.

Philip sighed. 'Well,' he whispered to the President, 'it looks as if we're going to have to do something about this. Have you got a clear line of fire?'

'Not very,' whispered Kasaboru. 'Let's wait and see what develops – the officer may intervene if the soldiers turn really nasty.'

'Well, we'll see,' said Philip.

Down below, Corporal Avakubi was again insisting that the younger nun should take off her clothes; he was holding her firmly by the arm, but the Sister was still resisting strongly. Angry voices were raised, with the soldiers and the other nuns all joining in.

At this point Duncan Grey finally roused himself. He stood up, with difficulty, from his chair at the table and staggered over to stand between his Corporal and the nun he was berating.

'Take your hands off that woman!' bellowed Grey in a voice thick with alcohol. 'And get back to the lorry! I'll deal with you later.' And he stood there, gently swaying.

Corporal Avakubi looked at his commander with the utmost contempt. He had never had much respect for this feeble little white man, whom everyone knew was a cuckold, and he now felt a burning hatred for him. Did the officer really think that he, a man who couldn't even keep his own wife, was going to prevent a Corporal in the Balembian army from raping a mere nun if he wanted to? Well if so, the officer had another think coming. The Corporal hawked loudly and then spat a large gobbet of saliva straight into Duncan Grey's face.

For a second Grey could hardly believe what had happened. But then he reached up to his face, found that he really had been insulted, and let out a roar of anger. He began groping for the Enfield revolver in a holster at his belt, but as he did so Avakubi stabbed him through the heart with his bayonet; then he stabbed him again. With a moan Duncan Grey fell to his knees, and after a moment he pitched forward on to his face.

Some of the nuns screamed and crossed themselves. Even the other soldiers seemed stunned and taken aback. But after only a slight pause, during which he stared down at the body in the dust, Avakubi carried on as before. He started shouting and pulling at the youngest nun all over again, even more determined to have his way than before.

The President nudged Philip's arm. 'Let's move into a better position,' he said, indicating a pile of rocks to their right. 'We'll still be hidden by the trees over there, and if we have to shoot we'll have some support to rest on.'

'Good idea,' whispered Philip. And while the soldiers shouted and gesticulated, he and the President quietly wriggled over to their new vantage-point.

Down in the square the soldiers had now shepherded all the nuns except the youngest into one of the classrooms, where they could be seen kneeling in prayer; one of the soldiers stood guard over them outside the door.

The youngest nun was now kicked and punched until she agreed to take off her clothes, which she did as slowly as possible. But eventually, after much bullying from Avakubi, she stood there quite naked. She was a woman with strong thighs and arms, the result of much hard physical work, and her breasts were large and well shaped; Avakubi was clearly delighted with her. Her skin was exceptionally white, and the Corporal commented on it admiringly; he attempted to stroke her back and buttocks, but the nun shrank from his touch.

Silently, Philip pushed off the safety-catch and cocked the Lee Enfield rifle.

'Now?' asked the President.

'Not yet,' said Philip. 'I'll take the Corporal, you take the one by the classroom door – then you take the shorter of the two others.'

Kasaboru nodded. He found that his heart was pounding with the tension.

Corporal Avakubi prodded the naked woman's bottom with his bayonet. She screamed and tried to fend him off with her hands, her large breasts swinging freely as she moved in panic. He poked her again and again, terrifying her with the flashing piece of steel, a wide grin on his face. She backed away from him, her eyes staring.

The other soldiers all chuckled with glee; they liked to see the fear in the nun's face, so they pushed her back towards Avakubi so that he could attack her once again.

The Corporal's eyes shone with a cruel joy, and his arm went back to slash a great arc across the nun's exposed flesh. But before he could deliver the blow, Philip Morgan shot him through the chest.

The bullet hit a rib just above Avakubi's left lung and deflected in a mis-shapen lump directly into his heart; it tore a gaping hole in his left ventricle and exited from his back in a shower of blood and tissue. The force of the impact knocked Avakubi clean off his feet: he went over backwards, with his legs straight out and slightly apart and his arms spread wide; he landed lifelessly in the dust, and the bayonet with blood on its tip flashed brightly as it flew out of his grasp and landed harmlessly some distance away.

The President almost simultaneously fired a single shot from his Sten gun into the body of the soldier by the classroom door; the man staggered, then clutched himself with a cry of agony and fell to his knees. Kasaboru shot him again, this time through the head, and the man sprawled sideways without a sound; a trickle of blood began to curl away on the ground.

One of the other soldiers remained frozen to the spot with horror. He was Philip's target, and a .303 bullet smashed into his skull where the jawbone meets the ear; fragments of bone and metal dispersed widely into his brain and he died instantly.

The other soldier was quicker off the mark: he ran for the lorry. But that, as it turned out, was a mistake: he ran into open space, and that meant that the President could safely fire bursts from his Sten gun. He fired two quick combinations of three rounds each, and the man went down kicking and squealing. He twitched awkwardly for a few moments and tried to get up, but the effort was too much for him and he turned over on to his back; his left hand flopped to the ground and the life visibly went out of him.

Philip hurried down the hill and unlocked the classroom door to let out the imprisoned nuns. They immediately rushed over to the youngest of their number, whose name it appeared was Ruth, and whisked her away indoors. In a few seconds there was almost total silence and stillness where earlier there had been panic, screaming and pain.

Left on their own for the moment, Philip and the President tried to decide what they should do now. They had no way of knowing whether the soldiers who had called here were part of a much larger force searching the whole area, or whether they were an isolated group. If the men were part of a larger force it was possible that other army personnel would come looking for them when they failed

290

to appear. However, after a brief discussion the two men decided to get rid of all evidence of the soldiers' visit first – they would consider what to do about any other enquirers later.

They dragged the five bodies over to the lorry and dumped them in a line in the back. Then they scuffled all the bloodstains into the dust and put away the folding tables and chairs. Finally they were just about to drive off to dump the lorry and the bodies some distance away, when Sister Mary appeared from the house.

Philip asked her if she knew of a ravine or a quarry within a few miles' radius, where the lorry could be abandoned with little likelihood of it being found in the next few days. But Sister Mary objected: she didn't like the idea of the dead being treated in such a disrespectful manner – not even *these* dead.

'But Sister,' Philip protested. 'What would happen if these bodies were found here? We have to get rid of them in order to protect you.'

'God will protect us,' said Sister Mary simply. 'And if anyone asks us what happened, we will tell the truth.'

Philip was not at all happy with that proposal. He strongly suspected that if any other soldiers came along and found some of their comrades dead, the nuns would get very little sympathy and respect for having told the truth. He glanced at the President, wondering how far he could go in telling Sister Mary who she was dealing with.

'All right then,' he said after a moment. 'Let me put it another way. It is necessary for the security of the state that no-one should know what has happened here today – or at least, not for a few days. We would much prefer that you did not tell anyone that we have been here.'

Sister Mary's eyes had followed Philip's to the President's face, and suddenly she reacted. She found herself looking at the handsome black-skinned man who was standing beside Philip with a new insight. It was as if she now understood something which had been bothering her unconsciously for some time.

'Ah,' she said. She smiled and nodded her head. 'Now that is a different argument – and one which in the circumstances I am prepared to accept. There are things I will do for the nation's sake that I would not do for our own. But you must still give me ten minutes with the dead – I must say a few prayers, even for those who in life were our enemies.'

Philip grinned and shook his head in amazement: this woman was really extraordinary. 'Be my guest,' he said, and helped her into the back of the lorry.

A quarter of an hour later the President set off in the army lorry and drove it five miles to a lonely stretch of cart-track which ran along the edge of a cliff forty feet high; Philip followed behind in the Morris.

Together they set the lorry up so that when the handbrake was released it would slide gently over the cliff, carrying its five corpses with it. Then, when everything was ready, they took the final step and moved smartly out of the way. The lorry rolled forward and pitched slowly over onto its back in the air; it landed at the foot of the cliff with an enormous crunch which generated a huge cloud of dust. And with that accomplished, the two men then returned to the mission.

In the evening they shared a highly appetizing meal with the nuns. They enjoyed it enormously, despite the fact that the nuns insisted on thanking them for what they had done over and over again; it was fortunate, Philip and the President felt, that nuns were discouraged from kissing anyone, or they could have been even more seriously embarrassed than they were.

Afterwards they waited until darkness was almost complete before leaving the mission. But eventually, when visibility was down to a hundred yards or so, they launched the Carlows' little Heron from its trolley and set out to sail across Lake Alberton to Sungbarta.

Sister Ruth was in an extremely shocked state as a result of her experiences at the hands of Corporal Avakubi – in fact she was still visibly trembling when they left – but she had recovered sufficiently to join them for the meal and to come out and see them off.

The light breeze filled the sails of the Heron, and the boat began to move away over the water. Philip was at the helm with the President in the bow, and for the most part they stared ahead into the enclosing gloom of the dusk. Occasionally, however, they looked back at the shore.

Sister Ruth's hand had been badly cut by a slash from Avakubi's bayonet and it was heavily bandaged; and the very last they could see of the mission, as the breeze rocked them over the water, was the white patch of the nun's hand, moving constantly against the dark background as it waved and waved goodbye.

Twenty-six

After leaving the Mayor's house, Joro Nyanga treated himself to a tour of the fallen city of Sungbarta. He took the precaution of keeping his large military escort with him, but in the event he found that the soldiers were not needed.

On the whole Nyanga was well pleased with what he saw. Naturally there was some disorder and confusion in the streets – he would have been surprised if there had not been – but the most important point was that there was no sign of any resistance. On the contrary, quite a number of the citizens, particularly the less well educated, seemed to have decided that it was more discreet to appear to welcome the Gabuti troops than to be seen to be gloomy and despondent. As soon as these particular Sungbartans realized that it was the victorious Nyanga who was driving by, they nudged each other and broke into forced smiles and loud applause. Nyanga waved and smiled back: he thoroughly approved of such hypocrisy because he knew that with repetition the emotion would come to seem natural and genuine. Before long, he felt, the Sungbartans would begin to love him as they had loved Kasaboru.

After about half an hour spent driving around the streets, Nyanga arrived at City Hall. He made a particular point of inspecting the police cells in the basement, and again he approved of what he saw; at the moment the cells were largely empty, and he ordered spaces to be reserved for the high-level prisoners whom he was expecting to have to accommodate before long. Then he went up in the lift to the fourteenth floor, where he found General Tchen, the Gabuti commander. The General had established his communications centre in the council chamber, which gave him a magnificent view of almost the whole of the city and of the lake to the east.

Nyanga arrived in the council chamber to find that General Tchen was being served coffee by one of his dusky and well-proportioned female 'assistants' – and that reminded Nyanga that it had been all of thirty-six hours since he had had a woman himself. He promptly telephoned Digara and gave orders for Jane Stuart to be brought to Sungbarta immediately; he felt that a second helping from that particular dish would probably taste even sweeter than the first.

293

In the meantime Conrad Hall and Eileen Grey had had another meeting, this time over breakfast at the President's palace, back in Digara. After dinner the previous evening they had gone to bed separately – neither was the other's type – but they had decided to keep in very close touch from then on; the situation was changing hourly and it was obviously going to be important to have up-to-date information.

This morning there was news both of the fall of Sungbarta and of the United Nations' decision to intervene in Balembi. And the Hall/Grey alliance soon decided that it was in both their interests to join up with Nyanga at once. The game, as Conrad Hall observed, was beginning to hot up, and Nyanga was clearly going to need a wise and experienced man to advise him; in Eileen's view he was also going to need the company of a good woman to take his mind off the worrying affairs of state.

Having reached these conclusions, Conrad Hall and Eileen Grey promptly persuaded General Juba to arrange a flight to Sungbarta for them; they arrived in a Gabuti helicopter just before noon.

Nyanga was not, in fact, very pleased to see either of them. He had noticed that Eileen's attitude towards him was becoming increasingly proprietorial, and he didn't like it; he also felt that Conrad Hall's Germanic concentration on work and efficiency was distinctly tedious. However, he recognized that both Hall and Eileen had their uses, and he greeted them with a nod when they entered the office in City Hall which he had recently commandeered.

Conrad Hall sensed the restraint in Nyanga's attitude, but he ignored it completely. 'Congratulations, my dear Joro!' be bellowed heartily, seizing Nyanga's hand and shaking it up and down. 'Congratulations – an absolutely magnificent victory!'

Elbowing Conrad Hall out of the way, Eileen Grey smothered Nyanga's face with kisses and squirmed her groin against his. Nyanga remained stony-faced at first, but after Eileen had worked on him for a few seconds he eventually grinned with pleasure and squeezed her warmly in return.

'Thank you,' he muttered to Hall. 'Thank you very much.'

Conrad Hall rubbed his hands together briskly. 'Well – now that you've polished off Sungbarta, Joro, we can really get things humming. In the next few days we'll get everybody back to work – we'll stop all this milling around in the streets – and in a week or two we'll be breaking all records for production, you mark my words. Of course, this decision of the UN's might cause us a bit of a problem. . . .'

'Oh no it won't,' said Nyanga firmly. He disentangled himself from Eileen in order to emphasise the point. 'It will be no problem at all. It will take the UN weeks to get properly organized, and in any case there's not a damn thing they can do to change the situation once they get here. I am the head of state – I am the king of the castle, and there's no way they can get around that, particularly after I have addressed the Congress of Independent African States. And in a way I quite welcome the UN's coming. Their arrival will mean that the Gabuti troops will have to go, and that's all to the good – we don't want them here for ever. And then after a while the Russians will see to it that the UN are also forced to pull out, and so before very long we shall be all on our own again – which is exactly what we want. And then, my dear Conrad, we shall be in like Flynn, as I believe the Americans say.'

Conrad Hall positively chortled with amusement at this last remark, making himself appear far more impressed by Nyanga's wit than he actually was. Now that Nyanga possessed real power it was going to be important to remain in his favour, and Hall was an old hand at flattery.

Eileen Grey was also very anxious to consolidate her relationship with Nyanga, and later that morning she persuaded him to have lunch with her alone. After they had finished the meal, which was served in the Mayor's private dining-room, she exercised all her seductive skills to get him to make love to her.

Nyanga obliged, but he worked out some of his resentment by calling in the waitresses and the cook to watch him at work. He deliberately humiliated Eileen in front of these spectators; he stripped her naked, slapped her around the room a few times, and punched her hard on the fleshy part of her upper arms until she screamed with pain. Then he had intercourse with her on the dining-room floor, still with the servants watching.

Eileen was hurt physically but she didn't care. She had been so desperate for reassurance that any kind of attention from Nyanga was better than none; and she took comfort from the thought that while he was beating her up he could not be with anyone else.

For the rest of the afternoon Nyanga found his time fully occupied with political matters, but towards eight o'clock in the evening his mind began to turn towards women once again. He decided to visit Jane Stuart.

Jane too had been brought to Sungbarta by a Gabuti army helicopter, though not the same one that had carried Conrad Hall and Eileen Grey. She was now safely installed in a cell in the women's section of the jail in the basement of City Hall; Nyanga had only to descend in the lift to be able to call on her very quickly.

Jane looked up as the heavy metal door of the cell was unlocked; there was always a faint hope that this time the face which greeted her would be both familiar and friendly. But when she saw that her visitor was Joro Nyanga she turned her head to the wall and ignored him.

Nyanga came and sat down on the bed beside her. This particular cell was at least clean and fairly comfortable, and he looked around with approval. Then he placed his hand on top of Jane's as it rested on her knee. He looked at her carefully, and seemed quite impressed by what he saw: her beauty was unimpaired, and the two police-women in Digara had provided her with clean underclothes, a brand-new shirt and a pair of slacks.

'You know,' said Nyanga thoughtfully, 'you really are a very desirable woman. . . . Of course, I would prefer to see you smiling and happy rather than sad and upset as you are now, but we could find ways of curing that. . . .' His grip tightened on her hand. 'I'm sorry I wasn't able to come and see you last night,' he continued.

Jane wasn't sorry at all: she still felt painfully sore and bruised from his first visit, but she decided not to say so.

'Unfortunately I just had to fly here to Sungbarta,' Nyanga explained with a sigh. 'There are some things which just will not wait, as I'm sure you understand.'

He stood up and went and leaned against the wall opposite so that he could look at Jane properly; he folded his arms across his chest.

'You know, Jane, I have been very much impressed by you in a number of ways. You are obviously intelligent. You have profes-sional qualifications which inspire respect – and above all you are beautiful. Yes indeed, you are exceptionally beautiful. . . . I have had a great many women in my time, women of all types and races, and I can tell you without exaggeration that physically you are the most delectable of any of them. With just a little encouragement I could become very, very keen on you, Jane. Very keen indeed. Obsessed, even.'

Jane said nothing. She kept her eyes on the floor.

Nyanga paused and then went on. 'Of course, I can have you any time I want you. Physically, I mean. That is why I have had you brought here. If you resist I can have you tied down, or I can beat you unconscious. But I would prefer, believe it or not, I would prefer you to be my partner willingly. I would very much like you to co-operate, and do whatever I ask without being beaten and coerced. And who knows – with a little practice you might even come to enjoy it. I could name a great many who have. White women, too, the wives and daughters of some very eminent men who have come to me and asked me – begged me, even – to make love to them.'

Nyanga sat down beside Jane once more; he put his arm around her shoulders, his face close to hers.

'Now I see from your face, Jane, that at the moment you find that hard to accept. Well, that's understandable. You've had a rough time these last few days, and you don't like being locked up in here. Well of course not – no-one would. And there's no reason why you should be locked up any longer. You can be out of here tonight if you wish – it's just a question of your attitude of mind. . . .'

Nyanga pulled Jane's shoulders round so that she had to face him; his voice was intense and persuasive.

'Be my lover, Jane,' he said fiercely. 'Be my woman. Make up your mind that you're going to be a winner, not a loser. A survivor, not a victim. All you have to do is make love to me, wherever and whenever I wish. And you have to do it with enthusiasm – play-act a little if you must, but make it convincing. You have to go down on your knees and beg for it if that is what I want – and it often is. . . . But in return for that simple service, just think what you will receive. You will earn your freedom for a start. You will be given money. Jewels. Position. Influence. Servants. You would become the acknowledged mistress of one of the most powerful men in Africa – and all because you are so beautiful.'

Nyanga removed his hands from Jane's shoulders and sat back a little.

'Think it over, my dear,' he said kindly. 'Think it over – I'm sure you'll make the right decision.'

Nyanga rose to leave, but even as he stood up Jane spoke.

'I don't need to think it over,' she said quickly. She was surprised by the sound of her own voice: cold and flat and unfriendly.

Nyanga turned back to look at her.

'I know how I feel about your suggestion,' Jane continued. 'I thought you might make a proposal like that, and I've already decided how I feel about it. And I know I shan't change my mind.' She looked up at him, her eyes steady.

'Oh?' said Nyanga. He was beginning to sense what her reply would be.

'Yes,' said Jane. 'It's very simple, really. . . . You see, I'd rather die than have you make love to me again. I really would. In fact I'd rather die than have you touch me again. If you so much as try to touch me, ever again, I shall fight and kick and struggle as hard as I possibly can, for as long as I possibly can. If you want me you're going to have to rape me, and if you rape me again I shall stop eating and drinking for good, until I'm dead – and then you won't be able to rape me any more, unless you fancy doing it to a corpse. And you're probably even capable of that.'

Nyanga placed his hands on his hips; his expression betrayed his anger. 'Oh, so that's your answer then, is it?' he said grimly. 'I should have known – I should have guessed that a girl like you would be a racist underneath. Like all the rest of you Europeans – you think that a black man is only acceptable if he's a slave – if he's prepared to stay in his place.' His tone was bitter.

'My attitude has got nothing to do with your being black, you half-wit,' snapped Jane. 'Don't you understand anything? It's not because you're black that I won't make love to you – it's because you're a liar and a thief and a torturer and a murderer. That's why – because of all those things, not because of the colour of your skin.'

Nyanga laughed shortly; he seemed genuinely amused. 'So, you'd rather die than be my woman – is that the position?'

'Yes,' said Jane hotly. She gripped the edge of the bed to try to control the violent trembling in her hands.

'Well, let me tell you something, little Miss Stuart.' Nyanga came back and stood in front of her, his eyes searching her face. 'Let me tell you this. You say you would rather die than have sex with me again. Well die you surely will, and soon too. I'm not interested in a lifeless lump of meat – making love to a woman whose heart is dead is no good to me, so we might as well kill you properly. And kill you I will – or rather Bulu will – in public, and slowly, until you beg me, beg me to cut your throat. Bulu has asked for you, and Bulu shall have you. And I will see to it that he makes you suffer.'

Nyanga seized Jane's throat and forced her chin up, trying to make her look at him.

'And let me tell you something else – something that I have only recently heard, something which I trust will cause you pain. It's no good hoping against hope that your boyfriend Philip Morgan will come running along to the rescue, because he won't. The only running Mr Morgan is going to do is straight into my trap. You see, this afternoon your beloved Uncle Duncan was found dead.'

Despite herself, Jane opened her eyes.

Nyanga smiled. 'Oh yes, that's right. Found dead, with four of his men. And do you know who killed them, my dear? Well, obviously it was Kasaboru and Morgan between them – who else would have done it? And that means only one thing – it means that Kasaboru and Morgan are almost here.'

Jane's eyes opened wider.

'Oh yes, my dear, they're almost here in Sungbarta, not very far away at all now. And tonight they're going to come sailing into the city, right into my open arms. I know what signals have been arranged to tell them that all is well, and I'm going to make sure that those signals are given. And tomorrow morning you and Philip Morgan can meet your death together. Just think about that as you try to sleep tonight.'

Roughly, Nyanga pushed Jane down on to the bed; then he left the cell, slamming its heavy door behind him.

For a long time Jane lay motionless where Nyanga had left her. She felt as if she had a temperature; she had a pounding headache and a feeling of sickness in the pit of her stomach.

But somewhere, somewhere deep down inside, there was a feeling of jubilation beginning to grow very slowly within her, and some time elapsed before she realized what was causing it.

Nyanga had tried hard to hurt her; he had deliberately tried to terrify her with his death sentence. But somehow she didn't feel terrified: she felt relieved and almost happy. Now why was that?

Then, at last, Jane understood.

Nyanga had told her that Philip was still alive. Philip had not been drowned in the mountain stream, and he and the President had somehow survived in spite of everything. Nyanga had not captured them yet, and now they were almost here – nearly here in Sungbarta, the city they had been trying to reach for so long.

Jane sat up on the bed. Salty tears ran down her cheeks and into the corners of her mouth. But if she was crying, she was crying with pleasure, not distress, and a single thought ran round and round in her head, repeating itself like a faulty gramophone record.

He's alive! she said to herself. Philip Morgan is alive! He's alive, he's alive, he's alive!

And nothing Nyanga had said could detract from the satisfaction of that.

PART THREE

The Arrival

One

The breeze on Lake Alberton was coming from the west; as a result Philip and the President had to tack back and forth repeatedly as they sailed towards Sungbarta in the small Heron. The sky was cloudy, but there were occasional glimpses of moonlight – enough at least to enable them to check their progress against the dark outline of the shore to the south. They stayed fairly well out in the lake, with the President in the bow keeping his eyes open as best he could for any possible obstacles in the water ahead.

After about half an hour they began to see the first faint outline of Sungbarta on the horizon. There were no streetlights on in the city, and very little traffic moving, but as they approached the western shore they could see a number of lights in the buildings facing east. They debated at length whether this was a good sign or a bad.

'It could mean anything,' said the President eventually. 'If the city has been captured, then of course there would be no reason for it to remain in darkness. But equally, even if it is still under attack, there is no need for buildings facing the lake to take any particular precautions, drawing blinds and so on. The Gabuti forces will be to the south. And anyway, African soldiers don't like fighting in the dark, as you know, so there's not much danger of attack by ground troops at this time of night. And I'm quite sure the Gabuti air force won't fly in the dark, either – they probably have enough trouble taking off and landing in daylight.'

Philip laughed. 'I bet you're right there,' he said. He prepared to swing the helm round to put the Heron onto the opposite tack. 'Lee-oh,' he called, and they went about.

Another half-hour passed and they were rapidly nearing the shore. There was nearly a five-mile gap between the two mouths of the river Sung which turned the city into an island, and by no means all of that five-mile shore-line was heavily inhabited. The jetty which the President was aiming for was well to the north, several miles from the south road bridge and in a quiet, sparsely populated district: it had been selected for that very reason, as a landing-point at which a small boat could come ashore at night without being noticed by anyone.

Philip brought the Heron close to the wooden landing-stage with no trouble at all; the time was five past eleven. As they tied up they heard the sound of shooting on the far side of the city, but again they did not quite know what to make of it: it might have been an attack from outside the city limits, or it might have been a light-hearted celebration by victorious troops. There was no way of telling except by seeing what sort of an answer they received to their coded message; so as they went ashore the President carefully checked the pocket torch which he had brought with him.

'Well, so far so good,' he said. 'Now let's see if we can find my friend the Mayor.'

Joro Nyanga had dined that night with Yuri Semenov and General Tchen. Before beginning his meal he had arranged for a number of reliable Gabuti officers with night-glasses to be stationed along the Sungbarta shore, and towards eleven o'clock one of them reported that a small dinghy had been sighted on the lake; it was being kept under careful observation.

Nyanga grunted. 'Well, this must be Kasaboru and his friend Morgan arriving,' he said thoughtfully. 'I suppose we'd better go and greet them, just to tidy things up. Semenov, you come with me.'

Together the two men then drove to the Mayor's house, which had been kept under heavy but unobtrusive guard ever since the morning. Now the house was completely surrounded by hand-picked Gabuti troops: Nyanga was absolutely determined that there should be no mistake on his side at this crucial stage of the game.

At this hour the Mayor's grandchildren were naturally asleep upstairs, but Jennifer Levene was sitting in the living-room, her hands folded: she seemed to be praying. Even Nyanga was surprised to see how shocked and ill she looked: the death of her daughter-in-law, followed so soon by the loss of her only son, had left her emotionally drained. On top of that, the city had now been captured and her husband had been arrested and dumped in the city jail. In the circumstances it was no wonder that Jennifer Levene looked ill.

Inside the house the night air was hot and humid, and even Nyanga was sweating as he came quietly into the softly-lit living-room and sat down on the settee beside the Mayor's wife. Jennifer Levene hardly noticed Nyanga's arrival: she was already so used to having her house full of unwelcome guests that she was beginning to be able to look straight through them.

'Now, my dear,' said Nyanga amiably, 'we are coming towards the end of this particular operation.'

Jennifer turned her head towards him. During the day she had been wondering whether she could somehow hide a knife or a hammer in her chair and attack him with it when he next appeared. But the white mercenaries who were chiefly responsible for guarding her had been too clever for that. And in any case, Nyanga was too quick and too strong for her; she could see that at a glance.

Nyanga explained exactly what he wanted her to do, and what would happen if she refused. 'You are to follow the agreed routine to the *letter*,' he emphasized. 'Do you understand?'

Jennifer nodded. Yes, she understood. Before being taken to the city jail, Dan Levene had impressed upon her that to save the lives of her grandchildren she was to co-operate fully with Nyanga. Every night for the last four nights she had watched her husband make the necessary signal to President Kasaboru, and tonight she would do it again; that way she could at least protect her grandchildren. And by now she had almost convinced herself that Paul Kasaboru would not be coming – when he found out that the city had been captured he would make other arrangements. He would go to some other city, some other country – anywhere but here, where Nyanga was waiting for him.

At five minutes to twelve precisely Jennifer went upstairs to her bedroom at the rear of the house. And at midnight she flashed out the letter K in Morse code three times: dash dot dash; dash dot dash; dash dot dash.

Of course there would be no answer, she was certain of that. She almost turned to go.

But then, to her horror, she saw the answering signal from the end of the garden: the letter L repeated in Morse three times. 'Oh no!' she said softly. And beside her Nyanga smiled in the darkness.

Nyanga took the Mayor's wife by the arm and led her downstairs. He whispered in her ear as they went, coaching her on the next move, reminding her of the penalties of failure. Jennifer almost stumbled and fell on the stairs, but he caught her in time and held her up. Nyanga then took her to the open back door of the house and left her there. There were no lights on anywhere in the house except in the curtained living-room.

Across the lawn two figures emerged from the shrubbery: they came quietly over the grass, silently jubilant that at long last they had reached their objective.

'Is that you, Jennifer?' called the President quietly.

'Yes,' came the answer. And then, before she could lose control of herself, Jennifer turned and almost ran back to the living-room.

The President and Philip were tired – deeply and bone-achingly tired. It was only as they had been resting in the undergrowth at the end of the Mayor's garden, waiting for midnight to come, that they had realized how desperately weary they were. But they were also exhilarated and pleased with themselves: while they were waiting, they had had time to think back over their experiences of the last few days, time to congratulate themselves on managing to survive the worst that their enemies and the landscape had been able to throw at them. And now, at last, they told themselves, they were here. They had arrived. And if they could achieve that, then surely everything else was now possible too: Kasaboru could establish a base here in Sungbarta; he could regain the presidency and he could restore democracy and the process of law. Everything was now possible.

But it was this combination of exhilaration and fatigue which proved deadly: it clouded their judgement and prevented them from seeing danger where normally they would have been fully conscious of it. And so now, quite unaware of any risk to themselves, the two men went happpily into the house through the back door. The President led the way through to the living-room, where Jennifer Levene sat waiting, her hands clasped over her mouth to stop herself screaming.

And even when he saw her, Kasaboru could not understand at first. He stood in the doorway of the room and looked at Jennifer Levene as she sat on the settee opposite him, the table-lamp behind her leaving her face in shadow. He could see that she was upset but his mind could not comprehend why. He went further into the room, a puzzled expression on his face; Philip followed.

'Jennifer – ' the President began.

And then two soldiers appeared in the doorway behind them, and Nyanga came in from the adjoining dining-room. All three of these men were armed and were obviously prepared to shoot if necessary; they moved swiftly into positions where they could fire freely without endangering each other. And then, of course, both Philip and the President recognised their mistake.

Nyanga smiled, his teeth gleaming white from a patch of shadow. 'Good evening, Kasaboru,' he said genially. 'How nice to see you again.'

Neither the President nor Philip felt anything at first. They had experienced too much, and come too far, for this sudden change in their fortunes to have any immediate effect. They simply stood there, silent and still, not knowing what to say or do. The fatigue which had blunted their reflexes had also slowed their emotional reactions: they felt numb and almost bewildered.

One of the soldiers handcuffed their hands behind their backs; then he searched them thoroughly and took away all their weapons. And when that was completed there was an almost tangible relaxation of tension in the room.

Jennifer Levene spoke hesitantly, her eyes filled with tears. 'Paul – Paul, I – he threatened the children, you see, that was why. We didn't want to tell him – please believe me. But he threatened the children, you see – unbelievable things. . . .'

306

The President made a conscious effort to overcome the despair which had belatedly begun to sweep over him. He smiled and spoke kindly.

'Don't worry, Jennifer,' he said. 'I know what this man is like – I know the kinds of pressure he applies, so don't distress yourself. I'm sure he gave you no choice – no choice at all.'

'That will do,' said Nyanga curtly. 'You can decide who takes the blame for your problems later on.' Now that his prisoners were safely restrained by steel handcuffs, he came a little closer. 'Well,' he said after a moment, 'it took you long enough to get here – what kept you?'

No-one answered.

'Lost your tongues, eh? Well, I don't blame you. It must be a bit of a shock, coming all that way only to end up in prison again. You could have saved yourselves a lot of time and energy if you'd stayed where you were in the first place. . . .'

Nyanga sat down on the arm of a chair.

'Well now, I'm anxious to attend to more important things, but let me tell you what's going to happen to you next. To put it at its simplest, we're going to take up where we left off. You, Mr former President, will end up by confessing to numerous crimes against the state – Semenov will see to that, and quickly too. We have all the evidence assembled, and the evidence coupled with a confession will seal your fate for good. When the UN get here in a week or two's time you'll be safely imprisoned for your various crimes, and no-one, absolutely no-one, either here or anywhere else, will be seeking to get you released.'

At the mention of the UN Philip shot an urgent glance at the President, but Kasaboru did not appear to have noticed the reference – or if he had, he wasn't going to show Nyanga how he felt about it.

'Later on,' Nyanga continued, 'when the outside world has had time to forget all about you, you will be shot while trying to escape. A few months from now an incident like that will merit all of one small paragraph on an inside page of the world's leading newspapers. Your career will end with a whimper rather than a bang.'

Nyanga switched his attention to Philip.

'Now Mr Morgan,' he said briskly. 'What about you? Well, I think we'll simply forge your signature on a statement confirming that you were recruited by the British government to assassinate me. That ought to do. Such a statement will embarrass the British and will give us a good reason for executing you first thing tomorrow morning. You and your girlfriend Miss Stuart will meet your end together.'

Now it was Philip's turn to try not to show any reaction to what Nyanga said; he was not entirely successful, because Nyanga noticed a distinct change in Philip's expression.

'Oh yes, Mr Morgan,' he added in confirmation, 'your girl-friend is still very much alive. Didn't you know that? She's alive for the moment, at any rate – but she won't be for very much longer. As I've said, she will be executed early tomorrow morning.'

Nyanga paused as if considering what to say next. But then he suddenly appeared to become bored by the whole business; he waved a weary hand in dismissal.

'Take them away and lock them up,' he said to the soldiers. 'I'm tired of looking at them.'

A few minutes later an army lorry drew up outside the Mayor's house and Philip and the President were thrown into the back of it. Then they were taken to the cells in the basement of City Hall; their handcuffs were removed and they were locked in for the night.

As soon as they arrived at City Hall Philip looked around anxiously for any sign of Jane; but the cells were constructed of brick with solid metal doors, so there was no chance to see who was in any of them. And in any case, Philip decided, Jane was probably in the women's section. Well, at least she was alive: that was the main thing.

Eventually the soldiers stamped away and the cell block fell silent. But the President and Philip soon discovered that they could hear each other's voices through ventilation grilles high in the wall between their cells. They began to discuss their situation in whispers, but they had hardly opened their mouths when a third voice broke in.

'Paul – Paul – is that you? It's me, Dan Levene, over here.'

'Dan?' said the President excitedly. 'Dan – where are you?'

'I'm in the cell next to you,' said Levene. 'On your left as you look at the door. Can you hear me O.K.?'

'Yes, perfectly,' said the President. 'How are you, my friend?'

'Fine, fine,' said the Mayor, though he sounded very depressed. 'How are you?'

'Well, we're O.K. There are two of us – we're all that's left of a party of five, I'm afraid, and we're a bit the worse for wear. But we're still alive, that's the main thing. What about you – when were you arrested?'

'This morning. . . . Yes, early this morning.' Levene's voice suddenly faltered; when he spoke next he sounded very guilty. 'Listen, Paul – there's something you ought to know straight away. Something I ought to tell you at once. I'm afraid it's my fault that you're in here.'

'No it's not,' the President broke in firmly. 'You're to say no such thing. . . . I've heard what happened already – Jennifer's told me. It was Nyanga – he threatened to torture the children.'

'Yes, that's right,' said Levene slowly. 'And he threatened to kill her, too. He told me in detail what he would do to her, and he caught me at just the wrong time. I was feeling bad – the city had fallen – so I'm afraid I told him what he wanted to know.'

'Well you're to forget this idea that our being captured is your fault,' Kasaboru repeated. 'If it was anyone's fault it was ours. We should have been a damn sight more careful – but we were so pleased with ourselves for getting here in one piece that we just weren't thinking clearly. Nyanga set up a trap for us and we walked straight into it – and we've only ourselves to blame.'

Philip sighed as he thought about their predicament. He could see now how they ought to have been much more cautious, much more suspicious. But it was easy to be wise after the event.

'Yes,' he said sadly. 'I agree with that completely – we've only ourselves to blame.'

Two

Soon after dawn the next morning, loudspeaker vans toured the streets of Sungbarta, announcing that a public execution would take place on the steps of City Hall at eight a.m.

By seven-thirty the three narrow streets leading to the square in front of City Hall were thronged with people. Many of them were Gabuti soldiers; some were bemused and illiterate villagers who had been drawn into the city during the recent disturbances, either to seek shelter or to join in the attack; others were Sungbarta citizens of Fanda origins who regarded Nyanga as their saviour; and finally there were a few Sungbartans, both black and white, who felt that if you couldn't beat 'em it was best to join 'em. Middle-class, educated Europeans, on the other hand, were very few and far between.

By eight o'clock a noisy and cheerful crowd of several thousand people had assembled to await the promised entertainment. Shortly after the hour the three prisoners who were scheduled for execution were brought out on to the steps, their hands tied behind them with rope. There were two men and a woman: Philip Morgan, Dan Levene and Jane Stuart.

Philip blinked as he emerged into the bright morning sunshine, and Jane jumped with surprise when he suddenly appeared at her left side. Jane herself had been brought out first, and although she had been told the night before that Philip was still slive this was the first time she had set eyes on him since the mountain stream had carried her away.

'Philip!' she said. 'Oh, Philip – ' And her voice started to tremble uncontrollably.

For his part, Philip smiled at her with as much confidence as he could muster, and winked. He did his best to look relaxed and confident though in fact he felt extremely tense. He liked to think that he was not a coward, but the prospect of being shot or worse had kept him awake all night; he had spent most of the time trying to think up ways to escape, but so far his mind remained an obstinate blank. Philip wondered if Jane knew why they had been brought out onto the steps of City Hall – and then he realised that unfortunately she would find out very soon even if she didn't know already.

'How's things with you, Jane?' he asked with a grin. 'O.K.?'

As soon as he had spoken he felt that this was a very inadequate sort of remark, but somehow it seemed to have the desired effect. Jane nodded and smiled, and then bit her lower lip to stop herself crying.

'Yes,' she said after a moment. 'Yes, I'm all right.'

At this point, two soldiers pushed the couple roughly apart, preventing any further discussion. Philip contented himself with continuing to try to work his hands loose from the rope tying them together: already the bonds were a little slacker than when they had first been put on.

The crowd was kept waiting for another five minutes, with tension building up all the time. Then an officer of the Gabuti army went to the microphone which had been set up on the top step. He announced over the public-address system that President Joro Nyanga would now appear; and, right on cue, Nyanga emerged from the doors of City Hall.

The crowd roared its welcome.

Many of the crowd were genuinely enthusiastic about Nyanga, but if anything those who were not genuine admirers made even more noise than those who were. Horns were sounded, bells rang, flags were flourished, and wave after wave of pulsating sound swept over those on the steps.

Nyanga came forward, beaming broadly, and basked in the screams of adulation; he was wearing the uniform of a general in the Balembian army, khaki and gold, lit up with rows of medals.

Conrad Hall also came out onto the steps, but he remained tactfully in the background. Semenov and Bulu appeared behind him.

The enormous welcome which Nyanga now received went some way towards improving his ugly mood. The day had started badly for Nyanga, and in fact the previous night had not gone well, either.

First there had been his rebuff at the hands of Jane Stuart; that had upset him more than he would have thought possible. Of course he had been rejected by women before, particularly white women, but not very often: in recent years the women had usually come seeking favours from him. To be turned down now that he was President, and by a woman who had nothing to gain by it and literally everything to lose – well, the blow to his pride had been considerable, and the incident had irritated him all night long.

In the meantime Eileen Grey's behaviour had done nothing whatever to improve the situation. After having told Nyanga for months on end that she cared nothing for her husband and regarded him as a spineless fool, it now developed that she was quite upset by Duncan's death. Or said she was, which amounted to the same thing. The result was no sex – or no willing sex anyway, and co-operative sex was what Nyanga was after. He had had to make do with one of General Tchen's assistants, which had been interesting

311

and certainly exhausting, but not the same thing as a depraved and besotted white woman – not the same thing at all.

And then, to cap it all, Eileen Grey had refused to take part in this morning's executions. That was really infuriating. Nyanga had intended that she should publicly administer the last rites to his three prisoners – he felt that the spectacle of one white woman murdering another would prove very entertaining for the Gabuti troops and for the others in the square – but oh no, Eileen Grey had suddenly got cold feet. She had stated flatly that at eight o'clock in the morning and stone cold sober she couldn't possibly murder anyone. In fact she didn't even want to be on the steps at all. She would watch, she said, from the back of the crowd, anonymous in dark glasses and a headscarf, with a Gabuti officer to look after her; she would enjoy the atmosphere better that way.

Nyanga had reluctantly agreed. He would never understand women, that much was certain, but if Eileen got her own way in this matter perhaps she would revert to her normal self. If not, she would have to go, of course. And in the meantime Bulu could act as executioner in her place.

Nyanga stepped up to the microphone and silenced the crowd with a brief wave of his hands. Then he began to speak. He had the prisoners brought forward one at a time by Bulu, while he explained what heinous crimes they had committed.

The Mayor was presented first. Well, said Nyanga, it had long been known, of course, that Dan Levene had been a corrupt Mayor. He was an enemy of the people, a man who manipulated municipal budgets for his own private gain and neglected the interests of the city. He deserved to die.

Philip Morgan? Well, he was a spy – an assassin sent by the British, but fortunately he was incompetent and had easily been prevented from firing the fatal shot. Numerous incriminating documents had been found in his possession and these would be released to the world's press in due course. He too could expect no mercy: the death sentence for spies was internationally acknowledged.

And the woman? A hush fell on the crowd as Jane Stuart was brought forward for their inspection; nearly every man present licked his lips at the very sight of her. This woman, said Nyanga, had been Kasaboru's mistress. She had seduced him with her lascivious witchcraft into handing over great chunks of the nation's wealth to her. She was a whore, and a diseased whore at that. She was to be exterminated, stamped out, removed from the face of the earth and her ashes scattered to the wind. Bulu leered with pleasure at the very thought.

Now that the crowd's attention was no longer on him, Philip continued to work desperately to loosen the rope which held his hands. What he was going to do if he got his hands free he didn't

312

quite know, but first things first. He twisted and contorted his fingers and hands, thankful that for the moment at least everyone's eyes were on Jane.

Nyanga now asked the crowd to express an opinion as to which of the three should be executed first. And he was not left short of suggestions.

The woman, said some, their eyes gleaming like those of greedy children. No, no, others insisted, leave her till last – take the Mayor first instead. No-one seemed very interested in Philip Morgan, thank goodness – that allowed him to concentrate on the rope. And at last – at last – he could feel it beginning to stretch – or was it just that his hands were slippery with sweat?

At that moment, out of the corner of his eye, Philip caught sight of a jet plane streaking in at roof-top height across the lake. The plane was moving so fast that it was far ahead of its sound, and the noise of the crowd was such that no-one heard it coming. It flashed right over the centre of the square, its shadow flicking across the spectators' heads, and the actual passage of the plane was followed almost immediately by the overwhelming roaring scream of its jet engine.

The effect of this event on the crowd was staggering. The sound of the jet's engine echoed deafeningly back and forth from the surrounding buildings; it was picked up by the public address system and amplified still further, and almost everyone, from Nyanga downwards, instinctively ducked their heads and flinched from the incredible din.

The plane which had flown so low overhead had been an F–86 Sabre, a single-seater jet fighter built in the United States – Philip had taken in that much in the split second of the plane's passing. But the markings certainly hadn't been American: green, yellow and red in horizontal stripes. What was that – Ethiopian? Philip couldn't quite remember.

A moment later, however, he had an opportunity to refresh his memory, because the first Sabre was followed by a second, screaming in even lower if anything than the first. And then a third, a fourth, a fifth and a sixth, one after the other, with no respite between them. Each plane came in so low that it seemed certain it would strike the roof-tops.

None of the planes made any attempt to shoot up the crowd, but they didn't need to; the fact that they were not friendly was crystal clear from their method of approach. The jets had arrived without any hint from Nyanga that they were coming, and the crowd had only to look at Nyanga to see that he was just as bewildered and taken aback by the incident as they were. So the conclusion was clear, both from the planes' behaviour and from the official reaction to them: these were enemy planes, and in all probability they were about to start enemy action.

313

Long before the sixth Sabre jet had filled the square with the racket of its turbo jet engine and had fluttered the flags wildly with the turbulence from its wings, large sections of the crowd had decided that perhaps it wasn't too healthy to remain where they were any longer. Perhaps it would be better to take shelter in a nearby building, or to go home, or to leave the city altogether and go back to the peace of their village.

The crowd began to move – slowly at first. Then those in the centre began to push and shove and urge those on the fringes to get a move on. And those on the periphery started to run, bumping into each other as those going one way met those who had decided to go another. Feet stumbled against unnoticed kerb-stones and bodies were slammed against parked cars. The strong began to wrestle the weak out of their way.

The jets came back again and again, the scream of their engines generating still more screams from the crowd in the square below. In a matter of moments panic filled the air. It was as if every single person in the crowd became filled with a blind and overpowering determination to get out of the area at once, at whatever cost to anyone else.

The cost in fact proved high. There were only three narrow streets leading out of the square, and the spectators ran for these exits in a mass. Some of the first runners fell, and others tripped over them, resulting in several piles of bodies which narrowed the available space still further. Those behind these obstacles pushed and yelled and cursed and battered their way forward, losing all sense of discipline and control as the terrifying silver jets howled across the sky, time after time.

Eileen Grey was in the middle of the very worst bottleneck of all.

Eileen had come into the square after Nyanga had started speaking; a demure little Gabuti officer accompanied her. There had been no rush or panic when she arrived; it had been easy to walk through a side-street and join the crowd at the back, unobserved except by a few.

The Gabuti officer stood as close to Eileen as she would let him, breathing in her expensive perfume. It was all he could do to keep his hands off her rounded breasts and buttocks; even standing beside her gave him a massive, throbbing erection. But his orders were clear: he was to stay with Eileen at all times, and see that she came to no harm. Feeling her up was no part of his brief.

When the jets first started zooming overhead Eileen had ducked like everyone else. But they were just jets, after all: lower-flying than most perhaps, but she had seen thousands of them in her time. Eileen badly underestimated the effect they would have on her uneducated and superstitious companions.

She was slow in turning to run when the crowd began to panic, and slower than everyone else when she did break into a trot: her

314

skirt was too tight for sprinting. She was jostled and jarred from the back, despite all that the Gabuti officer could do to protect her. And in a moment or two she tripped and fell.

Eileen made no sound herself as she went down but the Gabuti officer screamed on her behalf. He screamed a great high shrill cry of despair and horror and pain, for he could feel the huge weight of the crowd behind them, and he knew instinctively that no-one who fell in the middle of such a crowd would ever, ever get up again.

Eileen tried to get up, of course. Several times she pulled herself on to her knees, or lifted herself up on her hands. But each time she was battered back down again by bodies tumbling over her or by feet using her as a spring-board to leap over a tiresome barrier to safety. She was kicked and smashed back into the ground, until at her fourth and final attempt to get up, her head struck the kerb in front of her and she lost all consciousness.

After that she was finished. Bodies piled up all around her and on top of her, compounding her concussion and preventing her from breathing. Her bones were cracked and broken, her flesh left crushed and bleeding.

Most of those who fell eventually managed to pull themselves upright again, and they limped away, cursing and wailing, following in the wake of everyone else. But fourteen bodies in the square remained totally motionless, beyond all further movement. Eileen Grey was one of them.

Ten minutes later the Gabuti officer came back, wringing his hands and with tears streaming down his face. When he had confirmed that Eileen Grey was dead he sat on the kerb beside her and waited until his distress had eased a little. Then, rather than face Nyanga's wrath, he shot himself with his pistol, making fifteen fatalities in all.

Yuri Semenov was the first man on the steps to recover his nerve. Almost as soon as he saw the first jet pass fleetingly overhead he realised what had happened: the United Nations had arrived, and far sooner than he would have guessed possible. Well, he and Nyanga would just have to move that much faster themselves, that was all.

Semenov looked towards Nyanga and saw that the man was cowering in bewilderment as the first flight of Sabres passed successively and so threateningly over the square. Semenov went over to him; he seized Nyanga by the arm and physically shook him. He was surprised to see that Nyanga's eyes were glazed with terror: the noise and the power of the jets had momentarily paralysed him, and Semenov reminded himself that Nyanga had come a long way in a very short time – from being a barefoot boy in a village to being President, in less than thirty years. In many ways Nyanga was still very primitive, and a quotation from Lenin came into Semenov's mind: 'Every cook has to learn how to govern the state.' Well, this particular cook was going to have to learn fast, or he would lose everything he had gained so far.

'Come with me!' Semenov shouted. 'Come with me – we must get back to the top floor!' He pointed upwards, a gesture noted by Philip Morgan. 'We must get back to the command post!'

Nyanga's eyes followed Semenov's finger, and at last he seemed to pull himself together. He took a deep breath, nodded, and hurried away into City Hall.

Nyanga did not notice, but Conrad Hall had preceded him by all of half a minute.

Semenov now seized Bulu, who was too stupid to be terrified but seemed puzzled by why everyone was running away.

'Bulu!' Semenov bawled. 'Get the prisoners back into the cells. You understand? Back into the cells! Here – take this.' He reached out and grabbed a submachine-gun from a Gabuti soldier who was standing limply with his mouth open; Semenov handed the gun to Bulu. 'Get the prisoners back into the cells – do you understand?' he repeated.

Bulu nodded vigorously to indicate that he knew what to do. Then, as Semenov hurried after Nyanga, Bulu trotted over to the three prisoners: he pulled them closer together and shoved them angrily towards the entrance of City Hall. He gestured furiously with the submachine-gun to indicate that they should go ahead of him, and quickly too.

'Run!' he shouted. 'Run!' His voice had a peculiar twang because of his cleft palate and the word was barely recognizable. 'Run, run, run!'

The prisoners had no option but to obey.

Nyanga and Semenov went up in the lift to the fourteenth floor.

'We must keep our heads,' Semenov emphasized heavily, noting with relief that Nyanga's expression was more normal now. 'We must keep our heads.'

'Don't worry,' replied Nyanga. 'I am quite capable of doing whatever is necessary.' He wiped his face with a handkerchief.

When the two men reached General Tchen's command post in the council chamber, they found the General on the phone and his staff in a flurry of excitement.

'What's happening?' asked Nyanga abruptly.

'It's the United Nations,' said Tchen, after he had put his hand over the telephone mouthpiece. 'They're buzzing the city and the airport.' He did not seem unduly disturbed about it.

'Are you sure it's the UN?' asked Nyanga. 'It's only twenty-four hours since the Security Council made its decision.'

'Twenty-seven hours to be precise,' said Tchen calmly. 'And I am sure, yes. They want to land at the airport.'

'Keep them out,' snapped Nyanga.

'How can I keep them out?' asked Tchen. 'You don't really want me to take on the rest of the world, do you?'

'Keep them out!' roared Nyanga. He put his hand on the pistol at his belt. 'Give the order – now!'

General Tchen looked at Nyanga for a moment, as if judging his mood. Then he shrugged his shoulders and spoke into the telephone. 'Try not to let them land,' he said ambiguously, and broke off the connection.

At the other end of the telephone line, the officer who had been speaking to Tchen felt as if he were about to have a heart attack. 'Try not to let them land!' he said aloud. 'What kind of an order is that?'

The officer asked himself what on earth he was supposed to do. Was he supposed to shoot at the UN planes or not? What happened to officers who shot at United Nations forces – and what happened to officers who disobeyed a General's orders? He was doomed either way, and he knew it – caught in a cross-fire with no possible means of escape. He groaned and cursed everyone in sight. But in the end the wretched officer did not have to take any decision or issue any orders at all, for events developed without him. For several minutes Canberra bombers of the Indian air force had been flying low over the runways and airport buildings, scaring the wits out of the Gabuti infantry who were dug in on the perimeter of the field. The Canberras also frightened the pilots of the Gabuti MIG 19s, who were not exactly rushing to take off to retaliate.

Eventually one of the Canberras flew too close to a section of infantry on the eastern edge of the airport, and the soldiers began loosing off at it with every weapon at their disposal, rifles, submachine-guns, pistols, the lot.

That was all the excuse the Canberras needed. They attacked in earnest this time. They strafed the airport from one end to the other, destroying six MIG 19s on the ground with their 20mm Hispano cannon, chipping great lumps of concrete out of the airport buildings and blowing up half a dozen trucks.

The Gabuti forces suffered a number of casualties and evacuated rapidly on their own initiative. Behind them they left the airport entirely deserted.

Bulu shoved the three prisoners ahead of him as they hurried down the stairs to the cells; Jane went first, the Mayor second and Philip last.

Soldiers and civilians were running everywhere: through the lobby, up and down the stairs and along the corridors; all of them were shouting orders and questions but nobody was doing anything very effective. From outside there came the continual noise of the jets and the screams of the departing crowd. The atmosphere was chaotic.

Bulu and the three others reached the cells in which Philip and the Mayor had spent the night and in which the President was still imprisoned. Bulu shoved the prisoners towards the closed end of the cul-de-sac which was formed by the cell corridor; then he turned to the bewildered Gabuti soldier who was standing open-mouthed at the foot of the stairs. 'Keys!' he yelled in his strange voice. 'Keys! Lock up prisoners – keys!'

Eventually the soldier realised what Bulu wanted and handed over the bunch of keys. He seemed to be glad to get rid of them, and hurried away up the stairs, presumably to find out what was going on in the outside world.

Bulu now had a problem. He had to hold a submachine-gun in one hand and unlock the cell doors with the other – and apparently he was none too familiar with either automatic weapons or locks and keys. Philip noticed with pleasure how clumsily Bulu held the submachine-gun: if Philip could just get his hands free. . . . He went on twisting and squirming behind his back while Bulu fiddled with the locks. Bulu grunted and talked to himself constantly.

After a minute or two Bulu opened a cell door and shoved Jane roughly inside. Then he locked her in and began to battle with the next door. It was a difficult and tedious process for him; he tried several keys to see which one fitted, rejected some, went back, tried them again, and so on. . . . Philip was only too pleased by this delay, but his wrists were aching fiercely as he pulled and stretched, twisted and turned, trying as hard as he possibly could to get his hand back through one of the loops.

With a cry of triumph Bulu opened a second cell door. With an urgent nod of his head Philip indicated to Dan Levene that he should go next, and mercifully Levene took the hint.

Bulu laboured on the third door. It was no easier for him than the others. He tucked the submachine-gun under his arm to give himself two hands free. He muttered darkly about what he would do to the keys if they didn't co-operate; he went on rattling and shaking them in the hope of finding the right one.

Finally he did find the one he needed; the cell door opened.

Bulu turned with a smile of satisfaction and Philip kicked him full in the groin with the point of his toe. Bulu screamed and doubled up in agony. The submachine-gun clattered to the floor and Bulu fell to his knees after it. He clutched his groin and screamed every time he exhaled; the pain was excruciating. His stomach and chest were pressed tight against his thighs and his back was parallel with the ground. He rocked himself gently backwards and forwards in his agony, his eyes pressed tightly shut. It was many, many years since anyone had dared to strike at Bulu, and he lacked the sense to protect himself even though grievously hurt.

Philip looked at his target: it was the back of Bulu's brown neck, exposed above a dark blue tee-shirt. Philip had no weapon and his hands were still tied – so he jumped up in the air as high as he could, and as he began to descend he stamped down hard with his right foot. The force of that downward kick, plus Philip's weight, broke Bulu's neck with a crack like the snapping of a pencil. Bulu's face hit the ground with a squelch.

Philip repeated the blow to the back of the neck twice, just to make sure.

Then he rolled Bulu over onto his back. The body unfolded slowly until it lay with the arms and legs outstretched; there was a dark patch of blood at the groin. Philip watched carefully, but there was no sign of the chest rising and falling. The deformed mouth was open and still, the eyes were staring without seeing: Bulu was dead at last.

'What's going on out there?' called the President urgently. 'Are you all right, Philip?'

'Yes, what's happening?' Jane's voice also demanded.

'It's all right, I'm O.K.,' Philip told them. 'But Bulu isn't – he's dead. Just keep quiet for a few minutes, there's been enough noise already. I'm going to try to get us out of here. We aren't out of the wood yet, not by a long way, but we're not going to give up without one hell of a fight. Hold still till I get my hands free.'

Working desperately now, Philip began to rub the rope binding his wrists aginst the corner of a brick wall, just as he had done after he and the President had been captured in the sewer. The rope was weaker this time and it only took two minutes' rubbing to get free. Then he picked up the keys which Bulu had dropped and advanced on the President's cell door.

There were four keys on the ring and the first one didn't work. Philip had just fitted the second key into the lock when he heard a voice from somewhere behind him.

'That's enough, I think,' said Nyanga.

Three

Philip looked round. The blood drained out of his face and the pain of failure became physical and real; he almost groaned with despair. This time he was really finished. He could not imagine himself finding the strength and the determination to resist any further; it would be far, far easier to lie down and die.

'Put your hands in the air,' Nyanga said curtly. 'And keep them there.'

Philip obeyed. He turned his body until he was facing Nyanga directly rather than sideways on. It didn't matter any longer: the larger a target he presented the better in some ways – it would make the end come quicker.

Then he realized that he was still holding the bunch of keys in his right hand. And that Nyanga was alone. And at that point Philip's mind began to function once more.

Rapidly he reassessed his chances. To begin with, Nyanga was armed only with an automatic pistol – a deadly enough weapon in the right hands but not as useful in a tight corner as, say, a Sten gun. Philip glanced over towards the submachine-gun which Bulu had dropped, but it was too far away to be worth going for. However, apart from the little matter of the pistol the odds were one against one. Upstairs there was a good deal of shouting and running about going on, but no-one seemed to be interested in what was happening down in the basement. So perhaps the situation was not quite as irretrievable as Philip had first thought.

Nyanga moved a little closer: he came close enough to make his Tokarev pistol more effective, but not so close that Philip would have any chance to jump him.

'I've had just about enough of you, Morgan,' said Nyanga bitterly. 'More than enough, in fact. Another two minutes and you would have had Kasaboru out of here, and God only knows what sort of trouble that would have caused. But you're too late. Semenov keeps on emphasizing to me how important it is to keep a clear head, and my head *is* clear – beautifully clear. And what my head tells me is that if the UN have arrived it's important to kill Kasaboru. Right now. And kill him I surely will – just as soon as I've disposed of you.'

Nyanga was now about twelve feet away, and he raised the pistol to eye level to give himself a better aim. As he did so Philip hurled the bunch of keys directly into Nyanga's face and simultaneously dived forward and rolled head over heels. Nyanga flinched and swore as one of the keys caught him full in the eye. He squeezed off two rapid shots, one of which clipped Philip's sleeve as it passed; both bullets ricocheted noisily off the stone floor and whined around the cell block. But then Philip was onto him and both men were fighting for their lives.

Philip went first for the gun, to put him on equal terms. With his right hand he grabbed Nyanga's right wrist, and with his left hand Philip seized the barrel of the Tokarev, attempting to break it out of Nyanga's grasp.

Nyanga held on tight, and with his left hand he tried to gouge Philip's eyes out and claw his face. He kicked and punched towards Philip's stomach and groin, grunting and cursing obscenely. Philip butted him in the face, bringing blood from Nyanga's nose, and forced the Balembian backwards, slamming him hard against a wall. He cracked Nyanga's wrist violently against a sharp corner of brick, swinging the barrel of the gun dangerously close to his own head as he did so. This gave Nyanga the opportunity to squeeze off two more shots, and in the confines of the cell corridor the explosions echoed deafeningly.

In the cells the three other prisoners could only listen and urge Philip on in their minds: they could see nothing and there seemed no point in calling out.

With a final violent heave Philip cracked Nyanga's arm back against the edge of the wall once more, and this time the pain and the force of the impact loosened Nyanga's grip. The pistol fell away to the ground, and their struggling feet kicked it spinning along the floor, well out of reach of either of them.

Now, with the pistol gone, the antagonists were equally matched, fighting with their bare hands.

Nyanga was big and heavy and strong; he was snarling with rage and aggression. He lunged forward, reaching for Philip's throat, and Philip let him come. He rolled backwards, put his right foot into Nyanga's stomach and tossed him high over his head, turning the impetus behind the attack to his own advantage.

Nyanga landed flat on his back with a sound like a sack of cement falling off a lorry. Philip went after the pistol.

But Nyanga was up in a flash, and Philip was just reaching out for the Tokarev when his opponent's full weight crashed down on top of his body, knocking the wind out of him completely. Nyanga covered him like a great black bear. Philip was astonished by how fast the man's movements were, how strong and determined and agile he was.

Nyanga wrenched Philip round until he was sitting astride his chest; then he grabbed Philip's throat with both hands. A great rumbling roar of satisfaction rose up from deep within Nyanga's lungs as his fingers closed around Philip's neck. He began to squeeze and twist with enormous power and force, flexing the muscles of his arms and bearing down from the shoulders with his full weight behind him.

Almost instantly Philip's vision began to cloud over. The pressure on his throat was intense and unbearable. He couldn't breathe and he couldn't move – Nyanga's haunches were firmly astride his body. All he could see, swirling dizzily above him, was Nyanga's triumphant face, the lips open wide in a grimace of both strain and satisfaction. Nyanga's thumbs were crushing his windpipe and Philip almost gave up. His hands gripped Nyanga's wrists and he tried in vain to loosen the terrible grip. But he couldn't. He felt feeble and slow, and his muscles would not respond to his wishes. He was dying and there was nothing he could possibly do to prevent it.

But then he heard a voice. It was Jane screaming at him through the cell door: 'Philip! Philip! Philip! Philip!' Over and over again.

In some strange way the voice seemed to pierce the fog in his brain. Clean and bright, the sound seemed to separate his mind from his body; it enabled him to make an effort of will independent of the pain he was suffering.

Philip gripped Nyanga's wrists, and with a sudden violent snatch he managed to loosen their grip for a second, allowing him time to take a brief gasping breath. Then he bent his knees, drew his feet up high and hooked them under Nyanga's armpits. And finally, with all the force he could muster, he violently straightened his legs and propelled Nyanga away from him; and with the weight removed from his chest he rolled away to the right.

Nyanga was hurled several feet through the air and landed on his back with another hefty thump; but he was immediately up again, seeking to catch Philip at a disadvantage. Luckily Philip was on his feet too, his hands held high in front of him, ready to meet Nyanga's next attack. He was breathing hoarsely through a throat which felt as if it were filled with broken glass, but at least he was on his feet.

The two men circled each other, their eyes seeking warning of the opponent's next move; both of them were bleeding from the nose. Each of them was looking for a chance to grab the pistol or the submachine-gun from the floor, but they knew that such a chance would not come easily.

'I'm going to kill you, Morgan,' said Nyanga softly. His fists clenched and unclenched as he spoke. 'I'm going to kill you with my bare hands – and then I'm going to kill your woman.'

Philip stepped forward and slammed a left hook into Nyanga's right eye. Nyanga tried to grab Philip's arm and missed. Blinking with anger he stepped forward himself, and Philip jabbed him again, rocking his head back hard. Whatever else Nyanga might be, he was no boxer, and he certainly didn't intend to fight like one.

Nyanga waited as they circled until Philip had his back to a corner of the corridor; then, with a great roar of rage, Nyanga rushed forward, hoping to slam Philip backwards and trap him in the right-angle formed by the cream-coloured walls. But Philip neatly side-stepped and helped Nyanga on his way with a generous shove from the rear. So in the event it was Nyanga who had the breath knocked out of him by the solid brick wall, not Philip, and Philip followed up by seizing Nyanga in a strong full nelson. He slipped his hands under his enemy's arms and linked them behind the neck. Then, planting his feet firmly, Philip swung Nyanga round and bashed his head ruthlessly against the vertical brick wall. Nyanga's scalp split open and blood began to pour down his face. Philip swung him again, with Nyanga bellowing in pain and anger, and cracked the skull once more.

A Gabuti soldier appeared at the foot of the stairs. It was the same soldier who had been in the cell corridor when Bulu had brought the three prisoners down. The soldier had a rifle in his hands, and it was held ready for use. But he didn't use it; instead he just stood there mesmerized, watching the conflict raging in front of him with open-mouthed amazement.

Through a red veil formed by the blood which was running down into his eyes, Nyanga caught sight of the soldier. At last relief had come.

'Shoot, you fool!' Nyanga shouted. 'Shoot! Kill him! Kill him! Kill him!' Philip slammed him into the wall again and Nyanga howled with pain.

The soldier hesitated. Then he raised his rifle, aimed, and pulled the trigger.

Philip's vision was clearer than Nyanga's. What was more, he had the advantage of a solid, unshakable hold. He was not going to release that half-nelson until the man he was holding was either dead or unconscious – and as the soldier fired, Philip twisted Nyanga's body sharply round to the right.

The bullet hit Nyanga squarely above the heart, ploughing deep into his chest. The force of it knocked the pair of them backwards into the wall. But even then Philip did not let go; he staggered upright, keeping Nyanga between him and the soldier.

At first, oddly enough, Philip was not quite sure what had happened: he thought he might have stumbled in his urgency to swing Nyanga round to shield himself. But then he felt and heard the change in Nyanga's body. The Balembian drew in a hoarse breath, and then another, and a third, as if he could not get enough oxygen; and then he gave a great shuddering sigh, his body trembling. His knees gave way and Philip found himself supporting his opponent's entire weight; Nyanga's head dropped forward suddenly and lolled inertly on his chest; the hands ceased to pull and tear at Philip's, and instead slipped away and hung loosely by his sides.

Philip stared at the soldier and the soldier stared at him.

And then the soldier realised what he had done. He stepped back, his face reflecting his horror; all thought of using his rifle again was abandoned. Finally, with a sudden terrified yell, the soldier leapt bodily all of three feet backwards; he landed facing the other direction, and he raced away up the stairs, wailing and screaming like a man running away from a ghost.

And in a sense, of course, that was what the soldier was – a man running away from a ghost. For by a monumental error of judgement he had killed a man whom he and all his fellow soldiers believed to be a powerful and vindictive witch – and now, beyond a shadow of a doubt, the witch's soul would haunt his nights and blight his days for ever.

It was no wonder that the soldier ran.

Philip dropped Nyanga in a heap on the floor and quickly unlocked the three cell doors. There was no time for talk or explanations and the released prisoners could see at one mightily relieved glance what had happened.

Philip hugged Jane briefly and then hurried to pick up the submachine-gun abandoned by Bulu; the President found Nyanga's pistol. Only then, when they had established some means of defending themselves, did they pause for a brief council of war.

The fleeing soldier seemed to have attracted no particular attention: at any rate no-one had come downstairs to investigate the noise and the various shots which had been fired. But in the circumstances that was not very surprising: both the lobby of City Hall and the square outside were crowded with screaming and shouting citizens, and many of the soldiers were firing futilely at the planes passing overhead. The dead littered the pavements, and the wounded staggered about bleeding, ignored by everyone else – so a few shots and shouts were nothing exceptional at the moment.

'Well,' said the President, 'where do we go from here? And where did those planes come from?'

'Ethiopia, if I read the markings right,' said Philip. 'Which means, I suppose, that the UN have arrived. The Ethiopians are hardly likely to have launched an attack on their own initiative. And as to where we go from here – well, I suggest we get out of this basement as soon as possible. A couple of hand-grenades rolled down the stairs could easily finish the lot of us.'

'Agreed,' said the President. He turned to Dan Levene. 'Is there anywhere safe in this building?'

'Well there was, yesterday,' said the Mayor doubtfully. 'The whole building was fully secure. But what's happened since the Gabuti army took over I really couldn't say. They're probably everywhere.'

'No doubt they are,' said Philip. 'The only thing I do know is that just before he ran off inside, Semenov told Nyanga that they had to get back to the command post on the top floor. So presumably that's where the Gabuti army has its headquarters.'

'Under the leadership of General Tchen, no doubt,' said the President thoughtfully.

'What about him?' said Philip, looking at the President's expression. 'Do you know him?'

'Well, I've met him a few times.'

'What's he like – is he a realist?'

The President hesitated. 'Yes, yes, I think you could say that.'

'If he sees that you're alive,' Philip continued, 'and sees that Nyanga's dead, and if he realises that the United Nations have sent in some sort of a peace-keeping force, do you think he'll do the sensible thing? Will he order his troops to withdraw, or will he fight to the death in the name of communism?'

'I think he would order a cease-fire,' said the President at once. 'He's not fool enough to think that he can defeat a force backed by the UN, and I don't think his political masters would want him to try. What are you suggesting?'

'I think we should go upstairs and lay the facts before him,' said Philip. 'Let him see that you're alive and Nyanga isn't, and see what kind of a response we get.'

The President's eyes searched the faces of his three friends; he saw that they were ready to follow him if that was what he decided to do.

'All right,' he said. 'Let's try it.'

Two minutes' exploration found a door which opened into another corridor where there was a lift. It was obviously this lift which had brought Nyanga down from the top of the building, once he had decided to kill the President immediately. Now the lift would take the dead body of Nyanga back to the command post.

Philip and Dan Levene dragged Nyanga by the feet and dumped him in a heap on the floor of the lift: it was not an action which showed much respect for the dead, but the time was not right for attention to niceties. Then the rest of them crowded into the remaining space, and the Mayor pressed the button for the fourteenth floor. Despite her familiarity with death in all its forms, Jane shuddered several times as the lift moved steadily upwards.

In due course the lift stopped and the doors slid open.

Philip stepped out, the Gabuti submachine-gun held at the ready: the weapon was a Russian-made PPS, broadly similar in operation to the Sten gun.

There was no-one to be seen in the corridor to either side of the lift doors, but voices could be heard from the council chamber nearby, and Dan Levene pointed the way to it. For the time being they left Nyanga sprawled half in and half out of the lift, preventing it from being called away to another floor.

Carefully, keeping in a group but with Philip leading the way, the four of them advanced towards the council chamber. When they reached it Philip peered through the open door.

There were four men in the room: General Tchen, who was speaking into a telephone, two other officers who were looking to the south through binoculars, and a clerk seated at a large table in the centre. None of the men was armed, so Philip felt quite safe in stepping boldly through the doorway; the President promptly followed him, and Dan Levene and Jane cautiously brought up the rear.

When he became aware of his visitors, General Tchen stopped talking into the telephone and stared for a moment. Then he put down the phone and smiled.

Then he laughed.

He put back his head and roared with laughter – and it was genuine, unforced laughter which rang loudly round the chamber, aided by the sensitive acoustics. His men watched him in astonishment, and in view of the way Philip was holding the submachine-gun they took care to make no sudden or threatening movements.

The General laughed for at least half a minute, taking off his glasses to wipe his eyes. The President waited until the mirth had subsided before he spoke.

'Well, General Tchen,' he said eventually, 'I think I'll take over from now on.'

The General shook his head in amused disbelief. 'It really is quite extraordinary,' he said. 'Nyanga just went downstairs to shoot you. You're supposed to be dead.'

'Well I'm not dead,' said the President brusquely. 'But Nyanga is – and if you want proof I suggest you go and look in the lift.'

'I will,' said Tchen emphatically. 'I certainly will.'

Accompanied by the President, who was holding the Tokarev pistol in a business-like manner, General Tchen stepped out into the corridor and returned a moment later.

'It's true,' he said to his aides. 'Nyanga really is dead. Well, well, well. Who would have believed it. . . .'

'And I gather the United Nations have arrived,' the President continued. He tucked the Tokarev into his belt and moved forward to look towards the airport through the wide south-facing windows.

'Yes, that is correct,' said Tchen with a nod. 'Planes from the Ethiopian and Indian air forces are currently harassing my troops, and no doubt there will be infantry following on.'

Kasaboru turned to face the General squarely. 'As President of Balembi I sent a message asking for UN intervention soon after Nyanga launched his attempted coup. And as President of Balembi

I welcome their arrival. I thank you for your co-operation in maintaining law and order in the meantime, and I assume that you will now withdraw your troops.'

General Tchen pushed his glasses further back on his nose while he considered the matter. There was a long pause during which the room remained very quiet; there was even a lull in the shooting and the shouting outside.

Then the General held out his right hand.

'Mr President,' he said, 'let me be the first to congratulate you on your remarkable escape. I am glad to see you alive and well and I formally acknowledge your authority.'

Kasaboru and the General shook hands, and the tension in the room relaxed immediately. Taking the lead from their commander, the two officers broke into loud applause; they came forward and shook the President's hand in turn. Philip and Dan Levene glanced at each other, grinned and then cheered heartily; Philip put the submachine-gun down on the table in order to be able to join in the clapping. He clapped until his hands stung with the force of it.

'Major,' said the General, turning now to one of his aides, 'issue the following orders. Our forces are not, repeat not, to resist the arrival of United Nations troops in any way, shape or form. All units will withdraw from city limits at once and will await further orders.'

'Yes, sir,' said the Major with alacrity, and he reached out a hand for the telephone.

The telephone exploded into a thousand fragments as it was struck by a bullet from a gun – a Kalashnikov automatic rifle which was held by Yuri Semenov.

Semenov covered the room with this rifle, keeping a particularly careful eye on Philip Morgan, whose hand had already begun to reach for the submachine-gun which he had only recently put down on the table.

'Don't try it, Mr Morgan,' Semenov advised. 'Not if you want to live. In fact I advise none of you to try anything. Get over by the wall, all four of you.'

It was painfully clear which four Semenov was referring to, and with the open barrel of a Kalashnikov facing them, neither the President nor any of his friends were inclined to argue. General Tchen and his men remained where they were, cautiously awaiting developments.

'Now then,' said Semenov calmly, when he was satisfied that everyone was where he wanted them, 'we will make good a little of the damage that has been done. . . . I think you were rather hasty in issuing that last order, General.'

'Playing for time, my dear Semenov,' murmured Tchen diplomatically. 'Just playing for time.'

'Well, we shall have time enough to correct matters now,' said

Semenov confidently. 'Nyanga is dead, as I have seen for myself, and that is unfortunate. But there are plenty of other potential leaders in Balembi. We can soon find ourselves a figure-head to lead a government which will co-operate with the USSR. General Juba will do, at any rate until we can find someone better.'

'Ah yes, an excellent man is Juba,' General Tchen agreed hastily. 'An excellent man.'

'He is a fool and easily led,' said Semenov contemptuously. 'For a long time he has been Nyanga's puppet, and now he will be Moscow's puppet instead. . . . But first we must dispose of these four nuisances – dispose of them once and for all. General, please remove that pistol from Kasaboru's belt, and the PPS submachine-gun from the table – Mr Morgan is eyeing it hungrily.'

'Of course,' said Tchen, 'of course.'

He moved forward to pick up the PPS. And as his hands fell upon it, he pushed off the safety catch, swung the barrel round in one smooth movement, and fired a long and lingering burst directly into Semenov's body.

Semenov was knocked helplessly backwards by a whole spray of jacketed lead bullets which twisted and jerked his body in all directions. His finger tightened once on the trigger of his Kalashnikov rifle, but the shot went harmlessly into the ceiling. Then he sprawled in an ugly heap on the floor and lay still at last.

No-one moved or spoke.

General Tchen walked slowly across the room to check that his handiwork was complete. He fired a final burst into Semenov's prone figure, just to make sure. Then he walked almost casually back to Philip, who had watched the incident incredulously, and handed the PPS over to him.

'Your gun, Mr Morgan, I believe,' he said courteously.

Philip took it. 'But – I don't understand,' he stammered. 'Why did you do that?'

The General turned away without answering.

'I think I can tell you why,' said the grim-faced President Kasaboru. 'It's because our friend the General is not an admirer of Moscow. He obeys his political masters in Gabuti, of course. But his real loyalties lie further east – in Peking to be precise. My information is that General Tchen has been in the pay of the Chinese for several years – and he is naturally very reluctant to see the Russians get a foothold in a country right next door to his. Is that not so, General?'

The Gabuti commander raised a quizzical eyebrow and smiled. 'No comment,' he said. 'No comment at all. . . . I will say only this. Neither you nor I, Mr President, can alter the course of history – not in any significant respect. The triumph of the proletariat is inevitable in the long run, and both you and I may be killed in the course of that revolution. But for the moment, at least, you are still

the President of Balembi – and I will withdraw my troops, as I
promised.'

Four

Conrad Hall was very quick to understand what was happening when the Ethiopian Sabre jets swept in across the heads of the crowd in the square. As soon as Hall saw the foreign markings on the first fighter, and saw that although the plane was not shooting it was being flown with aggression and determination, he knew instinctively that it was time for him to go.

Despite the apparent success of Nyanga's coup, Hall had for some days been very conscious of a strong undercurrent of resentment against the man who had so ruthlessly seized power. That resentment had made itself felt most plainly in the stubborn defence of Sungbarta; and Hall suspected that now, with the UN about to descend from the sky, Nyanga's grip on the country would rapidly begin to weaken.

In any case, whatever the eventual consequences of the UN intervention, it was immediately clear to Hall that Sungbarta was no longer a safe place to be. He decided in a matter of seconds that he would make his way rapidly back to Tikiro. On his arrival there he would pause and review the situation: if Nyanga remained in power, so much the better; and if he didn't, well then Hall would fly in his own private aeroplane to South Africa, where his Swiss bank account would no doubt make life tolerable enough. Conrad Hall, or Konrad Höller as he had once been known, was a man who had made a tactful exit from a scene of imminent defeat once before, in the spring of 1945 – and now he was about to put on a repeat performance.

The former Nazi walked calmly through City Hall to the municipal car-pool at the back of the building. There he commandeered a three-month-old Ford Cortina police-car. He climbed in, checked its tank for petrol, and drove quickly out of City Hall and into the deserted side-streets: the crowd which had assembled for the execution was concentrated at the front of the building, and he carefully selected a route which he knew would be free of congestion.

To avoid any possible delays when passing the airport, which Hall rightly guessed might also be the scene of an air attack, he crossed the river Sung by the north road bridge, and then turned back in a wide circle westwards to begin his two-hundred-mile drive to Tikiro. And thanks to his frequent use of the horn and flashing headlights, he arrived home in a little under four hours.

The police-car had not been air-conditioned, and Hall was sweating heavily and feeling very hot and uncomfortable when he finally halted outside the front door of his magnificent mansion. He badly needed a beer, but even so he did not rush indoors immediately. Instead he paused for a moment and looked up at the beautiful house on which he had spent so much time and money. He sighed. He decided that it would indeed be a very great pity if he had to leave Balembi, and perhaps after all it would not be necessary. He hoped so, anyway – he would make a few phone calls and establish the latest position. The first call, however, would be to his mechanic; Hall owned a two-year-old Piper de luxe Super Cub 150 which he piloted himself and which he kept at a small aerodrome some three miles down the road.

Conrad Hall let himself in at the front door of his manor-house and at a leisurely pace made his way to the kitchen at the rear. He noticed as he passed through the various rooms that everything was immaculately clean and tidy – a great tribute to the leadership of his housekeeper, Mrs Schell. Discipline, thought Conrad Hall – that's what this God-forsaken country needs – discipline. Mrs Schell keeps her staff in order and they respect her and admire her for it – and look what marvels she achieves as a result. If only Nyanga would inject a little discipline into his handling of the country, how much more successful he would be!

Once in the kitchen, Hall paused to wipe the sweat off his forehead with a handkerchief. Then he pulled open the door of the six-foot-high refrigerator to provide himself with a cooling can of beer.

The refrigerator was empty except for one item.

That one item was the head of Mrs Schell: it stared at him, open-eyed, the mouth grinning hideously above the untidily severed neck; blood formed a pool in the tray below.

For the first time in his adult life, Conrad Hall screamed. He screamed in unconscious protest at the horrible shock to his system; and he screamed, above all, with fear for what that dreadful sight implied. For the head of Mrs Schell, leering lifelessly at him out of the refrigerator, meant that death could reach out and touch him, even here; death could make its way uninvited and invincible even into the sanctuary of his own home.

And as Conrad Hall stood there, temporarily motionless, with his whole attention centred on the appalling face on the refrigerator shelf, death crept up on him from behind. It came in the form of the four young Fanda servant girls who had waited on his table so often in the past – and who had been humiliated and beaten so often in return for their hard work.

The eldest and boldest of the four girls came up behind Conrad Hall and struck him a tremendous blow on the right arm with a razor-sharp eighteen-inch panga. The blade was swung with such venom that it sliced straight through the skin, flesh and bone; it sliced right through the limb and into the chest beneath. Conrad Hall's right arm and hand flipped through the air and fell to the floor like discarded meat in a butcher's shop.

The remaining girls followed up hard from all sides. They slashed and chopped viciously with their pangas, cursing and abusing the man as they did so at the tops of their shrill little voices.

Conrad Hall reeled and staggered, squealing and whimpering in terror, vainly trying to protect himself with his one remaining hand. His throat was congested with loathsome fear and panic. He wanted to speak words: he wanted to implore them piteously to stop; he wanted to offer them money, jewellery, clothes – he would offer life eternal itself, if only the girls would stop attacking him. But he couldn't speak coherently: he would only moan and scream and shudder as each fresh blow struck home.

The four Fanda girls slashed Conrad Hall to his knees; then the strongest of them split his skull with a single blow, parting the bone like the shell of a rotten coconut.

And finally, when he was dead, they dealt with their former master as they had dealt with Mrs Schell before him. They reduced the body to a dozen or so conveniently sized pieces; then they loaded the lumps into sacks and took them down the road to a farm which was owned by one of the girls' fathers. There they fed their enemy to the pigs. And they stood beside the pigs, watching and talking together, until the very last of the flesh had been consumed.

Five

General Tchen proved to be a useful man in a crisis. Whatever his motives, he gave President Kasaboru every possible co-operation once he had made up his mind to do so.

To begin with, General Tchen rapidly ensured that the runways of Sungbarta airport were made clear and safe for use: that allowed a number of US Globemaster aircraft to begin ferrying in Dutch and Swedish infantry under United Nations command; US C130 transports also ferried in two battalions of Ethiopian troops. During this air-lift the Gabuti army stood well to one side, making sure that the newcomers understood clearly that no-one was even thinking about resisting their entry into the city.

General Tchen also arranged for President Kasaboru to make a speech over Radio Sungbarta at eleven a.m.; the General saw to it that the speech was broadcast simultaneously in Digara, and that recordings were made available to both the Voice of America and the BBC.

Announcements about the forthcoming speech were made over the radio in both Sungbarta and Digara at fifteen-minute intervals from ten a.m. onwards; these ensured that Kasaboru's eventual audience was huge, and most of the listeners were absolutely over-joyed to hear his familiar voice once again.

The President began by explaining that after Nyanga's attempted coup he had been forced to leave the capital in order to avoid assassination. However, he had now arrived safely in Sungbarta, where he had resumed his position as head of state.

The President went on to say that Joro Nyanga was dead, and that at the request of the legally constituted government of Balembi, United Nations troops were now entering the country to help to restore order; the Gabuti troops, who had entered the country in good faith, were now withdrawing to their own territory. All law-abiding citizens were asked to co-operate with the UN forces in ensuring that life returned to normal just as quickly as possible. The President himself would be returning to the capital shortly, where he would be making new appointments to the Council of Ministers.

That was virtually all the President said, but the impact of the speech was remarkable. The Gabuti President, prompted by General

Tchen, immediately confirmed that his country's forces were withdrawing from Balembi post-haste; he was particularly gratified, he said, that Gabuti had been able to be of assistance to a neighbouring country at a time of need. Within ten hours, all Gabuti troops had re-crossed the border into their own territory.

In Sungbarta the relatively few supporters of Nyanga sidled away into the shadows; the Fanda villagers who had made their way to the city during the past week suddenly found pressing reasons to return home; a number of other citizens decided to take an extended holiday. In their place the great mass of those who abhorred violence, whatever their political views, demonstrated their delight and relief by dancing in the streets. The Mayor, Dan Levene, had time for only a brief and joyous reunion with his wife and grandchildren before he was carried away on the shoulders of a celebrating crowd to be acclaimed as the city's greatest hero; and his wife wept with relief.

Shortly after twelve noon, troops wearing the blue helmets of the United Nations began to be air-lifted into Digara, the capital city. An advance force cautiously approached the President's palace, but in the event they were able to enter it without any opposition; inside they found the dead body of General Juba, who had taken cyanide after listening to Kasaboru's speech.

It soon became apparent, even in Digara, that the revolution had been successfully reversed with barely a shot being fired. The UN forces quickly released the many loyal Balembian army officers who had been imprisoned by Nyanga, and these officers lost no time in resuming command of their various units. Those officers who had supported Nyanga – they were mostly young, and of Fanda origins – either followed the Gabuti troops eastwards or else headed north to the Congo; with their leader gone, there didn't seem to be much point in staying. As for the soldiers who had actually fired the guns in the attack on the palace – well, as they explained to anyone who was prepared to listen, and to many who were not, they were just simple military men who obeyed whatever orders they were given. If their officers told them to shoot at the palace, well, they shot at the palace. But now that President Kasaboru was back, well, of course, they were only too pleased to acknowledge his authority, just like everyone else; and they would continue to do what their officers told them. There was not much that could be done about men like that, except to ensure that any further political ambitions among their officers were eliminated at an early stage.

The middle classes, both black and white, had seen more than enough of Nyanga in one week to know that his regime offered nothing but trouble for them; they were delighted by the prospect of a return to constitutional government.

Almost as soon as Kasaboru had finished speaking over the radio, shops began to open again; within an hour all the policemen had returned to work. Intelligent Civil Servants now felt sufficiently safe, for the first time in days, to go back to their desks, and competent engineers resumed control of the electricity and water supplies; buses began to run again.

Before long, even the most ignorant and brutish citizens, such as those who had attended the mass executions in the sports stadium, came to recognize that while revolution had a number of superficial attractions, there was, after all, a great deal to be said for peace, stability and the rule of law.

President Kasaboru returned to Digara the following day. Dr Vanderwelt, Secretary General of the United Nations, had seen to it that the UN forces increased in numbers very rapidly, and by the time the President entered his capital the situation was firmly under control.

Kasaboru spent the afternoon touring the city. For the most part he travelled in an open car, but often the vehicle was brought to a halt by the crowds thronging the streets for a glimpse of him. He spent hours talking to the people, and he was greatly saddened by the tragic stories he heard and by the extensive damage he saw. However, he was also greatly encouraged by the genuine enthusiasm with which he was greeted. He sensed an enormous determination to make good the mistakes of the past and to build an even better future – and that, he felt, would give him the backing he needed if he was to help Balembi to recover from its self-inflicted wound.

On the Thursday of that week the President flew briefly to Accra, in order to make his long-planned appearance at the Congress of Independent African States. In the circumstances he had half-decided not to attend after all, but Dr Vanderwelt persuaded him that it would do nothing but good if he were to step into the world spotlight for one day; and by then Kasaboru felt sufficiently secure at home to know that his temporary absence would involve no risk.

In the event, Kasaboru's speech to the Congress in Accra proved to be a classic of its kind, equal in its impact to Macmillan's 'Wind of Change' speech to the Cape Town Parliament in 1960.

Kasaboru's theme was simple: it was that change was inevitable, and in any case desirable. He argued, however, that change should be brought about in a peaceful rather than violent manner, in a political context which allowed the free expression of a wide range of opinion, and which ensured that it was always possible to appoint an alternative government if the people of a state so wished.

In private, not all the presidents and politicians who were attending the Congress agreed with these sentiments. But they were faced with a man who had survived revolution and death by the slimmest of margins, an achievement which they greatly admired and respected; in fact many of them inwardly hoped that in similar circum-

335

stances they would be able to emulate the feat. And so for the moment at least the heads of state were prepared to give Kasaboru the benefit of their doubts about his views. They rose to their feet and cheered him for five solid minutes – and when he returned to Digara early the next day the President received an unparalleled ticker-tape welcome.

On Sunday the President gave a lunch party. It was attended by the members of his now reconstituted Council of Ministers and by Jane Stuart and Philip Morgan.

In many ways the lunch was a sad occasion. Kasaboru was reminded by the new faces around the table that so many of his old friends and colleagues were gone for ever: Joseph Uvira, William Maiko and four other Ministers had been murdered; Bob Fuller and Kelly Thompson had both died on the journey to Sungbarta.

In other ways, however, the party provided an opportunity for celebration: it was the first time the President had had a proper chance to relax for a very long time, and he was visibly delighted to be at ease among friends.

Richard Chokwe had now returned from New York and had been joyfully reunited with his wife and children. He was toasted by the President for his courage and skill in helping to secure United Nations intervention. Chokwe obviously enjoyed telling the tale of how he had escaped from Digara to Cape Town by shaving off his beard and moustache and pretending to be an airline steward; the South Africans had done their best to delay him, but he had eventually made his way to New York via Cairo, Rome and London.

When coffee was served the President took Philip on one side; at the President's suggestion they retired to his office for a few minutes so that they could talk in relative privacy.

'Well, Philip,' said the President, once they were comfortably seated, 'what do you intend to do now?'

Philip answered at once; his mind was made up. 'Have a holiday first,' he said. 'Jane and I thought we would go away for a while – if you'll release me, that is.'

'Of course,' said Kasaboru. 'Of course. In fact, as far as I'm concerned, I shall quite understand if you feel that you've had enough of this country altogether, and want to be released from your contract. You have only to ask.'

'No, no,' said Philip firmly, 'I shall do no such thing. Jane and I will definitely be back in a week or two, once we've had a rest. We feel that there are plenty of jobs to be done here – plenty for both of us.'

The President nodded. 'Good,' he said, 'I'm very pleased to hear it. And what you've said about a holiday ties in with what I wanted to say to you, as a matter of fact. It concerns finance. . . . I don't know whether he told you, Philip, but your uncle, George Morgan, had been suffering from cancer for some time. Did you know that?'

Philip shook his head. 'No,' he said. 'I can't say I did know for sure. But I knew he'd been ill, and I guessed that cancer might be the cause.'

Kasaboru glanced out of the window beside him. 'Yes,' he said sadly, 'your uncle would have died soon anyway, and he would have been a great loss to us whatever the cause of death. But it was typical of him to sacrifice his life in the way he did – he was an example to us all in many ways. . . .'

The President turned back to look at Philip.

'But his passing raises other issues,' he continued. 'You see, Philip, for many years your uncle sponsored a number of young Africans to go to Europe to get themselves educated. He used to ask me from time to time to help him find suitable young men, and of course I was happy to do so. He also made me an executor of his will, and discussed its terms with me in some detail. . . . He made a new will shortly after you arrived here, Philip. He leaves half of his considerable fortune in trust, to continue to help the youth of this country. And the other half is left to you.'

The President looked through the open door of his office. In the room beyond, both he and Philip could see Jane Stuart as she remained seated at the dining-table chatting with Richard Chokwe. The afternoon sunlight, filtered by a soft lace curtain, lit up her features and emphasized their perfection. At that moment Jane laughed and turned towards them: she looked even more beautiful full-face than in profile; she caught Philip's eye and blew him a kiss. He smiled back at her happily.

'I only mention this money,' said the President cautiously, 'because I thought it might perhaps have some bearing on your future plans – on what you intend to do.'

Philip glanced at the President's face, which was deliberately expressionless, and then he looked back at Jane.

'Yes,' he said with a grin. 'Yes, I'm sure it will.'